P9-DOB-793

NEVADA UTAH

CALIFORNIA

LOS ANGELES

ARIZONA

MEXICO

RIVERSIDE DRIVE

FRANKLIN AVENUE

SUNSET BOULEVARD

WESTERN AVENUE

FIGUEROA STREET

NORTH MAIN STREET

7TH STREET

OLIVE STREET

FIGUEROA STREET

MAIN STREET

CENTRAL AVENUE

ALAMEDA STREET

RAYMOND CHANDLER'S
PHILIP MARLOWE

RAYMOND CHANDLER'S
PHILIP MARLOWE
A CENTENNIAL CELEBRATION

BYRON PREISS, EDITOR

A BYRON PREISS BOOK

ALFRED A. KNOPF
NEW YORK, 1988

To Ed Victor

THIS IS A BORZOI BOOK
PUBLISHED BY ALFRED A. KNOPF, INC.

Copyright © 1988 by Byron Preiss Visual Publications, Inc.
Introduction copyright © 1988 by Frank MacShane
Individual stories copyright © 1988 by Simon Brett, Robert Campbell, Max
Allan Collins, Robert Crais, Loren D. Estleman, Ed Gorman, James Grady,
Joyce Harrington, Jeremiah Healy, Edward D. Hoch, Stuart M. Kaminsky, Dick
Lochte, John Lutz, Francis M. Nevins, Jr., Sara Paretsky, W.R. Philbrick,
Robert J. Randisi, Benjamin M. Schutz, Roger L. Simon, Julie Smith, Paco
Ignacio Taibo II, Jonathan Valin, and Eric Van Lustbader respectively. Individual
illustrations copyright © 1988 by John Martinez, Paul Rivoche, Javier Romero,
and Dennis Ziemienski respectively.

"The Deepest South" by Paco Ignacio Taibo II,
translated from the Spanish by Barbara Belejack

Grateful acknowledgment is made to Houghton Mifflin Company for permission
to reprint "The Pencil" by Raymond Chandler from *The Midnight Raymond
Chandler*. Copyright © 1971 by Helga Greene, executrix, estate of Raymond
Chandler. Reprinted by permission of Houghton Mifflin Company.

Library of Congress Cataloging-in-Publication Data

Raymond Chandler's Philip Marlowe.
1. Detective and mystery stories, American.
2. Marlowe, Philip (Fictitious character)—Fiction.
I. Chandler, Raymond, 1888–1959. II. Preiss, Byron.
PS648.D4R39   1988   813'.01'08351   88-45344
ISBN 0-394-57327-7

Manufactured in the United States of America

First Edition

Special thanks to Lee Goerner, Executive Editor at Knopf; to our publisher,
Sonny Mehta; Anne Caiger, Manuscripts Librarian, Department of Special Collections, University Research Library, University of California, Los Angeles;
Kathy Hourigan, Graham Greene, Harlan Ellison, Dominick Abel, and the other
representatives of the authors and artists in this book.

Produced by Byron Preiss Visual Publications, Inc.
Produced in conjunction with Philip Marlowe, B.V.

Associate Editor: Ruth Ashby
Assistant Editor and Map Coordinator: Gwendolyn Smith
Illustration Editor: Randall Reich
Copy Editor: Len Neufeld
Mechanicals by Mary LeCleir
Cover painting by Dennis Ziemienski
Textures and map illustration by Dean Motter

Jacket and book design by Alex Jay/Studio J

CONTENTS

FOREWORD

BYRON PREISS

Perfect anthologies do not exist. Very good ones are extremely rare.
. . . Some of the best collections . . . are not so much anthologies as
one-volume libraries. They give you a lot for your money, but only an
iron man can hold them up without getting a sprained wrist. If this is
the way I must read, I shall stick to *Webster's Unabridged.* There isn't
a dull page in it.   —Raymond Chandler

I had come to U.C.L.A. in search of some validation for what I was
already in the midst of doing. Nearly a hundred years after Raymond Chandler's birth, close to three decades since he had typed the last words of
Philip Marlowe's literary career, I had invited approximately twenty-five
contemporary authors of the mystery story to celebrate Chandler's work,
with the consent of his estate, by writing new Philip Marlowe stories.

My guide on that classically sunny Los Angeles afternoon was Edgar
Award nominee Robert Crais, a novelist and leading television screenwriter.
He looked about Marlowe's age, thirty-eight. Something told me Chandler
would have liked this man. He was a vindiction of Chandler's hopes for
the mystery writer, a well-paid, respected man who aspired to attain Chandler's highest standard, to have his mystery novels treated as literature.

Crais escorted me to the University Research Library, where a large
body of Chandler's existing letters and manuscripts is kept. After various
explanations, we were given six or seven brown boxes containing folders
and envelopes with such tantalizing labels as, "Chandler, Raymond, 1888–
1959. The Poodle Springs story. La Jolla, 1959. 23 1. 22 x 14 cm. Ty-
pescript with holograph corrections." I nervously pried open that particular
envelope and pulled out the contents. I was holding canary yellow pages,
standard typewriter sheets cut in half, typed the long way, and tripled
spaced. Chandler had used a blue typewriter ribbon, and the visual effect
was the exact opposite of what a person might expect from one of the
geniuses of hard-boiled detective literature. The manuscript was pretty.
The colors reminded me of Monet's china in his dining room at Giverny.
Canary yellow and royal blue. These were the final colors of Raymond
Chandler's Philip Marlowe.

We skimmed the pages and proceeded onto *Playback* and Chandler's
letters, including correspondence to Wilbur Smith of the U.C.L.A. Library
that explained the purpose of those yellow manuscript sheets. Chandler
wrote that they contained "125 to 150 words and they are so short that
you don't get prolix. If there isn't a little meat on each, something is wrong."

Immersed as we were in the papers, Crais reminded me that we only
had a few minutes left until the Department closed. I reiterated my desire
to find validation in Chandler's words for doing this book.

I returned to the library the next day. I found a missive dated June 3, 1957, written by Chandler to Edgar Carter, about a series of Philip Marlowe TV shows. In it, Chandler argues for his own participation in the shows, but only as the writer of Marlowe's dialogue:

> . . . it seems that if I could deliver the character of Philip Marlowe, at the risk—somewhat the certainty—of being thought unbearably conceited, I should still be able to believe that Marlowe existed, and not a travesty of him. . . . After all, a great many writers have been trying to steal him from me for fifteen years or more, and they have never made it yet. I suppose all writers are crazy, but if they are any good, I believe they have a terrible honesty.

At last I had found something in Chandler's own words that related to this book, but it was discouraging at best. Marlowe's intolerance for hypocrisy came to mind. Was there any justification to pursue Marlowe with other mystery writers?

I returned to the papers, to Chandler's favorable review of James Sandoe's anthology *Murder Plain and Fanciful,* a part of which opens this foreword. On the last page I found the words which gave me solace for what we intended to do. Chandler wrote about Sandoe:

> I have a feeling, although he has not expressed it, that he regards the chronicles of this irrevocable art of the mystery as the only really significant literature of our time, in the special sense that an intelligent preoccupation with the subject—macabre to some, delicious to others, attractive in some manner to almost all—is the frame for almost the only kind of writing we do better than it was ever done before.

It was writing that fired Chandler's mind. It was his love of the potential of the mystery that seized his imagination and propelled his work. His letters overflow with his thoughts about the art of the mystery. His greatest hope for his own work was that it would endure as literature. I think it would be fair to say that his deeply held respect for the mystery as literature is shared by all of the authors in this book. They are Chandler's peers. Many would not be the writers they are had not Chandler followed Hammett and Cain down the back alley of fiction into the realm of art. The contributors to this book are here to honor Chandler, not to steal from him. I think he would be flattered by their attention, just as he was flattered to be elected President of the Mystery Writers of America in 1959. I think he would have gone on to critique each story in this book, piece by piece, until he reached the end of the book and found one story that he liked more than the others, but not enough to call it perfect. Nothing was ever perfect in Marlowe's world, yet if it had a basic morality, a common man's nobility, it was worthy of consideration. Chandler's review of Sandoe made me feel that there was honor in this collaboration. For that reason, for the sake of the good intentions of the contributors, I risk this book, and regret only that Chandler is not able to read it.

INTRODUCTION

HE MADE WORDS DANCE: THE CENTENARY OF RAYMOND CHANDLER

FRANK MacSHANE

RAYMOND CHANDLER DID not write detective stories because he had something to say about crime in America but because he wanted to understand and come to terms with the contradictions that assailed him. Growing up as a young man with his mother in England, he had bitter memories of his childhood in America, where he was born one hundred years ago. His father was such a violent alcoholic that his mother had to divorce him, and the clash of their personalities made him wary and suspicious although he was by nature open and romantic.

As a student at Dulwich College in South London, Chandler received a vigorous classical education which led him to write incisive critical essays and reviews. But he was also drawn towards romantic poetry. What he sought as a writer was an art form that would bridge the gap between the two sides of his nature, one that would be truthful without being coarse and that would be beautiful without being sentimental.

To improve his own writing and develop his craft, Chandler took a course in short story writing in London. He wrote sketches and paragraphs that were wordy and literary, though well phrased, and he also produced a short story in the manner of Henry James. Not having a style of his own, he turned to writers he admired and modeled his work on theirs, but the results read like parodies.

Realizing he could not make a success in London as a literary journalist and poet, Chandler decided to return to America in 1912. He took a number of odd jobs across the country, but was eventually employed by the Dabney Oil Company in Los Angeles, where he rose to be vice president and office manager. During this period, Chandler read a lot of contemporary fiction, but he did not try to write. In 1932, however, he was fired from his job at the oil company because of his drinking and failure to come to work. He then decided to change his ways and to make another attempt at becoming a writer. He even listed himself as "writer" in the Los Angeles Directory.

Once again, he began with imitations, and this time his model was Ernest Hemingway. Unfortunately, his sense of humor led him into burlesque:

> Hank went into the bathroom to brush his teeth.
>
> "The hell with it," he said. "She shouldn't have done it." It was a good bathroom. It was small and the green enamel was peeling off the walls. But the hell with that, as Napoleon said when they told him Josephine was waiting without. The bathroom had a wide window through which Hank looked at the pines and the larches. They dripped with a faint rain. They looked smooth and comfortable.
>
> "The hell with it," Hank said. "She shouldn't have done it."

Chandler was right in seeking a model, for he knew that the emotions he wanted to express could not be naively or baldly expressed. He needed to find a form that would allow him to express his feelings in an honest way. Writing, he knew, is not a mere technique that can be learned: it is a process which allows novelists, poets, and nonfiction writers to understand the truth about their feelings. The act of writing is the only means by which this discovery can be made. It is a process which helps the writer make sure that his work is emotionally and intellectually accurate.

It was at this point that Chandler discovered pulp fiction and, in particular, the crime magazine *Black Mask*, which had been established in 1920. Chandler found that he liked mystery writing because it was entirely without pretensions. There were also practical considerations. "It suddenly struck me," he said, "that I could write this stuff and get paid while I was learning." Chandler was attracted to pulp fiction because it depended on a discipline that could be mastered. Unlike "literary" writing, it made demands on the writer regarding length and subject matter, and therefore required that he learn the art of storytelling, which was not absolutely necessary in literary fiction. Chandler began by studying the work of writers like Dashiell Hammett and Erle Stanley Gardner to see what he could learn from them. He copied their techniques and wrote and rewrote many stories in their styles until he understood the medium.

In later years, Chandler would write, "Analyze and imitate; no other school is necessary." That is what he did for months on end and with no intention to publish. Moreover, he was realistic. "No writer ever in my age got a blank check," he wrote. "He always had to accept some conditions

imposed from without, respect certain taboos, try to please certain people."
What was more, Chandler understood a basic truth that few writers like
to admit: "No writer every wrote exactly what he wanted to write, because
there was never anything inside himself, anything purely individual that
he did not want to write. It's all reaction of one sort or other."

When he thought he had progressed far enough in his training, he
sent his work off to Joseph T. Shaw, the editor of *Black Mask*, who immediately accepted and published it. These first stories were competent
and had more individuality than most of the other stories published in the
pulps, but there was little that was special or individual in them. It was
simply evident that Chandler had mastered the technique. Whether he
would produce anything that was truly original, and therefore capable of
expressing his feelings and ideas, remained to be seen.

Chandler had accepted the tough guy school of detective fiction as
the one that best suited him. The English school was to his mind hopelessly
unreal. In actual life, detectives are not aristocrats or country vicars; they
are men of limited intelligence who are just doing a job of work. In his
own writing, he therefore created detectives who fit the conventions of the
hard-boiled school. They had little individuality, however, and their names
said little about them: Johnny Dalmas, Ted Carmady, Johnny De Ruse,
Pete Anglich, Sam Delaguerra, and Mallory. Sometimes they told their
own stories; often there was an omniscient narrator. It didn't much matter,
because they all sounded alike, and the stories were so full of action that
there was little room for character or atmosphere.

Since he had been educated in England, Chandler found that he had
to start from scratch in writing these slangy stories. "I had to learn American
just like a foreign language," he said. The process genuinely engaged his
imagination. As a poet, he was in love with what he called the magic of
words, and he wanted to bring that quality into his detective stories. He
knew that taut storytelling was essential to hold the reader's interest, but
at the same time he wanted to express the feelings that accompanied action.

In later years, Chandler explained what he meant in a letter to Fred-
erick Lewis Allen of *Harper's* magazine: "A long time ago when I was
writing for the pulps I put into a story a line like 'he got out of the car
and walked across the sun-drenched sidewalk until the shadows of the
awning over the entrance fell across his face like the touch of cool water.'
They took it out when they published the story. Their readers didn't appreciate this sort of thing: just held up the action. And I set out to prove
them wrong. My theory was that they just *thought* they cared about nothing
but the action; that really, although they didn't know it, they cared very
little about the action. The things they really cared about, and that I cared

about, were the creation of emotion through dialogue and description; the things they remembered, that haunted them, were not for example that a man got killed, but that in the moment of his death he was trying to pick a paper clip up off the polished surface of a desk, and it kept slipping away from him, so that there was a look of strain on his face, and his mouth was half open in a kind of tormented grin, and the last thing in the world he thought about was death. He didn't even hear death knocking on the door. That damn little paper clip kept slipping away from his fingers and he just couldn't push it to the edge of the desk and catch it as it fell."

While the writing of description helps induce feeling, it is less effective than the human voice, whether used in dialogue or narrative. A distinctive voice carries conviction and authenticity. It takes the story into a new realm and captures the reader's sympathies. This voice becomes, in fact, the author's style. For Chandler, this style was expressed in a language that combined the strength of the classical English of Dulwich College with the vitality of American vernacular speech. Together, these made the bridge that allowed Chandler to unite the two sides of his consciousness, the romantic and the realistic.

Philip Marlowe was the vehicle Chandler used to make this union possible. Marlowe was physically tough, fair-minded, and intelligent. Evolving from the detectives of the earlier stories, he had some of Chandler's traits, but he was not Chandler. Nor was he the plodding detective of real life. He was not only tough and fearless but also witty and gentle. In real life such a combination is improbable, but by giving Marlowe a strong and vivid personality, Chandler made him believable and convincing.

To imagine that Chandler created Marlowe as an idealization of himself is to miss the point, for Marlowe is a figure of fantasy. He is, in Chandler's words, "the personification of an attitude, the exaggeration of a possibility," and little else. "The whole point," said Chandler, "is that the detective exists complete and entire and unchanged by anything that happens, that he is, as detective, outside the story and above it, and always will be. That is why he never gets the girl, never marries, never really has any private life, except insofar as he must eat and sleep and have a place to leave his clothes. His moral and intellectual force is that he gets nothing but his fee, for which he will, if he can, protect the innocent, guard the helpless and destroy the wicked, and the fact that he must do this while earning a meager living in a corrupt world is what makes him stand out."

Marlowe's energy and idealism helped Chandler develop Marlowe as a complex character. Chandler conceived him so completely and in such detail as a human being that he is able to carry the story. It often happens in writing fiction that after the author begins the story, it starts to have a life of its own. The author is so in tune with the psychology of his characters he is no longer obliged to invent. He just follows along where his characters take him and thereby reveals the inner logic of the story.

As the medium through which Chandler told his stories, Marlowe became as real for his creator as any actual human being. In 1951, Chandler even wrote a portrait of Marlowe, giving his habits, his educational background, his preferences for drink and women, his domestic arrangements, and the furnishings of his house. Yet despite many similar beliefs and habits, Marlowe is very different from Chandler the introspective artist. Like Joseph Conrad's narrator, Marlow, after whom Philip Marlowe was probably named, he was a kind of co-conspirator with Chandler. As he tells the story in place of an omniscient narrator, he can make comments which as author Chandler would not care to make for fear of being morally heavy-handed.

Usually a character who is repeated in one novel after another becomes a familiar stock figure. He is welcomed by readers who have come to like him, and he serves as a familiar point of reference for each new story. But as Chandler changed over the years, so too did Marlowe. After finishing *The Little Sister*, a novel which won Chandler a great deal of notice among literary intellectuals, Chandler told his London publisher, Hamish Hamilton, that he might stop using Marlowe. "I find the attitude more and more artificial," he wrote. "I am afraid Mr. Marlowe has developed far more than a suspicion that a man of his parts is beginning to look pretty ridiculous as a small-time private detective. He's getting self-conscious, trying to live up to his reputation among the intellectuals. The boy is bothered."

As Chandler aged, he became more tired and vulnerable. Aware that his wife was very ill, he hurried to complete *The Long Goodbye*. With this book he wanted to move into new territory and write a detective story that had the range and scope of an ordinary novel. He therefore broke some of the conventions of the form in an effort to make Marlowe a more feeling and sensitive man than he had formerly allowed him to be. Chandler has Marlowe make friends with the characters in his book and even fall in love with one of them. These experiences bring him pain and loneliness, and Marlowe becomes increasingly disillusioned and disappointed. To a considerable degree, Chandler succeeds in making Marlowe a far more interesting character than he was in the earlier novels, but much of the lightness disappears as the cynicism increases. Here is a description of Marlowe watching a pretty girl in a swimming pool: "A girl in a white sharkskin suit and a luscious figure was climbing the ladder to the high board. I watched the band of white that showed between the tan of her thighs and the suit. I watched it carnally. Then she was out of sight, cut

off by the deep overhang of the roof. A moment later I saw her flash down
in a one and a half. Spray came high enough to catch the sun and make
rainbows that were almost as pretty as the girl. Then she came up the
ladder and unstrapped her white helmet and shook her bleach job loose.
She wobbled her bottom over to a small white table and sat down beside
a lumberjack in white drill pants and dark glasses and a tan so evenly
dark that he couldn't have been anything but the hired man around the
pool. He reached over and patted her thigh. She opened a mouth like a
firebucket and laughed. That terminated my interest in her. I couldn't hear
the laugh but the hole in her face when she unzipped her teeth was all
I needed."

   After Cissy's death, Chandler's moods were subject to severe stress.
He wrote *Playback* and the opening of the Poodle Springs story, but emotionally he was insecure. In low spirits he became sentimental and self-
pitying; when up, he was exaggeratedly zestful. It is therefore better to
remember him when he was at his best, when he and Marlowe were a team
that worked well together and when he had the balance and control that
produced his best work. "Style is the man," said Buffon, and at sixty,
Chandler tried to explain what he meant by that word: "In the long run,
however little you talk or even think about it, the most durable thing in
writing is style, and style is the most valuable investment a writer can
make with his time. It pays off slowly, your agent will sneer at it, your
publisher will misunderstand it, and it will take people you never heard
of to convince them by slow degrees that the writer who puts his individual
mark on the way he writes will always pay off. He can't do it by trying,
because the kind of style I am thinking of is a projection of personality
and you have to have a personality before you can project it. But granted
you have one, you can only project it on paper by thinking of something
else. This is ironical in a way; it is the reason, I suppose, why in a generation of 'made' writers I still say you can't make a writer. Preoccupation
with style will not produce it. No amount of editing and polishing will have
any appreciable effect on the flavor of how a man writes. It is the product
of the quality of his emotion and perception; it is the ability to transfer
these to paper which makes him a writer, in contrast to the great number
of people who have just as good emotions and just as keen perceptions,
but cannot come within a googol of miles of putting them on paper."

   Chandler was a real artist. He created a character who has become
a part of American folk mythology, and in writing about Los Angeles, he
depicted a world of great beauty and seamy corruption—the American
reality. He made words dance, and readers continue to respond to his
magic.

RAYMOND CHANDLER'S
PHILIP MARLOWE
THE THIRTIES

THE PERFECT CRIME

MAX ALLAN COLLINS

1935

S HE WAS THE first movie star I ever worked for, but I wasn't much impressed. If I were that easily impressed, I'd have been impressed by Hollywood itself. And having seen the way Hollywood portrayed my profession on the so-called silver screen, I wasn't much impressed with Hollywood.

On the other hand, Dolores Dodd was the most beautiful woman who ever wanted to hire my services, and that did impress me. Enough so that when she called me, that October, and asked me to drive out to her "sidewalk cafe" nestled under the palisades in Montemar Vista, I went, wondering if she would be as pretty in the flesh as she was on celluloid.

I'd driven out the Pacific Coast Highway that same morning, a clear cool morning with a blue sky lording it over a vast sparkling sea. Pelicans were playing tag with the breaking surf, flying just under the curl of the white-lipped waves. Yachts, like a child's toy boats, floated out there between me and the horizon. I felt like I could reach out for one, pluck and examine it, sniff it maybe, like King Kong checking out Fay Wray's lingerie.

Dolores Dodd's Sidewalk Cafe, as a billboard on the hillside behind it so labeled the place, was a sprawling two-story hacienda affair, as big as a beached luxury liner. Over its central, largest-of-many archways, a third-story tower rose like a stubby lighthouse. There weren't many cars here—it was approaching ten a.m., too early for the luncheon crowd, and even Marlowe didn't drink cocktails that early in the day. Not and tell, anyway.

She was waiting in the otherwise unpopulated cocktail lounge, where massive wooden beams in a traditional Spanish mode fought the chromium-and-leather furnishings and the chrome-and-glass brick bar and came out a draw. She was a big blonde woman with more curves than the highway out front and just the right number of hills and valleys. Wearing a clingy,

3

summery white dress, she was seated on one of the bar stools, with her bare legs crossed; they weren't the best-looking legs on the planet, necessarily. I just couldn't prove otherwise. That good a detective I'm not.

"Philip Marlowe?" she asked, and her smile dimpled her cheeks in a manner that made her whole heart-shaped face smile, and the world smile as well, including me. She didn't move off the stool, just extended her hand in a manner that was at once casual and regal.

I took the hand, not knowing whether to kiss it, shake it, or press it into a book like a corsage I wanted to keep. I looked at her feeling vaguely embarrassed; she was so pretty you didn't know where to look next, and felt like there was maybe something wrong with looking anywhere. But I couldn't help myself.

She had pale, creamy skin and her hair was almost white blonde. They called her the ice-cream blonde, in the press. I could see why.

Then I got around to her eyes. They were blue, of course, cornflower blue; and big and sporting long lashes, the real McCoy, not your dimestore variety. But they were also the saddest eyes I'd ever looked into. The smile froze on my face like I was looking at Medusa, not a twenty-nine-year-old former sixth-grade teacher from Massachusetts who'd won a talent search.

"Is something wrong?" she asked. Then she patted the stool next to her.

I sat and said, "Nothing's wrong. I never had a movie star for a client before."

"I see. You come recommended highly."

"Oh?"

Her voice had a low, throaty quality that wasn't forced or affected; she was what Mae West would've been if Mae West weren't a parody. "A friend of mine in the D.A's office downtown. He said you got fired for being too honest."

"Actually, I like to think I quit. And I don't like to think I'm *too* honest."

"Oh?"

"Just honest enough."

She smiled at that, very broadly, showing off teeth whiter than cameras can record. "Might I get you a drink, Mr. Marlowe?"

"It's a little early."

"I know it is. Might I get you a drink?"

"Sure."

"Anything special?"

"Anything that doesn't have a little paper umbrella in it is fine by me."

She fixed me up with a rye, and had the same herself. I like that in a woman.

"Have you heard of Laird Brunette?" she asked, returning to her bar stool.

"Heard of him," I said. "Haven't met him."

"What do you know about him?"

I shrugged. "Big-time gambler. Runs casinos all over Southern California. More every day."

She flicked the air with a long red fingernail, like she was shooing away a bug. "Well, perhaps you've noticed the tower above my restaurant."

"Sure."

"I live on the second floor, but the tower above is fairly spacious."

"Big enough for a casino, you mean."

"That's right," she said, nodding. "I was approached by Brunette, more than once. I turned him away, more than once. After all, with my location, and my clientele, a casino could make a killing."

"You're doing well enough legally. Why bother with ill?"

"I agree. And if I were to get into any legal problems, that would mean a scandal, and Hollywood doesn't need another scandal. Busby Berkeley's trial is coming up soon, you know."

The noted director and choreographer, creator of so many frothy fantasies, was up on the drunk-driving homicide of three pedestrians, not far from this cafe.

"But now," she said, her bee-stung lips drawn nervously tight, "I've begun to receive threatening notes."

"From Brunette, specifically?"

"No. They're extortion notes, actually. Asking me to pay off Artie Lewis. You know, the bandleader?"

"Why him?"

"He's in Brunette's pocket. Gambling markers. And I used to go with Artie. He lives in San Francisco now."

"I see. Well, have you talked to the cops?"

"No."

"Why not?"

"I don't want to get Artie in trouble."

"Have you talked to Artie?"

"Yes—he claims he knows nothing about this. He doesn't want my money. He doesn't even want me back—he's got a new girl."

I'd like to see the girl that could make you forget Dolores Dodd.

"So," I said, "you want me to investigate. Can I see the extortion notes?"

"No," she said, shaking her white blonde curls like the mop of the gods, "that's not it. I burned those notes. For Artie's sake."

"Well, for Pete's sake," I said, "where *do* I come in?"

"I think I'm being followed. I'd like a bodyguard."

I resisted looking her over wolfishly and making a wisecrack. She was a nice woman, and the fact that hers was the sort of body a private eye would pay to guard didn't seem worth mentioning. My fee did.

"Twenty-five a day and expenses," I said.

"Fine," she said. "And you can have any meals you like right here at the cafe. Drinks, too. Run a tab and I'll pick it up."

"Swell," I grinned. "I was wondering if I'd ever run into a fringe benefit in this racket."

"You can be my chauffeur."

"Well . . ."

"You have a problem with that, Mr. Marlowe?"

"I have a private investigator's license, and a license to carry a gun. But I don't have a chauffeur's license."

"I think a driver's license will suffice." Her lips were poised in a kiss of amusement. "What's the real problem, Marlowe?"

"I'm not wearing a uniform. I'm strictly plainclothes."

She smiled tightly, wryly amused, saying, "All right, hang onto your dignity . . . but you have to let me pay the freight on a couple of new suits for you. I'll throw 'em in on the deal."

"Fine," I said.

So for the next two months, she was my only client. I worked six days a week for her—Monday through Saturday. Sundays God, Marlowe, and Dodd rested. I drove her in her candy-apple red Packard convertible, a car designed for blondes with wind-blown hair and pearls. She sat in back, of course. Most days I took her to the Hal Roach Studio, where she was making a musical with Laurel and Hardy. I'd wait in some dark pocket of the sound studio and watch her every move out in the brightness. In a black wig, lacy bodice, and clinging, gypsy skirt, Dolores was the kind of girl you took home to mother, and if mother didn't like her, to hell with mother.

Evenings she hit the club circuit, the Trocadero and the El Mocambo chiefly. I'd sit in the cocktail lounges and quietly drink and wait for her and her various dates to head home. Some of these guys were swishy types that she was doing the studio a favor appearing in public with; a couple of others spent the night.

I don't like to tell tales out of school, but this tale can't be told at all unless I'm frank about that one thing: Dolores slept around. Later, when the gossip rags were spreading rumors about alcohol and drugs, that was all the bunk. But Dolores was a friendly girl. She had generous charms and she was generous with them.

"Marlowe," she said, one night in early December when I was dropping her off, walking her up to the front door of the cafe like always, "I think I have a crush on you."

She was alone tonight, having played girlfriend to one of those Hollywood funny boys for the benefit of Louella Parsons and company. Alone but for me.

She slipped an arm around my waist. She had booze on her breath, but then so did I, and neither one of us was drunk. She was bathed gently in moonlight and Chanel Number Five.

She kissed me with those bee-stung lips, stinging so softly, so deeply.

I moved away. "No. I'm sorry."

She winced. "What's wrong?"

"I'm the hired help. You're just lonely tonight."

Her eyes, which I seldom looked into because of the depth of the sadness there, hardened. "Don't you ever get lonely, you bastard?"

I swallowed. "Never," I said.

She drew her hand back to slap me, but then she just touched my face, instead. Gentle as the ocean breeze, and it was gentle tonight, the breeze, so gentle.

"Goodnight, Marlowe," she said.

And she slipped inside.

"Goodnight," I said, to nobody. Then to myself: "Goodnight Marlowe, you goddamn sap."

I drove her Packard to the garage that was attached to the bungalow above the restaurant complex; to do that I had to take Montemar Vista Road to Seretto Way, turning right. The Mediterranean-style stucco bungalow, on Cabrillo, like so many houses in Montemar Vista, climbed the side of the hill like a clinging vine. It was owned by Dolores Dodd's partner in the cafe, movie director and producer Warren Eastman. Eastman had an apartment next to Dolores's above the restaurant, as well as the bungalow, and seemed to live back and forth between the two.

I wondered what the deal was, with Eastman and my client, but I never asked, not directly. Eastman was a thin, dapper man in his late forties, with a pointed chin and a small mustache and a widow's peak that his slick black hair was receding around, making his face look diamond shaped. He often sat in the cocktail lounge with a bloody Mary in one hand and a cigarette in a holder in the other. He was always talking deals with movie people.

"Marlowe," he said, one night, motioning me over to the bar. He was seated on the very stool that Dolores had been, that first morning. "This is Nick DeCiro, the talent agent. Nick, this is the gumshoe Dolores hired to protect her from the big bad gambling syndicate."

DeCiro was another darkly handsome man, a bit older than Eastman, though he lacked both the mustache and receding hairline of the director. DeCiro wore a white suit with a dark sport shirt, open at the neck to reveal a wealth of black chest hair.

I shook DeCiro's hand. His grip was firm, moist, like a fistful of topsoil.

"Nicky here is your client's ex-husband," Eastman said, with a wag of his cigarette-in-holder, trying for an air of that effortless decadence that Hollywood works so hard at.

"Dolores and me are still pals," DeCiro said, lighting up a foreign cig with a shiny silver lighter that he then clicked shut with a meaningless flourish. "We broke up amicably."

"I heard it was over extreme cruelty," I said.

DeCiro frowned, and Eastman cut in glibly, "Don't believe everything you read in the papers, Marlowe. Besides, you have to get a divorce over something."

"But then you'd *know* that in your line of work," DeCiro said, an edge in his thin voice.

"I don't do divorce work," I said.

"Sure," DeCiro said.

"I don't. If you gents will excuse me . . ."

"Marlowe, Marlowe," Eastman said, touching my arm, "don't be so touchy."

I waited for him to remove his hand from my arm, then said, "Did you want something, Mr. Eastman? I'm not much for this Hollywood shit-chat."

"I don't like your manner," DeCiro said.

"Nobody does," I said. "But I don't get paid well enough for it to matter."

"Marlowe," Eastman said, "I was just trying to convince Nicky here that my new film is perfect for a certain client of his. I'm doing a mystery. About the perfect crime. The perfect murder."

"No such animal," I said.

"Oh, really?" DeCiro said, lifting an eyebrow.

"Murder and crime are inexact sciences. All the planning in the world can't account for the human element."

"Then how do you explain," Eastman said archly, "the hundreds of murders that go unsolved in this country?"

"Police work is a more exact science than crime or murder," I admitted, "but we have a lot of corrupt cops in this world—and a lot of dumb ones."

"Then there *are* perfect crimes."

"No. Just unsolved ones. And imperfect detectives. Good evening, gentlemen."

That was the most extensive conversation I had with either Eastman or DeCiro during the time I was employed by Miss Dodd, though I said hello and they did the same, now and then, at the cafe.

But Eastman was married to an actress named Miranda Diamond, a fiery Latin whose parents were from Mexico City, even if she'd been raised in the Bronx. She fancied herself as the next Lupe Velez, and she was a similarly voluptuous dame, though her handsome features were as hard as a gravestone.

She cornered me at the cafe one night, in the cocktail lounge, where I was drinking on the job.

"You're a dick," she said.

We'd never spoken before.

"I hope you mean that in the nicest way," I said.

"You're bodyguarding that bitch," she said, sitting next to me on a leather and chrome couch. Her nostrils flared; if I'd been holding a red cape, I'd have dropped it and run for the stands.

"Miss Dodd is my client, yes, Miss Diamond."

She smiled. "You recognize me."

"Oh yes. And I also know enough to call you Mrs. Eastman, in certain company."

"My husband and I are separated."

"Ah."

"But I could use a little help in the divorce court."

"What kind of help?"

"Photographs of him and that bitch in the sack." She said "the" like "thee."

"That would help you."

"Yes. You see . . . my husband has similar pictures of me, with a gentleman, in a compromising position."

"Even missionaries get caught in that position, I understand." I offered her a cigarette, she took it, and I lit hers and mine. "And if you had similar photos, you could negotiate yourself a better settlement."

"Exactly. Interested?"

"I don't do divorce work. I don't sell clients out. It's a conflict of interests."

She smiled; she put her hand on my leg. "I could make it worth your while. Financially and . . . otherwise."

It wasn't even Christmas and already two screen goddesses wanted to hop in the sack with me. I must have really been something.

"No thanks, señorita. I sleep alone . . . just me and my conscience."

Then she suggested I do to myself what she'd just offered to do for me. She was full of ideas.

So was I. I was pretty sure Dolores and Eastman were indeed having an affair, but it was of the on-again, off-again variety. One night they'd be affectionate, in that sickening Hollywood sweetie-baby way; the next night he would be cool to her; the next she would be cool to him. It was love—I recognized it—but the kind that sooner or later blows up like an overheated engine.

Ten days before Christmas, Dolores was honored by a famous British comedian, so famous I'd never the hell heard of him, with a dinner at the Troc. At a table for twelve upstairs, in the swanky cream-and-gold dining room, Dolores was being feted by her show-biz friends, while I sat downstairs in the oak-paneled Cellar Lounge with other people not famous enough to sit upstairs, nursing a rye at the polished copper bar. I didn't feel like a polished copper, that was for sure. I was just a chauffeur with a gun, and a beautiful client who didn't need me.

That much was clear to me: in the two months I'd worked for Dolores, I hadn't spotted anybody following her except a few fans, and I couldn't blame them. I think I was just a little bit in love with the ice-cream blonde myself. But she was a client, and she slept around, and neither of those things appealed to me in a girl.

About half an hour into the evening, I heard a scream upstairs. A woman's scream, a scream that might have belonged to Dolores.

I took the stairs four at a time and had my gun in my hand when I entered the fancy dining room. Normally when I enter fancy dining rooms with a gun in my hand, all eyes are on me. Not this time.

Dolores was clawing at her ex-husband, who was laughing at her. She was being held back by Patsy Peters, the dark-haired rubber-faced comedienne who was Dolores's partner in the two-reelers. DeCiro, in a white tux, had a starlet on his arm, a blonde about twenty with a neckline down to her shoes. The starlet looked frightened, but DeCiro was having a big laugh.

I put my gun away and took over for Patsy Peters.

"Miss Dodd," I said, gently, whispering into her ear, holding onto her two arms from behind, "don't do this."

She went limp for a moment, then straightened and said, with stiff dignity, "I'm all right, Philip."

It was the only time she ever called me that.

I let go of her.

"What's the problem?" I asked. I was asking both Dolores Dodd and her ex-husband.

"He embarrassed me," she said, without any further explanation.

And without any further anything, I said to DeCiro, "Go."

DeCiro twitched a smile. "I was invited."

"I'm uninviting you. Go."

His face tightened and he thought about saying or doing something. But my eyes were on him like magnets on metal and instead he gathered his date and her décolletage and took a powder.

"Are you ready to go home?" I asked Dolores.

"No," she said, with a shy smile, and she squeezed my arm, and went back to the table of twelve where her party of Hollywood types awaited. She was the guest of honor, after all.

Two hours and two drinks later, I was escorting her home. She sat in the back of the candy-apple red Packard in her mink coat and sheer mauve-and-silver evening gown and diamond necklace and told me what had happened, the wind whipping her ice-blonde hair.

"Nicky got himself invited," she said, almost shouting over the wind. "Without my knowledge. Asked the host to reserve a seat next to me at the table. Then he wandered in late, with a date, that little *starlet*, which you may have noticed rhymes with harlot, and sat at another table, leaving me sitting next to an empty seat at a party in *my* honor. He sat there necking with that little tramp and I got up and went over and gave him a piece of my mind. It . . . got a little out of hand. Thanks for stepping in, Marlowe."

"It's what you pay me for."

She sat in silence for a while; only the wind spoke. It was a cold Saturday night, as cold as a chilled martini. I had asked her if she wanted the top up on the convertible, but she'd said no. She began to look behind us as we moved slowly down Sunset.

"Marlowe," she said, "someone's following us."

"I don't think so."

"Somebody's following us, I tell you!"

"I'm keeping an eye on the rearview mirror. We're fine."

She leaned forward and clutched my shoulder. "Get moving! Do you want me to be kidnapped, or killed? It could be Brunette's gangsters, for God's sake!"

She was the boss. I hit the pedal. At speeds up to seventy miles per, we sailed west around the curves of Sunset; there was a service station at the junction of the boulevard and the coast highway, and I pulled in.

"What are you doing?" she demanded.

I turned and looked into the frightened blue eyes. "I'm going to get some gas, and keep watch. And see if anybody comes up on us, or suspicious goes by. Don't you worry. I'm armed."

I looked close at every car that passed by the station. I saw no one and nothing suspicious. Then I paid the attendant and we headed north on the coast highway. Going nice and slow.

"I ought to fire you," she said, pouting back there.

"This is my last night, Miss Dodd," I said. "I like to work for my money. I feel I'm taking yours."

She leaned forward, clutched my shoulder again. "No, no, I tell you, I'm frightened."

"Why?"

"I . . . I just feel I still need you around. You give me a sense of security."

"Have you had any more threatening notes?"

"No." Her voice sounded very small now.

"If you do, call me, or the cops. Or both."

It was two a.m. when I slid the big car in front of the sprawling Sidewalk Cafe. I was shivering with cold; a sea breeze was blowing, Old Man Winter taking his revenge on California. I turned and looked at her again. I smiled.

"I'll walk you to the door, Miss Dodd."

She smiled at me, too, but this time the smile didn't light up her face, or the world, or me. This time the smile was as sad as her eyes. Sadder.

"That won't be necessary, Marlowe."

"Are you sure?"

"Yes. Do me one favor. Work for me next week. Be my chauffeur one more week, while I decide whether or not to replace you with another bodyguard, or . . . what."

"Okay."

"Go home, Marlowe. See you Monday."

"See you Monday," I said, and I watched her go in the front door of the cafe. Then I drove the Packard up to the garage above, on the palisades, and got in my dusty inelegant 1925 Marmon and headed back to my apartment at the Berglund in Hollywood. I had a hunch Dolores Dodd wouldn't be pulling down a wall bed in *her* apartment tonight.

My hunch was right, but for the wrong reason.

Monday morning, sunny but cool if no longer cold, I pulled into one of the parking places alongside the Sidewalk Cafe; it was around ten-thirty and mine was the only car. The big front door was locked. I knocked until the Spanish cleaning woman let me in. She said she hadn't seen Miss Dodd yet this morning. I went up the private stairway off the kitchen that led up to the two apartments. The door at the top of the stairs was unlocked; beyond it were the two facing apartment doors. I knocked on hers.

"Miss Dodd?"

No answer.

I tried for a while, then went and found the cleaning woman again. "Maria, do you have any idea where Miss Dodd might be? She doesn't seem to be in her room."

"She might be stay up at Meester Eastmon's."

I nodded, started to walk away, then looked back and added as an afterthought, "Did you see her yesterday?"

"I no work Sunday."

I guess Maria, like God, Marlowe, and Dolores Dodd, rested on Sunday. Couldn't blame her.

I thought about taking the car up and around, then said to hell with it and began climbing the concrete steps beyond the pedestrian bridge that arched over the highway just past the cafe. These steps, all two hundred and eighty of them, straight up the steep hill, were the only direct access from the coast road to the bungalow on Cabrillo Street. Windblown sand had drifted over the steps, and the galvanized handrail was as cold and damp as a liar's handshake.

I grunted my way to the top. I'd started out as a young man, had reached middle age by step one hundred, and was now ready for the retirement home. I sat on the cold wet top step and poured sand out of my scuffed-up Florsheims, glad I hadn't bothered with a shine in the last few weeks. Then I stood and looked past the vertiginous drop of the steps, to where the sun was reflecting off the sand and sea. The beach was blinding, the ocean dazzling. It was beautiful, but it hurt to look at. A seagull was flailing with awkward grace against the breeze, like a fighter losing the last round.

Soon I was knocking on Eastman's front door. No answer. Went to check to see if my client's car was there, swinging up the black-studded blue garage door. The car was there, all right, the red Packard convertible, next to Eastman's Lincoln sedan.

My client was there, too.

She was slumped in the front seat of the Packard, sprawled across the steering wheel. She was still in the mink, the mauve-and-silver gown, and the diamond necklace she'd worn to the Troc Saturday night. But her clothes were rumpled, in disarray, like an unmade bed; and there was a little blood on the front of the gown, coagulated rubies beneath the diamonds. There was a little blood on her face, on her white, white face.

She'd always had pale creamy skin, but now it was as white as a wedding dress. There was no pulse in her throat. She was cold. She'd been dead a while.

I stood and looked at her and maybe I cried. That's my business, isn't it? Then I went out and up the side steps to the loft above the garage and roused the elderly fellow named Jones who lived there; he was the bookkeeper for the Sidewalk Cafe. I asked him if he had a phone, and he did, and I used it.

I had told my story to the uniformed men four times before the men from Central Homicide showed. The detective in charge was Lieutenant Randall, a thin, somber, detached man in his midforties with smooth creamy gray hair and icy eyes. His brown gabardine suit wasn't expensive but it was well pressed. His green porkpie lightweight felt hat was in his hand, in deference to the deceased.

Out of deference to me, he listened to my story as I told it for the fifth time. He didn't seem to think much of it.

"You're telling me this woman was murdered," he said.

"I'm telling you the gambling syndicate boys were pressuring her, and she wasn't caving in."

"And you were her bodyguard," Randall said.

"Some bodyguard," said the other man from homicide, Randall's brutish shadow, and cracked his knuckles and laughed. We were in the garage and the laughter made hollow echoes off the cement, like a basketball bouncing in an empty stadium.

"I was her bodyguard," I told Randall tightly. "But I didn't work Sundays."

Randall nodded. He walked over and looked at the corpse in the convertible. A photographer from homicide was snapping photos; pops and flashes of light accompanied Randall's trip around the car, as if he were a star at a Hollywood opening.

I went outside. The smell of death is bad enough when it's impersonal;

when somebody you know has died, it's like having asthma in a steamroom.

Randall found me leaning against the side of the stucco garage, lighting up my second Camel.

"It looks like suicide," he said.

"Sure. It's supposed to."

He lifted an eyebrow and a shoulder. "The ignition switch is turned on. Carbon monoxide."

"Car wasn't running when I got here."

"Long since ran out of gas, most likely. If what you say is true, she's been there since Saturday night . . . that is, early Sunday morning."

I shrugged. "She's wearing the same clothes, at least."

"When we fix time of death, it'll all come clear."

"Oh, yeah? See what the coroner has to say about that."

Randall's icy eyes froze further. "Why?"

"This cold snap we've had, last three days. It's warmer this morning, but Sunday night, Jesus. That sea breeze was murder—if you'll pardon the expression."

Randall nodded. "Perhaps cold enough to retard decomposition, you mean."

"Perhaps."

He pushed the porkpie back on his head. "We need to talk to this bird Eastman."

"I'll say. He's probably at his studio. Paramount. When he's on a picture, they pick him up by limo every morning before dawn."

Randall went to use the phone in old man Jones's loft flat. I smoked my cigarette.

Randall's brutish sidekick exited the garage and slid his arm around the shoulder of a young uniformed cop, who seemed uneasy about the attention.

"Ice-cream blonde, huh?" the big flatfoot said. "I woulda liked a coupla of scoops of that myself."

I tapped the brute on the shoulder and he turned to me and said, "Huh?" stupidly, and I smacked him. He went down like a building.

But not out, though. "You're gonna pay for that, you bastard," he said, sounding like the school-yard bully he was. He touched the blood in the corner of his mouth, hauled himself up off the cement. "You go to goddamn jail when you hit a goddamn cop."

"You'd need a witness, first," I said.

"I got one," he said, but when he turned to look, the young uniformed cop was gone.

I walked up to him and stood damn near belt buckle to belt buckle and smiled a smile that had nothing to do with smiling. "Any time you want to pay me back, man to man, I won't be hard to find."

He tasted blood and fluttered his eyes like a girl and said something unintelligible and disappeared back inside the garage.

Randall came clopping down the wooden steps and stood before me and smiled firmly. "I just spoke with Eastman. We'll interview him more formally, of course, but the preliminary interrogation indicates a possible explanation."

"Oh?"

He was nodding. "Yeah. He says he didn't see her Saturday night after the party. Apparently he bolted the stairwell door around midnight. It's a door that leads to both apartments up top the Sidewalk Cafe. Said he thought Miss Dodd had mentioned she was going to sleep over at her mother's that night."

"You mean, she couldn't get in?"

"Right."

"Well, hell, man, she would've knocked."

"Eastman says if she did, he didn't hear her. He says there was high wind and pounding surf all night; he figures that drowned out all other sounds."

I smirked. "Does he, really? So what's your scenario?"

"Well, when Miss Dodd found she couldn't get into her apartment, she must've decided to climb the steps to the street above, walked to the garage, and spent the rest of the night in her car. She must've have gotten cold and switched on the ignition to keep warm, and the fumes got her."

I sighed. "A minute ago you were talking suicide."

"That's still a possibility."

"What about the traces of blood on her face and dress?"

He shrugged. "She may have fallen across the wheel and cut her mouth when she fell unconscious."

"Look, if she wanted to get warm, why would she sit in her open convertible? That Lincoln sedan next to her is unlocked and has the keys in it."

"I can't answer that—yet."

I was shaking my head. Then I pointed at him. "Ask the elderly gent upstairs if he heard her opening the garage door, starting up the Packard's cold engine sometime between two a.m. and dawn. Ask him!"

"I did. He didn't. But it was a windy night, and . . ."

"Yeah, and the surf was crashing something fierce. Right. Let's take a look at her shoes."

"Huh?"

I pointed down to my scuffed-up Florsheims. "I just scaled those two hundred and eighty steps. This shoeshine boy's nightmare is the result. Let's *see* if she walked up those steps."

Randall nodded and led me into the garage. The print boys hadn't been over the vehicle yet, so the lieutenant didn't open the door on the rider's side, he just leaned carefully in.

Then he stood and contemplated what he'd seen. For a moment he seemed to have forgotten me. Then he said, "Have a look yourself."

I had one last look at the beautiful woman who'd driven to nowhere in this immobile car.

She wore delicate silver dress heels; they were as pristine as Cinderella's glass slippers.

The coroner at the inquest agreed with me on one point: "The high winds and very low cold prevailing that weekend would have preserved the body beyond the usual time required for decomposition to set in."

The inquest was, otherwise, a bundle of contradictions, and about as inconclusive as the virgin birth. A few new, sinister facts emerged. She had bruises *inside* her throat. Had someone shoved a bottle down her throat? Her blood alcohol level was high—.13 percent—much higher than would have been accounted for by the three or four drinks she was seen to have at the Troc. And there *was* gas left in the car, it turned out—several gallons. Yet the ignition switch was turned on. . . .

But the coroner's final verdict was that Dolores had died by carbon monoxide poisoning, "breathed accidentally." Nonetheless, the papers talked suicide, and the word on the streets of Hollywood was "hush-up." Nobody wanted another scandal. Not after Mary Astor's diaries and Busby Berkeley's drunk-driving fatalities.

I wasn't buying the coroner's verdict, either.

I knew that three people, on the Monday I'd found Dolores, had come forward to the authorities and reported having seen her on *Sunday*, long after she had "officially" died.

Miranda Diamond, now Eastman's ex-wife (their divorce had gone through, finally, apparently fairly amicably), claimed to have seen Dolores, still dressed in her Trocadero fineries, behind the wheel of her distinctive Packard convertible at the corner of Sunset and Vine on Sunday, mid-morning. She had been, Miranda told the cops, in the company of a tall, swarthy, nattily dressed young man whom Miranda had never seen before.

Mrs. Wallace Ford, wife of the famed director, had received a brief phone call from Dolores around four Sunday afternoon. Dolores had called to say she would be attending the Fords' cocktail party, and was it all right if she brought along "a new, handsome friend?"

Finally, and best of all, there was Warren Eastman himself. Neighbors had reported to the police that they had heard Eastman and Dolores quarreling bitterly, violently, at the bungalow on Cabrillo, above the restaurant, Sunday morning, around breakfast time. When questioned on this point, Eastman revealed that he had thrown her out, and that she had screamed obscenities and beaten on the door for ten minutes (and police did find kick marks on the shrub-secluded, hacienda-style door).

"It was a lovers' quarrel," Eastman told a reporter. "I heard she had a new boyfriend—some Latin fellow from San Francisco—and she denied it. But I knew she was lying."

Eastman also revealed, in the press, that Dolores didn't own any real interest in her Sidewalk Cafe; she had made no investment other than lending her name, for which she got fifty percent of the profits.

I called Randall after the inquest and he told me the case was closed.

"We both know something smells," I said. "Aren't you going to do something?"

"Yes," he said.

"What?"

"I'm going to hang up."

And he did.

Randall was a good cop in a bad town, an honest man in a system so corrupt the Borgias would've felt moral outrage. But he couldn't do much about movie-mogul pressure by way of City Hall; Los Angeles had one big business, and the film industry was it. And I was just a private detective with a dead client.

On the other hand, she'd paid me to protect her, and ultimately I hadn't. I had accepted her money, and it seemed to me she ought to get something for it, even if it was posthumous.

I went out on a Monday morning—four weeks to the day since I'd found the ice-cream blonde melting in that garage—and at the cafe, which still bore her name, sitting alone in the cocktail lounge, reading *Variety* and drinking a bloody Mary, was Warren Eastman. He was between pictures and just two stools down from where she had sat when she first hired me. He was wearing a blue blazer, a cream silk cravat, and white pants.

He lowered the paper and looked at me; he was surprised to see me, but it was not a pleasant surprise, even though he affected a toothy smile under the twitchy little mustache.

"What brings you around, Marlowe? I don't need a bodyguard."

"Don't be so sure," I said genially, sitting next to him.

He looked down his nose at me through slitted eyes; his diamond-shaped face seemed handsome to some, I supposed, but to me it was a harshly angular thing, a hunting knife with hair.

"What exactly," he said, "do you mean by that?"

"I mean I know you murdered Dolores," I said.

He laughed and returned to his newspaper. "Go away, Marlowe. Find some schoolgirl who frightens easily if you want to scare somebody."

"I want to scare somebody all right. I just have one question . . . did your ex-wife help you with the murder itself, or was she just a supporting player?"

He put the paper down. He sipped the bloody Mary. His face was wooden but his eyes were animated.

I laughed gutturally. "You and your convoluted murder mysteries. You were so clever you almost schemed your way into the gas chamber, didn't you? With your masquerades and charades."

"What in the hell are you talking about?"

"You were smart enough to figure out that the cold weather would confuse the time of death. But you thought you could make the coroner think Dolores met her fate the *next* day—Sunday evening, perhaps. You didn't have an alibi for the early a.m. hours of Sunday. And that's when you killed her."

"Is it, really? Marlowe, I saw her Sunday morning, breakfast. I argued with her, the neighbors heard . . ."

"Exactly. They *heard*—but they didn't *see* a thing. That was something you staged, either with your ex-wife's help, or whoever your current starlet is. Some actress, the same actress who later called Mrs. Ford up to accept the cocktail party invite and further spread the rumor of the new lover from San Francisco. Nice touch, that. Pulls in the rumors of gangsters from San Francisco who threatened her; was the 'swarthy man' Miranda saw a torpedo posing as a lover? A gigolo with a gun? A member of Artie Lewis's dance band, maybe? Let the cops and the papers wonder. Well, it won't wash with me; I was with her for her last two months. She had no new serious love in her life, from San Francisco or elsewhere. Your 'swarthy man' is the little Latin lover who wasn't there."

"Miranda *saw* him with her, Marlowe . . ."

"No. Miranda didn't see anything. She told the story you wanted her to tell; she went along with you, and you treated her right in the divorce settlement. You can afford to. You're sole owner of Dolores Dodd's Sidewalk

Cafe, now. Lock, stock, and barrel, with no messy interference from the star on the marquee. And now you're free to accept Laird Brunette's offer, aren't you?"

That rocked him, like a physical blow. "What?"

"That's why you killed Dolores. She was standing in your way. You wanted to put a casino in upstairs; it would mean big money, very big money."

"I have money."

"Yes, and you spend it. You live very lavishly. I've been checking up on you. I know you intimately already, and I'm going to know you even better."

His eyes quivered in the diamond mask of his face. "What are you talking about?"

"You tried to scare her at first—extortion notes, having her followed; maybe you did this with Brunette's help, maybe you did it on your own. I don't know. But then she hired me, and you scurried off into the darkness to think up something new."

He sneered and gestured archly with his cigarette holder, the cigarette in which he was about to light up. "I'm breathlessly awaiting just what evil thing it was I conjured up next."

"You decided to commit the perfect crime. Just like in the movies. You would kill Dolores one cold night, knocking her out, shoving booze down her, leaving her to die in that garage with the car running. Then you would set out to make it seem that she was still alive—during a day when you were very handsomely, unquestionably alibied."

"You're not making any sense. The verdict at the inquest was accidental death . . ."

"Yes. But the time of death is assumed to have been the night *before* you said you saw her last. Your melodrama was too involved for the simple-minded authorities, who only wanted to hush things up. They went with the more basic, obvious, tidy solution that Dolores died an accidental death early Saturday morning." I laughed, once. "You were so cute in pursuit of the 'perfect crime' you tripped yourself, Eastman."

"Did I really," he said dryly. It wasn't a question.

"Your scenario needed one more rewrite. First you told the cops you slept at the apartment over the cafe Saturday night, bolting the door around midnight, accidentally locking Dolores out. But later you admitted seeing Dolores the next morning, around breakfast time—at the *bungalow*."

His smile quivered. "Perhaps I slept at the apartment, and went up for breakfast at the bungalow."

"I don't think so. I think you killed her."

"No charges have been brought against me. And none will."

I looked at him hard, like a hanging judge passing sentence. "I'm bringing a charge against you now. I'm charging you with murder in the first degree."

His smile turned crinkly; he stared into the redness of his drink. Smoke from his cigarette-in-holder curled upward like a wreath. "Ha. A citizen's arrest, is it?"

"No. Marlowe's law. I'm going to kill you myself."

He looked at me sharply. "What? Are you mad . . ."

"Yes, I'm mad. In the sense of being angry, that is. Sometime, within the next year, or two, I'm going to kill you. Just how, I'm not just sure. Just when, well . . . perhaps tomorrow. Perhaps a month from tomorrow. Maybe next Christmas. I haven't decided yet."

"You can't be serious."

"I'm deadly serious. I'll be seeing you."

And I left him there at the bar, the glass of bloody Mary mixing itself in his hand.

Here's what I did to Warren Eastman: I spent two weeks shadowing him. Letting him see me. Letting him know I was watching his every move. Making him jump at the shadow that was me, and all the other shadows, too.

Then I stopped. I slept with my gun under my pillow for a while, in case he got ambitious. But I didn't bother him any further.

The word in Hollywood was that Eastman was somehow—no one knew exactly how, but somehow—dirty in the Dodd murder. And nobody in town thought it was anything but a murder. Eastman never got another picture. He went from one of the hottest directors in town to the coldest. As cold as the weekend Dolores Dodd died.

The Sidewalk Cafe stopped drawing a monied, celebrity crowd, but it did all right from regular-folks curiosity seekers. Eastman made some dough there, all right; but the casino never happened. A combination of the wrong kind of publicity and the drifting away of the high-class clientele must have changed Laird Brunette's mind.

Within a year of Dolores Dodd's death, Eastman was committed to a rest home, which is a polite way of saying insane asylum or madhouse. He was in and out of such places for the next four years, and then, one very cold, windy night, he died of a heart attack.

Did I keep my promise? Did I kill him?

I like to think I did, indirectly. I like to think that Dolores Dodd got her money's worth from her chauffeur-cum-bodyguard, who had not been there when she took that last long drive, on the night her sad blue eyes closed forever.

I like to think, in my imperfect way, that I committed the perfect crime.

━━━━━━━━━━━━━━━━━━
━━━━━━━━━━━━━━━━━━

This story is based on a real case, specifically the probable murder of actress Thelma Todd. I have taken liberties, changing names and fiction-alizing extensively, substituting characters from Chandler at times (Laird Brunette coming in for Lucky Luciano, for example) and, while there is an underpinning of history here, "The Perfect Crime" must be viewed as a fanciful work. A number of books dealing with the death of Thelma Todd were consulted, but I wish in particular to cite Marvin J. Wolf and Katherine Mader, the authors of Fallen Angels *(1986).*

In Farewell, My Lovely *(1940), Marlowe visits, briefly, the sidewalk cafe that had been Thelma Todd's, and climbs the two hundred and eighty steps to Cabrillo Street. (The wonderful 1987 book* Raymond Chandler's Los Angeles, *by Elizabeth Ward and Alain Silver, includes several photos of the hillside stairway—in reality a mere two hundred and seventy steps— as well as a photo of the still-standing structure that housed the cafe, now home to Paulist Productions, a Catholic TV and film production group.)*

My novels about Chicago detective Nathan Heller focus on real crimes and the real people involved therein, and are set in the 1930s and '40s. It seemed fitting for me, then, to do my Marlowe story in the historical Heller manner. This does not mean that I have done a Heller story and substituted Marlowe's name. Heller does to divorce work, would surely have slept with Dolores Dodd and would have taken money from just about anybody who offered it to him; and he might have flat-out killed Warren Eastman. Heller has lines he won't cross, but they are drastically different from those Marlowe won't cross.

I owe Chandler a great debt. ("Mallory," the protagonist of several novels of mine, is named after an early incarnation of Marlowe.) In my Heller novels, the idea has always been to bring a first-person Marlowe-style voice—complete with his keen wit and sharp sense of observation—to a larger landscape than the traditional mystery allows. Chandler himself experimented with an expanded landscape in The Long Goodbye *(1954), which was the longest first-person private-eye novel written until my* True Detective *(1983). In Nathan Heller's "memoirs," the expanded landscape is a historical one, as reported by a private-eye witness in the Marlowe/ Chandler tradition.*

Chandler has had, and continues to have, many followers. We who follow him have a responsibility to honor his memory and his achievement, not by mimicking him, but by attempting to do what he did—break new ground in an rich old field.

Max Allan Collins

THE BLACK-EYED BLONDE

BENJAMIN M. SCHUTZ

1936

I WOKE UP WITH my nose in the newsprint and a telephone inside my head. I shook my head and the phone fell out onto my desk. My hand spider walked over to it, grabbed it around the throat, and silenced it.

"Hello," she said. Her voice fluttered all through both of those syllables.

When I didn't answer, she tried again. "Hello, Mr. Marlowe, are you there?"

I checked the inside of my jacket to be sure and said, "Yes, this is Philip Marlowe."

"Oh, thank goodness, Mr. Marlowe. My name is Francine Ley De Ruse. My husband is Johnny De Ruse. Do you know him?"

I knew Johnny De Ruse. He was a gambler out of Vegas. He'd taken over Benny Cyrano's place. I wasn't sure how much more I wanted to know.

"Yes, I know him."

"I'd like you to follow him, Mr. Marlowe. I think he's seeing another woman. If he is, I want you to get pictures."

"I'm sorry, Mrs. De Ruse, but I don't do divorce work."

"But Mr. Carmady said you were the best. You were the man I should talk to."

Good old Ted Carmady, throwing some work my way. Ever since he'd hooked up with Jean Adrian, he'd become Santa Claus to the rest of us working stiffs. And here it wasn't even November.

"I'm sorry, Mrs. De Ruse. Ted has me mixed up with another Philip Marlowe. Like I said, I don't do divorce work."

"Well, do you know where this other Philip Marlowe is?"

"No, Mrs. De Ruse, I haven't a clue."

"Well, I'm sorry to have wasted your time, Mr. Marlowe, if that's even your name." She replaced the receiver indelicately.

"No problem at all," I said to myself.

I rubbed my eyes and stared at the top of my desk. So this was as far as I'd gotten. I was just going to stop by and type up my notes before I went home. Guess I didn't make it. I reached into my pocket and pulled out my notebook and the novel I had been reading. *Fast One*, by a guy named Paul Cain. Rumor had it that Cain was a screenwriter in town whose real name was Ruric. Rumor had it that even Ruric wasn't his real name. Maybe it was Marlowe.

I flipped open my notebook. I'd spent all night watching a cop as a favor for a friend of mine from the D.A.'s office. Seems that the D.A. wasn't happy with the police investigation of a recent murder. They'd asked me to shadow the cop because he wouldn't know my face. He'd spent a long time over dinner with the decidedly ungrieving widow at Musso and Frank's before dropping her off at her house. I spent the next two hours following him as he drove aimlessly through our host, the City of Angels.

I went over to the sink in the corner, ran some water, and splashed it on my face. Toweling dry, I looked at the face in the mirror. We looked like the same guy, but we weren't. I did know where that other Philip Marlowe had gone. He'd disappeared soon after that visit from Delano Stiles.

I went back to my desk, spun the chair around so it faced east, and looked out over Cahuenga Boulevard. I closed my eyes and it was spring again. The late afternoon sunlight was streaming in so heavily it looked pooled, like butter, on the floor. And Delano Stiles was telling me about his wife.

He'd marched right into my office, sat down, leaned forward, and told me, "I need you to find my wife, Mr. Marlowe."

I looked up from a chess diagram I had been studying and asked, "And why is that?"

"Because she's gone. She's run away, Mr. Marlowe, and she's taken my son with her."

I took a moment to see what she was running away from. He was tall, slim, and well dressed in a pin-striped suit. His black hair was swept back and had a touch of gray at the temples. His strong, even features were marred by the presence of a ridiculous, pencil-thin moustache.

"Let's back up a step," I said. "What's your name, your wife's, and your son's?"

"I'm Delano Stiles." He stopped to take a deep breath. He sounded like he'd run up all six flights of stairs to my office. "My wife is Monica and our son's name is Brandon. He's five years old."

"How long has your wife been missing, Mr. Stiles?"

"A couple of hours, maybe. I got a call from a car dealer over on Wilcox. He said that she had come in and tried to sell her car. When he found out that the car was in my name he told her she couldn't sell it. He was calling me when she grabbed some suitcases out of the car and ran out of the showroom, dragging Brandon with her. As soon as I got the message, I drove right over and questioned the man. Then I went looking for them myself. But frankly, Mr. Marlowe, I'm not the kind of man who can make people answer my questions. So I looked up detectives in the phone book, saw that your office was nearby, and came right over to see if I could retain your services."

"I'm sorry, Mr. Stiles, but I haven't any experience in divorce work. My background has been in insurance and criminal investigations."

"This isn't really a divorce case, Mr. Marlowe. It's Brandon I want back, not my wife. He's only five, Mr. Marlowe, just a little boy. It must be terrifying for him to be dragged all over strange parts of this city by a woman who's no longer thinking clearly."

"Why do you say that?"

"Because there's no reason for her to do something like this."

"Has she ever taken it on the lam before?"

"No. She's never done anything like this before. It's so . . . so impulsive."

Nothing Stiles had said so far had overcome my aversion to divorce work. Besides that, I still had seven bucks in the bank.

"I don't know, Mr. Stiles. Domestic stuff really isn't my line."

That's because it always seemed like legitimized blackmail. Two people trying to dig up as much dirt as possible so they could hold each other's noses in it until one of them cried, "Enough!" I was not about to be anyone's spade. But then again, maybe this one was different. I waited to find out.

"Are you married, Mr. Marlowe?"

"No."

"Any children?"

"No."

"Then you can't know what it's like to lose one, can you? I love my son, Mr. Marlowe. I need him with me. I don't want Monica back. I'll offer her a fair settlement. You won't have to be peeping at keyholes, I assure you."

I thought it over. He just wanted his kid found. I wasn't being asked to prove that the mother wasn't fit to walk among decent, god-fearing people, let alone marry or raise one.

"All right, Mr. Stiles, I'll take the case. If she's trying to skip town, she'll need money. Did she tap the bank accounts?"

"No, I called the bank before I came over here. The accounts are all in my name anyway."

"Does she have any money of her own?"

"You mean family money? No, her people are farmers, I believe. They're not even from around here. They're in Arkansas, Little Rock, I think."

"How did you meet her? It doesn't sound like you two traveled in the same circles."

"That's true. But out here in Hollywood all the circles seem to overlap, don't you think? Anyway it seems that way to me. Monica was a showgirl at Cyrano's. That's where I met her. She wanted to be an actress. I admit I was quite taken with her, Mr. Marlowe. She's a stunning girl. These days I think she was more taken with my connections than with me."

As Hollywood marriages went this was no worse than most. It would last as long as her looks and his money made each other feel good. When that didn't work anymore they'd finally realize that they were strangers, get divorced, and go do the same damn thing again.

"Has she appeared in any movies? That might make it easier to track her down. People in this town are crazy about identifying actors and actresses. It brightens their days just being in the same city with them."

"No, she hasn't been in any pictures. Monica's dreams exceed her talents. Even my intercessions on her behalf can't change that. She seems to blame me for her failure. I tried to provide for her every need and want, and this is how she repays me."

Stiles was wandering off into his own melancholy reverie. I retrieved him with a question. "Does your wife have any friends she might turn to at a time like this?"

"No. Monica was, as they say, 'right off the bus,' when I met her at Cyrano's. We married shortly thereafter. She never made any effort to get along with my friends. She just stayed at home and doted on Brandon."

I pulled out my notebook, flipped it open, and prepared to write. "What things did she take with her?"

"I asked the maid to check the house when I got the call about the car. She said that Monica took two suitcases filled with clothes for her and Brandon, some makeup, her jewelry, Brandon's teddy bear, and his favorite blanket."

"What were she and Brandon wearing?"

"Roxana, that's our maid, says she was wearing a teal blue skirt and a cream-colored silk blouse. Brandon had on white knee-high socks, khaki shorts, and a green and white striped shirt."

"Good. Do you have a picture of either of them?"

"Yes, I do." He pulled out his wallet, slid the photo out, and handed it to me.

Monica Stiles was sitting in a chair with her arms around her son. He was leaning back against her so that their cheeks touched. Brandon was a little towhead with deep dimples and the assured smile of a well-loved child.

A billowing tangle of blonde hair framed his mother's face. I studied that face. A broad, high forehead tapered past prominent cheekbones to a small square chin. Her full upper lip was wide and downswept. She would smile and pout magnificently. Her eyes were hidden behind large sunglasses.

"What color are your wife's eyes?"

"Black."

I looked at him.

"Yes, black. Monica's coloring is very unusual. She's a natural blonde, too."

"I'll need to take this with me," I said, tapping the picture.

"If you must. Please don't lose it, Mr. Marlowe."

"I'll be very careful with it. Now what was the name of the car dealer who called you?"

"The man's name was Arthur Shuman. He's the general manager at Peabody Motors. They're on Wilcox, between Sunset and Hollywood."

"Okay. Where can I reach you today if I find your wife and son?"

"I'll be at my office the rest of the day. It's on Rossmore just opposite Paramount Studios." He gave me the direct line into his office.

"My fee is twenty dollars a day and expenses. If I don't find her today, I'd suggest you call Pinkerton's in Little Rock to catch her at the other end."

Stiles opened his wallet and began laying crisp twenties on my desk. "Here's twenty for your time today and forty against expenses. Please find her for me, Mr. Marlowe."

"That's what I'm about to do, Mr. Stiles."

He rose and turned to leave. I had one question left to ask but I wasn't sure I needed to know the answer. With his hand on the doorknob, I decided to ask it anyway.

"Mr. Stiles, why is your wife in such a hurry to leave town?"

He turned slowly, and looking down at me, he said, "Mr. Marlowe, I assure you that it's a personal and private matter between my wife and me. I'm sure you can respect that."

"Of course," I said.

I watched Stiles pull the office door closed behind him and stared at the bills on my desk. Los Angeles was the wrong town to be poor in. When the hoboes tried to enter, city hall made a fence out of the boys in blue and dared them to climb over it. With things as tough as they were, why would Monica Stiles put herself on the wrong side of money? When I found her, I just might ask her that.

I stood up, unclipped my holster, and locked my gun in my desk. I wasn't going to be shooting anybody today. With the money in my wallet, I locked up the office and went to work.

Peabody Motors was one block west and one south. Shuman was bald and fat, and judging from the way he rocked on his feet, his shoes hurt, too. He confirmed everything that Stiles had told me.

I thanked him for his help and walked out of the showroom. On the sidewalk I tried to imagine myself trying to get out of town and standing there with two suitcases and a kid and no money in my pocket. She was a long way from Union Station or the airport. The bus station was only two blocks away, on Vine. Buses were cheaper and left more frequently. If Monica Stiles was still in town at all, she was nearby. That much I was sure of.

I drifted down Wilcox and crossed Sunset, looking for the places where she might have gotten money. On Santa Monica, I saw a pawnbroker's gold trident and went inside.

The man behind the counter had a loupe in his eye and a bauble in his hand.

"Excuse me," I said.

He put the stone down onto a velvet pillow and looked at me. "Yeah?"

I took out the picture of Monica and Brandon Stiles. "Has this woman been in this afternoon?"

He took the picture and studied it. "Not while I've been here, and I'd remember. She's a looker, that one is."

"Okay, thanks. Any other pawnshops in this area?"

"No. We're the only one up this way. Most of the others are over in Smoketown. What's the skirt trying to move, anyway?"

"Jewelry."

"Good stuff?" he asked hopefully.

"Yeah, real good." I opened my wallet and put a fin on the velvet pillow. I put my card on the bill. "If she comes in, you call me. It'll be worth your while."

He slipped the bill into his shirt pocket and glanced at the card. "Sure thing, Mr. Marlowe."

"If I'm not there I'll be at Al Levy's Tavern. You know it?"

"Yeah, the one on Vine, next to the bus station."

"That's right."

I left the shop and headed east on Santa Monica to Vine. As far as

I could tell, Monica Stiles still had no money. Wearing a silk blouse and stockings she wasn't going to get much of a response if she tried to pan-handle. I didn't feature her doing a smash-and-grab routine either, not with little Brandon in tow.

I wandered into the bus station and checked the schedule. The next bus east left at 7:30, two hours from now. I did a slow circuit through the terminal, but they weren't there. I thought about sitting still for the two hours and letting her come to me, but I still had a couple of moves left to make and the silly idea that I should earn my fee.

Al Levy's Tavern was just up the block. I walked in, ambled around the bar, and nodded to Al. He grunted around the cigar stuffed into his cheek and continued washing dishes. I fed the phone a nickel and called a house dick I knew. The shops were going to close pretty soon, and since Mrs. Stiles wasn't in the bus station the only places left for her to lie low in were the apartment hotels north of Hollywood Boulevard.

"Gramercy Place Apartments," a voice said.

"Is Kuvalick there?"

"Hold a moment." I held.

"Kuvalick," he rasped.

"Stan, it's Philip Marlowe."

"Yeah, Marlowe, long time."

"I need a favor."

"What is it?"

"I'm looking for a woman. She's dragging a couple of suitcases and a kid. Teal skirt, cream blouse. A good-looking blonde. You want to keep your eyes open and call some of your buddies in the other buildings. If you turn her up, call me at Al Levy's, okay?"

"Sure thing, Marlowe."

"Thanks."

I swiveled around on the stool and stared into Al Levy's face. Al had a bulbous drinker's nose that got so bright when he was angry it looked like a tomato wedge between his eyes.

"What'll it be, Marlowe?" he growled. A shiv in the throat had left him with a one-tone voicebox.

"Whiskey."

Al poured with a friend's heavy hand, and I sipped a bit before I took it back to the far corner booth and waited for the phone to ring.

I sipped and waited for almost an hour. When the call came in, it was Kuvalick.

"Your girl's been made, Marlowe."

"Where?"

"Over on Kenmore, near Hollywood."

"The kid with her?"

"No. Just the doll. She was walking toward the Morewood Arms Hotel."

"Thanks, Stan."

"Nothing to it."

I finished off my drink and went back into the rapidly spreading dusk. The Morewood was two blocks away and on the far side of Kenmore. I took up a position opposite the entrance of the hotel but didn't see Monica Stiles there.

She was walking up the sidewalk arm in arm with an older man who looked and dressed like her husband. Maybe she was learning to make friends. She was dressed as the maid had described, but she was wearing the sunglasses I had seen in the picture.

As they approached the front door, she turned her head toward me and ran her hand through her fine blonde hair. I saw a diamond on her left hand, gold buttons in her ears, a gold necklace that encircled her long, delicious throat and a large red pin to keep her blouse closed. I shook my head. She was wearing Little Rock and back for her, the kid, and the teddy bear, and she was doing the horizontal bop anyway. But that was Stiles's problem, not mine.

When they went through the Morewood's revolving front door, I walked across the street and used the lobby phone to call my client. I told him that I had located his wife and that his son was probably close by. He thanked me and said that he'd be there right away. I told him not to hurry and hung up. I wasn't here to take pictures or set them up for anyone else.

Back at my roost, I lit a cigarette and waited for her to come back out. About twenty minutes later she came flying out of the hotel, clattering down the steps on her high heels. Her arms were out for balance as if the stone was bunching and flexing itself under her feet.

I tossed the butt away and fell in behind her. She had a raging case of foot fever and I was afraid she'd spot me if I tried to close on her. So I slowed down and settled for just keeping her in sight.

She turned right on Franklin and ducked into a doorway. It was the side entrance to the Golden West Apartments. My place, the Hobart Arms, was only a block away.

Just as I got to the entrance and reached for the knob, the door retreated and I came face to face with Monica Stiles. She had a large suitcase in her left hand and a smaller one under her arm. In her other hand were her son's small fingers. He looked up at me, but he wasn't wearing that assured smile. He had that wide-eyed stare you get when your world is collapsing around you and you wonder if you'll ever be able to see over the rubble. He clutched his teddy bear to his chest.

"Excuse me," she said, "I've got to get somewhere."

I reached out and gripped her elbow. "I'm sorry, Mrs. Stiles. I can't let you leave."

Her head snapped towards me. "Let me go. You have no right to stop me like this."

"It's not you, Mrs. Stiles. It's the boy. His father doesn't want him to leave town."

"No," she shouted. "He can't have him. No. No. No." She swung her right hand at my face. I dodged the blow. She dropped the suitcases on my foot and pummeled me with both hands. I reached out and snatched her wrists and shook her hard. She whipped her head back and forth and tried to bite me. Her sunglasses flew off and I pulled her close.

Stiles had told the truth. She was a blonde all the way down and her eyes were black. But there was also purple and yellow and red there too.

"Rough trade at the Morewood?" I asked.

"No, you bastard. These came today with breakfast. Courtesy of your boss." The discoloration of her face was about right for a punch-out over bacon and eggs.

"Why'd he hit you?"

"How should I know. Maybe the sun came up too early. I gave up asking that question a while ago. I don't care what the answer is. I just want out. I can't take it anymore."

The boy, who had stepped into the darkness when his mother swung at me, came forward and wrapped his arms around her and lay his head on her hip.

She stroked his head and murmured, "It's okay, Brandon. Mommy's okay." Her stare dared me to make a liar out of her. I passed on it.

"Where were you going?"

"To the bus station. Catch the seven-thirty back east. My people are in Arkansas. I have no one out here. Delano kept me a prisoner in the house. He wouldn't let me out for anything. He was so jealous of anyone who paid attention to me."

"Why didn't you hock the jewelry? You'd have been out of here hours ago."

"That's a laugh, mister. Don't you think I tried? They're paste. I couldn't get to Pomona on these. Delano never trusted me. He never let me have any money. I didn't realize that everything he's given me was a fake. The only thing I have that's real is Brandon."

"How did you know that the Morewood was a hot-sheet joint? You're supposed to be right off the bus."

"When I found out that the jewelry was paste, I was frantic. I had nothing else to sell. The pawnbroker saw how desperate I was. He told me about the Morewood."

"And what was his cut for doing you this kindness?"

"He said he'd get a piece from the front desk for each guy I came in with."

When this was over I was going to have a talk with the pawnbroker. Probably a short, painful talk.

"How much money do you have?"

"Just enough to get me and Brandon out of the state. It was easy enough to pick up the guys, but I couldn't do the rest. I only got into the room with the last one. I made him get undressed first. Then I took his wallet and ran out."

I thought about everything I'd been told today and was ready to dismiss it all as self-serving half-truths. All except her black eye. That I believed in. I didn't care how she might have failed Stiles as a wife, there was no excuse for that. So I reached into my wallet and slipped out sixty dollars.

"Here, take this. It'll get you home and you can eat, too."

She reached out slowly and took the bills from my hand.

"Thank you. I don't know how I can repay you, Mister . . ."

"Marlowe, Philip Marlowe. And you don't have to. The money isn't mine. I never earned it. I never found you."

I reached down for one of the bags, and when I turned I saw Delano Stiles striding across the street toward us. He had two Hard Harrys flanking him.

I pulled my car keys out of my pocket, turned, and pressed them into her palm.

"Go. It's the convertible on the corner. You can still catch the bus. Don't go to Little Rock. He'll be waiting for you there. Get lost."

She reached for the suitcase and I said, "Leave them or you'll never make it."

She tore a slit in her skirt, kicked off her heels, picked Brandon up and ran for her life.

I watched Brandon's face over her shoulder as she fled up the street and wondered why he didn't cry out for his dad.

Stiles pointed up the street and one of his goons sheared off in pursuit. I dashed out into the street and tackled him knee-high. He toppled over and slammed his head on the road. He was stunned for a second. I grabbed his collar, set him up, and closed his shop.

I heard footsteps behind me and rolled away. Stiles kicked at my head, but I grabbed his ankle, twisted it hard, and he fell over. I scrambled to my feet and saw the second guy standing in the intersection. My car was pulling away from the curb. He reached into his jacket and pulled out a pistol. He moved casually into his shooter's crouch and sighted down his rigid arm.

I ran up the street yelling, "No!" But I was too late and his aim too true. I saw my car close on him. He fired once, twice, and then slid sideways like a toreador as the car careened past him on its three good tires, veered sharply to the right, jumped the curb, and slammed into Monroe's Pharmacy.

The shooter holstered up and sauntered over to the wreck. I caught up to him, spun him around, and broke my hand breaking his jaw. Stiles ran past me and flung open the car's passenger door. The whoop of police sirens grew in the distance.

Stiles groaned, "Oh my god," and sank to his knees. I looked in the driver's window. Monica Stiles was crouched over her son. She held his head in her hands and was kissing him everywhere. Over and over she murmured, "Baby, Baby." But he couldn't hear her. Children's bones are soft they say, but no neck turns that far.

I walked over to the bus stop bench, sat down, and lit a cigarette. I took it out of my mouth, stared at its glowing red tip and wanted to put it out in my heart. Instead I waited for the sirens to drown out two sets of sobs.

They never did though, and these days I'm not the same man I was that day. The name's the same, and that confuses some people. That's why I have to remind them that I don't do divorce work.

I read my first Raymond Chandler novel sitting on a two-dollar-a-night cot in the staff quarters of a West Virginia V. A. hospital. It was The Long Goodbye. *When I put the book down two things stayed with me: Chandler's style and Philip Marlowe.*

Chandler's poetic images made the "same old scenes" fresh and vibrant and lodged them firmly in my memory. He wrote dialogue in the language we wished we spoke, and he made it sound natural anyway.

Marlowe, like all detectives, made trouble his business. Chandler made the cost of that decision a central part of his novels. Seven times Raymond Chandler told the story of Philip Marlowe's struggle to resist the corruption he saw all around him. The tale got better with each telling. It's fifteen years since I first met Philip Marlowe and I still feel the same way.

Benjamin M. Schutz

GUN MUSIC

LOREN D. ESTLEMAN

1937

CARSON MOLDINE HAD an office in the cellar of the Mammoth Pictures property department building, right between Mae West's wardrobe and a room full of breakaway bottles suitable for use in saloon brawls. It was a fragrant little room with no window, a dusty bulb in the ceiling, and a big yellow oak desk that Noah's children had carved their initials into on rainy days. Noah had inherited it from his grandfather.

Moldine was a little older than the desk. A big brown man with no hair, great white handlebars, and eyes like shards of broken blue glass, he was rumored to be wanted in Oklahoma on an 1899 murder charge. Whether or not the rumor was true, there was nothing false about the Frontier Colt he wore in a holster under his old plaid jacket. Its amber handle bumped the desk when he leaned forward to accept the letters I'd brought. The blue eyes darted over each in turn. "This all of them?"

"Aren't they enough?" I asked.

He laughed once, a short dry bark, and dropped the pages onto the old stained blotter. "The little tramp's more trouble than her contract's worth. Sooner or later the studio brass will see that and give her the boot. Then they can use the money they're wasting on these leeches to make good pictures for a change. Can we expect any trouble over how you came by these?"

"Naw, I dropped the bodies into La Brea." I grinned and set fire to a Camel. "I paid them a lot less than they were asking. They hollered, but they knew none of the Hollywood rags would print what's in the letters, and the real papers don't care."

"I'd have shot the bastards."

"Why didn't you?"

"I'm paid to end trouble, not start it. What do we owe you, Marlowe?"

"The ransom ate up most of the retainer. A C-note ought to do it."

"Hell." He drew a disreputable-looking leather wallet from his hip pocket, separated three fifties from the wad inside, and held them out. "The extra fifty's for the whiskey," he said.

"What whiskey?"

"The whiskey it'll take to wash the stink off your hands. I'd rather dress out a steer in the dark than shake hands with that crew."

"Who said I shook hands?" I gave him back one of the bills. "Mammoth doesn't pay bonuses to private stars. Put it in your retirement fund."

"Who's retiring?"

I started to go. When I was at the door he called to me. His weathered old face was unreadable. "If you won't take tips, maybe you'll accept work. There's a girl on this lot could do with a break."

"What kind of a break?"

"I don't know exactly. She turned down one picture too many and they put her on suspension. Before that she started showing up late for shootings, fluffing lines, things she never did before. She's got trouble but she won't say what kind."

"Who's got her contract?"

"Sam Whiteside."

I spat smoke. "She's got trouble."

"Whiteside's okay, if you don't work for him and never lost money on one of his pictures. That's one kind of trouble. Hers is another kind. I think she needs a shamus."

"What's she to you?"

The old head came up. "That means what?"

"It means what it means, Carson. If she's your daughter, okay. If she's your mistress, that's okay, too, but it makes a difference in the way I approach her. You know that."

"I guess. Maybe I *should* retire. I've been around these glorified pimps so long I'm starting to think people will take me for one. Christa's just someone in trouble to me. Whiteside asked me to talk to her when it started, but all I could get out of her is she doesn't belong in this town. A young swain like you could get more, probably."

"Christa's her name?"

"Christa Vine. She's a singer and a good one. She should be doing *Carmen* but they put her in musicals. You know, with Dick Powell and a bunch of fairies in tails. I like westerns myself."

"Where do I find her?"

"Laurel Canyon." He scribbled an address on a studio pad and held it out. "She's married to Sonny Bloom."

"The gangster?"

"Please. The Hollywood entrepreneur. He financed two of her pictures."

"He can afford to. When his boys wiped out Frank Nunzio's boys in New Jersey he inherited Atlantic City."

"So what are you, anti-Semitic? A girl can't help who she falls in love with. Nothing in Hollywood is what it seems." He was still holding the address.

I took it. "Who pays?"

"The studio, who else?"

"You mean you."

He sat back. His jacket fell open, exposing the big revolver. "They pay me too much to sit behind this desk, and I'm too old to leave it."

"Like hell you are." I left.

Sonny Bloom, right name Nathaniel Goldblume, would have been at home in a Horatio Alger story if it were filmed by Warner Brothers. Born to immigrant Jews in Newark in 1907, he had graduated while still in short pants from petty thievery to grand theft auto, spent two years in a reformatory, and landed a job driving a beer truck for Big Frank Nunzio when he was twenty-four. A couple of scrapes with rival bootleggers brought him to the attention of Nunzio, who promoted him to bodyguard, but he wasn't so good at that, because eighteen months later Big Frank was gunned down by persons unknown while strolling the Boardwalk. A beer war raged for months afterward. At its end, Sonny Bloom found himself, at age twenty-six, the vice king of New Jersey, with interests ranging from illegal alcohol to numbers to labor racketeering among the Atlantic City dock unions. After two years of that he had moved his operation to the West Coast, where his good looks, streetwise charm, and marijuana connections in Mexico soon made him the darling of the Hollywood community. At thirty, the tough-talking easterner with the slicked-back hair and knock-your-eye-out neckties was as much a fixture around the pools and tennis courts of Beverly Hills as an iron jockey. The American Dream is hard to overlook in Southern California.

The house he shared with Christa Vine had been built by some forgotten star back when heroines danced with roses in their teeth. It was Hollywood hacienda style, with red tile roofs on all the wings, arches everywhere, and outside staircases that curved between roses and cypresses growing in perfect harmony. Where the composition driveway swept past the front door a chauffeur in shirtsleeves and Erich von Stroheims's riding breeches was busy waxing the hood of a blue-black Auburn with hubcaps the size of cocktail tables. I pulled my crate up behind it and climbed the steps to the door.

The doorbell chimed "Juanita." A maid whose German ironclad features told me her name wasn't carried my card back into the shade of the house and returned five minutes later. "Mrs. Bloom will see you." She let me into the entryway, took my hat, and went home to the suburbs.

I waited. The floor tiles in the room were Spanish. Spanish needles grew in Mexican pots on either side of a curving staircase like the ones outside. A framed poster advertising a bullfight in Spanish hung on one wall. Inside the curve of the staircase stood a suit of English armor, looking abashed.

"Awful, isn't it? Sonny insisted on buying it and putting it there. I told him it wouldn't go with the rest of the house. But you don't tell Sonny anything."

She had come up on me while I was looking at the armor. She was a blonde, no rare commodity in that part of the world, but the shade wasn't Harlow's or Joan Bennett's or any of the thousands that come between; it was hers alone. It fell in waves to her shoulders, framing a face with slightly Oriental eyes and a chin that came almost too close to a point. She had a light tan, unusual in that pale picture crowd. The robe she wore was silk with a frosty gold cast. Belted at the waist, it left her collarbone bare and covered her feet.

"Maybe he thinks he needs a tin suit," I said when I came down from the clouds. "They'd sell big in Jersey."

She held out a hand that felt too light for the rock it was wearing. "I'm Christa Vine. Did Carson really send you, Mr. Marlowe?" I'd written "Carson Moldine" on the back of my card.

"He never got a chance to save the banker's daughter from a runaway horse and it's been killing him ever since." I gave her back the hand, one of the more difficult jobs I'd had lately. "He thinks you're in some kind of jam."

"Really, I'm not. He's such a dear old uncle. But I'd be no kind of hostess if I let you get away without a drink. Or are you on duty?"

"I'm not that kind of detective."

"Does that mean you'll have a drink?"

"Only if it comes in a glass."

She laughed a way only singers can, turned, and, lifting her robe the way they do in the costume pictures, led the way into what I guessed they called the parlor. It was done in blue and white, with French doors looking out on a garden that wasn't anywhere near as impressive as the one at Versailles. There was a small bar in one corner and a cabinet phonograph that had cost about as much as my car.

Behind the bar Christa Vine said, "This is the one thing I never let Greta—that's the maid—do for Sonny. I like mixing drinks. Which one can I mix for you?"

"Scotch and glass."

She poured it from a crystal decanter, fixed herself something in a tall glass whose color matched her robe, and brought them over to a blue chintz sofa. I accepted mine and we sat down. She crossed a country block of silken leg over the other and showed me a golden sandal and pink polish on her toenails. "I'm sorry you've wasted your time," she said. "Carson's a mother hen."

"That mother hen shot down three armed men in a bar in McAlester that wasn't quite as nice as yours in ninety-nine." I drank Scotch. "Where's your husband, Miss Vine?"

"In this house I'm Mrs. Bloom. He's back East on business. What did Carson tell you?"

"He said you've been turning down work and forgetting your lines."

"I'm a singer, not an actress. I remember words better if they're set to music. And you haven't seen the scripts they offer me."

"How do you get on with Sam Whiteside?"

"Sam's a dear."

"That's one I never heard anyone call him."

"Well, he has been to me. He didn't want to place me on suspension, but those are the rules. Sooner or later he'll want me for a part that's right for me, and that will be the end of it. Yes, Greta."

Some detective. I hadn't heard the German maid entering the room behind me. She stood with her hands folded in front of her apron. "Telephone, missus."

"Who is it?"

"He would not say. He said it is important."

"I'll take it upstairs." She set her drink down untasted on the white coffee table and rose. "Please excuse me, Mr. Marlowe. Make yourself comfortable. Put on a record if you like." She went out, followed by Greta.

Several of the records in the cabinet were Christa Vine's. I put on one, "The Man I Love." Her voice was heavy silk with a velvet lining, too good for a motion picture soundtrack, which made brass of everything. I stood looking out at the garden for a while, and then the detective in me kicked in. The bar was stocked with wines and liquors bottled before Prohibition. The carpet and drapes had been bought in Paris. And she had an automatic pistol in the drawer of a blue lamp table.

It was a .32 Browning with nickel plating and mother-of-pearl grips. The engraving on the backstrap read: "Something to watch over you. Sonny." One of Christa Vine's most popular recordings had been "Someone to Watch Over Me." I sniffed at the barrel and wrinkled my nose. The women never think to clean them after firing.

By the time the maid returned alone, the pistol was back in its drawer. She had my hat.

"Missus said she's sorry. She was called away."

"Has she left?"

"She is dressing. Call later, she said."

The chauffeur had gotten the word. He had put on his uniform coat and was sitting behind the wheel. The Auburn gleamed like oiled steel in the late afternoon sunlight.

I drove around the corner and parked next to a bougainvillea in a planter. Through its branches I had a view of the entrance to the Bloom estate. It was surrounded by a four-foot stone wall and that was the only way in or out. I killed the time fooling around with a portable chess set I keep in the glove compartment next to the Luger.

Bishop was working itself up to take Queen's pawn when the Auburn came purring out into the street and turned left, crossing directly in front of me. I slumped down until it passed, then lay aside the chess set, started the motor, and swung out behind it. There was no traffic on the shady street and I gave it two blocks.

We took the scenic route past orange groves and wooden oil derricks into Hollywood, where a really first-rate sunset was having a hard go at the neon. There the traffic was brisk and I closed up. On Sunset the Auburn glided into the curb in front of a coffee shop and the chauffeur got out to open Christa Vine's door, but he wasn't fast enough; she was halfway across the sidewalk before he reached it. She had on a yellow cotton shift that had sent some fairy designer's boyfriend to drafting school and dark glasses with a scarf covering her hair. She went inside the coffee shop and the chauffeur got back behind the wheel.

I found a space half a block up and adjusted my rearview mirror to include the coffee shop door. I didn't touch the chess set.

After about five minutes a burly party in a blue silk suit and a gray felt hat walked past my car carrying a leather briefcase. I slumped down again, straightening just as he stepped into the coffee shop.

Things were getting interesting. A thousand years ago when I was with the District Attorney's office, I had questioned Brock Valentine in connection with some slot machines that had been dynamited in West Hollywood. He had put on weight, but the bulldog features and natty little black patent-leather moustache hadn't changed. Two minutes after he went inside he came out and walked back the way he had come, without the briefcase.

Christa Vine had it. She came clicking back across the sidewalk, threw the item into the back seat, and followed it in. She was still closing the door when the Auburn took off with a chirp of rubber. Of course I followed.

In a little while we left the city and headed up Mulholland Drive into the hills. Here and there a lighted window hung like an orange overlooked during harvest, but after a few blocks the trees covered them. Ours were the only cars on the street. I killed my lights and used the moon. Finally, at the top of Mulholland, the Auburn's brake lamps came on. I turned off the pavement, cut the motor, and coasted to a stop on the grass.

The dome light glowed in the Auburn and someone got out. I waited a minute, considering the possibility of checking out the situation on foot. Then whoever it was got back into the car and it swung around. Once again I made myself insignificant in the seat while the big racer tore past. When its tires wailed on the curves down below I got the Luger and the big flashlight out of my glove compartment and climbed out. It was a warm night even for Southern California. Tree frogs were singing far back from the road.

I found the briefcase without having to use the flash. Leaning against a frangipani, it gleamed softly in the reflected glow of Hollywood glittering at the base of the hill. I didn't go near it. I had a pretty good idea what it contained.

The County of Los Angeles had installed a telephone booth at the top of the hill, where Daddy's girl could call for a tow when Romeo pulled the busted-starter routine on a nice warm night like this one. I opened the door far enough to reach in and unscrew the light bulb, then opened it the rest of the way and called Bernie Ohls's number at the District Attorney's office. He recognized my voice.

"Phil, how's the boy? I thought you'd be washing about in the surf off Palisades by now, wearing cement argyles."

"Not yet," I said. "Still working the afternoon shift, I see."

"You, too. Unless this call's social."

"What do you hear lately about Brock Valentine?"

"Nothing good, and I read the obituaries every day. Word is he's partnered up with that big eastern money. He don't hardly carry powder for nobody no more. What about him?"

"Would any of that big eastern money belong to Sonny Bloom?"

"That's the name I heard. The D.A.'s looking for Sonny, by the by. He forgot to show up for an appointment."

"A hearing?"

"Prelim. Nobody's seen him in a month. What's Brock up to?"

I couldn't answer the question. I probably wouldn't have, anyway. At that point someone jerked open the door to the booth. A shadow blocked out the moon.

"Too bad, shamus," said the shadow. I smelled garlic on its breath. Then something swished, a black light exploded in my skull, and I tasted salt and iron on my tongue, just before I ceased to care about such things.

I woke up with light in my face, but it wasn't from the sun; it was too bright and I thought I could read G.E. at its core. It was my own flashlight. I said, "Turn that off or I'll make you eat it." That's what I meant to say. It came out in some other language. I was lying on my back on something damp. I hoped it was anybody else's blood but mine. My head felt like a smashed Thermos. I knew if I moved it the shattered pieces would shift around inside.

"How many fingers am I holding up, Phil?"

I looked. I thought there were two. "October," I said. "Nineteen thirty-seven."

The man chuckled. I knew then it was Bernie. He snapped off the flash. As the purple spots faded from my vision I heard tree frogs singing nearby. I was lying on the dewy grass next to the telephone booth on Mulholland. "I had your call traced," he said. "That was as sweet a sap job as ever I saw. You always were hard-headed."

I said, "The briefcase."

"What briefcase?"

"Never mind. You answered the question. Got a light?" I patted my pockets for a Camel.

Supporting my head with one hand, he speared one between my lips and lit it from a match he struck off his thumbnail. The smoke tasted like a chocolate sundae.

"Care to share what's new with the guy that saved you from the pigeons?" Bernie asked.

I sat up. An invisible elf swung a shovel at the back of my head but I brushed him off. "I make it Sonny Bloom's been kidnapped. Christa Vine told me he was back in Jersey, but someone called the house and she was in a lather to leave after that. She met Brock Valentine in a coffee house on Sunset after that and he gave her a briefcase. She took it up here and left it. That's when I called you. After that the lights went out."

Bernie said, "Sonny Bloom's dead."

I looked at him. His pale bristly brows were just visible against the dark oval of his face.

"It came across my desk just as I was leaving to come here," he said. "Somebody put two in him and dumped him behind a restaurant in Bay City early this evening."

"That was just about the time his wife came here."

"I guess whoever it was was pretty sure she'd deliver."

"Who do you like for it?" I asked.

"The guy was a gangster. Tomorrow morning I'll sit down with the L.A. directory and check off the names of the ones I *don't* like for it. You okay? Maybe I should have called the croakers."

"It was just my head."

"Get a look at the sapper?"

"No, but I'd recognize him in a dark room. He must have had a clove of garlic for supper."

"Was his voice kind of raspy, like he gargled number five sandpaper?"

"You know him?"

"Stinkweed Hovac. He used to be in pictures, went from grip to character parts. Might've made a career of it, too, if he didn't think garlic prevented everything from boils to cirrhosis of the liver. Nobody'd work with him after a while and he got canned. He was freelancing strongarm work last I heard. You're lucky you've still got a skull. He's bigger than the Depression."

I smoked and thought. Bernie took my silence for something else.

"You sure you couldn't use some hospital time? I'd hate to have to visit you in Camarillo, help the attendant roll you out into the sunshine."

"I'm swell." I put a hand on his shoulder and we got up together. Sky and ground traded places a couple of times, but I held on until they lost interest in the game. "I'll need a lift home if my car's gone."

"It's there. I can't speak for the radio."

"Never had one. What studio did Hovac work for, Mammoth?"

"Yeah. How'd you guess?"

I grinned in the darkness. "I'm a trained detective."

"Funny guy, Marlowe, You're a regular Fred Allen. Here's your bucket. The slanty pedal means go." He put my hand on the door handle. "If you get any ideas, remember who gets them."

◆　◆　◆

Greta, the German maid, answered the bell in curlers and a fuzzy bathrobe. "Missus is asleep," she said through a space no wider than her face. "You come back tomorrow." She started to close the door.

I braced a shoulder against it. "It's tomorrow now. I slept through most of last night. Tell Mrs. Bloom it's me or the cops."

She left me there. I let myself in and smoked a cigarette. I smoked another and then Christa Vine came downstairs. She had on the robe I'd seen her in earlier. Her face was freshly made up. "What is it, Mr. Marlowe?"

"I thought you might like to know there's an all-points bulletin out by now for Stinkweed Hovac. When they get him he'll talk to the D.A. Murder's a little out of his league."

"I don't know anyone by that name."

"Sure you do. He's the one you hired to take me down while somebody else picked up the ransom you conned out of Brock Valentine for Sonny's release."

She looked at me, at the thread of blood that had crusted on my forehead and the grass stains on my suit. "You're drunk. Sonny's in New Jersey."

"Sonny's in formaldehyde and you know it. You put him there. They found him right where Hovac dumped him, or maybe it was your chauffeur. Men like to do favors for you. Ask Carson Moldine."

"Greta, call the police."

The maid was watching from the staircase landing. She turned away.

"Yeah, call them," I said. "Find out what's taking them so long. On the way here I left a message for a friend in the D.A.'s office. I was with him only a few minutes earlier and could have told him in person, but I wanted some time with you first."

"Maybe I'm the one who's drunk. I can't understand you."

"You should have ditched the gun after you shot Sonny, or at least cleaned it. Maybe that means you didn't plan it. You planned everything else swell. My guess is when the cops dig back they'll find out you did a picture with Hovac. You remembered him, kept track of the work he went into after he left movies. You needed him for the rough stuff. It doesn't matter why you killed Sonny. The point is you made the most of it, stashed the stiff someplace while you convinced his partner he'd been kidnapped by a rival mob and that they'd told you to deliver the ransom alone, with just your chauffeur to drive. Valentine came through with the cash tonight and you went through the motions of a drop because you guessed I'd be watching. Hovac hung around the drop to keep me from seeing who picked up the briefcase and where it went. He hits hard, Hovac."

Her face was an obelisk. "That's a lot to draw from a gun. I mean, without a laboratory."

"The gun didn't fit in till later. The capper was just before Hovac hit me, when he said, 'Too bad, shamus.' The only way he could have known I was a shamus was if someone told him. And you and Carson were the only people who knew I was on the case."

"Yes." It was just a word to fill the silence. Then the obelisk broke. A tear slicked her cheek. "I didn't want him to hit me any more."

"Who, Sonny?"

"He'd hit me so many times. I was so bruised I turned down work so I wouldn't have to show my face on the set. I don't even remember what it was we were fighting about this time. He came at me and I used this." She drew the Browning .32 out of the pocket of her robe and pointed it at me. "He gave it to me to protect myself with."

"You don't need protection now. You need a lawyer." Keep her talking. The gun coming out now was something I hadn't counted on. Sirens moaned in the distance.

"I needed it then. You read what he had engraved on it. I shot him and he fell." She held out the gun.

I took it and started breathing again. "As anybody would, with two slugs in him." I put the gun in my coat pocket.

She said, "I only shot him once."

The basement office smelled of dust and stale perspiration, like a deserted locker-room or the wings of an old theater. The naked bulb in the ceiling shed dusty light over the big yellow oak desk and the boxes of rubber swords and false beards stacked in the corners. I found a bottle and a glass in one of the desk drawers, poured myself a shot, and made myself as comfortable as possible in the worn old seat. After a long time the door opened and I had company. He had covered his bald head with a hat that shadowed his brown face and snow-white handlebars, but his old plaid jacket and the big Colt he wore under it identified him well enough.

He said, "Make yourself at home, Philip."

"You're late or I wouldn't have started without you," I said. "Did the telephone wake you?"

"I don't sleep so good these days." He stood just inside the door with his palms on his thighs.

"Sonny was shot twice. Once with a thirty-two and once with a forty-five, an old one. Bernie Ohls told me that at Christa Vine's house. He'll be here in a little while."

"She okay?"

"They took her in. Why'd you do it, Carson?"

"You're telling it."

"I figure you knew the situation and told her to call you the next time Sonny threatened to beat her. She did, but by the time you got there she'd plugged him once already. You finished the job."

"It wasn't the first time I killed a man to protect a woman."

"I heard it was three men."

"No, that was another time. Can you blame me for this one?"

"No. You shouldn't have tried to make a buck off it, though."

"The s.o.b. left her one dollar in his will. The house and everything else went to his sister in Newark. He'd told Christa that. He owed her that ransom for putting up with him as long as she did. Did you really think I was going to take any of it?"

"It doesn't matter what I think, Carson. If you'd left it alone, Christa would probably have gotten off on self-defense and you on justifiable homicide. The kidnapping gag makes it look like murder."

"Not from where I'm standing. Nor you either, if you'd see it my way."

I drank some of his liquor. "You used me, Carson. You needed a patsy to report to the cops he saw the ransom drop, so you hired me. You set me up for a sapping so I wouldn't see too much. I can see it your way up to a point; then my head starts hurting."

"It had to be you, Philip," he said. "You were the only one I could count on to take the case that far. I told Hovac to go easy."

"That's why I'm giving you the chance to hand over that hogleg before the cops get here. It'll look better at the trial." I held out my hand.

He shook his head. "I can't do that."

"I didn't think you could." I started to get up. He set himself with feet spread and I stopped.

"You go first," he said.

"Sitting down?"

"That's what I was doing when those three killers came for me in McAlester."

"That was thirty-seven years ago."

"Thirty-eight. I'm older and I need the edge."

"It doesn't have to be this way, Carson."

"Draw."

I took my Luger out of the open top drawer of the desk and drilled him through the shoulder while he was still hauling at the Colt. His back hit the wall and he dropped it. He grasped his shoulder.

"You had it out all along."

"It's been a long night," I said. "I needed an edge too."

"That's how it starts."

For the second time that night I heard sirens.

I came to Chandler fairly late, after I had published my first book, and was pleased to recognize a kindred spirit. Long before I read him I was experimenting with exotic similes and metaphors, and eight years of art training had convinced me of the importance of visuals, things closely associated with Chandler's work. I continue to reread all his fiction, using it as sort of a lodestone to remind me where I came from and how far I have to go. He was, and remains, regardless of genre, the finest American stylist of this century.

Loren D. Estleman

SAVING GRACE

JOYCE HARRINGTON

1938

THE PHONE CALL came in the middle of a dream of good, smoky Scotch and a laughing, green-eyed blonde just about to slip out of something a little more comfortable.

The operator asked me if I was Philip Marlowe and against my better judgment I said I was guilty. Then she asked me if I would accept a collect call from Santa Rosa. I was too groggy to catch the name. I wasn't dreaming the empty quart bottle that was giving me the glad eye from the windowsill. Despite the cement mixer between my ears and the sand dune in my mouth, I managed to sit up. It was the Santa Rosa part that had gotten my attention. I said, "Sure. Why not? Maybe I've been left a million simoleons by a long-lost relative."

The voice that came out of the phone's earpiece sounded about ten years old. "Philip? Is that you? You probably don't remember me. This is your cousin June."

"Who died?" I said. "And when do I collect my million?"

She giggled—a high-pitched titter that made me think of the automatic fun-house crone that tells penny fortunes and cackles mindlessly in her glass cage. "You always were a joker, Philip," she chirped. "Nobody died. Not yet, anyway. But that's what I've got to see you about."

"You don't got to see me about anything, lady. I never had a cousin June, or Moon, or even Spoon. And much as I hate to hang up on a sweet young thing like you, I suggest you go find somebody else to play telephone games with." I slammed the receiver down, stubbed out my butt in an ashtray overflowing with dead gaspers, and tried to catch up with the dream.

No such luck. Cousin or no, Santa Rosa June had started up a train of thought that I usually manage to keep shunted off on a siding. There is nothing stupider than a chicken, unless it's an egg. I came by this profound piece of folk wisdom honestly. I was born in Santa Rosa and my first job, while I was still in high school, was packing eggs at one of the local chicken ranches. Those eggs went off to places like San Francisco and Los Angeles, and I stayed put in Santa Rosa among the feathers and the smell of chicken dung. But not for long.

The phone rang again. I grabbed it and shouted, "No!"

This time it wasn't the operator. June said, "Well, you don't have to get so huffy. Even if you don't remember me, I remember you. Sometimes I read about you in the newspapers. Once they even had a picture of you. So, would you drive up to Santa Rosa so I could talk to you about this problem I have?"

"No."

She sighed. "I didn't think so. That's why I'm here in Hollywood. Me and my sister, January. She was pretending to be the operator before. Now do you remember us? We were the Abbott twins. Now she's married and I'm not, but we're still twins. And I know we're not really cousins, but after you kissed me behind the gymnasium you said we could be 'kissing cousins.' "

"I said that?"

"It was the nicest thing anybody'd ever said to me."

"When?"

"Oh, it must be fifteen years ago. Maybe sixteen."

"And you remembered."

"Yes. But you didn't."

"I guess I owe you something for that. Where did you say you were staying?"

She named a fleabag over on Melrose. "But I could come to your place. My sister and I. We've been driving all night, but we're not a bit tired."

"Well, I am. Suppose you come to my office in the morning."

"It is morning, silly."

"I mean later this morning. Make it . . ." I squinted at the alarm clock that never yet had been able to wake me up. It was nine-thirty. I had to assume it was morning. Venetian blinds and dark brown monk's cloth draperies kept whatever sunlight there was outside the single window of my bedroom. "Make it eleven-thirty." I gave her my office address and hauled myself under a cold shower.

I recognized them the minute I saw them. They were sitting side by side on the two straight chairs I keep in my waiting room just in case I should have more than one customer at a time. Or even in a day. My waiting room is never locked. There's nothing in it worth lifting and I

wouldn't want to discourage anyone from waiting around for me to finish
a case or a hangover.

June had been dead right about Santa Rosa and even about the kiss
behind the gymnasium. She and her sister were identical twins. Every high
school has an ugly girl. The girl no one likes or wants for a friend. Santa
Rosa was lucky. We had two ugly girls. The Abbott twins, June and January.
I had kissed June behind the gymnasium in a pouring rainstorm because
the other girls had stolen all her clothes and then pushed her down a ravine
into the world's biggest mud puddle. It was December and cold and it had
been raining for about three weeks the way it does in northern California.

I gave her my slicker, kissed her muddy forehead, and drove her
home in my junkmobile. Then I went back to the school, found the girls
who'd done it to her, took them out to the chicken ranch to sample some
bootleg hooch I had tucked away out there, and locked all four of them
up in one of the chicken coops for the night. They were dead drunk when
I snapped the padlock on them so they didn't mind very much. Not right
then.

Fifteen years hadn't done much for the twins. They were still ugly.
Ugly isn't so bad if you've got something else to take your mind off of what
you see in the mirror every morning. Look at Eleanor Roosevelt.

But the twins were trying to convince the world and themselves that
roly-poly platinum blondes with bright magenta cupid's-bow lips and eyebrows plucked to extinction were the cat's pajamas. On Harlow it had
worked, but she died. On them, it was grotesque and pathetic.

One of them got up and flung herself at me. The other one lolled in
the rickety wooden chair and crossed her beefy legs in my direction. They
were dressed identically, in green and white polka dot chiffon with lots of
ruffles and flourishes, and they reeked of Evening in Paris. Their fat little
feet were crammed into white kid T-straps that raised four pairs of hurtful
looking bulges across their insteps.

The one who was leaning on me smirked up at my chin and tried for
a husky whisper. "Remember me now? I remember you, but you're a lot
taller. And handsomer."

The other one piped up in a voice that bore a striking resemblance
to the squawking hens of Santa Rosa. "Quit the lollygagging, June. This
was your idea. I still think it stinks, but let's get on with it now that we're
here."

"Good thinking," I told her as I unlocked my office door. "Please
step into my parlor and tell me all about it." My parlor hadn't changed
much since I'd left it the night before. Even the air in it was the same,

thick and stale with too much cigarette smoke and not enough ozone. I opened the window to liven the mix with an injection of exhaust fumes from the traffic on Cahuenga Boulevard.

The twins sorted themselves out, January flopping into the visitor's chair and June draping herself against the bank of five green metal file cabinets I'd picked up at a flea market. If business didn't improve, I'd have to return them emptier than I got them.

It was easy to tell them apart, even though they were identical. January oozed an attitude of sullen discontent, the bitter aura of gin battling it out with her perfume. June, at least, had kept a spark of vitality alive in her little shoe-button eyes.

She twinkled at me and said, "I hardly know where to begin."

"How about the beginning," I suggested. I sat down in the lopsided swivel chair behind my desk and parked my hat on top of the telephone. It wouldn't keep it from ringing if it had a mind to, but the way business had been going lately, there wasn't much danger of that.

June sighed and opened up her white leather pocketbook, a twin of the one that lay sprawled on January's lap. She pulled out a deckle-edged snapshot and pressed it to her far from inconsequential bosom. January sat up a little straighter and flashed her sister a malevolent glance.

"Well, we are looking for him, aren't we?" June pleaded.

"I don't care if I never see the son of a sea cook again!" January's carefully painted lips twisted in a vicious snarl. It almost made her look good.

"But Jan, he's got Baby Grace with him. We want to get her back, don't we?"

"If he hurts that kid, I'll kill him. I swear to God, I'll twist his crown jewels off and stuff them down his throat."

The party was getting a little rough for my delicate sensibilities. "Ladies, ladies," I soothed. "Your sisterly affection is touching, but if we're going to get anywhere with this we have to take the unemotional approach. Is there a missing person?"

"No!" January shouted.

"Two," June outshouted her. "Jan's husband, Walter, and their daughter, Baby Grace."

"They're not just missing," January rasped between teeth that kept trying to grit themselves into tooth powder. "He's kidnapped her. When I get my hands on him, he's dead. And I don't care who knows it." She snapped open her pocketbook and hauled out the smallest gun I'd ever seen. It almost got lost in her pudgy pink paw, but there was no doubt in my mind it could do the job.

"You know how to use that?" I asked her in my softest, most reasonable voice.

"You damn betcha! Right between the eyes for old Walter Watson when I find him." She pointed the gun at me to show me how well she could aim.

"Well, that's just swell. But in the meantime, would you mind putting it away? If you shoot me, accidentally, of course, I won't be able to help you find Walter, will I?"

She swung the gun around to point it at her sister. "You might as well tell him. I just hate to tell anybody. It's all so disgusting."

"There, there, honey," said June. "You don't have to say a word. I know how it upsets you." She sidled over to her sister and held her hand out, palm up. "Why don't you just give me that. It's not polite to point a gun at somebody who's trying to help you."

While they pondered the intricacies of pistol-packing etiquette, I slid open my desk drawer and slyly let my hand fall to rest on the .38 I kept there for just such social occasions.

But January stuffed her deadly toy back into her pocketbook and dragged out a brown glass medicine bottle instead. "It's for my nerves," she muttered as she twisted off the cap. "I got terrible nerves." She swigged at the bottle, smacked her lips and put the lid back on without offering a dainty sip to anybody else. Emily Post would not have approved.

June waddled over and laid the snapshot down on my desk. "That's him," she said, "with Baby Grace on his shoulders."

I stared down at a tall, narrow gent in a bathing suit. He was squinting into the sun over an eagle beak and a broad grin full of snaggles. The kid on his shoulders looked to be about five or six years old. Her light hair was crimped into the obligatory moppet curls and her little hands were clamped onto the guy's ears. Her legs and bare feet hung down against his chest, and her toes were curled. But it was her face that told me she didn't like being where she was, up above the world so high. Her eyes were big and scared and her mouth was small and pinched. A vague stretch of water shone in the sunlight behind them.

"We took that at Clear Lake about three weeks ago," said June. "Walter was trying to teach her how to swim."

"Forget the swimming," January mumbled. "You should see her tap-dance. She could make a fortune in the movies before she gets too old. She's just the cutest little number in the world. Walter had no right . . ." She trailed off into a cascade of gin-soaked blubbers.

Mother love. Hollywood was full of it these days. They came from Iowa and Nebraska and Kansas. Hard-eyed hungry women and their primped and painted Kewpie doll daughters. All trying to be the next Shirley Temple. The way I read this one, the twins were hot on the trail of Walter, who either was trying to save his little girl from breaking her heart against the movies' indifference or had beaten Mommie Jan and Auntie June to the draw in selling their piece of merchandise. Either way, it wasn't my kind of case.

I pushed the snapshot back across my desk. "Don't they have police in Santa Rosa anymore?" I asked.

"Bunch of fatheads," January snapped. "I wouldn't ask them to find Jimmy Durante's nose. Besides, we think Walter's somewhere in L.A. His sister Lucille's a seamstress at one of the studios. I called her yesterday and she sounded nastier than usual. She said she hadn't seen or heard from Walter in months. But I don't believe her. She hates me and she'd just love it if Walter left me and took Baby Grace with him."

June had been perched on the edge of my desk while all this was going on. Now she leaned over and picked up one of my hands, which had just been lying there minding its own business. "Philip, you've got to help us," she breathed. "There's something more. We think . . . I mean, we have good reason to believe that Walter does things to Baby Grace." Her round face had turned the color of dried phlegm, making the rouge spots on her cheeks stand out like traffic lights in the Mojave.

"What kind of things?" I asked demurely. I know, I know, I'm not a nice guy, forcing her to name the unnameable.

"You know what I mean," she hedged. "He's always picking her up and kissing and hugging her. We've never caught him doing anything more than that. But he's home alone with her a lot. He takes cares of her while Jan and I work at the beauty parlor."

"Great balls of fire, girls! He's her father. What's he supposed to do? Treat her like a piece of furniture?"

June lifted her hand off of mine, leaving behind a sticky film of sweat. She heaved a hopeless sigh and drooped like a deflated rubber swimming pool raft. "I should have known," she said. "No one likes to believe that sort of thing. It took us a long time to even let ourselves think it. Now you know why Jan's so upset. And why we don't feel right about going to the police. If this got out, it could just ruin poor Baby Grace for life."

There was some truth in what she said. Small town gossip is deadly. The natural inborn American killer instinct isn't confined to gunsels and lowlifes. Character assassination is one of the greatest pastimes of the village righteous and, as I recalled, Santa Rosa had more than its share of sanctimony.

After her outburst, Jan had been nodding drowsily in her chair, whether in agreement with June's accusation or in a gin stupor, I couldn't tell. Now, she rose majestically to her tiny feet. "Let's get out of here," she rasped. "This guy turns my stomach." She rested her flippers on top of it as if to hold it in place. "He's a washout. He doesn't want to help us, so let's go find Baby Grace on our own." She marched to the office door and flung it open. Then she turned and mustered up all the scorn accumulated throughout her twenty-eight or thirty years of being one of the Abbott twins.

"I hope you rot," she told me sweetly. "I hope you die slowly and it hurts a lot. You're in a crummy business in a crummy town and it suits you. I wouldn't even hire you to haul garbage. You're too . . . too . . . loathsome for that."

I was beginning to like her. There was a kind of raw honesty about her that made up for the phony veneer of bottle-blonde hair and too much makeup.

"Hold on, ladies," I said. "I didn't say I wouldn't take the case. Happens I don't have anything else on right now. I can give it a day or two."

"Oh, that's wonderful!" burbled June, reinflating herself to full size. "I just knew you'd do it."

"But your sister has to stop calling me loathsome. I'm a very sensitive guy. I'll admit to crummy, but that's as far as I'll go."

After I got the particulars about color of hair, eyes, and so forth, what the missing persons were wearing when last seen, and what kind of car Walter was driving, I asked for his sister's address.

"Miss High-and-Mighty Lucille Watson lives in Bay City," said January, and she gave me a street number in the run-down area behind the amusement pier. "Do you have to talk to her? She'll say nasty things about me."

"I promise not to listen any more than I have to. Which studio does she work at?"

January named one of the big ones, a fantasy factory where an army of poor slobs thought they were lucky to hammer and saw and stitch and paint their lives away. I guess they were. They got paid every week.

There wasn't much else they could tell me, so I rode down in the elevator with them, a risky ride given the combined tonnage of the twins and the decrepit state of the mechanism.

After tucking them into their dented Dodge roadster and pointing them in the direction of lunch, I went back up to the office and started working the phone.

None of the bigger studios had casting calls out for moppets and only one had seen any new meat under sixteen in the past week, a pet Limey boy wonder brought in by the studio boss for not so obscure reasons of his own. That left the sad remnants of the independents over on Gower Gulch, but not even superannuated cowboys could get any work there these days.

On the other hand, Walter Watson did have a connection of a sort. It was time to pay a call on Miss Lucille Watson.

I drove over to the studio where she worked. One of the guards was a retired cop who knew the inside story of why I'd been fired from the D.A.'s office a few years ago. He was glad to see me.

"Ah, Philly," he groaned, "ain't it terrible what this town does to you. Here I should be tending to my fishing at some lake in the mountains, but try to do that on a cop's pension, and you should be making a hero's name for yourself on the side of the law. Instead, look at the both of us. Patsies from the word go."

"It's the law that's the patsy," I told him. "Whores are always patsies. They sell themselves to anybody who flashes a wad and forget what it feels like to be clean. I need your help, Ralph. Nothing that'll get you in trouble."

"You name it, you got it," he said, clapping me on the shoulder with a grip reminiscent of the way he used to haul felons into the wagon. I tried not to wince; he meant it to be friendly.

"I need to talk to Miss Lucille Watson. She works here as a seamstress."

"Sure," he said, "I know Lucille. A tall, skinny sourpuss with goggles like the bottom of a shotglass. But I didn't see her today. Nor yesterday, come to think of it. Lemme just check the sheet."

He ducked into the little two-by-four office beside the gate and came out moments later shaking his head. "On sick leave since last week," he said. "I don't know where she lives."

"That's jake," I told him. "She's in Bay City, but I was hoping to catch her here. They're not too fond of me in Bay City."

He laughed a big haw-haw and roared, "Give 'em hell, Philly! You make those bozos look like the clowns they are."

I drove away from the studio with the sun in my eyes and the heat pressing in through the open windows like the blast from a steel mill.

As as soon as I reached Bay City, I stopped at a drugstore and bought a box of chocolates from a small, clean old gent in a white pharmacist's coat. He smiled as he wrapped the box in green paper and tied it with yellow string. "A present for your sweetie pie," he murmured. "That's nice. She's a lucky girl."

"Thanks, pop," I said, pocketing my change. "I'll tell her you said so. She may not agree."

I found Miss Lucille Watson's dirty white stucco bungalow in a row of other bungalows exactly like it. Hers was different by virtue of the white picket fence around the front yard and the enormous hydrangea bush that it guarded.

I rang the doorbell and heard it clang somewhere inside the house. The red painted door regarded me with wooden indifference and stayed closed. I rang again and turned to look back at the front yard. There was a Charlie McCarthy doll lying under the hydrangea. His mouth was open but he didn't say anything.

The door creaked open about an inch and a watery eye peered out at me. A voice croaked, "I'm not buying any. Go away."

"I'm not selling any. I'm giving it away this week." I took my hat off like a good boy. "Are you Lucille Watson? If you are, you've just won the Blue Network's Radio Sweetheart of the Week prize." I brandished the box of chocolates. "All you have to do is answer a few simple questions."

The eye went away from the door and came back magnified by a thick lens. The lens gleamed down at the chocolate box and then up at my face. "What questions?" The door creaked open a little wider.

"Nothing much, but I need to verify that you listen to the radio. You do have a radio, don't you?"

"Of course I do," she snapped. By this time the door was open wide enough for me to see both lenses, a stiff headful of lacquered finger waves, and a starchy lavender and white housedress buttoned and belted onto a miserly frame. The lenses rested on a sharp inquisitive nose, not quite the equal of Walter's eagle beak but clearly related. She licked her thin pale lips and reached out a bony hand for the candy box.

"Ah, ah, ah," I said, hiding the box behind my back. "Mustn't touch until I see the radio and you tell me what your favorite programs are."

"Oh, come on in," she said. "I guess you're harmless. If you're not, a hatpin in the right place'll teach you some manners." Her nasal twang branded her an escapee from the tall corn country.

She led me through a small dark foyer into an even darker living room anchored down with chunky California mission furniture. The radio was a floor model Philco with a round green dial. It was churning out another chapter of afternoon agony in the life of *Young Widder Brown*. "There it is," she said. "My favorite programs are *One Man's Family* and Jack Benny. Do you get paid for doing this?"

"What about your children? What do they like?"

"I'm not married," she snapped.

"Beg your pardon, Miss Watson. I saw the doll out in the yard. I thought it belonged to a child."

"What doll?" She hiked over to the front window and pulled aside the heavy drapes.

"One of those Charlie McCarthy dolls. Every kid seems to have one these days."

"My niece," she said. "She was visiting here with her father. Poor little thing. She'll miss that doll. She loves it so. I guess I'll have to send it to her."

"Visiting from back home?" I asked.

"What business is it of yours?"

"None whatsoever," I admitted in my best clodhopper fashion. "It just seems to me that children have a better chance of growing up on the straight and narrow in a place where folks work hard and go to church on Sundays." I hoped I wasn't laying it on too thick. "I'd guess you're from Iowa."

"I work hard and go to church on Sundays. But you're right, young man. My brother's taking little Grace back home with him to Council Bluffs. Now how about that candy?"

I handed over the box. "Must be hard on a little girl not to have a mother," I remarked.

"Who told you that?" she demanded, ripping off the green paper.

"Nobody. But you didn't mention little Grace's mother. Did she die?"

"Be a blessing if she would." She opened the box, picked out a chocolate-covered cherry, and popped it into her mouth. "She's been a trial to poor Walter since the beginning, with her drinking and alley-catting around. I warned him about her. But he wouldn't listen. But when she started in on little Grace, well that was the living end. Tap-dancing lessons and permanent waves. Putting lipstick on her and making her stand up in a barroom and sing. I ask you." Her words were sticky with chocolate and moral indignation.

"Yes, ma'am," I said. "So they're well on their way home by now."

She ate another chocolate and peered at me through her lenses. "You're pretty curious about my brother and his whereabouts, aren't you? I never heard of any Blue Network Radio Sweetheart of the Week nonsense. But I have heard of curiosity killing the cat."

Her lenses were aimed somewhere over my left shoulder. Before I could turn around to see what was there, the whole roomful of mission furniture fell on my head. There was a smell of carpet dust in my nose and the taste of iron in my mouth. The last thing I heard was a tiny voice crying, "Mommy!"

And the first thing I heard when I could hear things again was "Gosh all hemlock, Jack!" from the Philco. Afternoon agony had segued into high adventure and the all-American boy was hot on the trail of evildoers in the steamy Amazonian rain forest. While the all-American booby was taking an enforced nap on the Axminster. I lifted one eyelid and saw a tiny black shoe three inches from my nose.

Charlie McCarthy sat propped up against a chair leg, smirking a superior kind of smirk. I expected him to pop off one of his wisecracks and wouldn't have blamed him if he had. I deserved it. But he just sat there and watched me scramble to my knees and finger the sore spot on the back of my head. No blood. Just a mushy lump that could have been made by a baseball bat or a crowbar. Walter Watson had good aim. The lump was neatly centered on my cranium.

When I finished exploring my tolerance for pain, I noticed that Charlie was clutching a piece of paper in one wooden hand. "Thanks, pal," I said as I took it from him. "Nice crowd you hang out with."

The note said: "June should have told you that she's been babbling about you ever since your picture showed up in the paper. We've been expecting you to turn up. Ask her about a Mr. Hap Delaney. And tell Jan that Grace is okay." There was no signature. I turned off the radio when it sang at me, "Have you tri-e-e-ed Wheaties?"

I stuffed the note into my pocket, tucked Charlie McCarthy under my arm, and made a quick tour of the bungalow. In a small back bedroom, a single bed and a folding cot had been slept in. Underneath the cot, I found a pink sunsuit with grass stains on the seat.

The other bedroom wasn't much larger. I learned that Miss Lucille Watson was a bedtime Bible reader and wore dentures. The kitchen told me nothing at all unless neatness counts. Lucille was a fanatic with the Fels-Naptha. And that was it. No hint of where they'd flitted off to. Only the certainty that Walter and Baby Grace had been here and now they were gone.

I did the only thing I could do. The name Hap Delaney rang a distant bell. Something to do with running a string of kid pickpockets in movie theaters around town. A regular latter-day Fagin. But that was a long time ago and I hadn't heard his name since. I went back into the musty overweight living room, picked up the phone, and asked the operator for the *Hollywood Citizen-News.* My sometime drinking buddy and all-purpose oracle, Benny Flinders, might have some current dope.

When Benny came on the line, he sounded more dyspeptic than usual. "Now just tell me this, Marlowe," he groaned. "What's a guy to do when his girl gives him the gate, the sawbones tells him to quit drinking, and his hair starts falling out in clumps the size of haystacks? Where've you been, kid? I haven't seen you in a month or so." Benny'd been sounding like an old man ever since I'd known him, but he was closer to my age than he was to Methuselah's.

I asked him about Hap Delaney and he laughed. "Easy," he said. "Out of the slammer about six months and busy as a birddog with a new scam. Knowing Delaney, it's got to be illegal, but nobody's got anything on him yet. He's got an office over on Highland, but he's hardly ever in it. He's been touring up and down the coast, interviewing talent. Calls himself an agent, specializing in kid actors. Between you and me, I think he's buying and selling. I don't know who's in the market, but there've been a few rumors surfacing about parties where young kids provide the entertainment. And I don't mean ring-around-the-rosy. You got something going with him?"

"I don't know yet, Benny. But as soon as I do, it's yours. Thanks."

On the way back to Hollywood, with Charlie McCarthy propped up on the seat beside me, I tried to get a little conversation going. "Now tell me this, my wooden-headed friend. If the Gold Dust Twins have been doing business with Hap Delaney, and if Walter knows about it, then why doesn't he blow the whistle on the deal?"

The dummy answered, "Don't be stupid, shamus. Walter wants to keep the money *and* the kid."

"What money?" I asked.

"The money the three of them got paid for the merchandise. Or maybe just the two of them."

"Which two?"

"You figure it out. You're the detective."

I wasn't much of a ventriloquist. The dummy's answers only raised more questions.

It was late afternoon when I finally parked on Highland Avenue across the street from the building where Information had told me The Delaney Agency was located. The elevator operator was a rosy-cheeked lad who looked ready to burst into song and dance. Delaney's office on the ninth floor had a candy-striped door and a sweet-faced granny type sitting at a candy-striped desk behind it.

"Hello," she cooed at me. There was a fishbowl full of gumdrops on the desk. A rocking horse stood in one corner and a dollhouse in another. "How may we help you?"

"We can tell me if Hap Delaney is in." I helped myself to a green gumdrop and dropped one of my cards on the desk.

The coo turned into a caw as she read my name out loud. "We're closed for the day. I was just leaving." She reached for a flowered straw hat and plopped it cockeyed on top of her gray topknot.

"He wouldn't be on his way to Santa Rosa, would he?" I asked.

"Santa where?" she muttered. "I don't know what you're talking about." She got up from her chair and looked wildly at a slightly open door on the other side of the reception room.

"Because if he is, he doesn't have to go so far. The merchandise that was stolen from him hasn't left town." I spoke right up, loud enough so that whoever was on the other side of the door could hear what I was saying.

The door opened and the sweet old granny sat back down. The man in the doorway looked a bit like a youthful Santa Claus—round pink cheeks, round button nose, a crown of curly red hair, and a smile as broad as Topanga Canyon. He was everybody's favorite uncle.

"It's all right, Bessie," he said. "You go on home now. I'll take care of this."

She scuttled out the door and Hap Delaney ushered me into his office. The candy-stripe decor ran riot. A soda fountain with three stools occupied one side of the room. There were dolls and teddy bears everywhere, including a couple of Charlie McCarthys. "So you're Philip Marlowe," he said. "I've heard about you. Sit down, sit down. I'd offer you a drink, but the bar runs strictly to sarsaparilla. What can I do for you?"

I sat down on a couch between a Shirley Temple doll and a Dionne quint. "I'm looking for a girl. Baby Grace Watson. A little bird told me I should look here."

He laughed jovially. "Do you know how many Baby Thises and Baby Thatses I see in a week? They all tap-dance. They all sing. They all look alike. What I'm looking for is the one who stands out in a crowd."

"What happens to the ones who don't?" I asked.

He shrugged. "How do I know? They go home, grow up, and marry the boy next door. If their mothers let them, that is."

"You wouldn't happen to steer them into some other line of work, would you?"

"Such as what?" He wasn't smiling anymore.

"Oh, I don't know. What other kind of work is there for a five-year-old girl?"

"Listen, Marlowe," he said. "This is a legitimate business. It may not be a *nice* business, but it's all legal and aboveboard. I don't know who told you to come to me, but there's nothing in it. I haven't seen your Baby Whatsit."

"Mind looking at a picture of her?" I pulled the photo out of my pocket and handed it to him.

He barely glanced at it. "Like I said, they all look alike. And all the mothers think they're gonna get rich off their kids. Some of the fathers, too. But if a plain little girl with freckles and pigtails should walk in that door, her I could do something with. She'd be different. You know what I mean?" He handed me back the snapshot. "Anything else I can do for you?"

"Well, if she should show up, you could give me a call. She'd be with her father. I left my card with Bessie."

Downstairs in the long shadows, I hunkered down in my car and watched the front of the building. It took him about twenty minutes to hustle through the revolving door. There was a cab waiting for him right at the curb. I watched it head down toward Melrose and then made a U-turn and moseyed after it. Something told me I knew where Delaney was going, so I took a chance and stopped to make a phone call. Ralph, the studio cop, told me all about where the hired help stayed when they had to work late. A few more nickels and Lucille had given me chapter and verse and Deuteronomy for good measure. I gave her a time and a place, and she said, "We'll see about that."

There was a coffee shop on the ground floor of the hotel where the twins were staying. Through the plate glass window, I saw a platinum blonde head and a bright red one bent toward each other across a small table. I parked in a no parking zone right outside and went into the hotel lobby. I rang the twins' room on the house phone. A muzzy voice answered.

"Get down to the lobby right away," I said.

"Wh-a-a-t?"

"Do you want Baby Grace back or not?"

"But I'm not even dressed," she wailed.

"Get dressed and get sober and get down here. I'll be waiting for you." I hung up on her before she could think of another reason why she couldn't. Then I went to stand by the lobby entrance to the coffee shop where I could keep an eye on June and Hap Delaney.

Delaney didn't look like everybody's favorite uncle anymore. He was yapping away at June and she was taking it with her head bent. Then she raised her head and started yapping away at him. This went on for about ten minutes. They took a break while the waitress refilled their coffee cups.

January hove to alongside of me, huffing and sleepy-eyed.

"Look at that man," I told her. "Ever seen him before?"

"Why, sure," she said. "He's the one who said he could get Baby Grace into the movies. He came to Santa Rosa looking for talent and said she was the greatest thing he'd ever seen."

"He just came right up to the door and said that?" I asked.

"Well, not exactly," said January coyly. "There was an ad in the paper about auditions for talented children. So I took Baby Grace. That's how it happened. He even came out to the house to meet Walter and June just to prove everything was on the up-and-up. Then we were all going to come down here to find a place to live while Baby Grace was getting started on her career. But Walter skipped out with her before we could do that. What's he doing talking to June?" Her pudgy hand flew to her mouth. "Oh, my goodness!" she gasped.

"What is it?"

"The contract! Walter and I signed a contract. Do you suppose Mr. Delaney could sue us?"

"Don't worry about it," I told her.

"But I want Baby Grace to be a movie star," she wailed. "She could do it. She's cute enough."

"Sure she is. She's cute enough for Walter and June to go behind your back and sell her to Hap Delaney, so he could turn around and sell her to some baby lover for nursery games."

She blinked at me, making a strange kind of keening way back in her throat. "That's dirty," she whispered finally. "That's the dirtiest thing I ever heard of. Even Walter wouldn't do a thing like that."

"You sure of that?" I asked her.

"I don't know what I'm sure of anymore," she moaned.

I liked her better when she was tearing off a piece of my hide. "Well, let's go in," I said. "Nothing like finding things out firsthand."

I opened the coffee shop door and led the way. January lumbered behind me like a mother elephant in search of her lost calf. June saw us first and half rose out of her chair. She pasted a smile on her face and fluttered her hands at the waitress. "Two more chairs," she called out. "It looks like we're turning into a party."

January bore down on her like the Bonus Army marching on Washington. "I want my baby. Where's my baby? How could you do this to me, June?"

"Shut up," said June. "You're drunk again. What kind of mother are you? Can't you see that Mr. Delaney's here? He wants to find her just as much as we do."

"No!" said January. "Not him. Where's the money, June? I didn't see any money. How much did he pay you for my baby?"

The waitress brought over two chairs and tried to edge them around us. "Please sit down," she whispered. "The manager's looking at you."

January kicked one chair over and raised the other one to chest level as if she were a lion tamer in a one-ring circus.

"Don't be ridiculous," said June. "Why don't you have a drink? Let's go out to the bar."

"You'd like that, wouldn't you?" said January. "Who is it who's always buying me bottles of gin? I think I'm just beginning to understand something."

Hap Delaney rose wearily to his feet, but his smile was back in place for my benefit. "Family squabbles," he said. "I hate to get in the middle of them. Don't you?"

I put a hand on his shoulder and shoved him back into his chair. I'd seen something on the other side of the plate glass window—an eagle-nosed man with a little girl on his shoulders. And a pair of shot-glass lenses lurking just behind him. I put my other hand on January's arm and helped her lower the chair to the floor. She was trembling.

"Let's all take a deep breath," I said. I picked up the chair that January had kicked over and sat on it. January sat on the edge of her chair. The waitress relaxed and the manager went back to whatever managers of hotel coffee shops do when they're not anticipating riots.

And then the street door opened.

January was off the edge of her chair and halfway across the room before anyone could say a word. She lifted Baby Grace off Walter's shoulders and came back and sat down with the little girl on her lap.

"Okay," said Hap Delaney. "Let's call the whole thing off. Give me back the three grand and I'll forget I ever saw you folks."

"I don't have it," said June. "I gave it to Walter."

Walter said, "Not three thousand, you didn't. More like three hundred. I wouldn't sell my Baby Grace for a measly three hundred."

"Did they do anything to you, baby?" January whispered into Grace's tousled curls. "You can tell Mommy."

Grace burrowed her face into her mother's green and white ruffles and burst into tears.

Walter shuffled over to the table and put his hands on January's shoulders. "I'm sorry about all this, Jan," he said. "But I tried to tell you it was no good. You never would listen to me. It was always June you listened to, and believe me, she's the one behind it all. She handed Grace over to him three days ago. When I found out, I came down here and got Lucille to help me find her. It wasn't hard. She knows where all the dirt is in this town."

"That Bessie Prince," Lucille muttered. "Running a regular baby ranch out in the Valley. Everybody knows about it, but I never thought I'd see my own niece there."

"Is that so?" June barked. "Blame it all on me, why don't you? But you two wanted it just as much as I did. Only you're just too feeble to admit it."

"All I wanted was for my baby to be a movie star," January whispered.

"That's what they all say," Delaney confided to me. "But I'm clean. Nobody can pin a thing on me."

"That may be, Mr. Delaney. But I don't think you should be doing what you do to anybody else's little girls." She sat there with Baby Grace on her lap and the little gun in her hand. "Don't you move, Mr. Marlowe," she said. "I know I really shouldn't be doing this, but I just can't help it. Walter, you'll use the money to get me a really good lawyer, and then we'll go home."

And I didn't move. It was a pleasure to watch Delaney try to crawl under the table. She shot him right through the breast pocket of his bright plaid jacket. Then she turned the gun on June. "Give Walter the rest of the money," she commanded.

"No!" said June. "It's mine. It's my ticket out of Santa Rosa."

"What's wrong with Santa Rosa?" said January. "It'll be just fine without you." And she shot June twice, just to make sure.

Lucille picked up June's white pocketbook, just slightly spattered with blood, and faded away to the lobby entrance.

When the police arrived, January was still sitting in the chair with Baby Grace asleep on her lap. She'd handed the gun over to me, and I handed it over to them.

They were pretty decent with her. They let her keep the kid with her, at least for a while. They didn't even give me a hard time, for a change. I guess they were glad that somebody'd put Hap Delaney out of business for good.

Walter cried a little and apologized for bashing me over the head. "I thought you were working for June," he said. "She kept telling us that you were her high-school sweetheart. I never had a high-school sweetheart. I never had anybody until I met Jan. She's a fine woman, you know. Just a little hot tempered sometimes. When this is over, I'm taking her and Grace back home with me. I'll make it all up to both of them."

After they'd all cleared out and I was wondering what to do with the rest of the evening, the waitress presented me with a bill for two coffees and an apple pie à la mode. I had to give her an I.O.U.—an evening at the Trocadero so she could be seen by the right people and get started in the movies. I didn't ask her if she could tap-dance.

When you grow up a movie-loving, library-haunting brat, it would be pretty hard to miss out on Raymond Chandler. And a whole lot of other writing people.

Of my two loves, I much preferred the library. Honestly. I could have spent my whole life there. But we were all shipped off in a slovenly clump on Saturday afternoons to the movies. I didn't mind, and I never minded what was playing. I got to see a lot of good stuff. Some of it was Chandler, but I didn't know that then. My dazzled childish eye saw only the Bogarts and the Bacalls. It was only later that I started looking for the writer, of the screenplay and of the book behind the movie.

I made a wonderful discovery in those days. The movies I liked best were often based on books, and that simple fact sent me back to the library where I would rather have been in the first place. Sad news. The libraries I went to weren't large on Chandler. Dickens, yes. Steinbeck, yes. L. Frank Baum and Jack London and Oscar Wilde. So I read all those people and many, many others whose books were or weren't made into movies before I got around to Chandler.

Did Chandler influence my work? Damned if I know. I'd like it if he had because he was a fine, honest, painstaking craftsman. I read and reread everything I could find of his, and everything I could find about him, while I was working on "Saving Grace." You can be sure he influenced that story. And it was fun. Both the writing and the reading. I like to think of all of us who contributed to this book immersing ourselves in Chandler the man and Chandler the writer. May the experience make us all better writers than we ever thought we could be.

Joyce Harrington

MALIBU TAG TEAM

JONATHAN VALIN

1939

H E WAS ABOUT six feet two, no wider than a beer truck, maybe forty, forty-five years old, with a gray felt hat crushed down around his ears, a checked sportcoat holding him in like a whalebone corset, and a cigar the size of a rolling pin wedged between the first two fingers of his right hand. His face, what I could see of it under the hat brim, was set in a scowl, somewhere between the casual contempt a really big man has for ordinary mortals and the kind of slit-eyed mean that's truly dangerous, the kind that doesn't give a damn about cops or damages or little toylike things such as the electric chair. I might have been wrong, but I thought he looked like trouble.

The huge man stared at the dingy office, then squinted with his whole face, like the view hurt his eyes.

"What's a guy like you charge?" he growled in a solidly contemptuous voice.

"Why's a guy like you want to know?"

"I got a job for you. Deliver a package. Take a few hours."

"I don't work by the hour. And I don't run a delivery service."

"Cute," he said softly. "That's very cute."

He put the cigar down on the corner of the desk and picked up my penset, pretending to study it for a moment like it was a ship in a bottle. With a tight-lipped grin, he held the thing out in front of his face and casually broke it in two. Still smiling, he dropped the pieces back on the desk.

"I'm cute, too," he said.

"I can tell that about you."

The man picked up the cigar and flicked ashes on the carpet, which was all it was good for anyway. And I'd been meaning to break the penset since January. Still there was something about him I didn't like.

71

"You're *gonna* do this job for me," he said, shoving the cigar in his kisser.

"I am?"

He nodded. "You're gonna go in a house and give a guy an envelope. Then you're gonna forget you saw me."

"Now how could I ever do that?"

He grinned again, as if that was so damn cute he thought he might have to break the customer's chair to keep from laughing. Reaching across the desk, he clamped a monstrous hand on my shoulder, like it was a game of tag and I'd just been chosen "it."

"Let's go," he said.

I didn't see any point in arguing.

Pulling me around the side of the desk, he pushed me toward the pebbled-glass door. With his free hand, he grabbed my hat from the hatrack and stuffed it on my head.

"I'd like to call Mom," I said to him, over my shoulder. "She'll worry."

The guy opened the door and shoved me into the hall.

"Cute," he said, under his breath.

There was a gray Packard parked at a meter in front of the Cahuenga Building, where I had my doghouse. It wasn't brand new, like a top-rank hood's would have been, or custom built and frosted in chrome, like a movieland flesh peddler's, but it was in nice enough shape to make me wonder about the guy behind me, the guy with the iron fist in my back. The car didn't go with the rolling pin cigar and the crushed hat and the tout's jacket. This guy should have had a Plymouth with a hole in the floorboard and an odometer that had flipped over the day the banks closed.

He laid me on the front seat like boxed china and got in on the driver's side. The car sank beneath his weight like a cheap mattress. Without a word he took off down Hollywood Boulevard.

There was just enough of an April breeze that morning to carry the scent of oranges over from the big groves in the Valley. It mixed peculiarly with the burning-rubber stench of the man's corona, like a crate of fruit that had been crushed by a truck.

The big fellow ran a light and gunned the Packard south on Western.

"Where are we headed?" I asked, just out of curiosity.

"I told you," he said, chewing over his cigar. "You're going to meet a guy and give him a package."

"What's in the package?"

He smiled his tight-lipped smile. "It's okay, shamus. It's just scratch."

"Who are we paying off?"

"A rat named Loma."

I raised an eyebrow. "Tony Loma, the fight promoter?"

The big man looked unpleasantly surprised.

"You know him?" he said icily.

"I know about him. Enough so that I wouldn't want to owe him money."

The dangerous look on the big man's face went away. "Well, you don't always get what you want. Didn't your momma teach you that, peeper?"

We turned left on Wilshire, passing the ornate facade of the Wiltern theater. It hadn't opened yet for the matinee double feature, but the marquee was lit like a vanity mirror. A kid on a ladder was making anagrams with the billing.

"*Secrets of French Police*," I read off the marquee. "How does that sound to you?"

The big man grunted. "I was in it."

"You're an actor?"

The big man actually laughed, although the laughter had to make its way around the cigar, so it came out sounding like the barking of a dog with a bone in its mouth. "Hell no, I ain't no actor. I was between bouts, and it was a couple days' stunt work for me and Elmo."

"You're a fighter, then?"

He didn't answer right away. "I wrestle, down at the Olympic there."

"Could be I've heard of you?"

The big man took the cigar out of his mouth and studied the ragged end. "Yeah, maybe." He picked a strand of loose tobacco off his lower lip. "Few years back I had a shot at Londes and the heavyweight title."

I waited and when he didn't say it, I asked, "What was the name?"

"My ring moniker was Crusher."

"Just Crusher? Nothing else?"

"The," he said without cracking a smile.

I smiled for him. "The Crusher, huh? How did the match with Londes work out?"

"Got my shoulder broke a week before the fight, in a prelim against Buddy Brewster." He screwed the cigar back in his mouth and puffed on it. "Gained a little weight. Got some gray in my hair. Now it's strictly tag team with Elmo."

I had trouble imagining the guy that could break this one's shoulder, gray hair or no. But I'd have bet even money that old Buddy Brewster wouldn't have fit in the front seat between us, maybe not even in the back by himself. It put me in mind of what a small fry like me was doing there. I couldn't see The Crusher hiring another man to pay a debt, even if it was owed to a thug like Tony Loma.

So I asked him, "Why'd you pick me to run this errand?"

Once again, the big man took his time about replying, as if each word was a coin coming out of his own pocket. "Guy I know tells me you're pretty straight. Says you can keep your mouth shut."

The world must have looked pretty crooked to him, from the way he said it. But that didn't answer the question.

"I mean, why don't you just pay Loma yourself?" I said.

The Crusher got that battened-down look on his face again, like his eyelids were a couple of wide-brimmed hats. "He don't like me, and I don't like him. Next time we meet . . . there's gonna be trouble."

"Guys like Loma don't travel alone."

"There's gonna be trouble," The Crusher repeated.

By then we were on Grand, heading south through Bunker Hill toward Exposition Park. It suddenly dawned on me where we were going, the Olympic Arena on South Grand. Pretty soon, I could see it, a huge block of concrete rising out of the pavement, like a mirage on the freeway.

The Crusher parked the Packard just outside the entrance on the south side of the building. On a good night, with a good card, the doorway would have been crowded with fans and reporters and a few well-dressed women with blood in their eyes, looking for one more bout to cap the evening. But at that hour of the morning there was nobody around, except for a couple of Spanish kids shadowboxing their way down the sidewalk.

"I gotta check something," The Crusher said, as he put on the safety brake.

He got out and I got out with him. I followed him through the entryway into the darkness of the arena.

The stands were built up on rafters, all the way to the ceiling, with spaced runways leading to the ring. An ingot of lead gray light fell onto the roped square of canvas in the center, illuminating it faintly, like an examination table in a morgue. Somewhere in the gloom someone was working a bag. You could hear the echo of his fists, pummeling the leather.

We circled the stands to a stairway, then went down a flight to the dressing rooms. The hallway was plastered with posters advertising main events from years gone by. I spotted The Crusher's name on one of them, way down in the undercard. Midway along the hall, the big man stopped at a dressing room door and rapped on the jamb—one short, two long.

"Yeah?" someone inside said.

Whoever the voice belonged to, he wasn't the guy The Crusher was expecting.

"Elmo?" he barked.

"He ain't in."

The big man's face turned red as rye whiskey. Taking one quick step back, he lowered his shoulder and plowed directly into the dressing room door with a force that had to be seen to be appreciated. Even for a guy his size, it was impressive. The door splintered and groaned, coming right off its hinges, like it had been hit by a Chevy.

The momentum of the big man's blow carried him halfway into the dressing room. He lost his footing on the concrete floor and ended up on his knees in front of a short, stocky, balding guy with a wrinkled, deeply tanned face. I'd seen that face before, in the sports page and, when I was with the D.A., pasted in the mug books. Tony Loma.

There were two other guys in the room with him, big, hulking torpedos in cheap black suits that looked like they'd been bought that morning at a mortuary fire sale.

Loma took a look at The Crusher, kneeling on the floor, and started to laugh. The two torpedos started laughing too, a second later. They could afford to laugh. All three of them were holding .38's.

From his knees, The Crusher looked up at Loma. I could see that he didn't care about the guns, and so could the bald man. He stopped laughing, cocked the pistol, and pressed the barrel against The Crusher's forehead.

"Don't even think about it," he said to the big man.

The Crusher's chest heaved. It took every bit of self-restraint he had to keep from attacking the guy. You could see him fighting it out with himself. The sane part eventually won, but it was a split decision. Taking a couple more deep breaths, he passed a hand through his iron-gray hair. He'd lost the hat on the way in. "Where's Elmo?" he said in a voice that was barely under control.

"That's what we were wondering. You don't have no ideas, do you, Crush?"

The Crusher glared at him.

Loma pulled the gun away from The Crusher's forehead and took a step back. "You never should have tied up with that punk. He's bad news."

The Crusher gave Loma his battened-down look. "If you done him, Tony, you're going to pay."

The bald guy chuckled. "You got guts, cracking wise with three .38's pointed at your head. I always said that about you, Crush. More guts than brains."

"You said a lot of things, Tony."

The bald guy flushed a little. "You got paid. Wha'd you got to complain about? It was business."

"Business," The Crusher said.

Loma glanced through the broken door at me. "Who's your pal?"

"Nobody," The Crusher said, slowly getting back to his feet.

"Tell nobody to take his hands out of his pockets and come in here." Loma nodded at one of the torpedos, and the hood trained his pistol on me.

I raised my hands and stepped through the door.

Loma looked back at The Crusher. "Elmo's got till two this afternoon, Crush, to come up with the scratch. His pals won't wait longer than that."

"*Your* pals," the big man said bitterly.

"Elmo's a big boy. He shouldn'ta mixed in this thing."

"He shouldn'ta mixed with you."

"You tell him to get the five gees, or he takes a dip in the Pacific."

The big man reached down and picked up his hat, dusting it off against his pants leg before putting it back on his head. "You'll get the dough," he said.

Loma pocketed his pistol and walked toward the door. The two torpedos followed behind him at a distance, as if they were carrying his train.

"Elmo knows the place," Loma said, from the doorway. "You tell him to be there. Ain't no good hiding out. We'll find him. You know we will."

The three thugs left. The big man stared after them with a look that would have given a normal man a nosebleed. After a while, he dropped his head.

"Do you know where Elmo is?" I asked him.

"I got an idea."

"Does he have the five gees?"

The big man laughed bitterly. "He ain't got a pot to piss in. Me, I can get the scratch." He shook his head. "It's all I got. Six years' work. And I gotta hand it over to that monkey Loma."

"How did your buddy Elmo get in dutch with these boys?"

He dropped his chin even lower, as if the thing were too embarrassing to look at head on. "When we was out on the movie ranch, Elmo fell in with some of that Hollywood trash, Loma's crowd. He's just a kid, nineteen. He don't know which side the bread is buttered on, but he thinks he knows it all. Some chippy winks at him, and he's falling all over himself to do her favors. She talks him into running down to TJ to pick up a package for Loma's pals. And the damn fool does it. On the way back up to Malibu, the package gets heisted."

"By who?"

"Who knows. Maybe some of Loma's torpedos. I wouldn't put it past the double-crossing rat."

"So Elmo's got to pay back for the goods."

"He ain't saved a dime," The Crusher said. "He hasn't learned that the money ain't gonna always be there, that you ain't gonna be nineteen forever."

"This kid a relative of yours?"

The big man raised his head and stared at me balefully. "A friend."

"A good enough friend to spend your bankroll on?"

The Crusher grunted. "How good does a friend have to be?"

We stopped at the big man's hotel before meeting with Loma's Hollywood pals. The Crusher didn't say why we were stopping, but I figured it was because the money was there, or nearby.

It was a cheap place called the Metropole, on Seventh and Spring. The lobby was a deadbeat's delight, but the rented room was surprisingly clean; or maybe it was just The Crusher who was clean. His place had the spare, neat, squared-away look of a soldier's billet. It was a look I recognized, the look of longtime bachelorhood. It smelled like a bachelor's flat too, of shaving soap and whiskey and the fat cigars the big man smoked.

While The Crusher rummaged through a linen closet in the bathroom, I took a look at a photograph sitting on the nightstand. It was a picture of The Crusher taken in a much better year, when his face hadn't looked like a crushed fedora and his hair hadn't turned to iron. There was a girl in the picture, pretty and pale and a little in awe of the big man beside her. Whoever she was, he still thought enough of her to keep her picture by his bed.

The only other decoration in the room was a poster on the door, featuring a picture of The Crusher and a red-haired kid billed as Young Wolf. I figured Young Wolf was Elmo. He certainly didn't look wolfish on the poster. He looked musclebound and callow and stupid, like a streetcorner bully. But I was probably seeing him with a jaded eye, knowing what a spot he'd left his partner in.

As I stood there staring at Elmo, The Crusher came back in the room carrying a zippered canvas gym bag. He had an odd look on his face.

"Somebody's been in here," he said. "And I think I know who."

"Loma?"

The big man nodded. "He probably stopped here, looking for Elmo, before he went down to the Olympic."

"Where is Elmo?"

"He and that chippy were shacked up in some cheap motel in Long Beach. The Enchanted Cottages. He probably lammed it back over there, to dodge Tony and the boys."

"I hope Elmo appreciates what you're doing for him."

"I told you. He's a friend." The Crusher set the canvas bag down on the bed and glanced at the photograph on the nightstand. "He's the kid of a dame I used to know." He looked back at the bag. "I owe her something."

He unzipped the bag and took out a couple of undershirts, some trunks, several pairs of rolled-up white socks, and a pair of shoes. When the thing was empty, he drew a penknife from his pocket and pried out the plywood bottom of the gym bag. Putting the board on the bed, he reached inside and his face turned white.

"Jesus," he said softly.

He lifted up the bag and looked directly into it. Then he turned it upside down. A little tag of paper floated out. The Crusher tossed the bag across the room, picked up the tag of paper, and stared at it.

"He done me again," he said incredulously and sat down hard on the bed. "The bastard done me again."

"Who?"

"Loma," he said and I could hear the rage rising in his throat. "He pays off that gorilla, Brewster, to bust up my shoulder, so's he can get his own boy a title shot. And now he takes my bankroll. Every penny I got!"

He crumpled up the piece of paper and threw it on the floor. "I'm gonna kill him."

"Now wait a minute," I said. "It's a pretty long shot that a guy like Loma, a stranger, could come in here and find that dough, without tearing the place up a little. Use your head. This room hasn't been searched. Somebody knew where to look."

"Read the damn note!" The Crusher said, jumping to his feet and pushing me out of his way. He went straight for the door, tearing it open as if he were tearing Loma's heart out.

I picked the crumpled note up and read it quickly. It was printed in a crude hand and said, "Thanks for the dough, T.L." I stuck it in my pocket and started after The Crusher.

I managed to catch up to him on the street.

"Where are you going?" I said.

"You know where," he snarled.

"At least let me tag along."

"This is the main event. No tags, this time."

"How are you going to find Loma?"

"I know where he's at. With the Hollywood bunch up in Malibu."

"Crusher, Loma's boys will kill you."

"So what?" he said and meant it.

When we reached the car, the big man pulled a fat cigar from his coat, bit off the end, and screwed it into his mouth. "Shamus," he said, "quit worrying about it. I've been getting mad most of my life, and it's always cost me something. It's cost me dough, it's cost me friends, it's cost me a good woman, and this time maybe it's gonna cost the decision. But at least this time I'm getting mad at the right guy. When it comes down to it, it's the only way this round could end." He struck a match on his heel and lit the corona. "So long, shamus."

He got in the car and drove off.

The first thing I did was phone Bernie Ohls from a pay phone in the Olympic lobby.

"There's a big guy in a gray 1937 Packard, California license number 53437. Pick him up."

"Why, Phil?" Bernie said.

"Because he's about to kill Tony Loma and get himself killed in the process."

"Too bad," Bernie said. "Loma could use killing. I'll put out an A.P.B. What's the guy's name?"

"He calls himself The Crusher. He's a pro wrestler. I don't know what his real name is. But you can't miss him. He's as big as a house. You better hurry on this, Bernie. The guy's dead serious."

"We'll try, Phil."

"Notify the C.H.P., too. And see if you can dig up a Malibu address for Loma. That's where the big guy is headed."

"Will you be in the office?"

"No, I'll check back with you. I've got to take a trip to Long Beach."

I caught a fast cab back to the office and picked up my car. It took me about a half an hour to make it down to Long Beach and another ten minutes to find The Enchanted Cottages motel. They didn't look enchanted to me. Haunted, maybe. I slipped the clerk in the office a fin to point me toward the right shack, then drove down the driveway and parked in front of it. Even though the clerk had claimed that the couple in 22 hadn't checked out, there was no other car around, and that worried me a little.

The cabin was made out of redwood logs with gingerbread appliqués over the door and window. The curtain in the window had been drawn. I pulled the .38 out of the gun holder beneath the dashboard and got out into the sun. You couldn't smell the oranges in Long Beach. Just diesel oil and mildew and the backwater smack of the pier.

I didn't have time for niceties, so I walked over to the door and kicked it open. I wasn't The Crusher, so it took me a couple of boots. When the lock finally sprang, I stepped in holding the gun in front of me.

A disheveled looking redheaded kid, the same kid I'd seen in the poster on The Crusher's door, was standing by the bed, a sheet wrapped around his torso. He looked sleepy and disoriented, as if my foot had been his alarm clock. He also looked mad. I could see a blush spreading up his neck into his freckled face.

"Who the hell are you?" he said.

"Marlowe," I said. "I'm a detective working for a friend of yours. A big guy named The Crusher."

"Jack wouldn't send a guy like you," the kid said, getting angrier.

"I guess that's what you were counting on, wasn't it, Elmo?"

"What do you mean?" Elmo said nastily.

"That Jack wouldn't tumble to your game. You always treat your friends like that?"

"I don't know what you're talking about."

"Sit," I said, pointing to the bed with the gun.

He sat.

"Where's your girlfriend?" I asked.

"Irene? She went out to eat, while I was asleep. She left a note saying she'd bring me back some chow."

"Want to bet?"

"Bet?" the kid said stupidly.

"Let's see the note."

He picked up a slip of paper from the nightstand and held it out toward me. I walked over to the bed. As soon as I got within arm's reach, Elmo went for my legs.

He was quick, but he was wearing a sheet. Besides, I was expecting it. I sidestepped him and smacked the gun barrel across his temple. Elmo groaned and grabbed his head.

"Jack was right about you, buster," I said, reaching down to pick up the note. "You've got a lot to learn."

Elmo blubbered like a baby.

I took a look at the note. It was written in a crude hand and said, "Gone to get eats. Back soon. I." I wasn't a handwriting expert, but I didn't have to be one to recognize the scrawl. It was the same hand that had scribbled the note in The Crusher's room.

I tapped the kid with the gun again, just hard enough to get his attention. He looked up at me with tears in his eyes.

"Whose idea was it to steal Jack's bankroll?"

The kid looked genuinely surprised. "Jack's bankroll?"

"The five gees he kept in his gym bag."

"Nobody knows about that," the kid said. "Nobody but me and Jack."

"You didn't mention it to Irene, maybe? Just in passing, in the night?"

The kid swallowed hard. "Oh, God," he said.

"You're a real sap, Elmo, you know that?" I stared at the boy disgustedly. "Because of your double-cross a friend of yours is in real trouble."

The kid shook his head helplessly. "It wasn't supposed to be like that. I was gonna get the money back to Jack, after he paid Tony off."

"And where were you going to get five gees, Elmo?"

His head sank to his chest. "The stuff. Irene was gonna sell the stuff."

"The stuff you brought back from TJ. The stuff you told Jack was heisted."

The kid put both hands to his head. "She said it was worth ten, maybe twenty thousand. She has friends who . . . they'd buy it from us."

"Well, now she has the drugs *and* Jack's five thousand. What do you think she's going to bring you back from the restaurant, Elmo?"

"Bitch," he said between his teeth.

"Get dressed, Elmo," I said. "Get dressed quick, while there's still a chance to save Jack's life."

"His life?" Elmo said with horror.

"Your girlfriend made it look like Tony Loma took his money. Jack's gone after him."

Elmo leaped up and started dressing.

We made the trip up the coast highway as fast as the car could run. Elmo had sobered up completely when he realized the spot his friend was in. It made me think that there might be something there worth saving— maybe the same thing that Jack had been willing to bet his life on.

The kid stared desperately through the windshield as we tore through Pedro and Bay City, rocking back and forth on the seat, as if he were trying to urge the car on with body English like a jockey. As fast as we went, it wasn't fast enough. I knew it before we got to the Colony, as surely as if it were already written. I knew it, but the kid didn't.

He started babbling and pointing, as soon as we hit the Malibu coast. I followed his sign language, down a little road off the highway that ran behind a row of beach houses. As soon as I saw the police cars and the ambulances, I slowed to a crawl. The kid flung the passenger side door open and hit the ground on the run. I pulled to a stop a few hundred feet away and stared at the little beach house, crawling with cops. I don't run toward tragedies unless I can do something to prevent them. And this time, it was too late to do anything at all.

After a while, I got out. The only smell was the smell of the sea, thick and salty like a taste on the tongue. I sat down on a big white rock beside the roadside berm. The beach ran right up the road, and the ocean stretched out beyond it, languid and sunstreaked and coolly oblivious to all the petty commotion on that tiny spot of shoreline.

Bernie Ohls walked over, throwing a long shadow across the sand. I looked up at him.

"The big guy's dead."

I nodded. "That's the way it figured."

"He got Loma, though. And one of his torpedos. The other one got him." Bernie looked back at the beach house. "The kid you brought along, Elmo Pritchard . . . he's pretty upset. He blames himself for what happened. He mentioned a girl, Irene Chivalo."

"Elmo was carrying drugs up from TJ for Loma. He told Loma the drugs had been heisted. But Elmo and the girl took them themselves, and left the big guy to clean up the mess."

"That's what the kid told us. We'll get an A.P.B. out on the Chivalo dame immediately. She and Elmo are going to do time. I think the kid knows it, too. He asked if he could talk to you."

"Why not?"

Brushing the sand off my cuffs, I got to my feet and walked up the road to the beach house. Elmo was sitting in the front seat of a cop car, staring at two attendants wheeling a loaded gurney over to an ambulance.

"Is that Jack?" I said to him, through the cop car window.

He nodded. "It's my fault."

"Yes."

Elmo put his hands to his face and started to cry.

"Everything's got a price tag, kid. The big guy knew that. You're learning it now."

He sobbed. "Call my mom in Oxnard, will ya? Tell her."

I walked back down the road to my car. Bernie was waiting there for me.

"Is there anyone to claim the body?" he asked.

"I'll look into it," I told him.

When I got back to my office, late in the afternoon, I picked up the county phone book and started thumbing through the various towns and municipalities, searching for a woman named Pritchard in Oxnard. It was going to take some time to drive up there. But time was all I had that afternoon, and I figured the woman would want to know.

The year I chose, 1939, was a good year for Chandler. It was the year of Farewell, My Lovely, *which happens to be the first Chandler novel I read. I've written my story in what I hope is an approximation of the style of that novel (although it's somewhat stripped down, because of limitations of length). Knowing that Chandler often "cannibalized" his short fiction, I've made an attempt to write a story that might have served as a springboard for* Farewell, My Lovely, *touching upon some of the same kinds of characters and themes.*

Along with many of your other contributors, I can honestly say that I wouldn't have become a detective story writer had it not been for Chandler. Reading him in grad school was a revelation. Here, for once, was a genre writer with style and wit. His sense of place and character were first rate. But it was his language, more than anything else, that impressed me. Chandler had a truly memorable voice; and through his narrator Marlowe, he showed me that a detective could be a lot more than a wisecracking stereotype (although Marlowe could crack wise with the best of them). Philip Marlowe remains, I think, the funniest, the most worldly wise, the most charmingly cynical, and the most original creation in American detective fiction. Marlowe was, and will always be, a model for us all.

Jonathan Valin

RAYMOND CHANDLER'S
PHILIP MARLOWE
THE FORTIES

SAD-EYED BLONDE

DICK LOCHTE

1940

THE THING ABOUT having an office on Hollywood Boulevard is that you never know what's going to come calling. Even if you're six flights up. That humid Monday morning, the list began with a butterfly. It cleared the sill, maneuvered past the lifeless curtain and paused to check out the room before committing itself further. It took in walls the color of a jaundice victim, a desk that had more scars than Primo Carnera's nose, a rump-sprung client's chair, five pond-green filing cabinets, three of them as empty as my stomach, and me, leaning back in a swivel chair that squeaked like a mouse that had expected Swiss cheese and got farina. In spite of everything, the butterfly decided to stick around. It soared to the ceiling, skimmed the cobwebs, then did a rollover and dived for the floor where it nestled on the edge of the worn red carpet. It had just settled in when a pair of black and white spectators waltzed through the door and sent it off to bug Valhalla.

The two-tone Sunday dogs were only a part of my visitor's sartorial splendor. Accompanying them were a wide-brim Panama with a pink band, a nutmeg brown silk suit, a dark red shirt, and a white dickey-sized tie with pink bubbles on it that matched the hatband. The guy's vaguely cherubic face was pink, too, and freshly barbered. His sunburned nose, which should have been on a larger, fatter man, was as red as a beefsteak tomato.

His nervous eyes shifted from me to the squashed butterfly. He said, "Aw, Christ," and dropped to one knee. He used a polished fingernail to scrape what was left of the bug from the carpet, whipped out a pink display hanky and rested the remains on it. "Aw, Christ," he repeated.

I watched him with a certain sense of wonder as he brought the handkerchief litter to my desk and placed it carefully on the glass top before sinking with a sigh onto the client chair.

"He was a beauty, too," he said. "It's not like we got so much beauty

87

in the world, we can afford to waste a little. I'm a goddamn Jonah is what I am."

I removed my dead pipe from the ashtray, picked up his handkerchief and dropped the ex-butterfly among the ashes and butts. I dumped the whole mess into the wastebasket and handed him back his pink linen. "Stir seems to have bared your poetic soul, Johnny. Or is this a new grift?"

He gave me a smile as thin as boardinghouse milk and said, "So sue me if I like insects. Try five years doubled up in a ten-foot cage with an ex–pin jabber who can't do nothing but play nose checkers, and see if you don't start giving pet names to cockroaches."

"I'll take your word for it," I said, waiting for him to get around to the reason he'd dropped by.

As he patted his handkerchief back into his coat pocket, he scanned the room. "You ain't exactly conquering the world, are you, Marlowe?"

"I'll leave that to Mr. Hitler and see how far he gets with it. Are we just waltzing here, or is something special going to happen when the band stops playing?"

His smile grew wider under his bright red nose. "Kathy'll be up in a sec. She stopped off at the Madison to grab some smokes, say hello to the old gang. She tole me how you helped out while I was inside."

Kathy was Johnny Horne's wife, a tall blonde with sad, China-blue eyes, who used to be a good cop. Her problem was, she had lousy taste in men. Johnny wasn't the worst of them. But he was determined to bounce checks for a living even though he had no aptitude for it. So Kathy had been forced to turn in her tin and get a job selling smokes at the Madison House while Johnny spent most of their wedded years in San Quentin sewing mailbags. That's where he'd been when Kathy had brought me into a situation involving stolen pearls.

It hadn't been quite the cakewalk she'd described; but four or five stiffs later, we wound up splitting twenty-five grand that the insurance company had posted for the recovery of the teardrops.

Johnny Horne ran his little pinkie along a crater a cigarette had scorched in the desk. "You musta put your share of the loot in the bank, huh, Marlowe? Saving it for a rainy day."

"I keep it in my bathtub in dimes and quarters so I can run my fingers through it on slow nights."

I was about to ask him how Kathy was when I found out for myself. "Hi, Phil," she drawled from the doorway. The last I'd seen of her, she'd been slightly seedy and as glum as St. Agnes on a cloudy day, even with a handbag full of twelve thousand five-hundred dollars. In the harsh sunlight that sneaked past the drapes, she looked like a new woman. Her blue eyes were so bright they glittered, and her simple aqua dress fit her lanky frame like pants on a lambchop. I wondered if the reward money had been responsible for the changeover, or if it was Johnny getting his wings.

He hopped from the chair and held it out for her as carefully as if it were a Chippendale.

Kathy asked, "How much have I missed?"

"We haven't left the starting gate," I told her.

Johnny cleared his throat and said: "Waitin' on you, angel cake."

Angel cake leaned back in the chair. "You still hide your gargle in that desk drawer, Phil?"

"Right next to the knitting," I said, pulling out the Old Forester and a couple of glasses. Ever the proper host, I poured them each a shot and took mine from the bottle. Johnny sipped his carefully. Kathy downed hers with a little chuckle, coughed once, and said, "I figure we owe you this one."

"You don't owe me a thing."

"You split that insurance loot right down the middle; and hell knows, you did all of the work and took all of the knocks."

"History doesn't pay the rent," I said. "So the hell with history."

"Phil, this one'll make us all fat as geese," she said earnestly. Johnny's eyes ping-ponged from her to me.

"Maybe I'm trying to lose weight."

Johnny chuckled nervously. He shook his head, and his Panama wiggled like it had caught a breeze. "Marlowe, the tag on this could be as much as one hundred gees."

I smiled at them both. "As much as that, huh?"

Kathy started to straighten the papers on my desk. Either she was a compulsive cleaner, or she was being evasive. "Are you in?" she asked.

"Not yet. But I love a good story." I had nothing pressing. The chicken pot pie wouldn't be ready at Musso's for another two hours.

She pulled a pack of gaspers from her purse, peeled away the cellophane, tore off a neat square of silver paper, and deposited it into my empty ashtray, all in one graceful motion. "A little touch I picked up pushing tobacco down at the Madison," she said, offering me a nail.

I used the desk lighter on her cigarette, then mine, and relit it for Johnny's. No sense tempting fate. After we'd blown enough smoke in each other's faces, Kathy said, "Ever hear of the Jeweled Skull of Lhasa?"

I replied, "You stepped in *what*?"

"The Jeweled Skull of Lhasa. About the size of an ostrich egg. Belonged to a holy man a couple of lifetimes ago. This tribe in Tibet inlaid it with sparklers, rubies, the works. A British expedition stumbled on it, twenty or twenty-five years back. One of the Brits pinched it when nobody was looking."

"Gee," I said. "Is there a curse on it? People dropping like flies just from the sight of it?"

Kathy said, "Crack wise all you want, Phil. But a Warbucks in Frisco wound up with it on his mantelpiece. And, though some may consider it to be in bad taste, he was goddamned fond of it. So when it got lifted he posted one hundred grand for its return."

"And you know where it is?"

"No," she said. "But I know somebody who knows."

"How'd you manage that?"

Her blue eyes sparkled. "The years I spent on the force count for something," she said. "I still got friends downtown."

Johnny Horne bent down and kissed his wife's cheek.

"An L.A. cop knows the whereabouts of a priceless doodad and he talks to you about it?" I wondered.

"That's the beauty part," Johnny said. "He can't move on it."

Johnny's grin was as big as his head was empty. I turned to Kathy. "I guess I missed a salient point."

Kathy stared at me for a beat. "I . . . the cop's named Beaudry."

In my head, a nickel started rolling toward a slot.

She continued, "You must remember him when you were working for the D.A."

The nickel dropped. A scarecrow with sawed-off hair and a chin like a towel rack who was always in dutch with the D.A., Taggart Wilde. Usually had his nose in a book. The day Wilde handed me my walking papers Beaudry looked up from his novel to grumble, " 'And so proceed ad infinitum.' " I didn't know what the hell that was supposed to mean and was not inclined at the time to care very much.

"If Beaudry's got a line on the skull, he's holding all the aces," I said. "Why deal me in?"

She said, "Because I told him we can trust you."

I grinned at her. "Yeah. But other than that."

She smiled back. "Beaudry knows where the thief is holed up. But, being a cop, he can't front the recovery. His boss, Captain Maclin, would get too curious."

"Maclin would also want a piece of the reward, like maybe ninety-nine percent," Johnny added.

"That's why Beaudry came to me. He'd heard about the Leander pearls. And how the payoff went down."

I exhaled a little smoke and looked from her to Johnny. She took her husband's hand and said, "Sweetheart, would you take a little stroll? Then we'll have us a nice lunch somewhere."

Johnny leaned forward and touched her cheek. He cleared his throat and croaked, "I think I'll take a stroll." At the door he added, "Sorry about your butterfly, shamus."

"He wasn't mine, Johnny. He dropped by to visit my bluebottle flies."

"Whatever." He left us with another of his halfhearted, crooked smiles.

Kathy wasted a minute after the outer door clicked shut before she said, "The last stretch took its toll, Phil. Johnny came out of Grey Castle like Ferdinand. He'd rather smell the flowers. But even if he wanted in on this, Beaudry would keep him out. You know how cops are about cons. So I suggested that you front the deal, and that was swell with Beaudry. He likes you."

"That must be why he looked the other way when Wilde lowered the boom on me."

"I wouldn't know about that. Anyway, wasn't somebody just telling me how useful history is?"

"Good point. How do we carve it up?"

She hesitated, then said, "Beaudry wants half. You and I split the rest."

Twenty-five grand. Enough for a good day's work. I nodded.

Kathy relaxed, tried a smile.

"You look good," I told her.

"It comes and it goes."

I poured her another finger of hooch and we toasted the future. Then she turned off the smile and said, "Beaudry's playing this close to the vest. He's kept me in the dark about the who and the where. You'll get it all tonight at his house—a bungalow over in Culver City, by the bakery. He'll be there by eight. I'll phone him you're coming."

I stared at her while she wrote out the address. The situation seemed a little more complicated than necessary, but that was typical of Beaudry. No matter how many times his backside got gnawed on by Taggart Wilde because of it, Beaudry never did things the simple way. He preferred to circle a problem and attack it from some odd angle. By that time, it was usually too late.

I took another swig. Recovering the skull was going to be a snap.

Sure it was. I put that thought in my back pocket near my wallet and told Kathy that Johnny was making noises like he might be staying on this side of the gate for a while.

She shrugged. "Maybe. But you know what they say about old habits, Phil. You can't beat 'em to death with a crowbar."

They were having some sort of do at M.G.M. studios, and Washington Boulevard, which was usually pretty empty at that time of night, was teeming with sleek limousines driven by sleek chauffeurs. Maybe President Roosevelt was in town. Maybe Greta Garbo had finally decided she wanted company.

The snarl made me ten minutes late for Beaudry. His bungalow was a fading matchbox on a patchy street full of potholes and weird ideas. Somebody had painted several trees bright yellow. Another had stuck baby dolls all over the top of his Packard. Maybe it was the air. Three blocks away, the Bialy Brothers Best Bread building, a place the size of an airplane hanger, was filling the still, humid night with bakery smells. It was the heady kind of odor that reminded you what the world was like when you were young. Which can be a pleasant thing. Or it can be murder.

There was a dim light inside Beaudry's, and the sound of tinny laughter. I walked past a parched lawn and a weed garden to a screen porch and dusted the door with my knuckles. Inside the house a familiar voice said, "Rochester, have you pressed my tuxedo pants?"

I called out, "Beaudry?"

"Not yet, Mr. Benny. Fella who rented 'em hasn't brought 'em back yet."

More laughter.

I slipped the .38 Colt Super Match from its shoulder holster and tried the screen door. It opened.

"Well, call him and tell him to bring 'em back now. I'm due at the Colmans in an hour."

I stepped onto a neat little porch with two white rockers and a metal glider.

"Can't call him, Mr. Benny."

"Well, why not?"

"I'm all out of nickels."

I moved through the open front door into a large living room illuminated only by the orange dial of a Philco console. The radio laughter subsided just as the shiny waxed floor creaked under my feet and I heard the click of a hammer being cocked.

"Beaudry?" I asked hopefully, not moving.

"That you, Marlowe?" came the baritone reply. "I must've drifted off. Lemme get rid of the noise."

A light went on in the corner of the room and Beaudry's scarecrow figure shuffled past me. His bare feet and ankles showed under pants that were too short for him. A white shirt hung down over his belt and flapped around his butt. His gun was still in his hand. I didn't put mine away either.

He clicked off the radio, stuck the gun in his belt, and yawned. I took a quick look around as I holstered my .38. The place could have stood in for a Christian Science Reading Room. One wall was filled with books. Newspapers and magazines were piled neatly on a shiny oak table next to the radio. On the coffee table next to the couch an open volume rested. George Santayana's *The Realm of the Spirit*, whatever that was.

I asked him if he read much.

He paused to look at his library and shrugged. "Like the feller said, 'Reading maketh a full man.' 'Sides, as you well know, most police work'd bore the horns off a mountain goat. So I read. Been doing it since my wife passed away. Eleven years, now. C'mon. I'll get us some milk and cookies."

I followed him through a neat little dining room with a polished hardwood table and six matching chairs. A bouquet of buttercups and baby's breath sat in a glass vase on a matching sideboard. Past that was the kitchen. White walls. Black and white checkerboard tile floor. A set of dirty dishes rested on a porcelain sink.

He found a bottle of Old Canterbury in the cupboard and dragged it and two tumblers over to a small wooden breakfast table where a book rested beside another vase, this one full of bright red wildflowers, the kind they call desert paintbrush.

Beaudry poured two heavy shots and said, "To crime, huh, Marlowe?"

I clicked my tumbler against his and wet the back of my throat with the harsh alcohol.

He emptied his glass, made a face, then let out his breath. "It's all in there," he said, indicating the book.

It wasn't a new edition. The blue jacket was battered and worn. The drawing on it was of a black bird and a hand emerging from water holding coins and jewelry.

"This is supposed to tell me how to find a holy man's skull?" I asked.

"Have you read it?"

Actually, I had. I'd heard that its author, Dashiell Hammett, was an ex-Pinkerton, and that had made me curious enough to plunk down the two dollars. I'd liked it, a hell of a lot more than I'd liked the film they made of it with a Latin-lover type as the sleuth, Sam Spade. I heard the

Hollywood boys gave it another try a year ago. That time they changed Spade's name. One day they'll learn that some books will never make a good movie.

"I don't see what this's got to do with the price of heads," I told Beaudry.

He grinned and filled our glasses. "There's a lot in there Hammett didn't make up, exactly."

I cocked an eye. "You mean the dame? Brigid whatever?"

"Well, he made her up from two dames he knew. And the fat man was somebody he followed for Pinkerton. It's the black bird I'm talking about. The falcon. It was supposed to have been a gift from the Order of the Hospital of St. John of Jerusalem to Emperor Charles V. A gold falcon encrusted with jewels as a sort of rent payment for their occupation of the island of Malta."

Just listening to him made my throat dry, so I took another pull at the hooch and said, "I think you been reading a little too much, pal."

"Maybe," he said. "But I never heard of a guy going broke because he read too much. You don't want to hear any more, adios, brother."

When I didn't ankle, he continued. "There never were any gold falcons. Historians like Jonathan Theil have written that the birds the Hospitalers gave in those days were made of feathers and claws, not precious metals. What got Hammett thinking about jewels was an ancient skull filled with diamonds and rubies. He saw it in San Francisco in the twenties, in the possession of a heavy holder named Grunwald who'd bought it off of a limey named Forbes-Ralston whose father had looted it from Tibet. Grunwald, who owns about five square blocks along Market Street, got his mansion broken into seven years ago. The skull was among the loot. The Frisco cops caught one of the crib crackers when he tried to fence some of the glitter. A little gyp known as the Midget Bandit. He'd been in and out of Q. since twenty-three, when he got nabbed with his mitt in the till of a gas station in Stockton."

"Are we getting to the point, Beaudry? Because if not, we're going to need another bottle."

"The point is, the Midget is still in Q., and he never spilled on his partner. But I know the bustard's name and I know where he's hanging his turban these days."

"Mind telling me how you came by all this information?"

He grinned at me. "A night three years ago, my partner, Ray Doyle, and I were sent out to Freddie March's house to check a disturbance. There was a hell of a party going on. Flynn was there, and a bunch of writers. This Fitzgerald guy. And Ernest Hemingway. And Hammett, drunk as the well-known skunk, and shouting that Hemingway didn't know nothing about women or how to write about women. Hemingway was responding to this by breaking all of the Marches' glassware against the wall, which is what made the neighbor call us in the first place.

"Anyway, we wind up driving Hammett back to his hotel, because he couldn't drive himself, and the woman who was with him, Lillian somebody, didn't want to leave the party. And he starts telling us about his days as a Pink. And that leads to him jawing about the *Falcon*, and the Skull of Lhasa. He talks about this Midget Bandit, who's in the *Falcon* under the name of Wilmer, and the Midget's partner, a wildman that Hammett swears he's going to use in a book some day. And he laughs about the coincidence of the real Wilmer finally getting his hands on the real falcon."

He screwed up his face so that his shovel of a chin almost touched the tip of his nose, then sighed and said, "I got another five years before I retire, Marlowe. Now, me, I don't see myself staying in blue another five years, what with guys on the right on the heavy grab and on the left turning 'em in. Sooner or later, somebody is gonna shoot somebody, and I don't want it to be me. So I got a list of potential tickets to the good life—gems that have never surfaced, missing persons, a couple real bang-bang daddies with prices on their heads. Ever' so often information blows in that strikes me as interesting. So I stick around after hours downtown and check out leads. None of 'em has paid off before. But this one ought to bring the average way up."

"How'd you run across the Midget's partner?"

"I just looked up one afternoon and there he was. Seems he's given up boosting in favor of a new grift, some sorta swami mumbo jumbo. This old Highland Park dowager swore out a complaint and so he got dragged in and booked. He has this beetle juice on his face to make him look Hindu and he's wearing a goddamn turban and he calls himself Sandor the All-Seeing. But according to his prints, he's the Midget's partner, Smiler Foy."

"And nobody asked him about the theft in San Francisco?"

"Nobody knew about it. Except me, of course. And now you."

He started to wet my glass again but I stopped him. "I want to be conscious when I meet the swami."

We both stood. "Any idea how you're going to approach him?"

"Head on," I said.

That wasn't in Beaudry's lexicon. He screwed up his face and said, "It's your play to call. But the man is slippery as a greased eel. I blinked my eyes and he was out of the lockup."

"Have you got a better suggestion?"

"Nope. But you don't want to spook him."

"Where do I find him?"

"He's got a crummy little rat trap in Venice. On the canal."

"You didn't brace him, by any chance?"

"Hell, no. Brace him? And tip him that I knew about the skull? What'd be the sense in that? You know me better than that, Marlowe."

I did at that. Bracing him would have been too simple, and simplicity was not Beaudry's style. It had cost him countless arrests. Now it was going to cost him twenty-five grand.

There was a green sedan parked in front of my car and a small man perched on my front fender. There was more than enough moonlight for me to see that it was Johnny Horne. He was wearing a dark blue suit so shiny it might have been dipped in brilliantine. His shirt was dark, too, with a cream-colored tie that matched his display handkerchief. A wild rose was stuck in his lapel.

As I opened my car door, I asked, "Catching the night air, Johnny? Or do I get to guess what's on your mind?"

"You going after the dingus now?"

I didn't reply.

"Lemme tag along."

"Why should I?"

He frowned and took a step to the right and a step to the left, like an anxious chicken. He finally blurted, " 'Cause I need to jaw with you about something."

I slipped behind the wheel and opened the other door for him. He got in eagerly. The engine kicked over and we were off to Venice. He coughed and cleared his throat for a few minutes, then asked, "Phil, when I was at Q., did you and, uh, Kathy . . . well, you know what I'm asking?"

My eyes went to his coat, which was stretched too tightly across his thin chest to be hiding a gun. Not that anything had happened between me and Kathy to make him want to draw down on me. I told him so.

He shook his head. "Yeah, that's what I thought," he said. "But I had to ask. My head's all screwed up. Those were five long years and my rhythm's jumbled now that I'm out again. Everything's a little off. It's me. I been imagining things."

I glanced over at him. He was staring out at the road, shaking his head. "Kathy's the greatest. She did some things for me, coulda got her in dutch, maybe even put away. Did 'em to keep me out. And when I screwed up so bad she couldn't pull any more strings, she came up once a week, like clockwork. For all five goddamn years. She's there when I get out and she drives me to a swell place she's bought out in Gray Lake. Painted it fresh for me. Neat as a pin. Got flowers planted all around. Like living in a rainbow." He pointed to the wild rose in his lapel. "This came from our own garden, unnerstand?"

I nodded. But I didn't understand. He sounded like he was ready to unspool on me and I didn't need any distractions. Not if I was going to have to deal with Sandor the All-Seeing. Still, it was interesting to hear about the house and garden. He said suddenly, "I'm not going back on the grift. If you ever hear I'm bouncing checks again, I want you to run me down and shoot me. You hear that, Marlowe. You shoot me."

"Relax, Johnny. Nobody's gonna shoot you," I told him. Which shows you how much I knew about anything.

We glided down Venice Boulevard, over the crest where the ocean breeze dropped the temperature at least ten degrees and puffs of fog passed in front of the headlights like spirit tumbleweeds.

Pretty soon we could see the Venice canals. And smell them. They were built in the early 1900's by a real estate mogul named Kinney who had patterned the town after its Italian namesake. But his dream went up in smoke, literally, in the twenties when his pier burned and the canals filled with slime and the bohemians and oddballs moved in.

Sandor lived not far from where Kinney's version of the doge's palace had once stood. I parked across the canal from his shack on an empty, weedy lot inhabited mainly by mosquitoes. Johnny asked, "What're we doing over here?"

"Trying not to make a hell of a lot of noise," I told him. "I want to get a sense of the place."

Sandor had put up a four-foot chicken wire fence around his property line. Its closest side was about ten feet out into the scum-covered canal. The little plaster square it guarded didn't seem to be worth all the trouble.

There were no lights in the yard area, but a bright glow flooded from the back window. A big man was wandering around inside. He was brown-skinned with long gray hair. He was wearing a black short-sleeve shirt and what appeared to be black trousers. He was gesturing with his hands and shouting angrily. It looked like he was arguing with himself.

Something moved in the yard, but I couldn't see what it was. Maybe a dog. On the canal, several gray shapes bobbed. First, it was an ex-con who liked butterflies. Now I had a con man who kept ducks. Maybe I would get a pet ferret to walk on lonely afternoons.

I told Johnny to sit tight and wait for me. Then I crossed a footbridge that put me on the other side of the canal, two darkened houses away from Sandor's. I unholstered the .38 and hopped the nearest fence, moving quietly through the sandy soil to the next, slightly higher fence.

I walked along it to the front of the house and crossed a front lawn until I was facing Sandor's square, flamingo-colored stucco house. A shade blocked the view through the front picture window.

I tried the far side of the house, following the stepping-stones to the rear of the place until I met up with the chicken wire fence. It was only as high as my waist. I waited for a beat, to see if a dog would sniff me out. When none appeared, I pushed down on the chicken wire and stepped over it easily and silently. I could hear Sandor, inside the house, railing on about the powers of the mind.

In the moonlight I could barely see Johnny standing beside my car across the canal. I waved to him, but he didn't wave back.

I moved closer to the back door, which was open a few inches. There were three wooden steps leading to it. My plan was simple. A bit too simple, all things considered. I was going to push through the door, draw down on Sandor, and force him to show me the objet d'art. I got as far as the top step when I was attacked from the rear. A pair of large gray geese took a sudden interest in my ankles and legs. They did not pursue me silently. I was so intent on guarding my flank that I did not hear Sandor until he was at the door, shouting, "Mine enemies I shall smite down." And damned if he wasn't a man of his word.

Consciousness was a thing with feathers. Flapping near my face. I was lying on my back. Sandor, or someone, had dragged me inside the shack, which was now dark. The goose was not attacking me, merely trying to get out of the closed back door. The hell with the goose. Whatever I'd been smote with had raised a knob the size of a gumball on the back of my head. I pressed it, winced, and sat up. My gun was still in my hand. I smelled it, and didn't like the odor.

There was more of it in the room.

The gray goose continued to try to flap through the closed door. I staggered to it, threw the door open, and the goose hopped out without a word of thanks. I leaned against a wall and tried to make the floor settle down.

There was a light switch near my hand and I used it. A red bulb disclosed a bedroom. That is to say a bed was in it. It was covered with a spread decorated with the signs of the zodiac, a nice touch. The walls had been carelessly painted black and silver.

Sandor the All-Seeing had been caught on his blind side. He lay beside his bed, face down. He'd been shot in the back, twice, and the blood had congealed in a dark pool under him. A .32 was near his body.

There was another corpse in the doorway. Johnny Horne was propped against the jamb. He'd lost his hat and one eye. His head was angled so that the blood had drained away from his face. His mouth was open in astonishment. His once ruddy nose might have been made of clay.

I moved past him into a larger room where a curtain was drawn over a picture window. No more bodies. No geese. No jewel-encrusted skulls. Only furniture draped in black. A long sideboard covered in black velvet contained a glass fortune teller's ball, black and silver candles, and little boxes of powders and foul-smelling vials. A desk yielded six guns of various calibers, a can of oil, and several little white patches of cloth. Sandor evidently took good care of his weapons.

On a coffee table near a black sofa was an ashtray that had been used as a candle holder. The ashes and butts it contained had been emptied, but a drop of wax had trapped something. A neat square of tinfoil.

According to my wristwatch, I hadn't been out longer than an hour. Two men had been murdered and the stage had been set to make it look like . . . what? Sandor had shot Johnny and I had shot the swami? And done what? Fallen over backward and knocked myself unconscious?

The Venice cops might have bought that. But I didn't feel like giving them the chance. I'd been lucky enough to have been awakened prematurely by the goose. It was time to see how far that luck would take me.

A police car was pulling up in front of the shack as I let myself out the rear door. I was looking for the geese this time, but they'd wandered off to the side of the fence, drawn by the noise the cops were making.

I moved quickly in the opposite direction, wading into the dark, brackish water of the canal. By the time Sandor's back door opened again, I was standing beside my car, dripping on the running board, shivering, and panting as quietly as I could.

I carefully unlatched the door and eased behind the wheel. Across the canal, a uniformed cop entered the backyard with a drawn gun and a flashlight. When the geese hit him, he discharged his gun. Several times. Lights went on all along the canal. People shouted. Two more cops rushed from the murder house.

I kicked my engine over and backed away from the edge of the canal. I didn't put on my lights until I turned onto Venice Boulevard, a full two miles from the murder scene.

◆　◆　◆

"Phil? Is that you?"

"None other," I said to Kathy Horne, who stood in her doorway wrapped in a silk robe, squinting at me and yawning. My wet duds were dripping all over the bedroom floor of my apartment. "Better get some clothes on, Kathy. We have to go see Beaudry."

"Did something go wrong?"

"A little snag. We'll discuss it at Beaudry's."

"I . . . Johnny didn't come home tonight. He left right after dinner and he didn't come back. Oh, Phil. He didn't do anything . . . ?"

"Let's worry about Johnny later," I said.

In another half hour, I parked in front of Beaudry's bungalow behind Kathy's green sedan. She eyed it nervously as she got out of my car. "Johnny's here?" she asked.

"I'd be very surprised," I told her.

I rattled the screen door, then put my knuckle to it. Someone moved inside the house. The porch light went on. The front door opened a crack and Beaudry's head, bad haircut and all, poked out. "Kathy?" he asked when he spied her. He opened the door wide.

We both went in fast. Beaudry didn't like my being there. He was in his bathrobe, with bare legs and the straps of a gray undershirt showing. He stared at us. Kathy took the sofa. I leaned against the bookcase, while Beaudry closed the front door.

I unbuttoned my coat and said, "Things went a little awry tonight." And with them staring at me attentively, I told them as much as I had observed at Sandor's, before and after I'd been sapped.

When I described in detail the condition of Johnny Horne's head, Kathy's blue eyes got their sad look back. But it was an act. I said to them, "What I don't understand is why you crazy kids just didn't run off together. Why put on this goofy Toby show? You always had a weird way of thinking, Beaudry, but jeweled skulls! Jesus!"

"There is one," Beaudry said angrily. "All that stuff is true."

"It's just that Sandor didn't happen to have it."

Beaudry shook his head. "Naw. It belonged to one of Hammett's Pinkerton pals. Far as Hammett knew, the guy still had it."

"How was it supposed to go down?" I asked.

"You figure it out, shamus. You're the bright boy."

Beaudry was moving away from Kathy. I didn't like that, so I edged toward him, keeping them both in sight.

"You and Kathy have been playing house for a while. Long enough for her to tidy up this place and fill the tables with flowers from her garden. The only things in the beds outside are weeds."

I turned to her. "I guess you couldn't spruce up the grounds too much, what with nosy neighbors and all."

"We can work on the garden later," Beaudry said, as if he meant it.

"Not after they hang two murders on you," I told him.

Kathy sighed and reached into her coat pocket. I tensed, but it was a cigarette she was after. She lighted up and said, "It seemed like a good idea at the time."

"How'd you get Johnny out here tonight?"

She said wearily, "He was getting wise that I was . . . involved with somebody, so I sort of hinted that it was you, Phil. I was hoping he'd follow you to the swami's. He did even better: He talked you into letting him come along."

I turned to Beaudry. "And Sandor was primed for our visit, right? Judging by his arsenal, the swami was also a hired shooter. You paid him to put the slug on me and take out Johnny. I'd wake up, see that Sandor had flown, and assume that he'd bumped off Johnny because of the jeweled doodad. Only something went wrong. What was it, Kathy? I know you were there. I saw the neat little square you tear from your cigarette packs. What was it that Sandor wanted? More money?"

"He wanted to kill you, too, Phil," Kathy said flatly. "Said it would be cleaner. He had his pistol pressed against your temple when I picked up your gun and shot him."

I didn't know if I wanted to believe her or not. I said, "Was that before or after he shot Johnny?"

"Johnny was already dead," she said and looked away.

"Johnny wouldn't have just walked in there. But he would have come running if you'd called to him."

She looked away but said nothing.

I continued, "He told me you'd done some things to help him out, things that might have put you in trouble with the cops. Maybe you played around with some evidence, misfiled a few papers. Was that what you were afraid of, that he'd spill if you ditched him for Beaudry and you'd wind up in the slammer?"

"Something like that," she said and took more smoke into her lungs.

Beaudry said, "What the hell good will it do to put Kathy through the wringer on this, Marlowe? You know damn well Johnny was no great loss."

"He liked butterflies," I told him. "Besides, maybe Sandor didn't kill Johnny."

"You can't think that Kathy . . ."

"You mean an ex-cop wouldn't dream of using a gun on a husband she wanted dead? Actually, Beaudry, I was thinking that this is your kind of play. Too complicated by half. Maybe you followed us there tonight and pulled the trigger yourself."

He dug his hand deeper into his robe pocket. He said, "I never been near the place."

I bent down and picked up something from the polished floor. A gray goose feather.

I saw his arm tense and pushed myself away from the wall of books, drawing my gun as I went. His robe pocket exploded and a bullet tore the hide off of a book on the shelf. He paused too long to stare at the ruined book and I shot him several times in the chest. The force of the slugs lifted him off his feet and knocked him back into the door he had just closed.

Kathy gave a sharp scream and ran to him.

She didn't cry. By the time the cops arrived, she was cradling Beaudry's ugly, lifeless head in her lap, but she still hadn't cried. She had the saddest eyes I'd ever seen, but she didn't seem to have a tear to put in them.

I never found out if she'd really saved my life in Sandor's shack. But I did finally discover, quite by accident, what Beaudry had been trying to tell me in Taggart Wilde's office the day I was fired. On a surveillance job that kept me holed up in the Bay City library for six days, I happened to open a book of poems by the guy who wrote *Gulliver's Travels*, Jonathan Swift, and read: "So, naturalists observe, a flea/ hath smaller fleas that on him prey;/ And these have smaller still to bite 'em;/ And so proceed ad infinitum." Some reader, that Beaudry. But he should have stuck with Swift and stayed clear of Hammett.

————————————————————
————————————————————

Thanks to a paperback cover depicting what I thought to be Gregory Peck with a gun in his hand discovering a naked girl in a closet, when I was thirteen years old I went directly from the Oz books by L. Frank Baum to Raymond Chandler's The Big Sleep. *Baum was no slouch at moving the action along, but Chandler's pace took my breath away. And while some of the aspects of the plot were beyond the comprehension of a very naive teenager, I remember being in awe of the narrative style and the marvelously funny dialogue. One of Marlowe's lines, "Don't go simple on me, Joe," served to toughen up my schoolyard act to a degree that now, several decades later, I still find myself using it to make a point.*

Since Chandler's novels introduced me not only to the mystery story, but to adult fiction, his influence has been profound. When, after a ten-year span as columnist for the Los Angeles Times book review, I finally decided to write a novel, I knew it had to be a mystery—a mystery featuring an honest, hard-boiled, but sentimental private eye who walked the mean streets of Los Angeles. Oddly enough, by the time that book, Sleeping Dog, was completed, a second protagonist had sneaked in—a precocious little girl who had lost her dog. I guess I couldn't ignore the Baum influence either.

Dick Lochte

THE EMPTY SLEEVE

W. R. PHILBRICK

1941

I WAS READING THE latest on Lepke when the man with the silk flower in his lapel entered the lobby of the Mansion House Hotel. Lepke had been born Louis Buchalter, and according to the newspaper he had matured into a thoroughly unpleasant item who had just been sentenced to die in New York, in the electric chair. I looked at his picture. Mr. Buchalter was a natty little dresser in a cashmere over-coat, a nice conservative tie, and a gray fedora, well blocked. The glint of handcuff at his wrist might have been an item of personal jewelry, the way he carried himself.

"Ahem," said a hesitant voice. "Mr. Marlowe?"

I looked up from Lepke and focused on the silk flower. Two pale, nervous fingers were twisting the green wire stem.

"What if I wasn't?" I said. "Then all the world would know."

The gentleman with the nervous fingers was Sydney Sanders. I knew that because of the corny trick with the flower.

"We could walk across the street and take the elevator up to my office," I suggested. "It's not too late to change your mind."

"Ahem," he said again, letting his small gray eyes flick around the seedy lobby. "That is, I prefer not."

He'd told me over the phone that he daren't risk being seen entering a private investigator's office. Apparently it was okay if he was seen dis-appearing into the haze of nickel cigar smoke in the lobby of a round-heeled hotel.

I lit up my pipe and looked him over. Sanders wasn't quite as natty a dresser as Lepke, but he was trying. Soft leather brogans, black silk socks, dove-gray flannel trousers, the kind that hold a crease, and a belted raincoat of the type that is popular with weather-beaten war correspondents but is rarely seen in sunny Los Angeles. Oh, and the silk flower.

His face was just another middle-aged, putty-colored face, or would

105

have been if it hadn't kept twitching. The twitch was a lively thing, flitting from the corner of his mouth to his cheek, then up to his eyebrows. I had to look away.

I said: "Spill it. It's only sixteen shopping days until Christmas."

"I feel like such a traitor," he said, passing a hand over his face. It didn't work. It only made his hand tremble. "If they find out, they'll throw me out of the game, and then where will I be?"

Out of the game. He made it sound as bad as being booted out of the country club, which for a man with dove-gray flannels can be a terrible thing indeed. I was about to get up and make my exit and let Mr. Sanders twitch in peace when he said:

"Do you play cards, Mr. Marlowe? This will never work if you don't play cards."

"Can't I play chess?"

"Poker," he said, fussing with the flower again. "High-stakes poker. And I'm very much afraid that one of us is cheating."

So I settled back and relit my pipe.

He sighed. "It started out sort of social, at a fellow I know's place out in Beverly Hills. Then the money part of it got more important and we were hooked, all of us. A month ago my friend started having trouble with his wife and we had to move it from Beverly Hills. And that's when the game started getting funny, if you know what I mean."

I said, "You better tell me the funny part."

Sanders yammered on for a while and then made his pitch. When he had finished and gone, I tapped my pipe in the brass ashtray, just because I like the way it rings, and went up to the cigar stand. The blonde behind the counter was reading a paperback with a lurid cover.

"The butler did it," I said. "Only he's not really the butler and that's the whole trick."

"Hello, Philip," she said. "I already guessed about the butler. I'm only reading so's I don't have to stare at the dingy walls."

"Got a pack of cards there?"

She put a sealed deck on the glass countertop and pushed it at me. "Your pal looked familiar," she said. "I seen him in the papers, I think."

I said: "Nah. A man as fine as that never comes in a place like this."

"Anything you say, brown eyes. Stick around, why don't you? We could play fish or something."

"Sorry, Jo Ann," I said. "Got a date."

She asked, "Who's the lucky number?" and squinted slightly.

"Nobody special," I said, "Four guys with whiskey to drink and money to lose."

I slipped the pack of cards into my side pocket and planted a small, friendly kiss on the corner of her mouth. Maybe it brightened up her day. It did mine.

Back in my office I closed and locked the inner door. It wouldn't do if a potential client caught me playing solitaire. I might give in to the impulse to put a red queen down on a red jack, and then where would I be if word got around?

At my apartment I showered and shaved, not too close. I wasn't supposed to be a tough guy, not the way Sanders had thought it through, but it wouldn't do to looked buffed and polished for the occasion, either. I wasn't hungry, particularly, but fried up a thick steak and made myself eat it, every bite. I kept chewing until I could see the shine on the plate, and in it a man who expects to imbibe a fair share of Scotch and wants meat in his belly to tame it.

How prudent. I must have looked full of myself when I hit the street because there was a Santa with a yellow smile lurking on the corner of Franklin and Kenmore, and he pointedly rang his bell at me.

"Merry Christmas," he said and jiggled the bell clapper again, in case I hadn't tumbled.

" 'Tis but the sixth of December," I said, flipping a quarter into his kettle. "Begone, oh shade of holidays past, and trouble us no more."

Santa gave me a sour look and scratched at his cotton-batting beard.

There was a new radio in my car, so I turned it on and listened. Britain was threatening to declare war on Finland, Rumania, and Hungary because said nations had refused to quit fighting Russia. Jap diplomats were meeting with Secretary of State Cordell Hull, and the Navy flyboys had gotten careless and crashed the world's largest flying boat.

Not a word about card cheats at Sydney Sanders' Saturday night poker fest, marooned for the last month in Bay City. Heading west on Wilshire, I kept a light foot on the pedal, not wanting to find out if it was true, as rumor had it, that there were two or three cops in Bay City who weren't dirty.

449 San Vicente Boulevard was a drab little building a few blocks from the sea. Pale yellow light came from the lower windows, where the silhouette of a thin woman drifted languidly through the artificial illumination. I parked on the opposite side of the street, a block away, and rolled down the window. There was a tang of cut grass in the air, and sea salt, and white wash. Especially the white wash. In Bay City it's the only brand of perfume the law allows.

I was purposely early. Ten minutes expired before a black Ford sedan, not new, pulled to the curb. The specimen who climbed out did so gingerly, as if afraid the potholed street might give way underneath him. The old-man carefulness was not a consequence of age: He was a thin boy with a mop of wavy black hair cut short over the ears. He wore an off-the-rack gabardine suit, the kind that lasts forever but never hangs quite right, and carried his hat in his hand.

He went up the steps. The door opened before he got there. The door went dark again.

Three minutes later a battleship veered around from the ocean end of the boulevard. It was a two-tone battleship, fawn on the fenders and puce on top, and it was not quite as long as Roosevelt's term in office. It managed to drift to the curb without the assistance of a tug, and an admiral climbed out. A Hollywood admiral with a braided cap and jodhpurs and knee-high boots that matched the paint job on the limousine.

He opened one of the rear doors. He didn't curtsey, but almost. Out came a debonair extrovert in velvet spats, size small. The little man wore a bowler, pushed back on his head at that certain special angle, and of course he carried a cane. I assumed he was going to flog the chauffeur with it, but he surprised me. He simply skipped up the steps and into the house.

The chauffeur took off the braided cap, dusted the billows of his jodhpurs with it, and appeared to be satisfied with life and where it had taken him. I wanted to tell him he'd stepped in something only it was the Christmas season and I was the kind who gave quarters to phony Santas.

Sanders arrived in a new Chrysler roadster. I got out to meet him at the bottom of the steps. He was nervous and that made me nervous and I rolled a cigarette around in my fingers, unlit.

He said: "I see Willy is here. That boat's a studio limo. He's got it on loan. Think you can fool him?"

"Try to look like you're not booked into the heist of the century, okay?" I said. "We're just playing cards, is all, and I'm going to pay attention. Where's the crime in that?"

"I suppose you're right. It's just—I still find it hard to believe Willy would cheat us. He sure doesn't need the money."

Sanders had taken out a cigar and was mimicking my trick of rolling it around his fingers. Not on purpose, near as I could tell, and before long he dropped it. Then he picked it up and dusted it off and slipped it into his pocket, as if it had never touched the ground.

"I'm probably making a terrifically big mistake," he said.

We went up to the door, Sanders leading the way, and it opened before he could ring the bell. A thinnish woman with a halo of fine, dyed-yellow hair held out a pallid hand and said, "Sandy, that's a new flower, isn't it? And this must be the new gentleman. Come in, come in. Ray's out in the kitchen getting ice for Willy. You know how he wants his ice."

Sanders pressed his lips to her wrist and said, "Cissy, this is Marlowe. He's going to try his luck with us this evening."

Until you took her in and examined the effect, Cissy appeared to be in her late forties, and carried herself even younger. Her face never stopped moving and neither did her hands, which she used better than semaphores, and the reason for all the movement was to keep herself out of focus. She was seventy if she was a day, and there were fine cracks in the expert glaze of makeup, and her hair was as unreal as the flutter of angel wings. The act didn't make sense until a few minutes later, when I met her husband, and then it made plenty of sense.

She gave me her hand. I followed Sanders' example and brushed my lips against a frail wrist scented with sandalwood and said, "Nice of you people to let me sit in. Have you lived in Bay City long?"

"We never live anyplace for long," she responded vaguely, and showed me where to hang my hat.

It was a four-room apartment, sparsely furnished. There seemed to be too many books and not enough chairs. The skinny boy with the old-man walk was sitting on a faded red davenport, holding a glass tumbler in both hands.

"Marlowe," I said, tipping a salute. "I'm the new kid on the block."

"I'm Nixon," he said. "They call me Nick here. It's very informal."

Sanders went into the kitchen, where someone was joking in a German accent. The accent may or may not have been the joke, it was too early to tell. The Scotch and swish had been set up on a little glass-topped tabouret. I poured myself a drink—I wasn't fussy about ice—and got Nick the oldish boy to light my cigarette, just to see if his hand was steady. It was.

"When do we start?" I said, nodding at a round table and the empty chairs surrounding it.

"When Mr. Farnum gets here. He's an amazing man, Mr. Farnum is, considering."

I didn't ask considering what. Sanders came back, accompanied by Willy Boy, and a diffident-looking gent who carried an ice bucket and tongs. Ice Bucket wore round horn-rims that failed to obscure mild, inquisitive eyes. Sanders introduced him as Ray, a poet.

"No kidding," I said. "The kind that rhymes?"

"Now and then," he said. "When it strikes my fancy."

This was a new experience for me. I didn't know that poets came with names like Ray. He was at least twenty years younger than Cissy, his wife, and that explained her curious, girlish affectations. Sanders, who had something to do with publishing, was "handling" a book of Ray's verses. He made it sound as if the book was a speckled trout he'd caught on a dry fly he'd tied himself. The way Sanders looked at it, the fly was the important part, not the fish.

Willy Boy sniffed at his drink and said, "Why must we always wait for this Farnum man?" with a lot of v's in place of the w's, which established to my satisfaction that the German accent was real enough. When he spoke, and he often did, he gestured with his thin, leather-handled malacca cane. I got the impression Ray didn't care for Willy or his cane, although Willy didn't appear to notice.

Sanders had recovered his nerve and remembered his lines. He smiled slightly and said, "Poor Mr. Farnum lost a pile last week, Willy. Remember? You won it off him, I believe."

"No excuse," Willy Boy said. His black, Brill-Creamed hair was so precisely parted the white mark on his skull looked like a scar.

Sanders wasn't ready to let it go yet. He said, "It's been nice of Ray and Cissy to let us play here, Willy, but I can't help thinking it was more convenient at your place in Beverly Hills. Any chance we'll get back in there?"

Willy Boy glared. "Shaddup, Sandy. You know my situation."

We sat down at the round table and waited for Mr. Farnum. Ray lit up a bulldog pipe and smoked. He didn't talk much. Thinking up verse, maybe. Cissy fussed around us with a tray of crackers and Yakima apples and sliced cheese. I nibbled a bit of cheese. It was sharp enough for surgery.

"This is nonsense," Willy Boy said, glowering impatiently. "We're here, let's begin. Deal the cards!"

Nixon said, "Mr. Farnum got a little out of sorts last week when we started without him. He likes to be here when the deck is cracked. Last time he wasn't and he lost a thousand or so."

Willy Boy glared. "What's that supposed to mean? There was nothing wrong with his cards except they weren't good enough to win."

Sanders coughed into his fist. "I'm sure Nicky didn't mean anything. Did you, Nicky?"

Nixon was working his lower lip in and out as he nodded, trying to pass it off as a smile. No matter what he did with his face, this is what came through: the perpetually aggrieved expression of a man who changed his socks either five times a day or never.

The doorbell rang.

Nixon said, "That'll be Mr. Farnum," and he was right.

The great man wore a heliotrope cape that hung in luxurious folds from a set of wide shoulders. His face was florid and puffy, his mouth small and moist, to match his eyes. I didn't like him much. He unclipped the cape with his left hand and caught it by the nape before it hit the floor, which took some doing. His right sleeve was empty.

He said: "I'll have a whiskey, please," and when he sat the chair under him creaked like an old wooden ship nudging an incoming tide.

Ray put down his pipe and peeled the cellophane from a deck of cards. He held the deck up. Farnum slurped at his drink and nodded. Willy Boy, upstaged by the cape and sleeve, could only glare.

The poet shuffled the cards and dealt.

I had five hundred of Sydney Sanders' dollars in my pocket before the game started, and more an hour later. It was basic poker, stud and draw. The only trick was knowing how to bet, and that was some trick.

"Turn that down," Willy Boy said quite suddenly, as Nicky was in the act of dealing. "I hate it."

He was referring to the radio. Cissy, smiling a dreamy kind of smile, had tuned in the Boswell Sisters, who were fronting for the Dorsey Orchestra. She drifted near the wall, feeling the music with her thin arms, like a butterfly that had loosed itself from the fading wallpaper.

Ray said, "Okay," and got up to turn off the radio. Cissy kept right on feeling the music. When Ray sat back down his eyes were very quiet and still.

"You got two aces showing, Sydney," Willy Boy said. "Are you raising?"

Sanders examined his manicure. Willy had four spades showing. "A hundred," Sanders said.

He and Willy and Nixon were still in the hand. There was over a thousand in the pot. I'd gotten out early with a pair of deuces that never meant to tango, so I could watch the act. Farnum watched, too, as his left hand planted the soggy end of a cheroot in his glistening mouth.

"See the hundred and double it," Willy Boy said.

Nixon spoke up in turn, his voice cracking: "See the double and double *that*."

We all looked at the boy. He had the makings of a low straight, if his down card was inside. Tiny beads of sweat came down from his hairline, like drops of fine oil on a pane of pebbled glass.

Willy Boy gave him a long look, then reached into his wallet, extracted five c-notes, and tossed them into the pot.

"Call," he said.

Sanders looked at the pile of greenbacks and the cards he was facing and sighed and folded.

"I'm calling you," Willy Boy said, nudging Nixon.

Nixon turned his bottom card. It made the straight. He reached out both hands to rake in the money. Willy Boy picked up his bottom card and flicked it into the center of the table. It was a spade.

"I believe that wins," he said.

Poor Nicky was having trouble getting his breath. He looked like a goldfish in need of a shave. Willy Boy tapped his malacca cane on the floor and said, "Deal."

I folded out of the next round and wandered into the kitchen, glass in hand. I'd seen enough, everything else was extra. Cissy was in the kitchen. She had a black Persian in her arms and she was purring along with the cat.

"Are we having fun?" she asked

"Tons," I said. "I've got cramps I've been laughing so hard."

The old woman stared at me. It was a long, lingering kind of look that started at the top of my head and slid down until she'd untied the knots in my shoelaces and tied them back up again, all in her head, just to see what kind of knot tier I was.

She said, "You remind me of someone I knew when I was younger— and he was younger, too."

"Ah, youth," I said. The words dropped like chips of ice into a broken cup, but it was too late to take them back.

"Mock it if you like," she snapped, hugging the cat to her breast. "Maybe someday you'll look into the mirror and see a tired old gentleman with his belt cinched too high."

I tried to make amends by patting the black cat. The Persian, sensing the distress of her mistress, bared small, perfect teeth. An ugly laugh brayed in the other room and someone swore in German. I went back in to take my medicine.

Nicky nodded as I sat down. "Mr. Wilder just won a bundle with trip tens. You're pretty clever with cards, aren't you, Mr. Wilder?"

Willy Boy lifted his cane, placed the gold-tipped end on a spot over Nixon's heart, and pushed gently. "You're all bluff," he said. "I think I'll sell you to Sam Goldwyn. Now keep dealing."

Ray won the next hand for a smallish pot, and then Sanders came back for a while, unwilting his green silk flower. It didn't matter. I knew the play by then. The work was in waiting for the third act.

The curtain came an hour before dawn. Nixon had the deal. A dark beard was showing through his boy face, like stub ends of frost-killed grass coming up in a blanket of gray snow. He licked his lips and shuffled the cards.

Willy Boy looked at him the way a toad looks at a wingless fly. "Don't be nervous," he said sweetly. "It's only money."

"You mean it's only *his* money," Farnum said suddenly. He'd been silent for more than an hour, losing in dribs and drabs. The empty sleeve hung at his side like a pennant on a windless battlefield.

"It's okay, Mr. Farnum," Nixon said. "I know what he means."

Farnum shrugged. The cheroot in his mouth was as cold and wet as the glint in his eye.

Nixon dealt.

Willy Boy showed a king.

Farnum had a jack up.

"Luck is with me," Willy Boy said after checking his down card.

Farnum said, "You call it luck? How amusing."

They began to bet into each other, raising like fiends. It was more than cards. There was a small war being waged as dawn came. The rising sun poured knife cuts of red light through the drawn blinds. When the last round had been dealt, only Willy Boy and Farnum remained in the game, facing a pride-swollen pot. Ten grand or more—I'd stopped counting.

The German, who'd been strangling the leather handle of his cane, got his third king.

"God is good," he said.

The man with one arm was showing three jacks.

"So," Farnum sighed softly. "Do you speak of the German god? Or the Hollywood god?"

Willy Boy said, "The god of money. A thousand times," and pushed a stack of bills forward.

"See it. And raise five grand more—if you have the guts," Farnum said.

Farnum reached into his pocket, removed his wallet, extracted five crisp bills, and fanned them into the pot. Done with one hand it was a beautiful thing to see.

Willy Boy looked at Farnum's three jacks the way he might look over three plain-faced Nebraska girls posing on stools at Schwab's Drugstore. His eyes narrowed.

"Call my chauffeur in," he demanded.

This was done, and after a bit of contrived rigmarole the chauffeur produced another fat wallet and handed it reverently to the German.

"See the five and raise you . . . ten thousand more."

That brought Sanders to life. He said, "Now wait a minute, Willy. The limit is five, we all agreed to it months ago."

"Ten is fine," Farnum said. He was gently rubbing his down card with a plump finger. "Provided you take my note."

Willy Boy nodded. "But of course. Your note as a gentleman."

Farnum borrowed paper and pen from Ray and wrote out the I.O.U. He placed it on top of Willy Boy's ten grand.

"Make your move," he said.

The German turned over his bottom card. "Full house, kings over."

Farnum said, "Never trust God in a game of chance," and turned over the fourth jack.

The black cat was sleeping in my hat. I shooed it away and soft-pedaled to the door. I wanted to be first out, before Sanders could ask me a lot of questions I wasn't yet prepared to answer.

Ray was on the steps, polishing his glasses. He held them up against the sunrise. He seemed to be aware that he was blocking me. He spoke without turning around: "You can just see the ocean from here. I wonder why they call it the Pacific?"

"You'll have to look it up," I said. "See you around."

"Do I look that dumb? Maybe I do."

I said, "I don't know what you mean by that."

He shrugged and smiled a secret kind of smile. "You know what's wrong with this crummy town?" he said. "There's too much water out there, too many drowned men."

I liked that, even if it didn't rhyme.

When the others spilled from the apartment I was hunched down in my car, hat tipped over my eyes. The hat smelled of the cat, and just a hint of sandalwood. It didn't bother me. There are worse things to smell.

Willy Boy did a funny turn just before his on-loan limousine pulled away. He got out, broke the malacca cane over his knee, and planted the pieces in Ray's lawn, like small, brittle trees. I rolled a cigarette around in my fingers and grinned. It was a Hollywood touch, and in the ephemeral light of Sunday morning it seemed fitting.

Nixon was the last to leave. Cissy came out on the stoop to hand him his hat, and he took it, ducking his head. Then Ray linked hands with his wife and they watched the youngster slouch out to the shabby Ford with the strange, old-man walk he affected.

They were still standing there when I pulled out to follow him.

♦ ♦ ♦

Nixon turned left on the Pacific Coast Highway, heading south. I hung back, giving him plenty of room. He hadn't gone more than half a mile before slamming the Ford into the rear bumper of a Dodge beach wagon.

I pulled over to the shoulder, slipped my gun into my pocket, and got out. The radios of both cars were on full volume. Nixon was standing by his crumpled fender, more interested in the broadcast than the damage. The driver of the Dodge leaned out his door, his mouth open. Both men were staring out at the purple-gray Pacific, transfixed.

"What gives?" I said.

Then I heard the bulletin and realized what had made Beach-wagon slam on his brakes.

"Them Jap bastards," Nixon said, grinning happily.

"They'll be heading this way now," Beach-wagon said excitedly. "The whole yellow fleet."

Maybe I should have left it like that. Just driven away, gone back to tell Ray that he had a few hundred more reasons to hate the sea. What did a twenty-five-grand grift mean now that the bombs had started falling?

Old habits die hard. I offered Nixon a ride.

He shook his head, as if coming out of a dream. "Thanks, no. I'll just make a phone call."

"You'll take a ride and smile about it," I said, sticking my gun in his ribs. Beach-wagon was too busy searching the horizon for the coming invasion to notice.

I pushed Nicky behind the wheel and got into the back seat.

"Just go where you were going," I said.

"I don't know what you mean."

I caressed his ear with the barrel. "You're cute," I said. "But you're not that cute. The two of you were in it together. You're the mechanic. You set him up."

"Mister, you've got it all wrong. I'm a lawyer. I'd never break the law."

I laughed all the way to the Waterfront Hotel. That was where Nicky and his partner were going to split up the cash. The boy confessed readily after I promised not to bring the cops into it.

"Bring in the Bay City cops?" I said. "Willy Boy was right. I oughta sell you to Sam Goldwyn. Now drive."

In the hotel lobby the early risers were huddled around a radio. Nobody paid us any mind. One man with one gun wasn't anything to get excited about, not that morning.

The elevator didn't respond to the call button so we took the stairs.

Three flights. That made me irritable. I pushed Nixon into the room ahead of me.

"Sorry, Mr. Farnum," he said.

The one-armed man was sitting on a narrow bed, puffing a new cheroot. The twenty-five grand was already divided into two piles on the pillow. He looked at me with eyes as black as spent bullets.

"Ah, nuts," he said. "We'll make it a three-way split."

I grinned and said, "Nicky is going to join the Navy, but what'll we do with you?"

Farnum blinked at the gun. He said, "How'd you cop us?"

"It's an old grift," I said. "You polished it up a little, but it's still an old grift. The kid here is the mechanic, he fixes the deck. You call the shots and you called it mighty cute. Willy Boy is the one with all the dough, so he was the pigeon. For three weeks you let him win, and fixed it so the others thought he must be cheating somehow. That takes the attention off of you and the kid. You just had to get Willy Boy in the right mood to bet wildly. So you fed him what looks like a winning hand, and then insulted his pride. He stayed in to prove he wasn't cheating. The I.O.U. was a beautiful touch. It convinced everybody but me."

Farnum blinked again. I almost fell for it, blinking along with him as his left hand went under the pillow. I squeezed off a shot, perforating a brass bedpost, and an ugly black revolver skittered to the floor.

"Don't tell me," I said. "If you still had the right arm I'd be dead."

Farnum shrugged. He'd made his move and it hadn't worked and now he was waiting for it to be over.

"How'd you lose it?" I asked. "At a card game by any chance?"

The dark, insect eyes glistened. I dragged the revolver back with my toe, got it into my pocket, and made Nicky stuff the twenty-five grand in a pillowcase.

"I'll bet you were one hell of a mechanic in your prime," I said, backing to the door. "I'll bet you made Nicky look silly. You taught him the tricks and with your coaching he's good enough to fool sailors, maybe, but he'll never be a tenth as good as you were. Spill it, Farnum. I've already promised the little shyster here there'll be no cops involved. Tell me who caught you and took off your arm."

He looked at his empty sleeve, his face a gray mask, and said, "Lepke took it. He never caught me; he just did it for kicks. And I pray the little squint screams when they turn on the juice."

I said, "They always scream," and left with the pillowcase over my shoulder.

◆ ◆ ◆

I was having a party in my office when the chauffeur arrived. Me and a bottle and Betty Grable. The bottle was in the file cabinet, under "C" for cheap Scotch, and Betty was smiling at me from a calendar.

"Next time try knocking," I said to the chauffeur. "You can take your gloves off. I don't mind."

"Mr. Wilder sent me up for the money," he said stiffly. Maybe he wanted to throw me a salute. There was a lot of it in the air, suddenly.

I leaned back in my chair and peered out the window, over the ledge. I was surprised. There was a different battleship in the street below.

"Is that Willy Boy in the limousine?"

The chauffeur nodded. "He and Mr. Sanders are discussing business. They want their money, sir."

He held out his hand.

I stood up and opened the window. It was a fine December day and the smog was light upon the city. I picked up the pillowcase and emptied it out the window.

"You better hurry," I said to the chauffeur. "It's snowing."

Flaubert once exclaimed that he was Madame Bovary (how embarrassing for his friends—and hers!), but Chandler was very firm in maintaining that he was not Marlowe, and so it should come as no surprise that the author and the detective, both of whom resided in the Los Angeles area, crossed paths at least once.

Although Marlowe is fairly coy here about not dropping any last names, the astute reader will know that Chandler and his wife Cissy were in residence at 449 San Vicente Boulevard in early December of 1941, when "The Empty Sleeve" takes place. Less certain is the true identity of the young poker player Marlowe identifies as Nixon. Can he be any relation to the future politician and trickster? Marlowe doesn't say.

And that is the great legacy Raymond Chandler left to those authors who choose to write about crime: the freedom not to say, not to have to spell out the solution to every puzzle. For Chandler the real mystery was Marlowe and what made him tick. That's why millions of readers have felt comfortable slipping into his shoes and walking the mean and beautiful streets of that compelling hallucination called Southern California.

If you have any questions about Chandler's genius, or who was cheating at cards on a certain night in December, feel free to take them up with Marlowe. He leaves the door to the outer office unlocked, for your convenience.

W. R. Philbrick

DEALER'S CHOICE

SARA PARETSKY

1942

S̲HE WAS WAITING in the outer office when I came in, sitting with a stillness that made you think she'd been planted there for a decade or two and could make it to the twenty-first century if she had to. She didn't move when I came in except to flick a glance at me under the veil of the little red hat that had built a nest in her shiny black hair. She was all in red; she'd taken the May's company's advertisers to heart and was wearing victory red. But I doubted if she'd ever seen the inside of May's. This was the kind of shantung number that some sales clerk acting like the undertaker for George V pulled from a back room and whispered to madam that it might suit if madam would condescend to try it on. The shoes and gloves and bag were black.

"Mr. Marlowe?" Her voice was soft and husky with a hint of a lisp behind it.

I acknowledged the fact.

She got to her feet. Perched on top of her boxy four-inch heels she just about cleared my armpit.

"I've been hoping to see you, Mr. Marlowe. Hoping to interest you in taking a case for me. If you have the time, that is."

She made it sound as though her problem, whatever it was, was just a bit on the dull side, and that if I didn't have time for it the two of us could forget it and move on to something more interesting. I grunted and unlocked the inner door. The muffled tapping on the rug behind me let me know she was following me in.

The April sunshine was picking up the dust motes dancing on the edge of my desk. I dumped the morning paper onto the blotter and reached into my desk drawer for my pipe. My visitor settled herself in the other chair with the same composure she'd shown in the outer office. Whatever little problem she had didn't make her twitch or catch her heels in her rosy silk stockings.

While I was busy with my pipe she leaned forward in her chair, looking at the paper; something on the front page had caught her eye. Maybe the Red Army bashing the Krauts along the Caspian, or the U.S. carving a few inches out of Milne Bay. Or Ichuro Kimura eluding the U.S. Army right here at home, or maybe the lady whose twin daughters were celebrating their first birthday without ever having seen their daddy. He was interned by the Japs in Chungking.

When she caught me watching her she settled back in her chair. "Do you think the war will end soon, Mr. Marlowe?"

"Sure," I said, tamping the tobacco in. "Out of the trenches by Christmas." We'd missed Easter by a day already.

The girl nodded slightly to herself, as if I'd confirmed her opinion of the war. Or maybe me. The bright sunlight let me see her eyes now, despite the little veil. The irises were large and dark, looking black against the clear whites. She was watching me calmly enough but those eyes gave her away—they could light up the whole Trojan backfield if she wanted to use them that way. But something in her manner and that hint of a lisp made me think they didn't play much football where she came from.

"I need some help with a man," she finally said.

"You look as though you do just fine without help." I struck a match against the side of the desk.

She ignored me. "He's holding some of my brother's markers."

"Your brother lose them in fair play?"

She gave a shrug that moved like a whisper through the shantung. "I wouldn't know, Mr. Marlowe. All I know is that my brother staked a— an item that didn't belong to him. My brother has gone into hiding, since he knows he can't pay up and he's afraid they'll break his legs, or whatever it is they do when you can't pay your gambling losses."

"Then I don't see you have a problem. All you have to do is keep supplying your brother with food and water and everyone will be happy. Your gambler will go after easier prey by and by. What's his name?"

I thought I saw a faint blush, but it was such a phantom wave of color I couldn't be sure. It made me think she knew where her brother was all right.

"Dominick Bognavich. And if it were just my brother I wouldn't mind, not so much I mean, since he was gambling and he has to take his chances. But they're threatening my mother. And that's where I need your help. I thought perhaps you could explain to Mr. Bognavich—get him to see that— he should leave my mother alone."

I busied myself with my pipe again. "Your brother shouldn't bet with Bognavich unless he can stake the San Joaquin Valley. I believe that's all Dominick doesn't own at this point. What did your brother put up?"

She watched me consideringly. I knew that look. It was the kind I used when I wondered if a chinook would accept my bait.

"A ring," she finally said. "An old diamond and sapphire ring that had been in Mother's family for a hundred years. My brother knows he'll get it when she's dead, and she could die tomorrow—I don't know—she's very ill and in a nursing home. So he anticipated events."

Anticipated events. I like that. It showed a certain thoughtfulness with the language and the people. "And what about your brother. I mean, does he have a name, or do we do this whole thing incognito."

She studied me again. "No, I can see you need his name. It's—uh—Richard."

"Is that his first or his last name? And do you have the same last name or should I call you something else?"

"You can call me Miss Felstein. Naomi Felstein. And that would be Richard's last name, too."

"And your mother is Mrs. Felstein, and your father is Mr. Felstein."

"Was." She gave a tight little smile, the first I'd seen and not any real sample of what she could do if she were in the mood. "He's been dead for some years now."

"And what is it you want me to do for you, Miss Felstein? Shoot Dominick Bognavich? He's got a lot of backups and I might run out of bullets before he ran out of people to send after me."

One black-gloved finger traced a circle on the arm of the chair. "Maybe you could see Mr. Bognavich and explain to him. About my brother not owning the ring, I mean. Or—or maybe you could talk my brother into coming out of hiding. He won't listen to me."

Sure I could talk to Bognavich. He and I were good pals, sure we were, and my words carried a lot of weight with him, about as much as maggots listening to protests from a dead body. I didn't like it, any of it. I didn't believe her story and I didn't believe in her brother. I was pretty sure she didn't have a brother, or if she did Bognavich had never heard of him. But it was the day after Easter and I'd been too savvy to let myself get suckered by the Easter bunny, so I owed the rubes one.

I gave her my usual rate, twenty-five dollars a day and expenses, and told her I'd need some up-front money. She opened the little black bag without a word and lifted ten twenties from a stash in the zipper compartment with the ease of a dealer sliding off queens to send you over the top in twenty-one.

She gave another ghostly smile. "I'll wait for you here. In case you have no success with Mr. Bognavich and want me to take you to my brother."

"I'll call you, Miss Felstein."

That seemed to confuse her a little. "I may—I don't—"

"I'd rather you didn't wait in my office. I'll call you."

Reluctantly she wrote a number on a piece of paper and handed it to me. Her script was bold and dark, the writing of a risk taker. Oh, yeah, her brother lost some big ones to Dominick Bognavich all right.

A guy like Bognavich doesn't start his rounds until the regular working stiffs are heading home for a drink. If I was lucky I'd make it to his place before he went to bed for the day. But when I'd wound my way up Laurel Canyon to Ventura, where Bognavich had a modest mansion on a cul-de-sac, I found he'd become the kind of guy who doesn't make rounds any time of day.

He was slumped against the door leading from the garage to the house. He looked as though he'd felt tired getting out of the car and decided to sit down for a minute to catch his breath but had fallen asleep instead. It was just that he had taken the kind of nap where six small-caliber bullets give you a permanent hangover.

I felt his face and wrists. He'd been dead a while; if I had a look around without calling the cops it wasn't going to halt the wheels of justice any. The door behind him was unlocked, an invitation for fools to go dancing in and chase the angels out. I listened for a while but didn't hear anything, not even Dominick's blood congealing on the floor.

The kitchen was a white-tiled affair that looked like the morgue after a good scrubdown. I gave it a quick once-over, but Bognavich wasn't the kind of guy who hid his secrets in the granulated sugar. I passed on through to the main part of the house.

The gambler had employed a hell of a housekeeper. She'd left sofa cushions torn apart with their stuffing spread all over the pale gold on the living room floor. White tufts clung to my trouser legs like cottontails. Marlowe the Easter bunny hunting for eggs the other kids hadn't been able to find.

Bognavich's study was where he'd kept his papers. He'd been a gambler, not a reader, and most of the books dealt with the finer points of cards and horses. They lay every which way, their backs breaking, loose pages lying nearby like pups trying to get close enough to suckle their dam.

I did the best I could with the papers and the ledger. There were

I.O.U.'s for the asking if I'd been inclined to go hustling for bread, but nothing that looked like a Felstein. I didn't feel like lingering for a detailed search. Whoever had put those six holes into Dominick might be happy for the cops to find an unwelcome peeper fingering the gambler's papers. I gave the rest of the house a quick tour, admired Bognavich's taste in silk pajamas, and slid back through the kitchen.

He was still sitting where I'd left him. He seemed to sigh as I passed. I patted him on the shoulder and went back to the Chrysler. Miss Felstein could have put six rounds into Bognavich without wrinkling her silk dress, let alone her smooth little forehead. It was the kind of shooting a dame might do—six bullets where one or two would do the job. Wasteful, with a war on.

I pulled the pint from the glove compartment and swallowed a mouthful just on principle, a farewell salute to Dominick. He hadn't been a bad guy, he just had a lousy job.

I half expected to find Miss Naomi Felstein, if that was who she was, not just what I could call her, planted in my waiting room like a well-kept jacaranda. I expected her because I wanted her to be there. I wanted to see if I could shake a little fire into those cool dark eyes and get her to tell me why she'd come to me after finding Dominick's dead body lying in front of his kitchen door this morning.

She wasn't there, though. I wondered if she ever had been there, if perhaps she was just an Easter vision, in red the way these visions always appear, leaving the faintest whiff of Chanel behind to undercut the tobacco fumes. I had a drink from the office bottle and the Chanel disappeared.

I didn't have much hope for the number the mirage had left, and my hope began to dwindle after fifteen rings. But I didn't have anything else to do so I sat at my desk with the phone in my ear looking at the front page of the paper, trying again to figure out which of the stories had caught my phantom's attention.

I finished the details of Errol Flynn's cruelty to his wife and why she had to get his entire estate as a settlement and started on why the army thought Ichuro Kimura was an enemy spy. I'd gotten to the part where he'd thrown empty sake bottles at the soldiers who came to arrest him for not reporting for deportation at Union Station last Wednesday when I realized someone was talking to me.

It was a querulous old man who repeated that he was the Boylston Ranch and who was I calling. Without much interest I asked for Miss Felstein.

"No one here by that name. No women here at all." His tone demanded congratulations for having rid Eden of all temptresses.

"Five feet tall, lots of glossy black hair, dark eyes that could bring a guy back from the grave if she wanted them to."

He hung up on me. Just like that. I stuck the bottle of rye neatly in the middle of the drawer and stared at nothing for a while. Then I got up and locked the office behind me. Oh, yes, Marlowe's a very methodical guy. Very orderly. He always tidies up his whiskey bottle when he's been drinking and locks up behind himself. You can tell he came from a good home.

The army had a roadblock set up just outside Lebec. I guess they were trying to make sure no one was smuggling empty sake bottles in for Ichuro Kimura. They made me get out of my car while they looked under the seats and in the trunk. Then they checked my I.D. and made me tell them I was looking for a runaway girl and that I had a hot tip she was hiding out on the Boylston place. That made them about as happy as a housewife seeing her cat drag a dead bird into the kitchen. They started putting me through my paces until the sergeant who was running the block came over and told them to let me through. He was bored: he wanted to be killing Japs at Milne Bay instead of looking for old men in Lebec.

The sun had had all it could take of Kern County by the time I got to the turnoff for the Boylston Ranch. It was easing itself down behind the Sierra Madres, striking lightning bolts from the dashboard that made it hard for me to see. I was craning my neck forward, shielding my eyes with my left hand, when I realized I was about to go nose to nose with a pickup.

I pulled over to the side to let the truck go by, but it stopped and a lean, dusty man jumped down. He had on a cowboy hat and leather leggings, in case the gearshift chafed his legs, and his face was young and angry, with a jutting upper lip trying to dominate the uncertain jaw beneath it.

"Private property here, mister. You got any reason to be here?"

"Yup," I said.

"Then let's have it."

I got out of the Chrysler to be on eye level with him, just in case being alone with the cows all day made him punch happy.

"You got any special reason for asking, son? Other than just nosiness, I mean?"

His fists clenched reflexively and he took half a step nearer. "I'm Jay Boylston. That good enough for you?"

"You own this spread?"

"My old man does, but I'm in charge of the range. So spill it, and make it fast. Time is money here and I don't have much to waste of either."

"An original sentiment. Maybe you could get it engraved on your tombstone. If your old man owns the place I'd better talk to him. It's kind of a delicate matter. Involves a lady's reputation, you might say."

At that he did try to swing at me. I grabbed his arm. It was a little tougher than his face but not much.

"What's going on here?"

The newcomer had ridden up behind us on horseback. The horse stopped in its tracks at a short command and the rider jumped down. He was an older, stockier edition of Jay. His face held the kind of arrogance men acquire when they own a big piece of land and think it means they own all the people around them as well.

"Man's trespassing and he's giving kind of smart answers when I ask him to explain himself," Jay said sullenly.

"Mr. Boylston?" I asked. The older man nodded fractionally, too canny to give anything to a stranger, even the movement of his head.

"Philip Marlowe. I'm a private detective from Los Angeles and I'm up here on a case."

"A case involving my ranch is something I would know about," Boylston said. His manner was genial but his eyes were cold.

"I didn't say it involved your ranch. Except as a hiding place for a runaway. Big place, lot of places to hide. Am I right?"

"The army's been all through here in the last week looking for a runaway Jap," Boylston said. "I don't think there's too much those boys missed. You're a long way from L.A. if you hope to sleep in your own bed tonight."

"This is a recent case," I said doggedly, Marlowe the intrepid, fighting on where others would have turned tail and run. "This is a woman who's only recently disappeared. And she's attractive enough that someone might be persuaded to hide her from the army."

Boylston had headed back to his horse, but at the end of my speech he turned back to me. He exchanged a glance with his son. When Jay shook his head the father said, "Who's the girl?"

"I don't have a name. But she's five feet tall, glossy black hair, probably a lot of it but she wears it in kind of a roll or chignon or whatever they're calling them this year. Very well dressed—lots of money in the background someplace."

"If you don't know her name how do you know she's missing or even what she looks like?"

I smiled a little. "I can't tell you all my secrets, Mr. Boylston. But I will tell you she's wanted for questioning about a murder down in L.A."

Boylston swung himself back onto his horse. "I haven't seen anyone like that. I can account for all the women around here: my two daughters, and three of the hands are married, and none of 'em has black hair. But if you want to look around, be my guest. There's an abandoned farmhouse on up the road about five miles. We just acquired the land so we only have one hand living out there so far; he can't keep an eye on the house and cover the range, too. That'd be the only place I know of. If you don't see her there you'd best get off my land. Now move your truck, Jay, and let Mr. Marlowe get by."

Jay got into the truck and moved it with an ill will that knocked little pebbles into the side of the Chrysler. I climbed back in and headed on up the track. In the rearview mirror I could see Boylston on his horse watching me, standing so still he might have been a knight on a chessboard.

The road petered out for a while into a couple of tire marks in the grass, but after four miles it turned into a regular road again. Not too long after that I came to the house.

It was a single-story, trim ranch, built like a U with short arms. It was made of wood and painted white, fresh as the snow on the Sierras, with green trim like pine trees. Whoever used to live here had loved the place and kept it up. Or the hand who was watchdogging was a homebody who kept the shrubs trimmed and weeded the begonias.

I rang the bell set into the front door, waited a few minutes, and rang again. It was sunset, not too unreasonable to think the man was done with his chores for the day. But he might be in the shower and not able to hear me ringing. I tried the door and found it unlocked. I pushed it open and went on in with a cloud of virtue wrapped around my shoulders. After all, I wasn't even housebreaking—I had Boylston's permission to search the place.

The hall floor was tiled in brown ceramic with a couple of knotted rugs floating on it. The tiles were covered with a film of dust—the hand who lived there didn't have time for the finer points of housekeeping. Opposite the front door, sliding glass doors led to a garden, a place which the previous owner had tended with care. I stared through the glass at the trim miniature shrubs and flowering bushes. There even seemed to be a pond in the middle.

I turned left and found myself in the kitchen wing. No one was hiding in the stove or under the sink. The other wing held the bedrooms. In one you could see the cowboy's obvious presence, several pairs of jeans, a change of boots, another of regular shoes. The other two bedrooms had been stripped of their furnishings. No one was in the closets or hiding in the two bathtubs.

The only thing that gave me hope was the telephone. It sat next to the kitchen stove, and pasted to it, in neat printing, not my mirage's bold script, was the number I had called. The number where the querulous man had hung up on me after I'd described her.

When I'd finished with the bedrooms I went back to the sliding doors leading into the small garden. Sure enough, a pool stood in the middle, bigger than it had appeared from inside the house. I climbed onto a bridge that crossed it and looked down. Immediately a trio of giant goldfish popped to the surface. They practically stood on their tails begging for bread.

"Go work for a living like the regular fish," I admonished them. "There's a war on. No one has time to pamper goldfish."

The fish swam under the bridge. I turned and looked down at them. They'd taken my words to heart—they were hard at work on the face and hands of a man who was staring up at me in the shallow water. In the fading light I couldn't make out his features, but he still had all of them, so he couldn't have been in the water long. His dark hair waved like silken seaweed in the little eddies the carp stirred up.

What a detective that Marlowe is. Someone strews bodies all over Southern California and Marlowe finds them with the ease and derring-do of a bloodhound. I wanted a flashlight so I could get a closer look at the face. I wanted a drink and a cigarette, and I was beginning to think I shouldn't stray too far from my gun. All these useful items were in the Chrysler's glove compartment. I headed back through the house, skating on the lily ponds on the tile floor, and climbed into the passenger seat. I had just unscrewed the bottle cap when I detected something else—a grand display of pyrotechnics exploding in my retinas. I didn't even feel the blow, just saw the red stabbing lights riding on a wave of nausea before I fell into deep blackness.

My head was a seventy-eight on a turntable that had automatic reset. Every time I thought I'd come to the end of the song and could stop spinning around someone would push the button and start me turning again. Someone had tied a couple of logs behind my back but when I reached around to cut them loose I discovered they were my arms bound behind me. I reeked of gasoline.

The time had come to open my eyes. Come on, Marlowe, you can get your eyelids up, it's only a little less horrible than the old bamboo shoots under the fingernails trick.

I was in the driver's seat of the Chrysler. Someone had moved me over, but otherwise the scene was just the way I'd left it. The glove compartment was open. I could see my gun and the bottle of rye and I wanted both of them in the kind of detached fashion a man lost in the desert wants an oasis, but I couldn't see my way clear to getting them.

Footsteps scrabbled on the gravel behind me. "You can't set fire to him here," someone said impatiently. "You may own the valley, but the U.S. Army is camped on the road and they will certainly investigate a big gasoline fire up here."

I knew that voice. It was husky, with a hint of a lisp behind it. I'd heard it a century or so ago in my office.

"Well, you're such a damned know-it-all, what do you suggest? That we leave him here until morning when the hands will find him?" The sulky tones of the kid, Jay Boylston.

"No," the woman said coolly, "I think you should let me drive him into the mountains. He can go over a ravine there and no one will be surprised."

"Kitty's right," Boylston senior said authoritatively.

Kitty? She was a kitty all right, the kind that you usually like a good solid set of iron bars around before you toss raw meat to her twice a day. There was a bit more backchat about who would do the driving, but they agreed in the end that the kitten could do it so that no one would wonder where Jay and his daddy were.

"You fired his gun?" Daddy asked.

"Yes," Jay said sulkily. "I shot Richard twice with it. When they find him they'll think Marlowe did it."

"Right. Kitty, just see that his gun falls clear of the car before you set it off. We want to make sure the law doesn't have any loose ends to tie up."

So she did have a brother named Richard. Or had had. That wavy black hair in the goldfish pond, that was what her dark leopard tresses would look like if she undid that bun.

"Sure, Kurt," the husky voice drawled.

Kurt and Jay shoved me roughly back into the passenger seat and Miss Kitty took my spot behind the wheel. I tried to sniff the Chanel, but the gasoline fumes were too strong. She drove rapidly up the track, bouncing the Chrysler's tire from rock to rock as though she was driving a mountain goat.

Things looked bad for Marlowe. I wondered if it was worth trying any of my winsome charms, or if I should just roll over on top of her and force both of us flaming into a ditch. It was worth a try. At least it would change the situation—give those cool black eyes something to look surprised about. I was getting ready to roll when she stopped the car.

Her next move took me utterly by surprise: she reached behind me and hacked my arms loose with an efficient woodsman's knife.

"You're kind of pushing your luck, Kitty." I moved my arms cautiously in front of me. They felt like someone had just forced the Grand Coulee's overflow through them. "I've been concussed before. I'm not feeling so sorry for myself that I couldn't take that knife from you and get myself out of here. You'd have to explain it to Kurt and Jay as best you can."

"Yes," the husky voice agreed coolly. "I'll tell them something if I have to—if I ever see them again, that is. But I need your help."

"Right, Miss Kitty. You lure me to Dominick Bognavich's body. You bring me into the mountains and set the sweetest sucker trap I've ever seen, including planting bullets from my gun in what I assume is your brother's body, and now you want my help. You want me to drive my car over a cliff for you so you don't have to chip those bright red nails of yours?"

She drew a sharp breath. "No. No. I didn't know they were going to knock you out. And I didn't know they had killed Richard until I got here. He—he was the weak link. He always was, but I never thought he would betray me."

The quiver of emotion in her voice played on my heart like a thousand violin strings. "The gambler. I know. He gambled away your mother's whoosis and so you had Kurt Boylston drown him in the goldfish pond."

"It didn't happen quite like that. But I don't blame you for being angry."

"Gee, sister. That's real swell of you. I'm not angry, though—I love being hit on the head. I came up from L.A. just to get knocked out. And then have gasoline poured on me so I couldn't miss the cars."

"That was never supposed to happen," she said quickly. "I was trying to get to Grandfather—to the ranch—before Jay did but I couldn't—there were reasons. . . ." Her voice trailed away.

"Maybe you could tell me what was supposed to happen. If it wouldn't strain your brain to much to tell the truth. Maybe you could even start with who you really are."

In the dark I couldn't tell if she was blushing or not. "My real name is Kathleen Moloney. Kathleen Akiko Moloney. My mother married an Irishman, but her father was Ichuro Kimura. I know I look Jewish to many people, and in this climate today it is helpful to let them think so. Dominick—Dominick is the one who suggested it. He suggested the name Felstein. And when I pretended to lose the title to my grandfather's land to him, he kept it under the name of Felstein." Her voice trailed away. "I needed help and I was so afraid you wouldn't help me . . ."

"If I knew you were Nisei." I finished for her. "And what makes you so sure I will help you now?"

"I don't know." She leaned close to me and I could smell her perfume again, mixed with the gasoline and a faint tinge of ladylike sweat. "I saved your life, but that wouldn't count with you, would it, if you thought it was your duty to turn me in and force me to go to Manzanar."

"You're not in any danger. A girl like you knows how to fight her way out of trouble."

"Yes. I have to use the gifts I have, just as you do, Mr. Marlowe. But we can argue about that later. Let me finish because we must move quickly. If you agree to help me, I mean."

In the moonlight all I could see was her shape. She'd shed the hat and the suit and was wearing trousers and cowboy boots. I couldn't see her features to tell if she was spinning me another long yarn into which she had somehow appropriated the tale of Ichuro Kimura from the morning paper. I shook a large portion of rye into me to give my brain a fighting edge.

"Don't drink," she said sharply to me. "It's the worst thing for a man in your condition."

"On the contrary," I said, tilting the bottle a second time. The first swallow had settled the nausea in my stomach and sharpened the pain in my head, but the second one went clear to the base of my spine and worked its way into the brain. "I think I can stand to hear your tale of woe now. Tell me about Richard, the weakling."

"Kurt Boylston has wanted to own my grandfather's land for a long time. It's a small ranch, only nine hundred acres, nothing compared to the Boylston spread, but it has the best water. My grandfather worked it as a field hand when he came here from Japan in 1879 and gradually came to own it.

"Boylston has tried everything to get his hands on it. Then, with the internments and the anti-Japanese scare, he saw his chance. He announced that Kimura was a Japanese spy and that his land should be confiscated. Boylston said he would farm it as a service to the government. Of course, in times like these, frightened men will believe anything."

Her husky voice was shaky with passion. I wanted a cigarette very badly but didn't want to send us up in flames lighting it.

"My grandfather would not go. Why should he? He is no spy. And he knew it was only a ruse, a trick by Kurt Boylston to get his land. I'm sure you saw in the paper how he fought the army and then disappeared. I took the title and gave it to Dominick, but I had to tell Richard. And Richard was weak. Kurt must have bought him. I saw—I saw when I got to Dominick's house this morning, how he had been shot, and knew it was Richard, shooting him six times out of fright, then tearing the house up to find the title. After he turned it over to Kurt, the Boylstons drowned

him in my grandfather's goldfish pond. I pretended all along to be in love
with Kurt, to be supporting him against my grandfather, but after tonight
even he will be able to understand."

I wondered if even now she was telling the truth. She sure believed
in it, but did I? "Why didn't you tell me this this morning?"

The moonlight caught leopard sparks dancing from her eyes. "I didn't
think you'd believe me. A Japanese spy, written up in all the papers? I
thought I would get here ahead of you and explain it all to you, but then
I saw Richard's body in the pond and knew that Kurt would figure out
my true involvement before long. I had—had to go back to his ranch
and—" Her voice broke off as she shuddered. "I used my special gifts,
that's all, and took the title from his pocket while he slept."

I put one of my gasoline-soaked hands on her soft leopard paw. Why
not? She'd told a good tale, she deserved a little applause.

"Bravo. You got your paper back. You don't need me. You want a
lift someplace on my way back to L.A.?"

She sucked her breath in again and pulled her hand back. "I do need
you. To smuggle my grandfather into the city. The army knows my car,
and they know my face. They would stop me, but they won't stop you."

I rubbed the bottle a few times, wondering if her grandfather would
pop out of it, a wizened Japanese genie.

"He's been hiding here in an old well, but it's bad for him, bad for
his rheumatism, and it's hard for me to sneak him food. And now, he could
climb down into the well, but not up, not by himself, but you—you are
strong enough for two."

She was the genie in the bottle, or maybe she just had a little witch
blood mixed in with the leopard. I found myself walking across the jagged
ground to where a well cover lay hidden beneath the sage. I pried it loose
according to the enchantress's whispered instructions. She knelt down on
the rim and called softly, "It's Akiko, Grandfather. Akiko and a friend
who will bring you to Los Angeles."

It wasn't as simple as Miss Moloney thought it would be, driving
around to pick up Route Five from the north, but then these things never
are. In the first place Kimura wouldn't travel without a little shrine to the
Buddha that he'd been keeping in the well with him, and it was a job
packing the two of them in the trunk under some old blankets. And in the
second place we ran into Kurt and Jay because the only way to Route Five
was along the trail that led past the Kimura Place. And in the confusion
I put a bullet through Kurt Boylston's head—purely by mistake, as I explained to the sheriff, but Miss Moloney had hired me to look for rustlers

on her grandfather's old place and when Kurt had started to shoot at us I didn't know what else to do. The sheriff liked it about as well as a three-day hangover, but he bought it in the end.

What with one thing and another the sun was poking red fingers up over the San Gabriels by the time we coasted past Burbank and into the city.

I dropped Miss Moloney and her grandfather at a little place she owned in Beverly Hills, just ten rooms and a pool in the back. I figured Dominick had been a pretty good friend, all right. Or maybe the Irishman who married her mother—I was willing to keep an open mind.

She invited me in for a drink, but I didn't think gasoline and rye went too well with the neighborhood or the decor, so I just left the two of them to the ministrations of a tearful Japanese maid and lowered myself by degrees through the canyons back to the city. The concrete looked good to me. Even the leftover drunks lying on the park benches looked pretty good. I've never been much of an outdoors man.

When I got to my office I tried the air to see if there was any perfume left, but I couldn't detect it. I wondered what kind of detective I was, anyway. There wasn't anything for me in the office. I didn't know why I'd come here instead of finding my shower and bed—that was the kind of thing I could detect all right.

I put the office bottle back in the drawer and locked it. I put yesterday's paper tidily in the trash can and looked around for a minute. There was a scrap of black on the floor underneath the visitor's chair. I bent over to pick it up. It was a little square of lace, the kind of thing a lady with the poise of a dealer would have tucked in her black bag, the kind of thing even the most sophisticated lady might drop when she was peeling off twenties. It smelled faintly of Chanel. I put it in my breast pocket and locked the door.

It's hard to describe the influence Chandler had on my own work. I think all modern PI writers create very much in his image, far more so than in Hammett's. It was Chandler who really framed the relationship of the PI to justice, law, and society, and my detective, V. I. Warshawski, certainly operates according to the values Chandler outlined in "The Simple Art of Murder."

There is a way, too, in which my work developed as a reaction to Chandler. After reading Farewell, My Lovely *almost twenty years ago I found myself wishing for a woman hero. Chandler's women are complex, some venial, some drunk, some sex cats, some gallant, but in most of his books the seductress, whether Dolores Gonzalez, Velma, or Carmen, is at the root of the trouble. I spent many years working on different ways in which a woman could play a stronger, less sexual role in a mystery and finally, in 1979 came up with V. I. Warshawski. So in a way Chandler is directly responsible for my decision to write a PI novel.*

Sara Paretsky

RED ROCK

JULIE SMITH

1944

S HE HAD LONG auburn hair that looked chestnut in the sun. It fell over her right eye, and her left one was green, a deep, clear emerald that had seen more than Kansas cornfields, but not much more. She had on shorts and a white halter top, but her skin was still white, still waiting for California to put its mark on her.

She stood before one of two rosebushes in the tiny bed outside her tile-roofed bungalow, a basket on her left arm, gathering her rosebuds. She looked like every kid from the Midwest whose old man drinks too much and works out on her old lady and who needs to get out of the house and who comes to Hollywood after winning a high school talent contest.

On the third finger of her right hand—the one holding the scissors— was an emerald-cut ruby not quite as large as a business card. To the left of the rock were two small diamonds and to the right were two more.

"Evelyn Merrill?"

"Yes?"

"Philip Marlowe." I gave her my business card. "I saw your picture in the paper."

She tossed her hair aside, letting me see both eyes. They flashed green fire. "I am already employed, thank you. I do not pose for artists. I am not looking for work as an actress. I do not wish to be a star." She turned and started up the two steps to her postage stamp of a porch.

"I thought you were a singer."

She turned around, furious. "How do you know that?"

I indicated the card. "Knowing is my business."

For the first time, she looked at it. "A private investigator? What business could you possibly have with me?"

"If you'll invite me in, maybe we could talk about it."

"How do I know you're on the level?"

"Forget it. Let's talk here."

135

"Oh, never mind. You look okay."

She went in and held the door for me to follow. There was a davenport on one wall, under a couple of windows, with a cocktail table and a couple of chairs opposite. On the wall were a few family photos. The rug was straw. I sat on the davenport, the girl in one of the chairs.

I pulled a couple of newspaper clippings out of my breast pocket. One was of Evelyn Merrill at the beach, one of those cheesecake pictures taken by passing photographers who get lucky. She was standing sideways, throwing a beach ball, the rock on her finger all but throwing sparks.

The other was a photo of a much older party, also a handsome woman, wearing a hat with a small veil, silk scarf and smart suit. The caption said she had just completed a successful charity drive—or it would have, if I hadn't discreetly removed it. The picture showed her shaking hands with the mayor. On her right hand, either the same rock or its twin was all but throwing the same sparks.

I passed the pictures over to Evelyn. "We need to have a talk about the rock."

"The rock?"

I pointed to her ring. "The red one. On your finger."

"I don't understand."

"Look at the pictures."

She did and then she looked at me, confused. "It's the same ring, isn't it?"

"It is if yours is engraved 'RR.' "

"It is. What's this all about?"

"That's my client in the picture. The ring was stolen from her shortly after the picture ran. When she saw your photo, she asked me to make discreet inquiries."

"She thinks I stole it?"

"She wanted to know if you'd mind saying where you got it."

"Of course not." The green eyes were stricken. "My fiancé gave it to me." She tossed the hair once again, even though it was already well out of her line of vision. It was a proud, defiant gesture. "You think my fiancé's a taxi driver? Maybe a sailor who can't find a ship to sail on? A pathetic clerk who deals with a cheap fence every now and then? He's not. He's Tony Bizzotto. Do you know him?"

"I know him." Meaning I knew of him. Tony Bizzotto was one of the biggest developers in the business—not some gaudy little crook with nothing more to recommend him than good taste in women. Nothing like that. Tony was a little less ruthless than a pack of Cossacks.

"How'd a nice girl like you get tangled up with a heel like that?"

"Please don't be fresh, Mr. Marlowe. I think I've helped you all I can." She smiled sweetly. "Except for one small matter—shall I phone Tony and let him know you're on your way?" I smelled fresh-cut flowers as I brushed past her.

I stopped somewhere for a sandwich and a martini and then I phoned Kenny Haste, a crime reporter on the *Chronicle*. After we had each showed the other how amusing we could be, he told me what I already knew from the phone book—Tony Bizzotto didn't go into any office. "He works out of his home," Kenny Haste said. "Probably out of his swimming pool."

He gave me an address in the kind of neighborhood where you need a car to go next door to borrow a stamp. Too bad I wasn't wearing my powder blue suit.

The driveway was slightly shorter than the Oregon Trail and I was on it when a black Packard demanded the right of way so forcefully I lightly smacked a tree trunk trying to comply. But I continued bravely on.

If Bizzotto didn't live in the Taj Mahal, he didn't occupy a railroad shack either. Maybe we could just say Scheherazade could have made the place up. I got out of my car, straightened my tie, walked to the door, fought off the urge to say "open sesame," and rang the bell instead.

A young Filipino answered the door. He had a flat face, beetle brows, and a sullen expression. He also looked smart, like maybe Bizzotto was pretty careful about whom he hired and his employees pretty careful about whom they let in the house.

"Marlowe," I said, handing him a card. "Mr. Bizzotto's expecting me."

"Mr. Bizzotto's not home."

"Damn! He warned me not to be late. Was that him leaving in the Packard?"

For a second, uncertainty flickered under the beetle brows. The kid was smart, but he might as well have said, "What Packard?"

"Mr. Bizzotto's not home," he repeated.

"Thanks for your trouble," I said, and headed back toward my car. A pair of smart, sullen brown eyes drilled a hole in my back and didn't stop watching until I'd turned around and started chugging back down the Oregon Trail. At the first curve, I pulled off the road, parked, and meandered back to the sultan's palace.

I slipped around the side, maybe taking to heart Kenny Haste's remark about the pool, maybe just looking for an open door or for a servant who could use a bit of the folding. I wasn't sure yet. I was sure Evelyn Merrill was in over her head, though.

Bizzotto was sitting by the pool, wearing swimming trunks. He was in his midfifties, maybe older, with hair that was gray like a frigate's gray, and plenty of it, on both his head and chest. He had a dark, even tan, but he was going a little bit to seed around the middle. While you wouldn't mistake his nose for a banana, it helped that it wasn't yellow. His mouth was very wide and very nasty. His neck was a little too thick. His eyes would have been surprised if they hadn't been glassy and empty. Someone had shot him in the chest, by the looks of things someone sitting in the chair next to his.

"I thought I told you to buzz off." The houseman had slipped out a back door I hadn't heard him open.

"Did you hear a shot a while ago?" I asked.

The Filipino came closer, took in the hole in the boss's torso, and puked in a bed of begonias. I figured that made him innocent, but Hollywood's full of actors. Finally he said, "I didn't hear anything. He was with a woman. I stayed in a different wing of the house."

"Why did you come out here now?"

"He had a phone call."

"Did you see the woman he was with?"

He pulled aside the chair that had been recently occupied by a murderer and sat down gingerly. "Only from a distance. She drove up, swished out of the car, and went around back like she owned the place. He told me he was expecting a lady. I guess he phoned her and said to meet him in back."

"You wouldn't make a bad dick yourself."

"Really?" The eyes that had recently changed from sullen to scared brightened up.

"Yeah. You're smart and you're observant. But stay out of the racket, kid. There's no money in it."

"Oh." He looked down at the concrete patio. I slipped a five-spot into the pocket of his white jacket.

"There's a little in talking to me, though. What did she look like?"

When he looked up, his face was sullen again. He looked as if he were trying to be tough, practicing for a new career as a shamus. "She was blonde and she was wearing a black hat and a blue print dress with a short jacket that was kind of mustard colored. That's all I could see. I only got a glimpse of the back of her."

I showed him the newspaper clipping of Evelyn Merrill wearing the rock. "Do you know anything about this?"

"Sure, that's Miss Merrill. Swell, isn't she?"

"What do you know about the ring?"

He shrugged. "Nothing, I guess. I never thought about it." He looked at Bizzotto, mentally hooking two up with another two. "The boss gave it to her, huh?"

If my client could have seen Tony Bizzotto's Turkish delight of a mansion, she'd probably have had to bite her lip to keep from laughing. She lived in a two-story Tudor house in Pasadena, furnished mostly in faded chintz. The garden ran to English lilac, the living room to family photos on top of the Steinway. Her name was Myra Heatley and she lived with her daughter, Nancy Daniels, who answered my knock.

Nancy showed me into the living room, left, and returned with her mother. Myra had eyes like sapphires, hair that had settled down to the gracious peachy color of cantaloupe flesh, and a little way about her that was as subtle as a California sunset. The peach hair, which had probably once been red as poppies, was parted on the left side and arranged in elegant waves. She wore a royal blue suit that did its best to look demure.

Nancy wore brown. She had brown hair, cut in a pageboy, straight and sober, while her mother's curled merrily. She had her mother's fine skin and blue eyes, but they were a darker blue and without the sapphire sparkle. She was thinner than her mother, not so lush, and she carried her shoulders hunched slightly forward. Something about her was wary and I wondered if it was Myra she was wary of.

Myra came close and shook hands. Her perfume was jasmine, I thought—something, at any rate, that could have wafted in the window on a spring day. "Mr. Marlowe," she said. "A report so soon?"

"Yeah," I said, and sat on the flowered davenport. She and Nancy sat as well, in overstuffed chairs facing me. "A report so soon. Evelyn Merrill received the ring as a gift from a man named Tony Bizzotto."

Myra drew in her breath and lost her color all at once. Nancy went rigid. After a moment, Myra spoke to Nancy. "Darling, could you excuse us?"

Nancy nodded, got up, and walked out with the gait of an old woman, one foot in front of the other, as if she were in danger of falling. I thought she could have used a shot of brandy, but I wasn't her mother.

When she was gone, I said, "You owe me some answers."

"I beg your pardon?"

"Bizzotto's dead."

"Dead!" Her color was coming back. She crossed to a sideboard and poured us both a drink.

"Murdered," I said. "That's why you need to tell me what's going on."

She swallowed her drink whole. "I see. If I don't you'll tell the police about the ring."

"Any reason why I shouldn't?"

"You be the judge, Mr. Marlowe. I'll tell you my story and let you decide. You see, Tony Bizzotto bought the ring for me—twenty-five years ago."

"So the bill of sale you showed me was false."

"On the contrary. It was quite genuine. Tony and I were—well— quite different people then. He had names for me, because of my hair. Pinkie was one and Red Rock was another; sometimes Pink Lady or Reddy Kilowatt or even Ruby. Usually Red Rock. I tell you this for a reason.

"One night a business acquaintance of his was shot to death. The next day he and I had lunch in a certain very nice neighborhood and we took a walk afterwards. We saw the ring in a shop window and I turned to him and said, 'I was with you last night.' Just like that. Out of the clear blue. I've often wondered since how I had the nerve to do it.

"He said, 'Come on,' and took me by the wrist, almost dragging me into the shop. He said to the proprietor, 'I'd like the red rock in the window, please,' and he had it engraved with the letters I told you about and he had the bill of sale made out to me. It was the most perfect communication I have ever had with a living soul."

"Don't tell me. You dumped him the day after that."

She lit a cigarette and gave me a smile that could have melted the snow pack at Mammoth. "Of course not. I kept my part of the bargain. I waited until he was clear of the murder investigation. And then I changed my name and moved—moved to a better neighborhood and in with a better crowd. I hocked the red rock to buy clothes. I wore the clothes to new places that I knew about and homes of new friends I made, and I met men. Invariably, the men gave me tiny tokens of their affection. I would cash in enough of the gifts to get the ring back, and when I had to I'd hock it again."

She blew smoke out her nostrils. "Eventually, I met a very nice man and married him. And when that ended I met another and married him. My second husband died a year ago." She paused. "Do you blame him?" she said finally, giving me as level a gaze as an accountant might.

"I think I get the point of the nickname."

"I'll ignore that and say only that I had no money, no education, and to my mind, no choice. And I had to make a home for my daughter."

"Your daughter! Nancy was born . . ."

"Out of wedlock. She was six when we moved to Los Angeles. Her father was killed in a mining accident."

"I'm sorry."

"Thank you. If he hadn't been, our lives would have been different. But he was, and I got mixed up with Tony Bizzotto. For a long time afterward I was afraid he'd find me. I even dyed my hair to hide from him. But after so many years it hardly seemed to matter. I thought he'd have found me if he'd wanted to. So I stopped being cautious. And then that picture ran in the paper. And the ring disappeared. When I saw the other picture, I thought I knew what had happened, but I had to be sure." She gave me the level gaze again, a look like the sky at night. "I didn't kill him. Do you believe me?"

I shrugged. "I'll think it over and let you know."

It was nearly dark when I got back to Hollywood, but I could see her through the venetian blind slats—Evelyn Merrill sitting on her davenport, knees drawn up under her chin, staring at a spot on her green wall. It was a dull landlord green, but with her hair and eyes it looked good. She was wearing a satin hostess gown, blue-gray like the dusk outside.

She wasn't wearing makeup, but her eyes weren't red either. If she'd been crying, it didn't show. "I found him," I said.

"Wayne told me. The houseman. Would you like a drink?"

Without waiting for an answer, she poured me a stiff one, moving mechanically, like a person in deep shock.

"I'm sorry about Bizzotto," I said.

A sound came out of her, the kind of sound you might expect from an animal whose front paw has just stepped into a trap. The tears came too, and I held her while she cried it all out. Then I got her a drink and made her swallow some of it.

"My client says he gave her the rock twenty-five years ago," I said. I told her the story, leaving out nothing that would have protected Bizzotto's privacy, wanting her to know, for the record, the kind of man he was. When I got to the part about the nickname, she winced. "He called me that," she whispered. "Red Rock." She swallowed. "He told me there was another one. That he had been in love with another woman once—that I reminded him of her. Mary Daniels."

"Myra."

"Myra! That was her in the picture! Myra Heatley. Oh, God, what have I done?" The tears started again. I held her some more, and after a while she could talk again.

"I looked her up. I pile my papers up on the back porch and then throw the whole pile away at once. That picture you showed me was only a couple of weeks old. So I just looked through till I found it. I knew there was something funny going on as soon as you showed it to me. Because of the picture of me. It wasn't any accident—a passing photographer stopping for a cheesecake shot. Tony called up a newspaper friend and arranged it. He knew everybody, and everybody owed him. It wasn't any effort for him." She gave me a faint rueful smile.

"He said it would help my career. But when you showed me the other picture, I knew that wasn't it. Only I didn't know what was going on— and I had to know. He'd asked me to marry him, you see." She let me have the smile again, a smile that said that was an idea she could hardly believe she'd ever entertained.

"So I called Myra Heatley. I told her you'd been here and I asked her if she knew Tony Bizzotto. And she said no, she'd never heard of him. But if she's Mary Daniels, she and Tony had a daughter together."

I was finding it hard to keep up. "They were married?"

She shrugged. "He never said. He just talked about his long-lost daughter and how much he missed her." She stopped and took a deep breath. "I fell for it, too. I felt really sorry for him and I wanted to give him something warm and soft to replace her. To replace both of them. Tell me—what's she like?"

"Myra? She was probably a lot like you once. She had some bad breaks and she did the best she could. You'll do better."

I was starting to feel like a yo-yo that plopped down in Pasadena and fetched up in Hollywood, but I couldn't conduct my next interview on the telephone. And I couldn't conduct it without a search of my client's garage.

I did the search before I rang the bell. There was a black Packard parked where I expected it. Nancy answered the door. "I'll get my mother."

"Don't bother. I need to talk to you." She looked as if I'd struck her. But she led me into the living room and sat me down. She didn't offer me a drink.

"Bizzotto contacted you after he saw your mother's picture, didn't he?"

She nodded.

"And you saw him."

Again she nodded, barely perceptibly, as if she were frozen and couldn't thaw enough to move.

"May I ask why?"

She shook her head for no, and her whole body shook as well—the thaw had been sudden and violent.

"Easy," I said, and put out a hand to steady her. She jerked away as violently as she had shook. The way she moved told a story all its own.

"He wasn't your father, was he?"

"No!"

"You've never told anyone about him, have you?" She shook again. "But you can tell me. I won't tell your mother."

"He said *he'd* tell my mother," she cried. "That's why I saw him."

Myra Heatley strode into the room, looking as nearly panicked as I supposed she ever got. She was very white. "Tell me what?"

"You know what," I said. "That's why you dumped Bizzotto and changed your name. You knew what he was doing to her—maybe you even caught him; or maybe she told you; or maybe you just knew. You've spent your whole life trying to make her forget, and she'd rather see the scum again than take a chance you'd find out."

Nancy was crying and shaking and keening. I wondered if she would have to be hospitalized. But her mother took her head in her arms and held it against her breast, as if Nancy were a small child, and rocked her, and then gave her some kind of pill and got her to bed.

When she came back, she was calm. "He did it all out of revenge, didn't he? He set up the picture of Evelyn Merrill, but that wasn't enough." She poured herself a drink and knocked it back. "He knew the one thing that would really get to me. Hurting my baby." Despite the drink, her face contorted and she covered it with her hand for a moment. "Just like he did before."

She looked at me again, resolve all over her face, her square jaw set as if there were no turning back and no tomorrow. "And so when Evelyn Merrill called and told me he'd given her the ring, I knew he'd stolen it from me, and he knew where I was. But there hadn't been a burglary. That meant Nancy must have given it to him. I knew that he'd seen her." She shrugged, as if reporting that she'd had to let her maid go. "So I drove over and killed him."

"How did you do that?" I asked.

For a moment she looked utterly bewildered, but she pulled herself together without missing more than a beat. "I bought a cheap dime store wig so I wouldn't be recognized. I'll show it to you." She disappeared and came back with a blonde hairpiece.

"Uh-huh," I said. "And what did you stab him with?"

She looked at me hard, like a poker player trying to read the opposition, and then she said, "I shot him."

"Can I see the gun?"

"Of course not. I threw it over a cliff—into the ocean."

"You didn't kill Bizzotto. You didn't know where he lived, and if you could have found out, you wouldn't have had enough time to get there before I did—or maybe you would have, just barely. But you couldn't have known I stopped for a sandwich. You had every reason to think I'd go straight from Evelyn Merrill's to Bizzotto's. If you'd wanted to kill Bizzotto, you'd have picked a more convenient time."

"I didn't even think about that. I was in a fury."

"You're good. You could probably convince the D.A. And he probably wouldn't look any further once he had your confession. But what good would it do? What would happen to Nancy with her mother in prison?"

She looked at me as if I'd hit her. She hadn't even thought about it, meaning that the whole performance had been improvised within the last ten minutes. She really was good.

"Look," I said. "Do what you said you did. Find the gun and get rid of it. Burn the wig and the clothes she wore. And do it fast. Evelyn Merrill might mention you to the cops."

"You're not going to them?"

"Why should I? By the time I got there, you'd have destroyed the evidence."

Her shoulders sagged with relief.

"By the way, there's something you should know. Evelyn Merrill's a nice kid. She'd probably remind you of yourself at her age."

She smiled. "I'd like her to have the ring."

There was something about the red rock. It had a funny quality. It could inspire perfect communication between two people.

———

I can't imagine that any American writer hasn't been influenced by Chandler, at least indirectly, as he or she will certainly have been influenced by writers whom Chandler influenced. Surely every American writer of mysteries must have been, no matter how funny, fluffy, or cozy, no matter how hard-boiled, street-wise, or tough their own books may be. Quite simply, Chandler set the standard and everything else is a deviation therefrom.

In my work, I've wanted to deviate a lot. I've wanted, for instance, to write about women as I know them—widely varied, sometimes murderous, often heroic, almost always hardworking—as opposed to the tarts, gold diggers, spoiled rich girls, and ruthless criminals who comprised Marlowe's female acquaintanceship. I've wanted my men to be more lifesized in their own eyes than larger-than-life superhero Marlowe, with never a thought for himself.

Surely that is as it should be. A hero like Marlowe would be a derivative hero (and has been, often). An attempt to recreate Chandler's vision would be pathetic and tatty. We must all write the way we write.

Chandler's influence, for me, has been in his use of language—or rather, in the inspiration afforded by it. I don't see how it is possible to read his books without being dazzled by the author's economy, his originality, his brilliance—all of that—but most of all by his precision. Who among us doesn't hear his cadences, his turns of phrase, when we sit down to work? We may never write that well—or even write similarly—but nonetheless we have internalized his work in a way that we couldn't escape even if we wanted to. We have used it as a jumping-off place for our own work and those among us who are masochists may also use it as the standard of excellence by which they judge themselves. Those with a better-developed sense of self-preservation wouldn't dare.

Julie Smith

THE DEEPEST SOUTH

PACO IGNACIO TAIBO II

1945

THE SUN, A perfect, orange-colored ball on the horizon, almost made up for the difficulty the breeze was causing me. I lit the third match and tried to cover the flame with my left hand. Alex had taken off his shoes and was squatting down, in deep conversation with a group of fishermen. He was speaking Spanish at full speed, eating his vowels, charming the three men. Seen from a distance he looked like the best vacuum-cleaner salesman in the world. He wasn't. Halfway through the conversation, the monologue, he looked up and nailed me with those two blue eyes. I was about twenty yards from him, next to his abandoned shoes. I released the smoke from the cigarette in his direction; the wind blew it away.

I was already becoming accustomed to this relationship—distant, yet in a way affectionate—that turned us into phantoms, shadows of each other. Four days before, one of the lawyers who handles his father's business had placed an envelope full of cash in front of me. "Alex will probably travel to Mexico sometime this week. Take care of him," he said.

I didn't like the lawyer's tie, red dots on a metallic blue background, and I didn't like his cross-eyed look. I liked even less his presumption that I knew who Alex was and why I had to take care of him. At any rate, as the sun entered through the cracks in the Venetian blinds in my Los Angeles office, the smoke from my cigarette made me remember a cup of steaming Mexican coffee I had drunk years ago.

Four days later Alex and I were looking at each other while the sun was setting on that beach some miles from Ensenada, in Baja California. If Alex was getting bored, soon we would be able to eat supper (at separate tables, of course) in some restaurant in Ensenada and I would be able to drink the coffee I remembered.

Alex seemed to get my message and, patting the fishermen on the back, walked toward his shoes. I didn't move. Alex approached, reeling like a sailor in a Hollywood musical comedy, and picked up his shoes without looking at me.

"Dinnertime, shadow," he said while speaking to the sea.

We walked toward the automobiles: his, a cherry-red Fleetwood convertible; mine, parked so close that it almost scraped his bumper, a green Oldsmobile that showed its scars and could have used a paint job.

I gave him a few seconds' advantage, tossed my cigarette on the ground, took one last look at the sun which was beginning to set in the sea, and got into the car.

Alex was no vacuum-cleaner salesman on vacation south of the border. He was the only heir to the Fletcher supermarket chain. Not that it mattered to me, but this seemed essential to the lawyer who slipped the envelope with dollars across my desk. He offered me very little else: a photograph of a boy of twenty-three with wild, blond hair that seemed to want to rise into a horn over his forehead, and a little bit of chatter about how "reckless" and "unstable" Alex was, "how sick he had returned from the Pacific," and "how bad it had been for him during the war in one of those Japanese concentration camps in Burma or the Philippines or Malaya." When I tried to determine the exact nature of my obligations as nanny, I couldn't find out anything more concrete. ". . . gets into too much trouble, you know? You can stop him from getting himself stabbed in some bad-luck brothel in Tijuana, that sort of thing." When I asked whether Alex should know that I was following him, he answered, shrugging his shoulders, "Do as you wish. One way or the other, Alex will find out and I'm sure he'll blame me. It's difficult to hide things from Alex, as you'll soon realize."

Monday. Alex fulfilled the lawyer's predictions and went south, first toward San Diego and later following the border to Calexico. He entered Mexico through Mexicali and stopped the Fleetwood right at Revolution Park, a few yards from the borderline. He rubbed his eyes as if he had just woken up and approached my automobile. Through the open window he said, "They told me that a China-Mex jumped that green fence seven times in one day. They captured him all seven times and sent him back to Mexico. He holds the local record. No one saw him, no one seems to know his name, but everyone knows the story. Maybe he never existed. I always wondered why he had to be Chinese. Why choose a Chinese guy for a myth?"

He didn't wait for my answer and walked left toward the Hotel Palacio, carrying a suitcase. By the way he was carrying it, it must have been heavy. We ran into each other a half hour later in the hotel bar. I was weighing the possibilities of a margarita as opposed to a gimlet, when Alex made his appearance on the scene. The ceiling fans seemed to be bothered by arthritic pains. A pair of Central European refugees were sweating copiously while drinking an acid wine, their silent faces fixed on a horizon that must have been thousands of miles away. Just watching them made me hot, the worst kind of hot, sad and exhausting. A girl of about fifteen, probably German, was playing the piano in the corner and humming. Alex came over to me.

"I don't know why the Chinese guy wanted to go to the United States. It's much better down here. We're the ones who ought to be jumping the green fence, not them," he said. Then he sat down at the next table and in Spanish ordered a pitcher of sangria.

Mexicali at that time was a way station for refugees from all over Europe who were seeking permission to enter the United States. It had been, and probably still is, the trampoline for thousands of Mexicans who illegally cross the border to make themselves a few dollars in the north. Above all, it was a languid city; dirt was everywhere; clouds of dust tried to cover the poor tracks of progress and return the city to its ancient desert condition. It was a city where you heard songs in many languages, songs that were almost always melancholy.

That first day on Alex's tracks turned into a pilgrimage that seemed absurd, erratic, but at other times motivated by some obscure design. He entered a shoe store and spent hours trying on Mexican boots, only to end up not buying anything. He stopped by the local newspaper and placed an announcement (for two dollars I got hold of a copy: "I've already arrived, Ana. I'm at the Palacio. Alex."). He visited three doctors. (I duly noted the names and addresses and promised to stop by later on. One of them had a marvelous bilingual sign in the window: "We cure incurable diseases, the others cure themselves.") He went to the fair on the outskirts of the city and with absolute seriousness dedicated himself to winning rounds in the shooting gallery, in between flirting sessions with the gypsy woman who ran the booth.

At the end of the afternoon, with his white linen suit and my black shoes covered with dust, we went walking toward the border, bound for the hotel like a pair of defeated gamblers. As we went inside, he looked at me with curiosity. His two blue eyes were shining with a strange intensity. I entered the bar to kick around some ideas and get rid of the taste of dust with a pair of margaritas.

"Marlowe, you work for that *guero*, that blond guy?" a man at the next table asked me as I was finishing the first drink. I should have looked up before. The tables around him were empty. I never liked Mexican police, but Mexicans liked them even less than I did. The man had a big scar that went from his right eye to his throat. Through his open jacket you could see the butt of his .45.

"I don't know. It seems he doesn't like me very much." I laughed.

The policeman smiled. "I don't like him either."

"And me?" I asked, returning the smile and signaling the waiter to bring me the next margarita.

"No, amigo. You're in the business. With you, we always know what's going on, and if we don't, we guess, or we ask. No, the one I don't like is that blond guy. He came here to go crazy. Do you know what he has in that suitcase?"

I kept on smiling. There's nothing like candor when engaged in chit-chat with the police.

"He's carrying a pile of dollars and a Thompson submachine gun. *'Ta loco el pendejo ese.* That asshole's crazy."

"And why didn't they take it away from him at the border?"

"He must have paid a *mordida*, a bribe. You figure it out."

The heat kept me from sleeping.

The morning of the second day I ran into Alex in the corridor. The bathroom was around the corner and we were both on the way to shave. Alex wasn't wearing a shirt; an enormous whitish scar crossed his back.

"You can call me Alex," he said, turning his back to me, knowing that my eyes were mesmerized by the scar. "I'll call you Marlowe. It doesn't matter to me if that's your name or not. It's the name you used to register, and that's good enough for me. By the way, if you talk to the doctors I saw yesterday, they'll tell you that I have a fatal disease. There's no point trying to cure me; it's a matter of months." He was speaking without looking at me, not even granting me a gesture over his shoulder. He presumed that I, with my towel on my shoulder and my shaving brush and razor in hand, was following him.

"Try not to cut yourself shaving. There's nothing that bothers me more than blood in the bathroom sink," I said.

He laughed forcefully. Neither of us could shave. There was a Mexican in the bathroom, sitting on the toilet and playing the guitar. He had the face of a man with few friends. Disturbing him didn't seem like a good idea.

In the afternoon he took off in his Fleetwood at seventy-five miles an hour down the terrible roads that go to Ensenada, crossing canyons and desert. Every once in a while, despite the best efforts of my Oldsmobile, I lost sight of him.

We got to Ensenada as it was getting dark. At the entrance to town he swerved off the road and drove directly onto the beach. I took all the time in the world to light a cigarette, because I hadn't been able to enjoy one during the roadside chase that afternoon. Alex appeared in between the shadows; he seemed annoyed that I hadn't followed him.

"I'm in love with a woman who lives around here. Her husband is a famous Mexican poet. He threatened to kill me if he saw me near his wife again. What do you plan to do, Marlowe?"

His eyes sparked with fury. He was about to take a walk when I landed a direct hit on his jaw. He collapsed in silence onto the white sand. I walked along the beach, guided by the lights of a cabaña some two hundred and fifty yards away.

"I saw Alex's car a while ago. Did he come with you?" asked a young man with curly hair who was smoking on the cabaña porch.

I nodded.

"Are you his doctor?" the man asked.

"No. I'm a kind of nursemaid."

"In my country they're called bodyguards."

"It's specialized work. More like soul guards."

"Raul Cota," he said, extending his hand.

He must have been about forty, with a full beard capped by a mustache. There was a sad look about him.

"Marlowe," I answered, extending my hand. "How do you know Alex?"

"He comes around here; he spends his time roaming around my cabaña and telling everybody that he's in love with my wife. But that would be difficult. I've been a widower for two years. Maybe he knew her before. . . . I don't know. I don't think so."

I sat on the porch, pushing the sand around with the tips of my shoes. Cota went inside and returned a little later with two cups of coffee. I could hear the sea. Alex suddenly appeared in front of us, rubbing his jaw. I smiled.

"A cup of coffee?" offered Cota.

Alex nodded.

As the sun came up, Alex drove his Fleetwood north at full speed bound for a port on the Pacific called Rosarito. There we had lobsters with tortillas and frijoles for breakfast. I didn't pay more than two dollars for mine. If things kept going like this, I would never get my expense money from the lawyer in Los Angeles.

Alex began to walk along the beach. I was getting fed up and stayed at the shack where they had served us the freshly captured lobsters. I was ready for a second cup of coffee with cinnamon. Alex, seeing that I wasn't following him, came back looking like an angry child.

"Come, Marlowe, let's walk along the beach and I'll tell you about the caves and the rock drawings."

"What's the hurry, gringo? Let him drink his coffee," the fisherman who had waited on us said.

"We have important things to discuss," Alex said in his rapid Spanish.

I left the coffee to one side. At any rate it was too hot. I lit a cigarette and tried to catch up to Alex, who was walking in a great hurry at the edge of the sea. The doves began to keep us company.

"Miles south of here there are prehistoric caves, full of rock drawings. They were painted thousands of years ago by a tribe of tall men, much taller than the *guaycuras* who later settled in this area. You know what we can do, Marlowe? We can get a couple of good cameras and cross the sierra. The caves are incredible: men of two colors, turning themselves into animals with horns . . ."

He waited an instant for my answer. Then he seemed bored and left me still smoking a cigarette while he went toward the sea, getting his shoes wet every time the cusp of a little wave would reach the shore.

Alex was getting drunk, like a soldier who just realized he had been fighting on the wrong side. Mezcal after mezcal; not even enough time to warm his tongue.

I was sitting at the next table surrounded by the noise of fifty simultaneous conversations and a mariachi band whose cornet player tried to blast my brains out by playing his instrument four inches from my ear. The Club Camalias had been the one and only stop after Tijuana. The Fleetwood, full of dust, was parked outside the den, which was a center for nervous drug addicts, sailors from San Diego, pimps and their merchandise, Mexican workers from a nearby construction company who didn't have the time to remove their hard hats, and a group of policemen headed by my old friend, whose name was Ramirez. After distributing his boys throughout the club, he came to sit at my table. I couldn't make out his words through the noise, only his smile.

Alex took note of the presence of my companion and sent for a double mezcal to welcome him.

"The Mexican police are *putas*, whores," said Alex, looking straight at our table and taking advantage of the break in the mariachi music.

Ramirez smiled, raised his cup, and toasted Alex.

"Your friend is completely crazy. Surely he wants to commit suicide."

"Seems like that to me," I responded.

"Why doesn't he do it on the other side?" asked Ramirez.

I was left looking for an answer. After all, it wasn't such a bad question.

Alex's eyes were glassy; his jaw slightly disconnected. Seeing that Ramirez wasn't reacting, he looked for something else to grab his attention. He found it easily. One of the American sailors was sitting at a nearby table, absolutely enthralled with a prostitute. Alex stood up and walked toward him. The mariachis began to play "La Paloma," possibly the only Mexican song to which I know the lyrics, but Alex gave me no time to enjoy it. He was arguing about something with the sailor. Suddenly Alex slapped the woman in the face. I jumped out of my chair. Ramirez didn't even make an attempt to follow me. The sailor took out a knife and stuck it in the first thing he found—Alex's left hand, resting on the table.

Violence, as always, provoked screams and abandonment. Nevertheless, the mariachis continued to play. I pushed the sailor aside and pulled the knife from the table, freeing Alex's left hand. Blood gushed out profusely. At his table, Ramirez limited himself to a smile.

Alex insisted on being treated in Mexicali, which is how the front seat of my car became full of blood. I knew I should be mad, but I wasn't. Alex's behavior just made me feel melancholy. While he was resting in an overstuffed chair in the waiting room, I spoke to Dr. Martinez about Alex's supposedly incurable disease.

"Incurable? It would have been fifty years ago, amigo. Now it's perfectly curable. All he has is a venereal disease, syphilis, and it's not even an advanced case. He's already being treated for it."

The nights in Mexicali are dark. Music lures you, like bait, from several places at once. Every once in a while a group of drunks crosses you, or a taxi driver stops to try to convince you that the doors of his automobile lead to the gates of paradise. There's a sense of asphyxiation, from the dirt in the air, the dry heat. It's a small city, stolen from the desert. Without my hat and jacket, I went walking in the night looking for answers. Maybe the questions applied to me, too. We went down to the south to leave our nightmares there, our worst dreams. Instead, we found ourselves, looking in the mirror, face to face with the dark side of our sadness and our solitude. What fault was it of the Mexicans that Alex had chosen their country to go crazy in?

"If I swim out there for a hundred and eighty-one days, I'll be back . . ." Alex said, pointing to someplace on the other side of the Pacific where he had left a piece of his soul.

"You should probably wait until your hand is better," was the only thing that occurred to me to say.

We returned to Rosarito, this time the two of us in my Oldsmobile. We were eating lobsters on the beach, and Alex allowed himself to drift off to sleep in the hammock. I decided to fight my drowsiness by walking on the beach. I had a few cigarettes with a group of women and gave them a hand cleaning sea snails. In return they gave me a couple of dozen for supper. When I returned I found that Alex had disappeared from the hammock and from sight. His suitcase was still in the automobile. I opened it.

There really was an old Thompson submachine gun, unloaded and rusty. There were also four or five stacks of Japanese money, printed during the occupation of the Dutch East Indies. Underneath them was a pile of photos of ragged English soldiers, Americans, Australians, and New Zealanders, saluting their flags, probably right after they had been liberated from a concentration camp. Many of them were covered with bandages, or they were on crutches, their hands in slings, with months-old beards, long hair, skeletal bodies consumed by fever, dysentery, and malnutrition.

Alex offered me a match to light the cigarette hanging from my lips. I accepted it.

"They want me to return, but I'm staying here. They want to put me in a cage in Los Angeles. Have you heard the Mexican song 'Jaula de oro,' about a cage of gold?"

He started to walk toward the ocean. I tried to take him by the hand, but he freed himself with a quick movement.

"Don't you realize, Marlowe?"

He turned his back to me and continued toward the sea. Then he turned and looked at me with his ice-blue eyes. A wave broke near the shore; the sun was beginning to set.

I saw him hurl himself into the water, swimming madly straight into the horizon, foam rising with every stroke. The sun floated over the sea. Alex was going further and further away. Fifteen minutes later you could hardly see his head in the distance. Then it disappeared.

The sunsets in Baja California are unforgettable. I would have to return the money to the lawyer in Los Angeles. I turned my back to the sea. My joints ached. It must have been the humidity. I walked toward the Oldsmobile.

The first Spanish edition of The Long Goodbye *appeared in 1973. I read it three times. I added it to what I had learned from Simenon, Durrenmatt, Hammett, and Le Carré, and was certain that crime literature offered me the best possible scenario for the stories I wanted to tell. Three years later my novel was published. I don't know how much of Chandler was left in it; probably little, because what I was trying to do with* Dias de combate *was launch a new genre, the new crime novel in Mexico, and not simply follow the tradition of the hard-boiled with a change of scenery. But no doubt Chandler was there; in stories built on dialogue and characters and atmospheres, rather than anecdotes, but which still managed to tell a story. For me, influenced by the Mexican baroque and magical realism, neorealism in the style of Chandler was the best option. Maybe no one can find traces of these influences in my books; it's not that important. I know how to recognize my debts; I know that Chandler is there somewhere in my novels, and I'm grateful to him.*

Paco Ignacio Taibo II

CONSULTATION IN THE DARK

FRANCIS M. NEVINS, JR.

1946

N THE DEPTH of night I gave up trying to roll over the edge into sleep. It had been dark for a year and I had tossed around in the lumpy bed in unit six of that isolated auto court for six months. Too many hours behind the wheel of the U-drive coupe, too much road grub, gallons more coffee than I could handle, endless time to stew in the juices of loneliness—sleep was out of reach. I twisted free of the blankets and flicked on the bedlight. My watch curled on the night-stand read fourteen minutes after two. I decided to stroll around the auto court, breathe in some of the night's peace, look up at the stars I never could see in L.A. Later I wished to God I'd stood in bed.

The thirteen months since Hiroshima and the Jap surrender had been boom times for private investigators. Hundreds of newly discharged vets, maimed by the war in ways the military didn't care to deal with, were wandering across the map in a search for the missing pieces of themselves. Some of those guys had families willing to spend a little money to find them. A few lucky Joes had come into inheritances while they were over-seas, and the banks and law firms that were handling the estates needed their signatures on the paperwork. One of those banks happened to be my client. Which explains why a peeper by the name of Marlowe had boarded the Santa Fe Super Chief in L.A. and changed trains in Chicago and taken a local into the heart of the upper Midwest and hired himself a U-drive jalopy to follow a cold trail, and also how this same peeper wound up huddled in his prewar trenchcoat and pacing the perimeter of an auto court in the middle of nowhere on a crisp and star-speckled night in October 1946. The trail I was following turned out to be the wrong one. I learned weeks later that my lost vet had taken a new name and drifted east early in '46, and that in a fit of the screaming meemies he had jumped off the twelfth-floor ledge of a downtown Poughkeepsie hotel on Mother's Day, tying up traffic for an hour. The guy had been raised in the upper Midwest, the bank had a report that he'd been sighted there, but in fact there was no reason for me to have traipsed across that turf, none at all. Life likes to play cute tricks on us like that.

The auto court sat on a gentle rise a few hundred feet off the state highway. Most of its customers these days were relatives or buddies visiting one of the thousand-odd discharged servicemen using the G.I. Bill to pick up a degree at the branch of the state university a mile to the east, beyond the highway and some hills. In October the auto court was a graveyard. Keeping the line of cabins between myself and the road, all I could see was the night and a wedge of moon and the twinkling stars. The only sounds came from crickets, except when a trailer truck growled along the invisible highway. An owl swooped down from nowhere in total silence, almost brushing my face. I froze and waited for the scream of a rabbit being torn apart in the woods and heard nothing but the crickets. Maybe the owl was on a false trail too.

Then I heard a cough in the night and I wasn't alone anymore. A tall thin man, bareheaded, light-haired, several days of whitish stubble on his cheeks, darted out from the edge of the woods and planted himself between me and the row of cabins. He was wearing jeans and sneakers and what looked in the moonlight like an army fatigue jacket. "Mr. Marlowe, sir?" His voice was low, nervous. "Could I bother you for just a minute?"

I was startled by the sound of my own name half whispered in the night. The idea in setting up shop at the auto court for a few days had been to give people a chance to get in touch with me, help me out with leads to the vet I was hunting, but I hadn't expected anyone to sneak up on me out of the woods at half past two in the morning. I formed my face into a mask of professional politeness and looked at the man. He didn't look at me but through me, into the cold nothingness that surrounded us. I guessed his age as somewhere in the late twenties. He kept his pale gloveless hands dangling at his sides as if he wanted to make sure I didn't think he had a weapon. If he was my lost vet, I was Eleanor Roosevelt's hairdresser.

"I'm Marlowe," I told him, trying to keep my tone mildly amiable. "What can I do for you? And can't it wait till morning?"

"I saw the story in the county paper the other day," he said, still so softly I could just make out the words, "about the young G.I. who was raised around here and has come into some money, and how you're trying to locate him. The article said you were staying at unit six of this auto court for a few days. I've been out here since ten-thirty last night, but I decided it was too late to knock on your door. Then when I saw you come out for a walk I decided there was no reason to wait till morning. Thanks for saving me a cold night in the woods!" He laughed, a short harsh bark that made me think of wolves, and fumbled with the belt of his fatigue jacket. "I don't know anything about the fellow you're looking for, but I do have a problem of my own on which I'd value your help very highly indeed."

I tried to avoid his eyes and groped for a diplomatic way out of this unwanted consultation. "Look, kid," I said, "whatever your problem is, I can't help you. I'm a stranger here. I'm not licensed in this state. Maybe the cops, or some local private . . ."

"No one else will do!" he shrieked, and tore at his jacket's zipper. For one mad moment I was sure he was going to expose himself. Then I saw the squat black box belted around his waist like the change-making machines that trolley conductors wear.

"Can you see the button?" he asked me, soft and gentle as the beautiful maiden in a fairy tale. "No, I don't suppose you can. But if I press down on it," he said, "we both turn to dust. You see, Mr. Marlowe, this consultation is literally worth your life."

He didn't move and I didn't move. We stood there at the edge of the woods, perhaps ten feet apart. A thousand miles from us a lumbering freight truck's highway beams bleached a patch of hillside as it topped a rise and vanished. The crickets kept chattering as if the world were on an even keel.

"My name is Hume." The white-skinned young-old man gave me a wistful smile as he introduced himself. "Charles Henry Hume II. I'm sorry I can't offer you my hand, Mr. Marlowe, but if I did you just might grab it and try to undo my belt. Mind if we keep it formal?"

Somehow I managed a dumb nod into the night.

"It's not my own problem I need to discuss with you," Hume said. "It's that of—well, of my dearest friend. We'll call him Chuck. Poor Chuck is inhibited about being seen in public. I speak for him."

I gulped down the bile in my throat and breathed deep. Nothing like crisp clean night air to make a guy feel bursting with health.

"Chuck never knew his father." Hume's voice dropped another notch. I had a hunch that it wasn't me he was talking to. "His parents married when they were both in high school. They—they had to marry. Six months later they had a little girl, born prematurely, weighing less than two pounds. There was irreversible brain damage. The baby never lived to walk or talk. She died when she was four months old. Chuck's mother told him later that the child had the face of an angel. She became pregnant again, but a few months later Chuck's father was drafted and sent to fight in the war to end war. Remember that one, Mr. Marlowe? The year was nineteen-seventeen. Chuck's father never lived to see his son."

I peered into the star-punctuated darkness, hunting for Hume's face, trying to read in his expression whether he expected a reply or comment. The pale-stubbled features were blank as a granite slab. I took a chance, said something I hoped was innocuous.

"So his mother had to support herself and the boy?"

"Yes," he said. Nothing hostile in his tone or look, but his splayed fingers kept playing with that change-maker's belt.

"Even in the first war they had death benefits," I said. "Widows' pensions."

"The money they paid her you couldn't raise a dog on," Hume said. "She had to find a job. She went back to Louisiana where she had grown up, and a small businessman in Opelousas hired her as his secretary. But she hadn't trained for a real career—how many women do?—so she was never able to get ahead of the bills and save anything. She spent almost nothing on herself, just a Chaplin picture now and then. You know what she did for fun? She invented her own recipes for special dessert treats." He began to chuckle as if he could taste them as he talked, a low throaty sensuous sound that put a coating of ice along my backbone. "Those treats changed her life."

Another pause. I let it hang there, kept my mouth shut, waited for him to pick up the thread of the story.

"Ever hear of Louisiana Lady?" he asked.

It sounded like the name of a movie, maybe something with Dorothy Lamour and Bing Crosby. In another place and time I might have told him so. Not then, not there. A smart-mouth remark like that could kill us both.

"Louisiana Lady!" he repeated impatiently as if I were a backward child who hadn't done his homework. "The mail-order gourmet food business. Jellies, pastries, cakes. People send them to other people on special occasions."

Not in my line they don't. Maybe that's the trouble with being a private snoop, you don't get to meet many people you want to send gifts to. For the second time in ten minutes I chose prudence and kept my flip remark to myself.

"In the twenties and even during the Depression it was the most profitable business of its kind in the country," Hume said proudly, as if he had been its founder. "The fellow Chuck's mother worked for set it up for her. She created all the recipes. Suddenly she was a wealthy woman, and the hard work of marketing her products was done for her. Within a few years Chuck had a grand new life. Private tutors, servants, a second home up here in the hills where they spent half of each year." I thought I heard a low sob somewhere in his voice. "Except that along the road to riches he lost his mother."

"She married again?" I guessed.

Bad move. The question touched a raw nerve and he shrieked, "No! No! No!" and made me think of someone I had once heard shrieking like that when his face had collided with a barbed-wire fence. God, why didn't the auto court manager hear him and look out the window and see something was wrong and call the cops? Hume's fingers tapped a code message on the belt of his black box. For an instant I thought the two of us were dead. Then the next moment the unshaven young lunatic was calm as a summer lake at dawn.

"Several times a year," he said, "she'd go away for a week or ten days at a time. Even as a child Chuck dimly understood. A different man went with her each trip. She'd never bring any of them home. Oh, she was the soul of discretion." He gave another of those throaty chuckles.

I stood stiffly in the darkness and measured the distance between us and tried to nerve myself to risk a flying leap that would pin the madman to the ground, and I couldn't make myself do it. That kind of play was for movie heroes or their stuntmen, not for me. Maybe he was bluffing, maybe there were no explosives in that belt, and if I lived through this encounter and found out he'd run a bluff on me I might curse myself as a gutless wonder, but at least I'd be alive. This was too cold a night to die in for no reason.

"I understand her better than Chuck did at the time," Hume went on. "She had loved her husband and her first child so much, and then she'd lost them both less than a year apart, and afterward she just couldn't bring herself to make that kind of emotional commitment again, not to another man and not to Chuck. Oh, she recognized her obligations to the boy and went through the motions, but a child can tell the difference. Chuck grew up alone. He had no money worries but lived a withdrawn and solitary life." Hume began to giggle gently and moved a few steps closer to me until his back was against the trunk of a sycamore, or maybe it was an elm. "I was his only friend," he said.

I didn't want to ask him where the two boys had met, first because it might have prodded him to tap the button and second because I knew the answer already: somewhere behind his pale wormy eyebrows. With the cricket symphony as background music I was trying to figure my next move when all of a sudden the crickets had competition, and so did the stars. There was the hum of a well-tuned auto engine and the crunch of tires on gravel. Headlight beams painted a cone of acid whiteness in the woods and came pivoting along the tree trunks toward us like the searchlight in a prison-break movie as the invisible car rounded the corner of the building line and turned our way. "Down behind those rocks," Hume hissed. "Now!" He dived for cover and lay on his side, his right hand caressing the black box, forefinger poised above what I had to take for the trigger button. I didn't want whoever was in that car to be blown apart for no reason and I didn't want myself to be either. I hit the dirt Marine-style and crawled into the screen of bushes within Hume's line of sight but as far from his own position as I dared. We flattened ourselves against the earth as the headlights bathed the bushes for a few seconds. The car circled the rear of the auto court and braked at the far end of the building line, maybe a hundred feet from us, parking at an angle so that I could make out the state cop insignia on the driver's door. A heavyset guy in uniform shirt and trousers and Sam Browne belt slid out of the car and stretched and yawned in the dimness of his parking lights and sauntered to the edge of the woods and stood facing the tree line and fumbled with his pants for a moment and relieved himself. He sauntered back to the car and slid behind the wheel and put on his headlights and completed his circuit of the auto court. His taillights winked out around the far corner of the line of cabins. Hume stepped out from his cover and made a hand motion that ordered me to do the same. His other hand never strayed from his belt box. As soon as the crunch of the cop car's tires on gravel had receded into the noises of the night, Hume went on with his life story as if the interruption had been a dream.

"Chuck was a solitary adolescent," he said, "but he learned to amuse himself. In fine weather he'd stay outdoors for hours, catching insects that he later mounted, or sitting in the grass watching the squirrels and birds. Sometimes he'd sit out in the woods all night. On rainy days he'd play indoors, making clever little mechanical devices out of scraps of wood and metal. And he read constantly. Pulp detective magazines were his favorites. If he and his mother exchanged a dozen words a day it was a lot."

"Great life," I said.

"In the summer of nineteen-thirty, when Chuck was thirteen, that life ended. Their second home in the mountains was about sixty miles west of here, at the end of a dirt track that curved off from a two-lane paved road that wound around the mountainside like a macadam snake. Chuck used to call the road Old Twistibus." Hume raised his face to the crescent moon and in a sweet choirboy voice, to the tune of the old Christmas carol *O Tannenbaum*, he began to sing:

O Twistibus!
O Twistibus!
A corkscrew's straight
Beside thee.

My breath went ragged. The way he stood there at the edge of the tree line singing softly up at the stars told me we were both going to be dead or mutilated before morning if I didn't make exactly the right move soon. I started to edge closer to him. First we were a dozen feet apart, then ten, then eight or nine. A few more steps, another half minute of his fit of abstraction, and I'd be close enough to aim a quick kick into his groin and then pin his hands behind him before he could touch the trigger button.

Then right in the middle of one of his cockeyed verses he shoved out at me with both hands. I hit the ground hard on my left hip. The impact went through me like an explosion. Hume towered over me, right forefinger on the button, smiling inanely. "I can read your mind, Mr. Marlowe," he said politely. "And I'd really appreciate it if you would allow me to finish my story."

As if I could stop him while I lay there like a dummy.

"One muggy summer afternoon in nineteen-thirty, Chuck's mother went off in her Duesenberg to do some errands in the village at the foot of the mountain. She never made it. At one of the nastiest bends of Old Twistibus she lost control of the wheel and went over the cliff. The gas tank blew and she was burned to a cinder. The Duesenberg was left a twisted hunk of steel. Believe it or not, the police had the absurd idea that it wasn't an accident, that poor innocent thirteen-year-old Chuck had sabotaged the brakes or something and turned the car into a death trap. Well, I did say he was clever with mechanical devices. . . . Anyway, the experts examined the wreck and found no signs of tampering. But they couldn't figure why she'd lost control of the wheel. She was a careful driver and it hadn't rained in weeks, so there were no wet spots where she might have skidded. The only piece of possible physical evidence was the burned fragments of some sort of small cardboard box that they found down the mountain from the wreck, and they couldn't even prove she'd had that with her. And anyway Chuck was far too young to be prosecuted for murder even if they had found evidence."

I lay prone on the cold earth and tried to weigh my chances of seeing the sunrise.

"So there Chuck was," Hume said, "suddenly a millionaire at age thirteen. His mother's gourmet jellies and cakes selling like wildfire. Naturally a guardian had to be appointed for him till he turned twenty-one. All sorts of earnest lawyers popped out of the woodwork to volunteer their services. I wonder how many of them had slept with Chuck's mother. But after the will was read they all crawled back into their holes. Can you guess why, Mr. Marlowe?"

"She, she . . ." Tough guy private peeper couldn't make anything come out of his smart mouth but a stutter. "Didn't leave him anything?"

"She cut me out like a cancer!" He screamed the words into the night like the death cry of an animal being disemboweled by a predator. "No apology. No explanation. 'It is my intent that no part of my estate shall pass to my son Charles Henry Hume II.' Can you see what a blow to Chuck that was?" The split between the two halves of him was wide open again. "She was flogging him from her grave, the bitch! Everything—the house and land, the stock in Louisiana Lady, personal effects—everything went to endow a foundation to do research into brain damage in newborn babies." He pointed into the far distance, beyond the highway and the hills. "That foundation is on the campus of the state U a mile from here."

My only interest that night was in living through it, but keeping him talking looked like the best way to do that, so I asked him a question. "You contested her will?" Good boy, Marlowe. Logical query under the circumstances, the voice halfway under control. There may be hope for you yet.

"The local lawyers said I had no grounds," he told me. "Oh, I was handed a few scraps. Exempt property, a maintenance award, stuff an unmarried minor child is entitled to in this state no matter what the will says. Didn't amount to a hill of beans next to the value of Louisiana Lady." He looked at me the way a snake looks at the bird it wants for breakfast and nervously licked his lips. "I suppose you're wondering how I've lived since then."

I didn't like his oh-so-casual tone and I liked even less the way he arched his upper body over me waiting for my answer. Survival instinct told me he was setting a trap. "I don't wonder anything," I mumbled.

"Oh yes you do, you do, you do!" That disemboweled-animal howl again, cutting the darkness like a butcher knife. "I've been locked up and let out and locked up again! My mother—my lawyer—my life—" Maybe he said "wife," I couldn't be sure. "I'm a victim too! Don't you care about justice, Mr. Marlowe? I want my life back. Everything that's mine has been taken from me."

"Sounds like you need a new lawyer," I said.

He let loose a horselike snort of disgust. "Lawyers are jackals. A lawyer stole my inheritance. I need a detective. I need you." He slithered closer to me as I lay still on the hard-packed ground. When he bent over me like a combat medic ministering to a wounded soldier I saw a tear forming in one eye. "Help me. Defend poor Chuck's rights. If A is planning to kill C but C has a detective dig up all the dirt in A's filthy past and C tells A that all that dirt will become public knowledge if anything happens to C—well, that guarantees C a long and happy life." I had no idea what he was babbling about. He wiped his jacket sleeve across his eyes, and the tears were replaced by the sly serpentine look I had seen there before. His finger strayed toward the belt button. "Help me. Be my detective. Save your own life."

This time his groin was within range of my foot. I kicked out with everything I had and he let loose an agonized whoop that was music to my ears and doubled over on his knees with his hands clutched to his testicles. That put my hands within reach of his face. I wasn't gentle with him. When he stopped thrashing around I whipped off the belt of my trenchcoat and tied his hands behind him and pulled off his shoes and socks so that even if he came to and got loose he couldn't run far. The mechanism around his middle I didn't touch or even stare at too closely. My breathing was still a wheeze when I stumbled across the rear lot of the auto court and around to the front and kicked in the door of the cabin marked MANAGER and hit the light switch and found the phone and asked the operator to put me through to the state police.

"You bet your ass it was a real bomb. Disposal squad just finished deactivating it." Major Fry, the officer in charge of the neighborhood cop barracks, was no taller than Alan Ladd and had a roll of fat around his belly that would have fed a European refugee camp for a week. He poured coffee from the pot in his private office into two chipped mugs and splashed in tots of whiskey from a bottle he pulled out of a file drawer. Through the dirty windows fronting on the barracks parking lot I watched the sun glow over the eastern hills. "Dynamite and percussion caps stolen from a highway crew the other day. He wasn't kidding about how good he is with mechanical devices. That auto court would have turned into a twenty-foot crater if he'd pressed the button."

"Christ," I muttered, and downed half the cupful in a gulp. The overboiled coffee made roadside java taste like nectar of the gods, and the raw hooch must have been left over from Prohibition. I had never enjoyed a drink so much. "I'm meant to live a while yet."

"If you're a good boy," Fry said, and glanced at his wristwatch. "Miss

Dunkel ought to be here any minute now, Marlowe. She wants to thank you personally for the way you handled the situation and, ah, her client." Miss Amanda Dunkel, he'd told me earlier, was Hume's lawyer, and I got the distinct impression she was a big noise in this state. "She'd rather you didn't press charges against the kid. I feel the same way. Let nature take its course."

"He's a loony," I said. "Someone has to put him away. Jail or the nut farm, doesn't matter where. You'll need me to testify about what happened."

"Marlowe," he sighed, "we need you like we need higher taxes. As soon as Miss Dunkel has thanked you properly we're packing your valise and escorting you out of here. But just so you won't get too curious and come back poking around, I'm going to tell you a few things. Have you figured out why Hume talks about himself as if he were two people?"

"I can make an educated guess." I downed the rest of the spiked coffee and held back a shudder. "Back when he was thirteen years old, he killed his mother."

"Smart peeper. I was new on the force when it happened but I got a good memory. I bet you could even tell me how he did it to her."

"Not in detail," I said. "But my guess is it was another cute mechanical device. He said the cops found fragments of a small cardboard box on the mountainside near where his mother had the crackup. Was that it?"

Fry's jowls wobbled like gelatin mold as he nodded. "He'd caught some hornets and stuffed them into that box and rigged it so the top would fly off a couple minutes after he set the thing on the front seat of her Duesenberg. The lid flew up and the hornets flew out and all over her and she lost control of the wheel just like he'd counted on and the car went over the cliff. We think he got the idea from one of those pulp detective magazines he was always reading. It was clever enough for a thirteen-year-old but it only fooled us for a few hours. Of course he was too young to be charged with murder, so they sent him to an institution where he belonged. Then eight or nine years ago Miss Dunkel came into the picture and got him out. A lady with money and clout, Marlowe. One of her brothers is on the state supreme court and the other's lieutenant governor. When the kid was free she started a suit to overturn his mother's will."

"Yeah," I said. "He mentioned something about that too. Said there were no grounds."

"He misspoke himself." Fry swept his pudgy hand toward the steel-gray bookcase behind his desk. I noticed then that most of the volumes on the shelves were law school casebooks. "I take night law courses at the state U when I have the time. Hume was right that in this state and almost every other state a parent can cut a child out of a will for any reason or no reason. But Miss Dunkel's got brains as well as money and clout. She didn't file suit here, she did it in Louisiana, where the Humes had lived half of each year. Louisiana's the only state in the union where the law isn't based on English common law, it's based on the Napoleonic Code. They've got a rule called *legitime* that says if you have a child and die with a will, you have to leave the kid at least one-third of your property. You can't disinherit a child except for just cause. Mrs. Hume's will was drafted by a lawyer up here, not in Louisiana, and the guy never figured it might be contested under Louisiana law, so the will didn't give any reason at all why the boy was cut out and everything was left to set up that medical research facility. Well, after Miss Dunkel had the kid released from the loony bin, she claimed his mother had died—what's the damn word?—domiciled in Louisiana and filed suit down there to give him his *legitime*. The case was settled. Twenty-five per cent of Louisiana Lady's annual income goes into a trust fund for Hume's benefit. Guess who's the trustee."

I heard the crunch of tires on gravel and saw a gleaming black 1939 Cadillac sedan turn into the front yard of the barracks building. A wizened chauffeur in livery opened the rear door and out came a biscuit-faced peroxide blonde at least fifty years old and fifty pounds overweight, wrapped in a tentlike ankle-length car coat which she wore like a royal robe of office. She gestured to the old geezer to watch the Cadillac and rolled majestically toward the guardpost at the front door.

"She got a settlement that good? Major, I've never been to law school but isn't there a rule that a murderer isn't allowed to benefit from his crime and can't inherit from his victim?"

"Sure is." I detected a note of impatience in his voice. "Damn good rule, too. Otherwise everybody'd be killing everybody else for inheritance money and we wouldn't have a civilized society. So what? Remember, because of his age and his mental condition Hume was never convicted of murder. The rule doesn't apply." He jerked his thumb toward the window in which the Cadillac was framed. "That was her argument anyway. Now, Marlowe, before that fat bitch waddles in here and I can't talk freely, let me ask you one more question. If anything should happen to young Hume, who do you suppose would come into the money he gets each year from the settlement?"

I was tired of guessing and tired of talking and sick of the smell of corruption. I kept my mouth glued and let him tell me.

"It goes to her," Fry said. "You see, Marlowe, after she got him out of the asylum she had one of her judge friends certify he was sane again, and then she married him and they made wills in each other's favor. They live in the fanciest house in the country, up in the hills fifty miles from here. Used to belong to Hume's mother. I've heard rumors she keeps him locked in the basement. Looks like he flew the coop a couple nights ago. Anyway, I figure someday soon she's going to make an accident happen to him or he'll make one happen to her, and I'm just letting nature take its course like I said. I'll be waiting for the survivor."

So that's what Hume had been babbling about just before I had kicked him. A heavy knock sounded on the door, and the overstuffed fiftyish phony blonde who would have reaped another fortune if her young husband had blown himself and me to powder in the woods behind the auto court billowed across the office and extended a cool plump hand and with a queenly smile fixed on her mouth but not in her eyes she murmured thanks.

I turned in the U-drive and caught a bus to Chicago, where I promoted myself a Pullman on the next Super Chief to L.A. With every added mile of distance between myself and the affairs of Mr. and Mrs. Charles Henry Hume II I felt cleaner, but I couldn't get to sleep. At fourteen after two in the morning I was sitting alone in the rear lounge car, staring out the window at the farmhouse lights winking by in the black void, wondering which of that pair of intertwined spiders would empty its venom sac first into the other.

A lot of the mystery writers I know are Chandler junkies and almost all of them got hooked when they were in their early teens, the years when we find or are handed most of our passions. I'm the oddball. I read The Big Sleep *when I was fourteen or fifteen and didn't like it. It left me confused and disturbed as I had never been by the classical detective fiction I was used to. I was several years older when I read* Farewell, My Lovely *and* The Long Goodbye *and understood precisely what gifts Chandler had that most of his contemporaries didn't. I still think his best work is endlessly rereadable, but I've never been tempted to try writing in his style. In "Consultation in the Dark" I've tried to be evocative of Chandler's motifs and approaches without imitating them too slavishly. The true Chandler junkies among both the writers and readers of this book will surely let me know if I've pulled it off.*

Francis M. Nevins, Jr.

IN THE JUNGLE OF CITIES

ROGER L. SIMON

1947

T HEY SAID THE Kraut was a Commie and he sure seemed strange to me. I was introduced to him by another Kraut with the unpronounceable name of Feuchtwanger and they said *he* was a *phenomenologist*. I didn't know whether that was better or worse than a Communist, but my friend Eddie seemed impressed. Eddie was a screenwriter.

It all began on a torrid Sunday in October when my neighbor with the pockmarked face was determinedly weeding every inch of his dichondra bed even though the temperature was cresting ninety-four. Eddie peeled up in a brand new Buick convertible that made it look as if Jack Warner had just given him the assignment of a lifetime. I wasn't used to Eddie this way. He was usually unemployed about nine months a year and rarely wrote anything more important than voice-overs for Daffy Duck cartoons.

"Hey, Marlowe," he said, leaning out of the Buick with that self-satisfied grin of the new-car owner. "How's the wheel of fortune treating you?"

"Not half as well as you, Eddie, I see."

"Yeah, well, a couple of writers named Reynolds and Lipman got the sackaroo and I ended up with a new term contract at Metro. Won't give you the exact figures but let me tell you it's enough to switch to the imported stuff. And I've got an office in the Thalberg Building too. . . . Hey, ever met a genuine literary celebrity?"

"Sure, Eddie. You. Weren't you writing an historical novel once? What was it about? Ancient Greece?"

"The Punic Wars," said Eddie. He looked insulted that I didn't remember, although as far I knew, he had never finished the book. He had bills to pay, he frequently explained, and there were a lot of hungry writers nipping at his heels for those coveted Daffy Duck slots. "There's a party tonight I want you to come to. You'll meet some *real* intellectuals."

"You mean the rest of the Daffy Duck staff?"

He didn't think it was funny. "I'm talking about Mann," he said. "*Thomas* Mann! And Feuchtwanger—the phenomenologist." I didn't bother to ask what that was at the time because I had a sneaking suspicion Eddie couldn't explain it anyway. But I had to admit the name Mann did mean something to me. He was one of those German eggheads who had escaped to L.A. during the war in order to avoid ending up as one of Schickelgruber's lampshades. I could hardly say I blamed them.

Then Eddie leaned over the side of his convertible and whispered to me. "I think Bertolt Brecht is going to be there. You know—the Commie who writes plays."

"I thought knowing Commies was bad news for guys in your racket, Eddie. Fella could be out of a job faster than you can say Josef von Stern-berg. And I hear they keep a list."

"Paranoia." He waved dismissively. "Look, I'll give you a ride in my new short. Come around seven." He winked conspiratorially. "I think there's a job in it for you."

I didn't have the slightest idea what that could be and even less of an idea when I walked into the party that night in Feuchtwanger's Spanish house overlooking Santa Monica Canyon. It didn't help matters that most of the people there were speaking foreign languages. They were congregated in a living room lined with more books than any store in L.A., if that meant anything, listening to a scruffy Russian with thick eyebrows play peculiar-sounding music on the piano with no discernible melody.

When the music stopped, I heard some Brit who looked nancy talking about short stories he was writing about Berlin and then some lady named Anita holding forth on what barbarians the movie moguls were. I had been around film people enough to know this kind of bitching was pretty standard fare and was relieved when a pinch-faced man took me and Eddie by the arm.

"I am Lion Feuchtwanger," he said, leading us into another book-lined study. I must say he pronounced it very well. "And this is Bertolt Brecht . . . Mr. Marlowe, Mr. Brecht."

He nodded to a small nearly bald man in a severe black leather jacket puffing a cheap cigar and staring at us through a monocled eye that seemed to penetrate every secret you ever had or imagined.

"Marlowe's what they call in America a shamus," Feuchtwanger said to Brecht, indicating me with some amusement. The playwright didn't react but continued to puff his cigar, staring at me in that same penetrating, unnerving manner.

"He's one of the best," said Eddie, talking me up in a way that somehow I felt didn't mean much to the German refugee.

"So what do I want him for?" Brecht said at length in heavily accented, but entirely grammatical English.

Feuchtwanger glanced over at Eddie. "As Mr. Brackwell has explained, it will be necessary to have a bodyguard." Feuchtwanger turned to me. "On Tuesday next, Herr Brecht will testify as a friendly witness before your House Un-American Activities Committee investigation of the motion picture industry."

"A *friendly* witness?" I made no attempt to hide my astonishment. The newspapers had been filled of late with reports of the ongoing HUAC investigation of Hollywood lefties with much discussion of "unfriendly" and "friendly" witnesses—the "unfriendly" being those who stood on their rights, shut up, and looked as if they were headed for the slammer; the "friendly" being those who talked to the committee, ratted on their buddies, and continued to work. That didn't sound like Brecht.

"Is this true?" I asked him.

Brecht simply nodded.

I looked from him to Eddie and Feuchtwanger, wondering what was up. "I don't get it," I said. "If you're going to be a 'friendly' witness, why don't you get the feds to guard you?"

"I will not have those people around me under any circumstances," said the playwright with a sudden vehemence.

"Hey, we're only doing this for your benefit, Bert," said Eddie. "The committee's going to want you to name names and—"

"I will tell the truth as I know it. That is all."

"But you promised you'd allow someone to stay with you until you testified. If you don't cooperate, you can't expect them to cooperate with you. It's the American way. Besides, they could deport you and that'd be the end of your contract with Republic. Weren't you going to write the next Laughton picture?"

The playwright half smiled, inhaling on his cheap cigar. "All right," he said. "As you say, a deal is a deal. I hope you like schnapps, Mr. Marlowe?"

"Never tried 'em."

That night I did. I sat in the kitchen of Brecht's place drinking schnapps while the playwright read some books. The schnapps weren't bad but the books looked inscrutable. But this didn't deter the Kraut, who pored over them, jotting down quotes and underlining phrases.

"What're you reading?" I asked finally.

"My own plays."

"You don't know them already?"

"More or less. But I want to see which ones sound as if they are written by a Communist. The committee will no doubt ask me about them, and since they have surely not read any of them, I will be able to substitute one for the other and leave them completely confused."

"Not a bad plan," I allowed. "So I take it, Mr. Brecht, that you are a Commie . . ."

"Of course I am. And a capitalist. And an atheist. And a believer. And a lot of other things."

"Sounds a little inconsistent, if you don't mind my saying so."

"I am a writer, Mr. Marlowe, and that is my job—to be a lightning rod for ideas. To try them on the way other people do winter coats. If I didn't, I would be terrible at what I did. And a coward."

"Are you going to tell the committee that?"

"I do not think they would understand it. In fact, I do not think they would understand the truth about anything. Besides, those of us who have lived in Germany recently have a habit of distrusting politicians. And I have the distinct impression things will get worse here before they get better. . . . And now, if you will excuse me, I must get some rest."

And with that he nodded to me, stubbed out his cigar, and left. I sat there a moment before pulling over his stack of books for a look-see. They were all in German and I was about to push them aside when I saw an envelope sticking out of the bottom one. It had an Air France logo on the front, and inside was a one-way ticket to Paris in Brecht's name for October 31—the day after he was scheduled to talk to the House committee.

I was mulling that one over when there was a sharp tap on the window near where I was sitting. Eddie was standing outside motioning for me to come out and gesturing across the street.

I met him under a jacaranda tree standing next to a wire-haired man with the ramrod posture of a retired Eagle Scout.

"This is Mr. Pierson," said Eddie, nodding toward the wire-haired man, who flipped open his wallet. An F.B.I. badge glinted in the reflection of a streetlamp. "We were wondering if you'd seen anything."

"What do you mean?"

"You know—anybody call, come by, anything suspicious?"

"I haven't seen anything. And I thought you worked for Metro, Eddie. On a term contract."

"Of course I do. But these are difficult times. These guys need help."

"Some of the writers around here are a little naive," said Pierson. "They think some kind of witch-hunt's going on, but the security of the nation's at stake. And we just want to be sure the Kraut'll be straight with the committee on Tuesday. Otherwise he's gonna land in stir with the rest of those pinkos."

"Uh-huh," I said.

"Now don't be gettin' smart, Marlowe," said Eddie. "I vouched for you, you know. And remember who's paying your salary."

"Yeah. Just who *is* paying?" I cracked, but continued before they could say anything. "But don't worry. I haven't seen or heard anything. And if I do, you'll be the first to know. . . . Now buzz off before the Kraut starts getting suspicious." And with that I headed back across the street, leaving them standing under the jacaranda.

Brecht was waiting in the kitchen when I got there.

"Who was that?" he asked.

"**J. Edgar Hoover's younger brother. When's your flight to Washington?**"

"Tomorrow evening."

"Too late. They're looking for any excuse to hang you, and they're not beyond a plant if you don't do it to yourself first." I paced about a moment. "Let's get you on the morning flight. I think there's one at seven a.m. I'll drive you to the airport. And do yourself a favor—between now and then, don't answer the phone and don't talk to anybody. And when you get to Washington, lay low, don't let anybody know where you are, and keep your mouth shut. . . . Now get some rest. And by the way . . ." I flipped open the book and handed him the Air France envelope. "Whatever you do, hide your Paris ticket."

Brecht stood there a moment, silently digesting this until we heard the car drive off. Then he took his pen and started to autograph one of his books to me.

"Don't bother," I said.

"It is *The Three-Penny Opera*," said Brecht with some pride in his voice.

"Yeah, I heard of it," I shrugged. "But I could never read German."

The playwright nodded and went to bed, but I could see he was hurt. These writers are very sensitive about their stuff.

Three days later I caught his testimony in the paper. I had to admit it was pretty funny. The Kraut pretended he could barely speak English and he ran so many rings around the committee by the time they were through with him they were begging him to leave. Some of it went like this:

Committee: Have you attended any Communist Party meetings?
Brecht: No, I don't think so. . . .
Committee: Well, aren't you certain?
Brecht: No—I am certain, yes.
Committee: You are certain you have never been to Communist Party meetings?
Brecht: Yes, I think so. . . .
Committee: You are certain?
Brecht: I think I am certain.
Committee: You think you are certain?
Brecht: Yes, I have not attended such meetings, in my opinion.

That appeared in the paper on November 1, the same day Brecht arrived at his final destination, Switzerland. At the same time, I decided to drive over to M.G.M. Studios to take care of some unfinished business. I slipped a sawbuck to the guard to let me through the gate, parked directly in front of the Thalberg Building, and hurried inside. I didn't stop at the reception desk but waltzed right by the secretary like a producer who had just signed a two-picture deal with Rita Hayworth.

Eddie Brackwell's office was on the third floor with a corner view of the entire lot and was more than big enough to write an encyclopedia, let alone a script. It had a couple of mock Louis XV couches and a Chippendale bar filled with enough champagne for an Oscar party.

Eddie was sharing a glass of the bubbly with a starlet when I came in and didn't look too pleased to see me, so I walked straight over to him and disconnected the phone before he could call the security service.

"Didn't you get your check, Marlowe?" he said, looking at me strangely.

"Sure did, Eddie. And I split it up the moment I got it for the old tenants of this office. I sent half of it to Mike Lipman and his family, who are living down in Mexico now that you cost him his writing job. And the other to Sherman Reynolds, who's back in New York trying to stay out of jail because you bastards smeared him."

"You didn't save anything for yourself?" he asked, his voice squeaking.

"No. I wanted something else for payment."

And with that I let him have a left to the solar plexus and a vicious right to the head. He flew backward into the Chippendale, breaking the glass and crumpling to the floor. Blood trickled from his forehead as I stared down at him.

"You know, Eddie, you guys don't give a good goddamn whether these guys are Communists or what they are—Brecht or anybody else. You just want their jobs, you pathetic assholes!"

Then I kicked him one for good measure and left, leaving the starlet screaming like a lost ingenue at a casting call.

Let me be blunt. Raymond Chandler saved my life. This is how it happened:

In my early twenties, I published two novels to respectful reviews and virtually no sales and, like many writers before me, hied myself to Los Angeles to take a shot at the screen trade. But also like many before me I didn't exactly get a kick out of sleaze balls with German cars and Spanish houses telling me what to write.

So I saved my money and tried my hand at another novel which was even more "literary" and unsalable than the previous two. I could see that in the eyes of my friend Alan Rinzler, who had just been appointed head honcho of Rolling Stone's *new publishing division, when he was reading the manuscript in the back yard of my house in L.A.'s Echo Park.*

"This is pretty good," he said, sounding like a freshman English teacher grading a paper. "But couldn't you do something more . . . Rolling Stone?"

I racked my brain. The Stone *was hot (this was 1972) and I sure wanted to work for it, but nothing came to mind when I blurted, as if out of nowhere: "Y'know, I've been reading a lot of Raymond Chandler lately.* Farewell, My Lovely. The Long Goodbye. . . . *Somebody oughta update the old genre. Do a private dick of our generation—hip, political, you know . . . a longhair."*

"Great idea," said Alan, dollar signs exploding under his Afro cut. "What do you want to call him?"

"Moses Wine," I replied, as quickly as that. I didn't give it any more thought.

Three months later, The Big Fix *was finished.*

Now, in May 1988, my sixth Wine novel is about to come out. They've been published in fourteen languages in umpteen editions and made into a film. Thanks, Ray.

Roger L. Simon

STAR BRIGHT

JOHN LUTZ

1948

FEED A NICKEL to the jukebox, Marlowe," Artie Duke told me. I did. Frank Sinatra started crooning about perfect love. I thought, Frankie should know.

Artie winked at the teenage waitress as she sashayed over to our booth with his toast and eggs. Artie was about fifty, a weasely little guy with a greasy black pompadour and ears that stuck out like open car doors. He was sporting a natty, double-breasted gray suit with white stripes not quite as wide as bowling alleys, and a withered red carnation from yesterday still snagged on a lapel.

I'd ordered only coffee. It was too early in the morning for food. Too early for Artie. Too early for Frank Sinatra. Especially too early for that.

Artie was the publisher of *Duke and Duchess*, a low-level Hollywood magazine that revealed "inside information" on the stars but specialized in predicting success for struggling young actors and actresses. Mostly actresses, because they provided the magazine with plenty of cheesecake layouts. *Duke and Duchess* wasn't quite a plain-brown-wrapper kind of magazine, but Hollywood dealt in sex, sublime or otherwise. Flesh was the name of Artie's game.

On a case I'd worked on in forty-seven, last year, Artie had provided me with information I couldn't have obtained elsewhere. I owed him a favor. He'd phoned last night and set up this meeting at the Meteor Diner on Figueroa to tell me how I could settle the debt. In my business, private investigation, it was the kind of debt I had to pay, and Artie knew it. And Artie never left leverage unused.

"I ain't gonna ask you to do anything sleazy," he said around a mouthful of toast, spraying the back of my hand with spittle and crumbs. "I mean, one thing about me's I got a certain amount of class."

I didn't argue with him. After all, he ate his eggs with a fork. I sipped

179

my coffee, gazed past dead flies out the grease-spotted window, waited. The traffic signal at the corner bonged, and a parade of cars accelerated in a cloud of exhaust fumes that rose wavering in the hot morning air. Some of the fumes found their way into the diner.

Artie spooned so much sugar into his coffee I thought I might get cavities from watching. When he stopped shoveling he said, "Has to do with murder."

Swell. "Who's the lucky victim?"

"Photog name of Corcoran."

"One of your photographers?"

"Naw, free-lancer. But he did some work for us now and then on contract."

"Cops know who bumped him?"

"Cops know from nothin'." Artie used his toast to sop up egg yellow and concentrated for a while on eating. He swallowed, loud, and said, "Corcoran phoned me a few days ago all excited. Said he had a layout on a new blonde bombshell, a sexy sorta child-woman Warner Brothers is planning on making into a major star within a year. The studio's keeping it all hush-hush, but I told him I wanted her photos for the magazine. Offered him plenty, too."

"Pay him before he died?"

"Sure."

I doubted it, knowing Artie. Just thinking about money caused his fingers to break out with glue. "So you want me to get the photographs."

"And find out the girl's name and address."

I was surprised. "You don't know her name?"

"First name only. Ella Lou. But that's her real name. I got no idea what her stage name's gonna be; maybe whoever's handling her ain't even picked one out yet. She's that fresh on the market." Artie wiped his mouth with the back of a hand. He'd finished breakfast the same time Sinatra finished singing. Body and soul were sated.

"So what's the problem?" I asked. "You go to Corcoran's office and search through the files till you find an Ella Lou. Get your pictures and her address."

Artie shook his head so violently his ears flapped. "Uh-uh, Marlowe. I ain't goin' anywheres near that place. This has gotta be on the Q.T. The cops have got Corcoran's office sealed and maybe they're even watching it in case whoever rubbed him out comes back. That's why I need you to figure a way in, get me what I need."

I added more cream to my java and stirred, tapped the spoon handle a few times lightly and musically on the mug's rim. What Artie had told me didn't feel right. I said, "This girl really that big a deal?"

His narrow little eyes flared so you could almost see the pupils. "Corcoran told me the camera loves her more'n anybody he ever pointed a lens at. He wasn't a man that raved about much, Marlowe, but he raved about this Ella Lou whazzername." He straightened up and sat back in the red padded booth with something like indignity, as if struck by delayed shock that I should ask such a question. *"She that big a deal?* Damn right she is! That's why she's being kept under wraps by the people wanna make millions outta her if she hits right, which is just how she'll hit. This little gal's a genuine can't-miss proposition. You know how rare that is?"

"Rare enough I never saw one." I tossed back my head and drained my coffee mug. The sun had edged across the sky and was beating in through the window, warming my right shoulder and arm. I wanted to get out of there, away from Artie Duke, and fulfill my obligation to him. Get it over with like a trip to the dentist and then move on to things more pleasant.

He was studying me, absently probing with a fingernail at a morsel lodged between his crooked front teeth.

"Okay," I told him, "It doesn't sound like much. I'll give you a call when I get what you need."

He handed me a folded piece of jagged-edged paper with the address of Corcoran's studio scrawled on it in black ink, and I tossed a dime and a nickel on the table and stood up. One of the coins spun with a descending, noisy clatter.

"By the way," I said, "how'd the photographer get it?"

Artie grinned kind of funny, like he might be sick to his stomach and tasting metal. "Shot behind the ear, finally."

"Finally? Isn't it always final when somebody shoots somebody else behind the ear?"

"I mean, after he was tortured."

"Tortured how?"

"I dunno. Burned with cigarettes and all. And I heard stuff was done to him with a knife."

I knew then why Artie chose to have me go after the photographs rather than going in himself. But if that question was answered, a lot more were raised.

He was still beaming that silly half grin at me, a spot of egg yellow on his chin. I gave him a good-bye nod and got out of there. The heat bouncing off the pavement on Figueroa slammed into me like a truck.

I felt a little nauseated myself as I crossed the street, and I wondered if I was wearing the same sickly look I'd seen on Artie. I didn't like murder. It could be messy. For the victim. For the murderer.

For the detective.

Corcoran's studio was on Alameda, a low, beige stucco building with flowering jacarandas out front and a sign that said Jack Corcoran Portraits in flowing red letters on a gray background. I drove past it slowly in second gear and saw a black '48 Ford coupé with a chopped-off antenna parked half a block down. There was a musclehead type slouched behind the steering wheel, actually pretending to read a newspaper. Even cops were going to the movies these days.

I parked in the next block and cut through a grassy field dotted with orange trees. A million insects droned and chirped that I was trespassing, and a warm breeze brought me a sweet scent of blossoms that clung like cheap perfume.

Back on concrete, I made my way down a narrow gangway and located the back of Corcoran's studio. I'd made sure the cops didn't have the place staked out in back, only assigned the block-jawed newspaper buff to keep watch for whoever might come by the studio to see Corcoran, not knowing he'd been killed.

It was easy to force a rear window and climb inside. Illegal, but easy. Too many laws worked that way.

I found myself in a vast, well-lighted room with high windows, pale gray walls, and a plank floor. There were photographic backdrops propped all over the place: stand in the right spot and you could be at the beach, in front of a snow-peaked mountain, in a plush boudoir, or in New York. Here, in Los Angeles, there was a three-section, silk Chinese folding screen in one corner that set off the area Corcoran had used as an office.

Sidestepping a bulky Speed-Graphic camera on a tripod, and a tilted white umbrella used for deflecting light, I walked over to the desk and file cabinets behind the screen. I moved quietly, as if the plainclothes cop outside in the Ford had rabbit ears and might hear me.

Alongside the desk, I noticed I was standing in the middle of a large dark stain. At the stain's edge was a yellow chalk outline of a man curled in the fetal position. I moved off the ugly stain and got down to business, keeping in mind that murderers did now and then return to the scene of the crime, death having given birth to the death wish.

Since I didn't know Ella Lou's last name, I started with the top file drawer and worked my way down. The gray folders were stuffed with photographs and personal information; usually eight-by-ten glossy shots of

Hollywood hopefuls, mostly women, and their vital statistics. I thumbed through this jumble of perfect teeth and clear eyes and flawless flesh until finally I spotted Ella Lou's name after a comma and her last name, Harrison. The blue, typed info sheet in her folder said she was seventeen years old, five foot two, a natural blonde, and measured 36-24-36. They all measured 36-24-36.

Also, her folder contained no photographs.

Quickly I rummaged through other folders, other drawers. Hers appeared to be the only folder in which there were no photographs. That was odd. This was, after all, Corcoran's photo file.

It didn't take me long to figure out why Corcoran had been tortured before his death. He'd known what his assailants would want and had hidden the photographs. The torture was to get him to say where.

I looked again at the bloodstain that had seeped into the hardwood floor. I was sure Corcoran had talked, or he'd still be alive somewhere— wishing he were dead.

It would be a waste of time to search the studio for the photos of Ella Lou. Anyway, the cops had no doubt made a thorough, routine search, and even they probably would have stumbled across hidden photos of a can't-miss blonde bombshell. It was a good bet that whoever had killed Corcoran now had the Ella Lou photographs.

The question was why. It was a question I knew I had to answer, not just for Artie but for myself.

And maybe for Ella Lou Harrison.

I unclipped my Eversharp from my shirt pocket and copied Ella Lou's address on the slip of paper Artie had given me in the diner. Then I left the same way I'd entered.

The plainclothes cop was still looming behind the steering wheel of the black Ford, sweating and pretending to read about how Dewey was sure to stomp Truman.

Hadn't even turned the page.

Half an hour later, I rang the bell of a three-story rooming house on Franklin whose address I'd gleaned from Ella Lou Harrison's file. Years ago a palm tree had been planted too close to the house, and its swaying fronds rattled gently against the clapboard siding. Sounded like a lazy typist who now and then got a burst of energy. Oleander bushes with fragrant red flowers ran wild beyond the porch rail.

On the other side of the door, floorboards creaked like the moans of the damned. Then the door opened, and a stocky, gray-haired woman about sixty stood squarely blocking my path. She was wearing a wrinkled flower-print dress, with sagging bobby socks and what looked to be nurses' regulation white shoes. Foot trouble. Varicose veins slightly thinner than ropes were networked over her unshaved legs. She had droopy, watery eyes and a dewlapped jaw, and she glared at me in the manner of a mastiff whose bone I'd just snatched.

I said, "I'd like to see Ella Lou Harrison."

"I'm Mrs. Galton, owner and manager here. Who should I say's callin'?"

"Philip Marlowe. Tell her it's about some photographs."

The woman's weary blue eyes got flinty and suspicious. "What kinda photographs?"

"I'll discuss that with Miss Harrison."

"Not today, you won't. She ain't home. Ain't been home the past week."

I felt the flesh on the back of my neck trying to bunch up. Once it got started, murder could be as contagious as the common cold.

"I'm a private detective," I said, and flashed her my I.D. "I've been hired to find Ella Lou."

"Private detectives ain't real cops."

"There aren't many real cops, even on the department."

"Just 'cause the family hired you, that don't mean you got special rights."

"Nope." I didn't bother correcting her assumption that I was working for Ella Lou's family.

Mrs. Galton propped her fists on her wide hips. "The old man called me all the way from Missouri day before yesterday. Said him and the missus was worried about their daughter 'cause she hadn't phoned when she was s'pose to. Way I see it, they was lookin' for me to put their minds at ease. But I couldn't do nothin' but tell 'em the truth, which is I ain't seen Ella Lou the past week and her bed's not been slept in."

"What did the old man say to that?"

"Said thank you and hung up, is what he did. Sounded all choked up and mad."

"How about if I look over Ella Lou's room?"

She said no to my request; it was against her rules. Said yes to the three dollars peeking out between the fingers of my right hand. Rules were rules, but commerce was king.

"First door at the top of the stairs," she said, as I was climbing the creaking steps. "You won't find nothin', though, 'cause that big fella was here before you."

I turned and looked down at her. "Big fella? A cop?"

She grinned with yellow teeth. "Real cops don't slip me money like you and him did."

"What did he look like?"

" 'Bout twice the size of you, with red hair and a mean smile."

"What did he say?"

"Same as you, that he was sent by the family to find Ella Lou. Only he said he was a friend, not a private dick."

I went on up the stairs, and the old woman followed and let me into a small furnished room. After closing the door, I listened to her clomp back down the steps.

I was looking at faded, rose-pattern wallpaper, dark mahogany furniture, a drab gray carpet with paths worn in it. Here was the kind of impoverished environment beginning show-biz types traditionally lived in, and then escaped from when they were discovered pumping gas or waiting tables. That was the dream, anyway, before it faded like the wallpaper.

I looked in vain for a photograph of Ella Lou. Then I checked the closet and her dresser drawers. There were a few dresses draped on wire hangers in the closet. In a drawer, with lingerie and a girdle, was a black lace nightgown. No nylons. Only one pair of high-heeled shoes. No luggage.

As I was leaving, I gave Mrs. Galton my card and asked her to phone me if Ella Lou showed up. She poked the card between sagging breasts inside her loosely buttoned housedress.

"Find anything upstairs?" she asked, as I pushed through the street door into brilliant sunlight.

"Not as much as there should be."

Which meant that Ella Lou, voluntarily or not, had packed some of her things and taken a trip.

The next morning Artie Duke, wearing the same suit but a fresh carnation, slithered into my office on Cahuenga and asked if I'd gotten the photographs.

"There are no photos," I told him, settling down behind my desk. I gave him an account of yesterday's activities, and the longer I talked the more nervous he looked.

When I was finished he said, "Listen, Marlowe, I found out the big boys are very interested in Ella Lou."

"Big boys? Should I hide my lunch money? What big boys?"

"Talent agents, syndicate types—crack wise and call 'em whatever you want. They're the people that control valuable show business properties like Ella Lou's gonna be. They play plenty rough, Marlowe, with other people and with each other."

"They played rough with Jack Corcoran this time. They must have killed him as part of a power struggle over who owns a percentage of Ella Lou Harrison."

"There's no way to prove it, though," Artie said. "They never leave a way to prove things like that."

" 'Never' isn't a word to use lightly."

Both our heads jerked around as the office door flew open.

The man standing in the doorway was tall and gangly, with a kind of rawboned power about him. His ill-fitting dark suit was so wrinkled the material might have been prune. Gnarled, big-knuckled hands on thick wrists dangled at his sides. He had a long, weather-battered face. Fierce blue eyes glinted under caterpillar brows. "Which of you's Marlowe?"

Artie piped up, "He is," and pointed at me.

With a towering awkwardness, the man shuffled all the way into the office. "Mrs. Galton, over at Ella Lou's rooming house, tol' me about you." He had a flat midwestern drawl, as if his words hurt as they slid over his tongue. "I'm Cletus Harrison, Ella Lou's daddy."

Artie jumped up, said, "Clete, glad to meetcha!" He extended a hand, which Cletus shook almost absently as he moved in on my desk.

"These last two days, I come all the way here by train from Farmington, Missouri. Been told you was a detective, so what can you make of this? I got it in the mail four days ago and knew I was needed."

I noticed he'd brought some of Missouri with him under his fingernails, as he gave me a postcard with a photo of a row of cabins next to a pine-bordered lake. BIG ROCK RESORT was lettered across the front of the card. The writing on the back was in a cramped, feminine hand:

Ive got to seak peace at this place for a while so I can keep my sanety and survive. Its where I am if you cant get in touch with me. Don't worry please!!!

Love—Ella Lou

"Kinda thing makes a father fret," Cletus said. "You know where this Big Rock Resort is, Marlowe?"

"I heard of it," Artie chipped in. "Place up north on Route 101. We can take my car."

Artie protecting his interest. Scared as he was, he didn't want to lose whatever part he might play in Ella Lou's future. It was a future that everyone seemed to be fighting over, and that had already caused one death.

I got the .38 from my desk drawer and slipped it into a belt holster under my suitcoat, where it rested bulky and meaningful. Then we hustled outside, and I climbed into the shotgun seat of Artie's new turtle-back Buick sedan while Cletus folded himself in back. Artie drove with a lead shoe.

Big Rock Resort was so named because of the large boulder alongside its entrance. The Buick roared and bucked over a winding dirt road, and Artie parked in a gravel lot shaded by tall pines. There was one other car on the lot, an old Chevy coated with dust and with a canvas water bag slung by a strap from its chrome hood ornament.

As we got out of the car I recognized the redwood cabins in the post-card photo, and beyond them the placid blue lake. From a nearby branch, a squirrel chattered furiously at us for intruding. The pines gave the clear air a sharp, fresh scent. The resort seemed like the kind of place where nothing ever went wrong for anyone, except maybe squirrels, but I knew better.

"I'll do the talking," I said as we strode toward the nearest cabin, with the OFFICE sign nailed over the door.

Cletus said, "Hell you will."

Nothing like a game plan.

The crunching of tires on gravel made us pause and turn.

A long black Packard had pulled into the lot. A tickle of alarm ran up my spine as I remembered the car's smiling chrome grille from the right-side fender mirror of Artie's Buick.

We'd been followed from L.A.

There were two men in the Packard. They got out, slamming the car's doors in unison so they made one solid *thunk*, and ambled toward us. One was short but double wide, with shoulders like curbstones. The other was a gigantic, thick-necked redhead wearing a nasty smile. Probably the man who'd beaten me to Ella Lou's boarding house and searched her room. I heard Artie mutter fearfully, "It's Red Mallory."

Another man, wearing boots, a green plaid shirt, and a broad smile, had emerged from the resort office and was approaching us from the opposite direction. His face was youthful and sunburned, and glowed with the open expression of the outdoorsman.

He said, "Hi, I'm Dan Dillon, manager and guide here. You folks are lucky; you'll be the only guests."

Red Mallory pulled a German Luger from the pocket of his tent-sized jacket and said, "Right there's fine. Don't nobody move."

None of us knew quite what to do, but Mallory's advice seemed sound.

After a few seconds Dillon, putting on a young man's bravado, broke the silence: "Say, what's the deal here? What is it you guys want?"

"All of us wanna see the guest you say ain't here," Mallory said, "a Miss Ella Lou Harrison."

Something hard came over Dillon's features; it was obvious he'd succumbed to Ella Lou's magic, like everybody else who'd met her.

"What cabin's she in?" the broad man asked. He was balding on top and had a couple of long strands of black hair strategically plastered sideways across his skull. Fooled nobody.

Dillon didn't answer until Mallory prodded him under the chin with the barrel of the Luger. "End cabin, number seven."

Mallory said, "Butch," and kept the gun on us while the broad guy swaggered off to see Ella Lou.

The cabin door was locked. Butch wasn't one for etiquette. He kicked it open and disappeared inside.

After a few minutes there was the sound of voices arguing, one of them female. Then a long silence.

Cletus had endured enough. It was the silence that set him off. As loud a silence as I'd ever heard.

He took a step forward and Mallory grinned, skillfully caught Cletus off balance, and shoved him back.

Cletus ignored the gun in the redhead's hand and charged him. Still grinning, Mallory sidestepped and whacked him alongside the head with the gun butt. This was all sport for him. Invigorating.

He said, "Calm down, you old bastard. I killed plenty during the war, so one more won't matter. Be fun, in fact."

Cletus rubbed the side of his head, spat on the ground, and set off walking toward Ella Lou's cabin.

Mallory laughed. "C'mon back here. Don't try runnin' a bluff on me or you'll get a gut fulla lead."

Beside me, Artie whispered, "Jeez! Don't that Cletus wanna live?"

Mallory's eyes darted from Cletus to me and Artie, then back to Cletus. The Missouri-stubborn farmer wasn't going to stop. He had a long, furrow-skipping stride; the distance between us was widening fast. "Get back here now, old coot, you don't wanna be buzzard meat!"

Cletus kept walking.

"Good enough," Mallory said calmly. He swung the Luger around and widened his stance to fire at Cletus.

I had my gun out in half a second, but he caught my motion from the corner of his eye. He took a quick shot at Cletus before whirling to blast me. I got a glimpse of Artie diving to the ground. Dillon jumping back. Cletus still standing. The .38 jumped in my hand. Mallory's gun barked and blazed.

The big redhead danced around slowly, almost dreamily, through the smoke and stench of gunpowder. Tripping with an invisible partner.

Then he dropped abruptly, as if every nerve in his body had lost life simultaneously. He'd landed facedown, and the bullet's exit hole in his back was gaping and ugly.

Artie was sitting on the ground with his head between his knees, retching. Cletus had resumed clomping toward the cabin, as if nothing had happened. Dillon bolted after him. I followed Dillon.

Butch had heard the shot and was out of the cabin, standing like a marauding bear on the plank porch. In his right hand was something metallic and shiny—not a gun. He immediately sized up what was happening and tossed the object away, trying to wrestle a gun out from beneath his jacket.

I stopped walking, aimed, fired.

I had to have hit him, but the wide man showed no effect. He had his gun out and snapped off a shot at Dillon, who spun to the ground and started writhing around and kicking. Butch was aiming at me now, and I knew I was as exposed as DiMaggio in center field.

I held my own aim, squeezed off a shot.

Again no reaction from my target. Was the guy real?

I dropped and rolled, knowing a bullet would be coming my way. And in my dizzying vision saw Cletus grab Butch's thick arm and hurl him from the porch. I lay on my stomach, sighted along the barrel, and blasted three shots as Butch was struggling to his feet, the gun still in his right hand.

This time he rolled his eyes almost tenderly in my direction, as if I'd hurt his feelings. He started to raise his gun to take another shot at me, but it was suddenly too heavy. His arm fell.

The front of his shirt was red and his life was pumping out onto the ground. Scarlet arterial blood splattering into the dust at his feet. He stared down at it, hypnotized, then got down on his hands and knees as if he might attempt to crawl.

Instead he curled up and died.

Dillon was lying still now. He'd lost a lot of blood and looked dead. Even if he was alive, he couldn't be moved. He needed an ambulance and plasma in a hurry, and that wasn't possible out here in the wilds. His luck and his life had run out.

Artie was still sitting by Mallory's body.

Cletus was nowhere in sight.

As I trudged toward the cabin, I stepped on the shiny object Butch had tossed from the porch—a straight razor. Dread and fury dropped through me like a cold weight. I ran the rest of the way.

Cletus was inside hugging his daughter to him, swaying from side to side like an oak tree caught in a storm. Ella Lou was sobbing, wearing only panties and a bra. Her body was smeared with blood and her face was a red mask.

"He cut her, Marlowe," Cletus moaned, stroking golden hair with his big hand. "Cut my baby so's she'd be ugly." He began to weep, out of his head. "Looka here what he done, Marlowe! Lord, look what he done! . . ."

I didn't want to look closer, but I did.

Two days later, Artie and I saw Cletus and Ella Lou, her face swathed in white bandages, off on the train for Missouri. She'd suffered half a dozen clean slashes; they'd been stitched up and she'd be okay. She'd even look all right after the doctors were done with her—but only all right. She'd never be the same. Never again be the stuff of mass fantasy.

Cletus helped her up into the pullman car, then glanced back and waved tentatively at us before boarding.

"Damned shame about her," Artie said. "Coulda been somethin' special. But they hadda fight over her like dogs over raw meat. This way everybody loses."

"Not necessarily," I said.

He missed my drift. "Yeah, that's true. I hear there's this hot blonde taking singing lessons over at Columbia. Same child-woman type as Ella Lou. Camera loves her the same way. Gonna be big. Name's Norma Jean somethin' or other."

The streamliner cleared its throat and inched forward. Steel clanked as the slack was taken up between cars.

I watched the train growl slowly out of the station, carrying Ella Lou Harrison back to the Midwest, to vast skies and rich farmland and probably marriage and kids and growing old and enjoying grandkids. A normal life. A good life. It could happen for her.

Good-bye, Ella Lou.

Good luck, Norma Jean.

———

I owe Chandler for showing me the true potential of detective fiction. For demonstrating that, far from confining the writer inside a formula, the detective story provides almost endless possibilities and directions. In many ways it sets the writer free. The detective, observing, commenting, influencing, illuminating the clockwork of his corner of the world, is something like a novelist within a novel. It was Chandler who used this freedom and dimension to best advantage, lacing his perfectly balanced prose with wicked social insight as well as beauty and poetry. Like a skilled photographer, he seemed to realize that the object in the lens is sometimes not as important as the light that falls on it. There are few genuine innovators in writing, and Chandler was one of them. Most of us who write this kind of fiction, whether we know it or not, or acknowledge it or not, emulate Raymond Chandler. I consider it an honor and a gesture of respect to emulate him consciously and publicly for this collection.

John Lutz

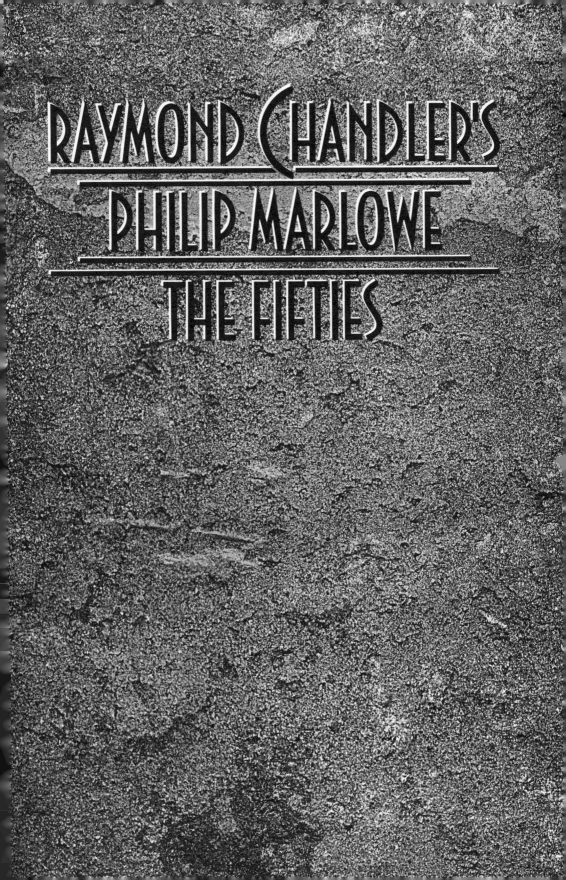

RAYMOND CHANDLER'S
PHILIP MARLOWE
THE FIFTIES

STARDUST KILL

SIMON BRETT

1950

THE HOUSE WAS in Malibu, backing on nothing but the beach and the ocean. Low, a white bungalow spreading like a melted ice cream in the white-hot sun. Terra-cotta tile roof, lots of purposeless curls of metal on the edges. Trying to look like it had history, and failing. A new building built with new money. A lot of new money.

The gates in the high white wall looked more purposeful than the rest of the curled metal. They were there to keep out unwanted guests. The Japanese houseboy who came when I pumped the bell-push had been trained to make all guests feel unwanted. I handed over a plain business card. "Miss West's expecting me."

He scowled as he opened the gates. He kept right on scowling as he led me up to a front door garnished with more gratuitous metal, into a dim hallway and through another door. The light in the sun porch was so bright I almost missed his farewell scowl, but I saw enough to know he'd been saving that one up specially.

My eyes adjusted quickly to the light when I saw the redhead on the chaise-longue. She was a nice piece of construction work and I wasn't the first man to think it. Most men evidently told her their thoughts on the subject, which explained the smug look on her face. Smugness aside, the face also had straight dark eyebrows, a cute nose, a pointed chin, and cherubic lips the Pope would have given up Lent for. For the eyes, black as olives, he might well have called in the valuers to give him a price on the Vatican. She wore a silk lounging robe with maybe enough underneath it for plunging into the ocean that winked away to the horizon. Certainly not more.

The Jap had had just enough strength left from scowling to hand her my card and she fingered this like it was ash and might blow away. "Mr. Marlowe," she said in a voice that hadn't been designed to be audible more than six inches from a pillow. The accent was thick Spanish.

I sat on a low tasseled sofa and threw my hat down beside me. "Got it in one," I said. "Did the card help?"

"Yes," she said. God had put so much into the rest of the package there hadn't been any room left for humor.

"I have a job for you," she said, moving straight to business.

I said nothing.

"Obviously you know who I am, Mr. Marlowe."

I did. You didn't have to be the biggest movie fan in the world to know who Lila West was. One of those actresses who spends more time in newspapers than in pictures.

"Fame is all very fine and dandy," she said, "but it attracts a lot of crazy people."

She wanted some reaction to this. I gave her a nod.

"People sick in their heads. Screwballs see you smile from their seat in the movie theater and think you're smiling at them. Half-baked saps write you letters, even call you up. You get used to it. Go into movies, that's part of the deal. But when some psycho says he's gonna cut you up, well, baby, you're reading from a different script."

Finally she'd made it to something worth hearing. "You've had threats?" I said.

"Yes," she said. She reached under the chaise-longue and pulled out a sheaf of blue papers.

I took them. Plain paper, no headings. Plain language, too. Sure, the guy wanted to cut her up. But he wanted to do a few fancy things to her before that, while she was still pretty.

I put the letters down on the floor. It was a still day. The salt smell rose off the ocean like incense. Not a day for cutting up beautiful dames. I said: "Why don't you take these to the cops?"

A little petulance tugged at her cherubic lips, making them look less cherubic. Making them look downright mean.

"Cops, what do they know? They won't take this kind of stuff seriously. They'll think it's a publicity play."

"And is it?"

Now it was hard to remember that the lips had ever been even slightly cherubic. "What's your game, bozo?" she snapped. "I can get insulted without paying you to do it."

"I had to ask," I said mildly. "And I'm glad to hear about the paying."

"What do you charge for your kind of work?" she asked.

I told her. About the daily rate. About the retainer. About the expenses.

"I figured it'd be more," she said.

Suddenly she came to life. Or as near life as you can get without moving from a chaise-longue. She reached underneath and produced a photograph in a worn leather frame. "That's the punk," she said.

It was a studio shot, so the photographer must have made the guy look his best. I didn't want to see his worst. The neck and the head didn't stop and start, they were one continuous feature. The eyes had been banged in close like tacks, and the mouth was one thin, hard line.

Lila West stretched to a box beside her for a cigarette. Pink, silver tip, a woman's cigarette. Or a pimp's. She snapped open a table lighter and sucked in the flame, then blew out a ribbon of smoke. "His name's Johnny Escalito. Hangs out as a doorman and part-time pug at the Stardust Club in Bay City."

"And he wrote these letters?"

She nodded curtly.

"How'd you know?"

"Hell, I know. What's with all these questions? I want questions, I'll hire a cop. I hire you because I don't want questions. All I want is you to do the job, take the money, take a powder. We never met, okay?"

"What is the job?" I asked quietly.

"I told you. Johnny Escalito." I reckon if the Pope had seen the viciousness in her eyes then, he'd have pulled the plugs on the Vatican sale. "I want Johnny Escalito dead."

I picked up my hat. "You got the wrong man, Miss West."

"Hell, you're a private investigator, aren't you? I was told—"

"You were told wrong."

I turned towards the door and found myself looking down the muzzle of a big Savage. The old coot who held it was too fat to be wearing Bermuda shorts, too bald to look good with sunglasses hiked up on his forehead, too flabby to look convincing with a gun in his hand. The face was kind of familiar, but I couldn't think from where.

His voice didn't sound tough, either. A nitpicker's voice, a vote-counter's voice, a jealous voice. "What's this slime doing in the house, Lila?"

He didn't worry her. Not enough to get her up off the chaise-longue. "Mr. Marlowe was recommended to me for some domestic work," she said languidly.

He moved forward, sniffing the air for lies. But he moved like he owned the place. Come to think of it, he probably did own the place. Lila West hadn't pulled in that kind of sugar from her lousy movies. Some sucker had to be picking up her tab. And this one had sucker written all over him.

"But it turns out," she went on, "that Mr. Marlowe is nothing but a cheap cheat."

"Glad you recognize your own kind, sweets," I said, cramming on my hat. At the door I stopped. "And at least I conduct my business standing up."

When I got into the car, I noticed a dusty black Packard parked way back in the shade of a pepper tree. The driver was slumped over the wheel. Asleep. Maybe dead. I was too hot to care that much.

I drove down the coast road, hungry for sea breezes. There weren't any. The sky was uniform blue, the sun dealing out its punishment to everyone rich enough to live on the coast. The road ahead sparkled and fragmented jeweled layers in the haze.

Suddenly I remembered who the sugar daddy was. A face seen in the papers as often as hers. Bud Cone, head of Ingot Pictures. Rich enough for the Malibu house to be among his small change. Good fish for an ambitious actress to leech onto.

I had given up on sea breezes by then and was on Wilshire, driving into the city. The traffic was heavy, hot, and angry. In the mirror I saw the dusty black Packard three cars back. The driver had woken up or been resurrected. Either way he was tailing me.

When I took a left onto Highland he was still three cars back. At the intersection with Santa Monica I tried to dust him off at the lights, but he stayed with me. So I cut a little square dance I'd done before around Yucca and Vine. That lost him.

The gods were smiling—there was a space to park outside the Cahuenga Building. I remembered the office bottle was empty. Five minutes later I had a pint under my arm and the virtuous, exercised glow of a man who's walked to the liquor store and back.

I don't know where he'd lost the Packard, but he was waiting for me in the lobby with a Colt automatic. It wasn't there to persuade me to do anything. It was there to kill me.

His dim outline flashed on the glass of the door as I entered, and I hit the carpet at the moment the gun spoke.

It barked a couple more times. I heard the slugs bite the floor as I rolled towards him. I caught his shin hard with the bottle and hooked my legs round his. He came crashing down.

I was up first and kicked at the hand along which he was sighting the Colt. The automatic skittered across the lobby. He grunted in pain. I planted a second kick firmly in his gut.

Another grunt, but he was tough. And quick. On his feet again, huge as a windmill, he swung a fist at my head. I felt its wake on my hair as I dropped to one knee.

I lunged a right to where his belt was, then, as the square chin came down, caught its edge with a left hook so sweet it should have been in a box with red ribbons on top.

His head clicked back. His eyes rolled blank. He thudded against the wall and trickled down to a heap on the lobby floor.

His face was only a little blanker than when he was conscious. Solid cement from ear to ear. Not Johnny Escalito, but school of Johnny Escalito.

I checked his pockets. Nothing you wouldn't expect to find in a bottom league pug's pockets. A spring blade, a brass knuckle, a lead-filled leather blackjack, a book of matches from the Stardust Club, a small notebook.

I pocketed the arsenal and added the Colt to my collection. Saw with satisfaction that the pint bottle had survived intact. I lifted the hood's lids. The eyes registered two big zeros. He'd be out a while longer. I took the notebook with me up to the sixth floor.

I swiveled in my swivel chair as I checked it through. The book was a kind of diary. Names, addresses, times. Some details recurred. Thursday afternoons three o'clock there was "Trudi." An address for her in the back of the book: 2397 Railton Street, part of the city where the only class you see is the rats. There were other repeated entries. Particularly the initials "S.C." These always came after a name, suggesting a place rather than a person.

"Stardust Club"? Maybe too obvious. If it was "Stardust Club", he had a meeting there that evening with someone called "B.C." Bud Cone? Or was that being obvious, too?

The net curtains at the open windows bellied outwards, drawn by invisible breezes that had no effect on the ambient temperature. I drew in the hot smoke of a cigarette and drummed my fingers on the glass top of my desk.

I could have called the police. But then I don't have that many friends who are cops. So I called the Sanitation Department. Complained to them about the trash in the lobby.

My memory had been too kind to Railton Street. It had slid a long way since I was last there. Even the rats had probably moved out, looking for a nicer area to bring up their babies.

It was a street of cracked sidewalks, flaking paint, and broken windows. Frame houses tired with the effort of staying upright. Boarded-up drugstores, hollow-eyed restaurants under faded lettering, defunct beer parlors. Snatches of cheap music and cheap quarrels surged and died from unseen rooms.

In spite of the afternoon heat, the front windows of 2397 were closely curtained. Sad jazz yearned from behind the door.

The woman who opened it carried enough weight to find the heat real hard, but she wore an evening dress that was all glitter and dangles. Makeup as thick as piecrust. Her hair, immobilized by a permanent, wasn't in God's color chart. Jet beads throttled a wrestler's neck. Her feet must have been fed into the French shoes with spoons.

"Yes?" she said, waiting to find out who I was before she committed herself to an intonation.

"My name's Marlowe," I said, trying the obvious. "Johnny Escalito sent me."

The obvious worked. She led me through the hallway into a dimly lit room of dark velour and davenports. Bottles on a small bar winked in the corner. The jazz mourned louder from an old gramophone.

She gestured me to a velour sofa which shuddered as she lowered herself down beside me. "How is Johnny?" she wheezed.

"Good," I said.

"And his new job?"

"Good."

"Hey, I never offered you a drink." She flopped around the sofa, like a whale trying to get up and tango. "Mind helping yourself?"

I moved to the bar. She wanted one of those liqueurs that leave your lips sticky for weeks. I loaded myself a glass with scotch and ice.

She went on talking. "Johnny never really fitted here. Too clumsy for a barkeep. And then he's only got a coupla words of English. Do better at the Stardust, where they just need muscle. Only here two weeks and I'm glad he shifted before I had to take a crowbar to him. Took him on as a favor to Rocky Hernandez. You know Rocky?"

"No," I said.

"Runs a joint in Mexico City. I started out there, so I owe him. Sure Johnny did fine in that kind of trash can. Lot of rough stuff there, punks beating up on girls, dopeheads, you know. In this city you gotta have more finesse."

I nodded. I'd seen all I wanted of the finesse of Railton Street. "Johnny mentioned a girl called Trudi."

The woman smiled. Her eyes disappeared. They could have got lost in the fat forever. "Trudi's kind of busy right now. You could come back in an hour. Or wait. Or then again"—a puffy hand brushed my knee—"does it have to be Trudi?"

I drained my glass and stood up. "I'll come back in an hour, beautiful," I said, lying on two counts.

As I drove along Santa Monica toward Bay City, the sunset went through its usual party pieces of flames and pinks and yellows and apricots and golds and was trying to invent a new color. Damn near succeeding, too.

The heat had hardly lifted with the evening. My shirt clung to my back like an extra skin. Too much driving that day. Still, the second visit to the office hadn't been wasted. Calls to Mexico City and to an old lush who owed me a favor. Used to work in movie publicity till the booze made him careless and he started telling the truth. Gave me some good answers to a few questions, though.

What's more, the Sanitation Department had depugged the lobby.

I lifted the dash lighter to a new cigarette. Smoke mingled with the lethargic perfume of jacarandas and the salt sting of the ocean.

A couple of prowl cars passed. The cops inside eyed me, bored and curious. Not enough crime on the streets of the city that night. Or not enough crime that they hadn't been told to ignore.

The Stardust Club was smart. Smart place for smart people, the kind who had shaken their dice out lucky in the movies. The kind whose only redeeming feature was money. Though most of them were way beyond redemption. The pug in my lobby hadn't been carrying Stardust Club matches because he went there, only because he worked there. As did the lump of pot roast in purple uniform who came forward to open the door of my car. Johnny Escalito. I'd have recognized him anywhere.

His face said it expected more expensive cars than mine. When I stepped out and tossed him the keys, it said it expected more expensive people.

"Mr. Cone in?" I asked him.

He jerked his head toward the door, for a fleeting moment giving the illusion that he had a neck. He was a man of few words, and he was saving those up for someone else.

Inside, the Stardust Club was all cool pale columns and flounced pink curtains. I felt like Jonah in the belly of an anemic whale. In the bandshell a colored combo played the kind of tunes that don't begin and don't end but just pour on out like water from a faucet. With about as much taste. Couples who liked that kind of thing circled aimlessly on the dance floor.

Two slabs of granite in purple tuxes had registered my entrance and I felt their eyes making dents in my back as I drifted across to the pale, pale bar. A barkeep who had escaped from some corps de ballet somewhere pirouetted across to me. I took a lot of Scotch with a lot of ice, parked on a tall stool, and looked around.

It was early yet. Most of the expensive people were still at the studios being overpaid. But, as Johnny Escalito had promised, Bud Cone was there. A white tux did more for him than Bermuda shorts, but that wasn't saying a lot.

Lila West had managed by this time in the day to get upright, or at least into a sitting position. The dress that adhered to significant bits of her body was flame-colored silk. She looked as inconspicuous as a watermelon in a basket of currants.

She didn't see me. Too busy giving a hard time to the tuxedoed bank account beside her. Bud Cone had done something to get her goat, and she wasn't rationing her feelings on the subject. My ears shriveled in sympathy.

Reading from the Latin flurry of gestures that garnished her conversation, it seemed her beef was with the Stardust Club itself. She wanted Bud to take her someplace else. Any place.

The old sucker was equally determined to stay put. And for some reason she didn't just follow her sweet nature, irrigate his bald head with her drink, and walk out. She seemed afraid to leave him there on his own. I figured I knew why.

One of the purple-tuxed tombstones lumbered toward their table and handed the girl a note. Her eyes flashed fury at its contents and raked across to the doorway. Johnny Escalito loomed there, the line of his mouth ruckled in a dumb grin.

Lila West seethed across the dance floor. At the doorway she tugged Escalito behind a pink drape, out of Bud Cone's line of vision. But not out of mine.

The speed her lips moved, she had to be talking Spanish. Spanish words that don't come in school textbooks. Escalito just grinned as the waves of her anger broke over him.

Suddenly she gave up, reached into her flame-colored purse, and pulled out a folded wad of bills. She thrust them into Escalito's hands and boiled back to her seat.

The dumb grin on his face crinkled wider as he counted the payoff. He pawed the bills into his purple uniform and moved back toward the main door.

Then he stopped and turned. The grin was wider and dumber than ever. Skirting the dance floor, he hunkered toward Lila West's table.

I slipped off my bar stool and moved after him.

I was close enough to hear when he spoke. "Miss West." The voice was thickly Spanish.

Her head spun round, the black eyes spitting fire. They took in my presence over Escalito's shoulder. "Behind you!" she hissed. "He's got a gun!"

If I'd had a gun, I wouldn't have got it out of the holster before a fist like a cement mixer caught me in the jaw. I staggered back, skittling over a couple of honeymooners on the dance floor.

Escalito's other fist was on collision course with my temple. I barred it with my left forearm and poked a stiff right into the spread mass of his nose. It was like punching Mount Rushmore.

A huge hand gathered the lapels of my jacket, and a forehead like a runaway tramcar smashed into mine. Through the fog I saw salami fingers bunching into a fist.

"Johnny!"

Lila West's voice froze him. He half turned toward her and I drove my knuckles into the side of his head, feeling the rasp of stubble.

He didn't notice I'd hit him. He still looked at Lila. In her hand was a gun. A small gun, like a toy. A lady's gun. Mind you, that didn't comfort me any. A lot of ladies kill people in this city.

She spat Spanish at him. Then, slowly, deliberately, she pulled the trigger. His body shuddered as the first slug thudded into his chest. Same with the second. And the third.

Johnny Escalito made no sound. To the end he was a man of few words.

Blood pumped through the lightweight worsted of his vest. A bubble of blood swelled at the corner of his thin mouth, burst and trickled.

He went down, straight as a plank. The dance floor shook.

No point in checking for a pulse. Guys with three bullets in their hearts don't have pulses.

The two rocky outcrops in purple tuxes were standing either side, looking down at the lump of dead meat that had been Johnny Escalito.

Lila West's flesh was white as milk against the blaze of her dress. She replaced the gun in her purse. She shut the clasp with a click.

Bud Cone looked like the embalmers had got halfway with him, but hadn't started putting the fluid back in yet.

The siren of a prowl car whined outside. If there's one thing cops are good at, it's arriving too late.

The homicide skipper had set up shop in the Stardust Club manager's office. He was a jovial fat man who only needed the suit, beard, and reindeer to pass for Santa Claus. He hadn't got that fat on what the police paid him.

He checked my I.D. and I got the usual wince of reproach when he saw my profession. If there's one thing cops don't like, it's competition.

But he handed the papers right back with a smile, all cream and two sugars. "Well, Mr. Marlowe, thank you. I'm sorry you got caught up in this jam, but the bruising'll go in a coupla days. If I were wearing your pants, I'd be straight home for a drink as big as a bathtub."

"And you'll call me in the morning?"

"Hell, what for?" he asked.

"I'm a witness."

"I got plenty of witnesses," he said. "Mr. Cone . . . the two heavies in the tuxes. That's enough."

"But what did they see?" I asked.

His eyes narrowed. He stopped looking jovial and started looking piggy. "They all saw the same," he said. "They saw that goon approach Miss West's table, they saw him pull a gun on her, they saw her shoot him in self-defense."

"They weren't using the same make of eyes I was. He didn't pull a gun."

The cop shrugged. "There was a gun on him. Savage, ugly great brute. He had a shoulder holster."

"I didn't say there wasn't a gun on him. I said he didn't pull a gun."

"You'd just had a smack in the jaw, brother. Maybe you weren't seeing so straight."

"I was seeing straight enough to know that Lila West plugged him in cold blood."

He shook his head. "Not the kind of thing you should go around saying, bozo. Don't you private dicks know anything about the law?"

"Plenty," I said. "And about justice."

"Phooey. Listen to me, Marlowe, the guy was a psycho. He'd written this whole raft of crazy letters to Miss West. He was a public danger."

"I doubt that goon could write his own name," I said. "And if he could write, it'd be in Spanish, not English. The reason Lila West shot him was that he had dirt on her. He'd worked in a Mexico City whorehouse where she'd been one of the main attractions. He was threatening to pull the plugs on that to Bud Cone."

The skipper put his hands on the table, palms down. He smiled, the picture of reasonableness. "Mr. Marlowe, maybe I'm not making myself clear. This Escalito character was crazy. He'd got this fixation on Miss West from seeing her in the movies. He wrote her hate letters. Then when he saw her in this club, he flipped and tried to kill her. She," he repeated with heavy emphasis, "shot him in self-defense."

"The shooting was in public. The club's full of people who know that wasn't the way it happened."

"I don't think you'll find anyone who'll *say* that wasn't the way it happened," he said casually.

"Here's one," I said, standing up.

He moved fast for a fat man. Suddenly he was up too, his hands tight on my lapels, his nose inches from mine. Close to, there was nothing jovial in the eyes. They were dead, like pebbles.

"Listen to me, Marlowe. The police don't like operators like you. We tolerate you, but if we want to put the lid on you, we can do it easy as squashing a ladybug. We run this city, we keep it neat and tidy, we trim the edges when necessary, we square things off. The last thing we want around is saps who think they're fighting the crusades. Understand me?"

"I understand you." He released the hold on my jacket. "But I'm not going to keep buttoned up about a whitewash like this."

"Mr. Marlowe, men like Bud Cone draw water in this city. You don't draw nothing—not even a disability pension if you get too curious. I make myself clear?"

"Clear as sewer water," I said.

He flopped back into his chair. The joviality had returned, in spades. "Just one word of advice, Sir Galahad. We got laws in this state about defamation, slander—I'm sure we could find a few others if we needed them. All I'm saying is—you repeat your allegations about Miss West and we'll bury you so deep in charges you couldn't dig your way out with a shovel. You try to take us on, Mr. Marlowe, and it's war."

"Suits me," I said.

He laughed. Maybe he thought I'd made a joke. I hadn't.

As he reached back to the tray of drinks behind the manager's desk, I saw the smallness of his life. All the little bits of grifting, all the shaved corners of his conscience, all the inadequate reassurances with which he had quieted his soul.

I stood up. He still had his back to me as he said, "Now come on, let's forget all this stuff. I'll bet there's nothing you'd like more at this moment than a large drink."

"No," I said, "there isn't. But not with you."

For me the great achievement of Raymond Chandler is his humor. His books prove that it is possible to put jokes into crime fiction without sacrificing tension, and indeed he frequently manages to use jokes to heighten tension. Nor does he allow humor to detract from character; again it has the effect of reinforcing character. And his jokes are always exemplary lessons in economy of phrasing.

Simon Brett

LOCKER 246

ROBERT J. RANDISI

1951

THE FIRST GRAND Central Station was built in New York in 1871 by Cornelius Vanderbilt. Vanderbilt wanted to build the largest railroad station in the world, and he succeeded. New York's high-society members were building at the time along Fifth Avenue and Madison Avenue between Thirty-fourth Street and Forty-second Street, and this was where Vanderbilt chose to erect his monument. It had to be large, but it also had to be elegant—and again, it was.

Between 1903 and 1913 the station was modernized, and today—in 1951—it is virtually a city within a city. All of this I learned by reading during the train trip from California to New York. Why was I taking a train ride from California to New York? I was wondering that myself, even as I stood in the center of Grand Central Station on a Saturday, in awe of what I was seeing.

According to my reading material the main concourse of Grand Central Station is a room 470 feet long, 160 feet wide, and 150 feet high. The New York Yankees could have played baseball there.

I had just gotten off the train on one of the lower track levels and as I entered the station itself I had to stop and stare.

Since it was Saturday most of the shops—including the famous Oyster Bar on the lower concourse—were closed. Add to that the fact that it was 7:15 a.m. on a Saturday, and I was virtually alone, which probably made the place seem much larger than it really was—if that was possible.

Getting over my shock and awe I approached one of the ticket windows underneath the schedule boards and asked the clerk, "When is the next train back to California?"

No, I wasn't *that* intimidated, but I did want to get back home as soon as my business was concluded. You see, I never *wanted* to make this trip in the first place. It is one of my failings that I take my friendships—few that they are—very seriously, and it was an act of friendship that had taken me three thousand miles or more from my home.

The ticket clerk looked at me and asked, "Did you just get off the train from California?"

"That's right," I said, "and I want to get right back *on* the next one. You got any objections to that?"

"Hell, pal," the clerk said, "that's up to you. You want to ride back and forth from California to New York like you was going from Brooklyn to Manhattan, that's your business. Next train leaves at eight-oh-five a.m."

"I'll take a ticket."

The ticket that I had been provided with *to* New York was one way, so it was necessary for me to buy my own ticket back. A further act of friendship on my behalf. I couldn't really complain about it to my friend, because he was dead.

I took my ticket, paid for it, and asked, "Where are the lockers?"

"On this level they're on the Lexington Avenue side."

"Where's that?"

Sighing heavily he leaned out a bit and pointed to my left.

"Thanks, pal. You've made the trip worth my while."

"Comedian," he said, and I didn't correct him. If he wanted to think I was a comedian instead of a private dick, let him. Sometimes I thought the two were one and the same, anyway.

I walked the length of the concourse until I reached a tunnel which, according to my new friend, led to Lexington Avenue and the lockers I was looking for. The key in my pocket was burning itself a hole there.

I stopped when I came within sight of the lockers and took a moment to reflect on the circumstances that had brought me to the brink of what was bound to be a monumental discovery—what was in Grand Central locker 246.

Three years ago I had been the only thing standing between Leo Carstairs and a long stretch in prison. Leo was a born fall guy. Other hoods would call him in on a heist only when they needed someone to throw to the cops. He was already a three-time loser, but I knew that Leo was innocent because at the time of the heist in question he'd been with me. This time the hoods hadn't even bothered to bring him in on the deal before trying to pin it on him.

Anyway, to cut it short, I pulled Leo's bacon out of the fire for him, and he swore eternal gratitude.

"Leo," I remember saying, "just do me one favor and stay out of trouble from now on?"

"Sure thing, Marlowe. You can count on me. From now on I keep a gun taped to the roof of the bread box. They'd never look there."

"That's not what I meant, Leo."

"Thanks, shamus," he'd said, pumping my hand. "You're aces in my book."

I watched him walk away from the Cook County courthouse that day, a spring in his step, and wondered how long it would take him to get himself all jammed up again.

It took three years.

Three years was actually a record for Leo Carstairs staying out of trouble. Of course, he could have been involved in lots of things during those three years and simply avoided being caught—or taking the fall for somebody else.

A week before my trip to New York I was at home in my house in Laurel Canyon trying to avoid a mate in three—my opponent was me—when the phone rang.

It was Leo and—surprise, surprise—he was in trouble.

"I did it big this time, Marlowe," Leo said, without preamble.

"Leo? Is that you?"

"Sure it's me, Marlowe. You didn't forget me in three years, did you?"

"Leo, you were supposed to stay out of trouble," I reminded him.

"I have, Marlowe, for three years—"

"And now?"

He took a deep, shuddering breath that almost blew my eardrum out and said, "I really did it this time, Marlowe."

"Leo, where are you?"

"New York."

"What the hell are you doing in New York?"

"I figured a change of scenery would change my luck."

"And did it?"

"Yeah, from bad to worse."

"Tell me about it, Leo."

"I ain't got time, Marlowe. This time they don't want me to take the fall, they want to kill me."

"For what?"

"I've got the stuff."

"What stuff?"

"I wanna give it back, Marlowe. You gotta help me."

"*What* stuff, Leo?"

"I can't . . . talk now, Marlowe. I been in one place for too long as it is. I'll call you again from someplace else."

"Leo, Leo, don't hang—" I started, but he hung up in my ear.

I didn't hear from Leo for three days, and then I really didn't hear *from* him, I heard *about* him.

He was dead.

If there was one cop I didn't automatically take for the bearer of bad news it was Lieutenant Violets McGee—except when he showed up at my front door before breakfast.

"Lieutenant," I said, "to what do I owe the pleasure."

"Back up, Marlowe," Violets said, "I'm coming in."

"I was just about to invite you."

He was alone, so I still didn't expect *real* bad news.

"You remember a weasel named Leo Carstairs?"

"Leo was okay, Violets. He just needed a break."

"Sure, they all need a break," Violets said. "Heard from him lately?"

"No," I lied. It was easy, sort of like falling off a log.

"Well, he's a dead weasel now."

"What happened?"

"Somebody snuffed him."

"Where?"

"A bullet in the heart."

"No," I said, "I mean, where did it happen?"

"Get this," he said, "New York City, outside of Grand Central Station. I always wanted to go to New York and see Grand Central Station, the Statue of Liberty, the Empire State Building, Yankee Stadium, Joe D.—"

"Before you take me on a tour of the whole city, tell me what happened? How did you get involved?"

"I got a call from the New York cops asking me to check up on a peeper named Marlowe. Seems your name and number were in his pocket. They checked you out, found out what you did for a living, and called me."

"And?"

"I told them I'd talk to you," he said, "and I've talked to you. Have a nice day."

He started for the door, but I still wanted some information without sounding too nosey about it.

"Exactly where did they find him, anyway?" I asked. "Grand Central Station is a big place."

"Outside somewhere. He was lying right under a mailbox."

"Any witnesses?"

"None," Violets said, opening my front door. "You're in the clear on this, Marlowe. You got three thousand miles in your favor."

"It's nice to be in the clear, Violets."

"Yeah," Violets said, "don't let it go to your head. Stay out of trouble, okay?"

"Sure, Violets," I said. "You know me."

"Yeah," he said, sourly, "I do for a fact."

Two days later the envelope came in the mail. No return address, and my name and address hastily scrawled across the front. I opened it and the key fell out. I picked it up, palmed it, and took the ticket out of the envelope. That was it, one train ticket, and one locker key with the number 246 on it. Both of them from Leo Carstairs, no doubt. The postmark on the envelope was New York City.

I stared at the ticket—an invitation to trouble for sure—and then at the key.

Leo had been involved in a heist, and he wanted to give the stuff back, that much I knew for sure. I didn't know *what* heist, though, but it didn't take a genius to figure out that he'd stashed the booty in a locker in Grand Central, and had sent me the key.

I had two options.

I could bury the key in a flowerpot, or I could do what Leo obviously wanted me to do—go to New York, retrieve the loot, and give it back for him.

Friends are a real pain in the ass, sometimes, but dead friends are the worst.

You can say no to them, but they won't hear you.

So here I was, in Grand Central, doing a favor for a dead friend. Stay out of trouble, Violets McGee had said.

Sure.

I took the key out of my pocket and approached the bank of lockers. They weren't that large, about fifteen inches square. What could fit in there, I wondered?

Trouble, that's what.

Wait for the 8:05 train Marlowe and head for home, I told myself, but sometimes even *I* don't listen to me.

I walked to the locker, hearing my own footsteps on the floor, stuck the key in the lock, and opened it. There was a bag inside, the kind fighters use to carry their gear to the gym. I was about to take it out when I heard the other footsteps behind me.

When trouble comes it doesn't creep up on you on tippy toe.

I turned and saw the two of them. They both held guns. I looked around, but there was no one else in sight. Saturday morning in New York. On a Monday or Tuesday or any weekday this place would have been teeming with people. On this Saturday there were only three of us, and two of us were pointing a gun at me.

"Have you fellas got the right guy?" I asked.

The one on my right had a droopy eye and an anvil jaw. The one on the left was slight, with a pronounced Adam's apple.

"You got the key to that locker, we got the right guy," Droopy said.

"This locker?"

"If it's got a gym bag in it, yeah, that locker," Adam's Apple said. It bobbed up and down when he talked.

"There are gym bags," I said, "and then there are gym bags. What's in this one?"

"If you don't know," Droopy said, "then you don't need to know."

"What makes you think this is your gym bag?" I asked.

"We been staking out these lockers for a week," Adam's Apple said, "waiting for somebody to show up with the right key."

"You been sticking up everybody who opened a locker? In New York that must have been a big job."

"Not so big," Droopy said. "You're the only mug who opened a locker what's got a gym bag in it."

"Lucky me."

"Where'd you get the key?" Adam's Apple asked.

"It came in the mail."

"Yeah, right," Droopy said, "with your subscription to *Life* magazine."

"And the bills," I said.

"Comedian," said Adam's Apple. I wondered if he was related to the ticket clerk.

"All right," Droopy said to Adam's Apple, "take it out."

Adam's Apple moved towards me and waggled his gun, a .32. Droopy was a bigger man, so he was holding a .45. That one would put a hole in me and the lockers behind me.

I moved aside.

"See if he's heeled," Droopy said.

Adam's Apple patted me down and took my Luger from under my arm.

"Nice piece," he said.

"Keep it," I said. "It's a gift."

"Thanks," he said, and dropped it into his jacket pocket.

"Stop socializin' and get the stuff," Droopy said.

Adam's Apple reached into the locker and took out the gym bag. He tossed it to Droopy, who caught it with his left hand. The gun in his right never wavered.

"See if there's anything else in there," Droopy said.

Adam's Apple peered inside the locker, then ran his hands over the bottom and the two sides.

"Nothing."

He stepped away from the locker and I stepped in front of it again. It was waist high and I stood directly in front of it, remembering what Leo had said about his bread box: "They'd never look there . . ."

Adam's Apple went and stood next to Droopy, who finally moved his gun away from me so he could unzip the bag. He opened it and whatever was in there must have been something, because they forgot about me for about ten seconds.

That was plenty of time.

I reached behind me and touched the top of the locker. It was there, taped tight. I grabbed it and pulled, and the tape gave.

Droopy picked that moment to look at me and I brought the gun out of the locker. The tape was still stuck to it, flapping around as I raised it and pointed it at him.

"Look out!" Droopy yelled, but he didn't have time to heed his own warning.

He dropped the bag and tried to bring the .45 up, but I shot him in the forehead. As he went over backward Adam's Apple gaped at him, then looked at me.

"Don't," I told him, but he didn't listen to me any more than I listen to myself.

I shot him in the chest as he tried to bring the .32 up.

The shots echoed and I looked down the concourse to see if anyone was going to come running. The ticket clerks in New York are smart. They stayed where they were and didn't even stick their heads out.

I stared down at the two dead men and then at the .38 in my hand. I turned around and stuck the gun back to the top of locker 246. I didn't have to wipe it because there was enough tape on it to keep my prints off it. I was lucky it had even fired with all that tape in the way. I went over to Adam's Apple then and retrieved my Luger. From there I was stuck for what to do.

The gym bag was lying on the floor, partially open. If I'd wanted to I could have looked inside. I like to think I wouldn't have been tempted by what was inside, but I'm only human. I leaned over, picked up the bag, and zipped it shut. I put it back in locker 246, closed it, removed the key—I had to put a coin in it first before it would release it, and me not even on an expense account—and then stuck the key in Droopy's jacket pocket.

I had a couple of ways to consider what had happened. One was that Leo really wanted me to find the stuff—whatever it was—and return it.

The other was that Leo purposely sent me a ticket that would get me to Grand Central Station at 7:15 a.m. on a Saturday morning, when the only three mugs who would be there were me and his two ex-partners. I wonder if he knew when he mailed it that he was going to be dead moments later? Maybe he thought that giving me to them would keep them off his trail. No, that wasn't right. I had never been Leo's patsy before, and there was no reason to think that he was looking to make one out of me now.

I *had* been set up, all right, but to kill, and not to *be* killed.

Leo probably thought he was really doing the right thing, this time.

I knew I was going to do the right thing.

I had five minutes to catch the 8:05, and I was going to catch it.

———

The first private eye books I read were the Lew Archer novels by Ross Macdonald. Little did I realize at that time—I was fifteen years of age—that Macdonald was refining a form that had been created by the big three of the pulps, Carroll John Daly, Dashiell Hammett, and Raymond Chandler.

I went back and read the big three, and found that I enjoyed Chandler the most. Daly was coarse and undisciplined, Hammett perhaps the most literary in style. However, I found Chandler fairly straightforward, and I found Marlowe the perfect tarnished knight, and the P.I. from which all P.I.'s have sprung. Further, Marlowe—although never "Marlowe" in the pulps—is the series P.I. who sprang from the pulps and went on to great success.

Chandler's influence on my work is, to my way of thinking, almost nil. Instead, what he did was hook me on a form—he and Ross Mac—that I read voraciously from that time forward, but when I began writing my own stories, my "eyes" were far from what Marlowe was, and my writing certainly borrowed nothing from the master. Yet, it was Chandler and Marlowe who made me realize that I wanted to write P.I. fiction. For that I owe them a lot.

Chandler is the master, and fifty years after Marlowe made his first appearance he is still the quintessential hard-boiled P.I.

Robert J. Randisi

BITTER LEMONS

STUART M. KAMINSKY

1952

WARREN HLUSHKA HAD the kind of face that made people say, "He'll never win a beauty contest." In fact, that's just what the bartender at the Cascadia Lounge on Broadway said to me when Warren burst nervously into the perpetual darkness of the bar bringing an unwelcome blast of sun behind him and reminding me that there were hours to go before I called it a day.

"Close the door," the bartender called, and Warren shifted the weight of the oversized book under his arm, pulled himself together, and closed the door. Then he squinted, blinked, and tried to adjust his eyes to the amber darkness.

Warren's nose was pushed to one side as if his face were permanently pressed against a store window. His large popping eyes made him look amazed at even the most inconsequential contact with other human beings. Warren was short, bald, and so thin you wondered how well he could stand up against an evening breeze off the Pacific.

Coils Conroy, the barkeep, was wrong. Warren had heard his beauty contest comment. Warren had won a beauty contest in Baker, Kansas, when he was a kid. He proved it to us by dropping what proved to be his family album on the bar and opening it to a brittle, crumbling, yellow newspaper clipping. The clipping showed that a boy named Warren Hlushka, son of Peggy and Marcus Hlushka, had won the 1912 Baker County Fair Best Looking Child ribbon. A photograph of a smiling blonde boy with yellow curls looked up at me. I turned the album around so Coils Conroy could see the clipping. He looked at it sourly, grunted, and turned away.

"That's me all right," Warren insisted. "That's me right there, Mister Marlowe."

I turned the album back around to look at the pretty young woman in the photograph holding the hand of the little boy. She wore a little hat and held her free hand up to her face to shield her eyes from the sun.

I looked at the kid in the picture and then at Warren. The long eyelashes were still there and the features, they were there too, but exaggerated, grotesque.

"And that, holding my hand, is my mother," he said. "And there, the next picture, that's my father, he's holding my baby sister, Louise. I want you to find her for me. That's why I came here looking for you. I thought it through, came looking for you. You're not in your office so . . ."

"Your sister?"

"Sister, right," said Warren, looking in amazement at the photograph as if he had never seen it before.

"The one you want me to find?"

"The one," he agreed. "I want to see her. I got something important to tell her."

"What?" I asked unwilling to reach for my beer and not offer Warren one.

"Can't tell you, Mister Marlowe," he said, lowering his voice and glancing at Conroy to be sure he wasn't listening. "Family stuff."

"How long has it been since you saw your sister?" I asked.

"Louise?" he asked and then considered the question as he bit his lower lip. "Twenty, twenty-five years maybe. I got a letter."

He turned album pages quickly, passing photographs, postcards, matchboxes, and even candy wrappers.

"Here," he said, triumphantly slapping the page with his palm.

I had come down to the bar to nurse a beer after a long morning of listening to the radio and reading the newspaper from cover to cover, including the car ads. The phone hadn't rung. The mailman hadn't brought a desperate cry for help, and no one had knocked at my door pleading for my services. I was tired from doing nothing. I wanted to look at Conroy's homely face and feel the cold moisture of an amber beer bottle. I didn't want to think about going back to my office or my apartment.

I had nothing better to do, so I listened to Warren Hlushka.

Warren fidgeted around, behind, and nearly on top of me, pleading, giving information as I tried to read the letter.

"Letter's from Louise," he said pointing at the neatly scripted name in the corner of the envelope neatly pasted next to the letter.

"I know," I said.

"She's not in Baker, Kansas, anymore," he said. "I called, asked. Long time ago. I looked for her a couple times. I asked."

"This letter's almost twenty-five years old," I said.

"I know. I know. I told you," he said shifting from one foot to the other and looking around the bar. There was no one there but me, him, and Conroy. "I just want you to find her for me. Tell me where she is, is all."

"She's gone, Warren," I said gently.

Conroy walked over, examined my almost empty, and looked at me. "Another?" he asked

"On me, Mr. Marlowe, on me," said Warren eagerly.

"No, thanks," I told both of them.

"You want privacy?" Conroy asked me, looking at Warren and making it clear that he would lead the man and his album to the door if I gave the word. Coils had lost his patience and most of his left leg on Guadalcanal. Warren was shaking his head no. I couldn't tell if the no was for Conroy, in response to my saying his sister was gone, or in answer to the prodding of some private demon.

"No, thanks," I told Conroy. "Warren and I are old friends."

I had known Warren for a couple of years, but we weren't friends. He did odd jobs in the neighborhood, washed windows, ran errands, swept up in exchange for free food from the restaurants, an odd pair of shoes or pants from a shoe store or clothing store, and a place to bed down in the basement of the building where I had my office.

I was now engaged in the longest conversation I had ever had with the man.

"I got drunk, Mister Marlowe," Warren said as Conroy shrugged and turned his back on us to clean some glasses. "I got drunk to get up the nerve, you know. Then I was ashamed of being drunk so I sobered. So my head is hurtin' fierce."

I gulped down the last of my beer, patted Warren on his shoulder, and got off the bar stool.

"She's gone, Warren," I repeated. "Get drunk again and get some sleep."

"I've got money," he said stepping back to dig into both pockets of his faded blue pants. Crumpled singles, fives, and tens appeared in his gnarled fists. He piled them on the bar next to his album and went back for more.

"See," he said. "I can pay."

More dollars. Lincoln and Washington looked up at me from the top of the heap of bills. They were on Warren Hlushka's side and I found them convincing.

"What's the discrepancy here?" Conroy said turning back to us, towel in one hand, glass in the other.

Warren was hyperventilating now, his large eyes fixed on my face waiting for the answer to all his prayers.

"Life's savings," he said earnestly, his face pressing against the window of his expected failure. "All I've got. I'm not asking for favors here. Oh no. I'm hiring just like any Joe. You too busy? O.K., but I'm a . . . a . . ."

Warren wasn't sure what he was and I didn't want to tell him.

"Give me a bag, Coils," I said, and Conroy shook his head and reached under the counter in search of a bag, his eyes never leaving the pile of bills, mine watching him. He came up with a brown paper bag and handed it to me. I shoved Warren's money into it and handed him the bag. He offered it to me again.

The last time I had met a client in a bar I wound up finding a woman for him. The situation wasn't quite the same. Warren wasn't about to break heads the way Moose Malloy had done. And I didn't figure to nearly get myself killed the way I had done looking for Moose's woman. Besides, I needed the money now, but more important I needed to have something to do.

"Twenty a day and expenses," I said. "If I don't find her in five days, I give it up and you promise to give it up. Deal?"

Warren went stone still.

"Give me fifty in advance," I went on. "I'll bill you for the rest if there is a rest. I'll need your album."

Warren shook himself out of his funk, smiled, and reached past me for the album. He handed it to me.

"That's business," he said, brushing his bald head in memory of long-departed hair and digging in to pull out my advance. "Alls you got to do is find her, tell me where she is. I'll do the rest."

"I'm closing for lunch," Coils Conroy said behind the bar as he removed his apron. "Place's a morgue."

I drove home with Warren's album on the seat next to me and his fifty bucks in my pocket. My car needed work. It was pitted with acne, but fifty dollars wouldn't cover the body work. When I got through my door, I took off my jacket and tie, turned on the table fan next to my chessboard, and sat down to look at the Hlushka family album. I wondered once or twice if I were doing a good deed or conning a sap who would never make it off the bottom rung of life. I wondered, but I didn't think about returning his fifty.

Warren's album contained six more photographs of Louise. She was about fifteen in the most recent one, a pretty girl in a white Sunday dress with a big white bow in her short auburn hair.

Judging by Warren I guessed his little sister would be in her midforties now. The one letter Warren had shown me didn't help much. It was postmarked Baker, Kansas, and said that Louise was thinking about getting married and that she and her fiance were considering a move to California. She asked if he could come home for the wedding. The address on the envelope indicated that Warren had lived in Dayton, Ohio.

I played through a Capablanca game from the 1921 international, had a cheese sandwich, took a shower, and went to bed early, turning the fan toward me. I had no trouble sleeping.

In the morning I shaved, stopped for a carry-out coffee and donut from a hole-in-the-wall called Casey's on La Cienega. Casey's coffee was awful, but his wife made great donuts. I took donut and coffee to my office, gathered in the three letters waiting for me in the morning mail, went to my desk, pulled over the phone, and got to work.

Two phone calls later I was talking to a woman named Ethel Murray at the *Baker Weekly Dispatch*. Ethel didn't sound young, but she did sound impressed by a long-distance call from California.

"Ethel," I said, "your editor, Mister Stanfield said you might be able to help me. Sometime back in May or June nineteen twenty-one a woman named Louise Hlushka probably got married in Baker. I'd like to know who she married and where . . ."

"Alton Cash," she broke in. "Married by Reverend Sawyer at the First Methodist."

"I'm impressed," I said.

"Needn't be," said Ethel. "I'd like to string you along, tell you I have one of those photographic memories like the boy in *American Weekly*, but it's not in me. I was Louise's bridesmaid. Not a big wedding, but I stood up and so did Alton's brother Jess."

"Where are Louise and Alton?"

"California," she said.

"Big state," I said, tucking the phone under my chin and reaching for the morning mail.

"I'll narrow it some," she said. "Alton said he had relatives in some place called Bay City. You heard of it?"

"I've heard of it," I said, opening a phone bill and shoving it in the lower right-hand drawer of my desk. "You have a picture of the happy couple or Louise alone? That's my final request and I'll send you five dollars for your time and effort."

"I'll take a look," she said, "Mister . . . ?"

"Marlowe," I supplied.

"Why are you looking for Louise after all these years? If it's about the Taylor girl, believe me it was an accident. I knew Louise. She had a temper, yes, but under it. . . . It was the rumors, the talk, that drove them off, not any fancy job. Alton was doing just fine in Baker."

"What did Alton do?"

"He was chief of police," Ethel said.

"Ethel, put together whatever you have on the accident and on Chief Cash. I'm sending you a check for ten dollars. You can cash it before you send whatever you find. Louise's brother is looking for her, just wants to make contact, and I'm helping him out."

There was a long pause, a sigh, and Ethel said, "I thought Warren was dead by now. I'll see what I can find for you and get it in the noon mail tomorrow. No charge. Just if you see Louise, tell her Ethel Murray said God bless."

I told her that if I had the chance I'd give Louise Cash her message. I thanked her, gave her my address, and hung up. It could have been easy from this point on. Bay City was less than thirty miles from where I was sitting. I'd had some run-ins with the police there, but that was a few years back. It could have been easy, but it didn't work out that way.

The second of my three morning letters was an ad for the latest in sidearms. I junked it. The last letter I didn't open. I recognized Terry's handwriting from the address. I junked it and pulled a Bay City telephone book from the same drawer I'd put the phone bill in.

There were five Cashes. No Alton. No Louise. I tried all five. Two were Negroes. Two were surly and said they didn't have any relatives named Alton or Louise. The fifth was a lonely old man who didn't want to lose this lucky contact with a fellow human. He said he thought he had a cousin Louise from the East but she had never come to Bay City. He suggested I come see him. He would make lunch and we could talk it over. I thanked him and said I'd get to him if I needed more help.

Warren Hlushka came by just before noon as I was leaving the office for lunch. He played with his sleeve, looked at me in wonder, and asked if I had found anything yet. I gave him what I had from Ethel and the phone book.

"There was some trouble back in Baker," I told him. "Something to do with a girl named Taylor. You know anything about it?"

"Me?" asked Warren.

"Unless Eisenhower just walked in behind you, yes," I said.

"I don't know anything about anything," he said.

"Your sister and her husband probably left because of the Taylor business," I explained. "Probably changed their name, that is if they even moved to Bay City. I'm waiting for some information from Baker. It'll take a few days to get here. No charge till it does."

"You favoring me, Mister Marlowe?" he asked. "Or is that the way of it? You're not trying to give me no free ride?"

"It's the way of it, Warren," I assured him and went out for lunch.

I didn't quite forget about Warren and the Cashes for the next two days but I did manage to push them into some dark space while I helped out on an insurance stakeout for the World Detective Agency. It was an around-the-clock surveillance on a trio of ex-cons who'd probably taken down a Brink's truck in Encino the month before. World called in free-lancers like me to fill in while the regulars were out beating the bushes. After two days, somebody at World decided we had the wrong men or it was costing too much. I was given a check for fifty bucks and the offer to join the staff. I took the check and turned down the job.

The package from Ethel Murray of Baker, Kansas, was under my door the next morning. It helped. There were newspaper clippings of the Cash-Hlushka wedding. Alton had gotten married in his chief's uniform. He looked lean, trim, and proud and his smile showed a small gap between his top front teeth. Louise had been married in a white dress. Her hair was short, her face pretty and clean, and her body full but not quite plump. There were no other pictures of Louise but there were several of Alton over the next year and a half after the wedding. He'd aged quickly. The Taylor case, on which there were four clippings, probably helped age him. Sharon Rose Taylor, twenty-four, had fallen or been pushed out of a window of the Equity Building, the tallest building in Baker, which meant that she had fallen about six floors at most. Alton and Louise had been with her at the time. Their tale was full of holes, but Cash was the chief of police and he'd said Sharon Rose had gone inexplicably mad and leapt out the window. Sharon Rose's father, according to the clippings, was incredulous in spite of the fact that his daughter had spent a few weeks in the state mental hospital earlier that year. The county coroner's inquiry accepted Alton and Louise Cash's story. The town of Baker might have had more trouble with the tale than the county coroner. Three months after Sharon Rose Taylor's death, according to a small clipping, Alton resigned as chief and announced that he had been offered a big job in California.

That was it. Not much, but something. I drove to Bay City with the windows open, half dreaming in the heat, not thinking about the drive. The smells of Los Angeles guided me. Each neighborhood has its own smell and look: the dry summer dust of the string of flatland towns; the suburban grass and steep hills as you head west; the smell of salt and the craggy coast as you hit the ocean and the coast highway. I drove south down the western end of the continent. This was as far as you could go, as far as your dreams would carry you in the United States.

Bay City was full of people who had run as far as they could go. It had been taken over more than thirty years earlier by men with dollars and guns who made a profit from the dreamers and high rollers. Bay City was known as the place where you could buy anything if you looked right and kept your mouth shut. I'd had a run-in with a Bay city cop named Degarmo some years back. Degarmo had been one of the dreamers. He was dead now, but Bay City was still alive, though the high rollers weren't rolling quite as high as they once had.

I drove straight to the police station, a freshly cleaned stone three-story at the end of a park. The lobby was empty and the polished stone floors recently scrubbed. The rubber soles of my shoes squeaked as I went through the door marked Inquiries/Detective.

The place had been through some remodeling since I had been there last. A counter ran from wall to wall protecting the police from the public. The desks beyond the counter were steel and small, with a few cops and robbers strewn around the place. Behind the counter facing me was an old cop whose face I remembered but whose name I couldn't place. He was overweight and uncomfortable in his stretched and starched uniform complete with tie.

He looked me over, didn't show any sign of recognition, which was fine with me, and decided I wasn't high priority.

"You got a problem?" he asked.

"Looking for a guy," I said leaning on the counter to face him. He was my height, about six feet, but I had the feeling he had once been taller. I pulled out a clipping of Alton Cash and shoved it toward him. The old cop looked down at the clipping and then looked up at me.

"Old picture," he said.

"Very old," I agreed. "But he has the kind of weathered face that probably doesn't change much and that space between his teeth wouldn't go away."

The old cop scratched his head and looked at Alton's picture again.

"What's your angle?" he asked.

"I'm a friend of his brother-in-law," I said. "Brother-in-law is sick, very sick, probably dying back in an L.A. hospital. Hasn't been in touch with his sister for more than twenty years and suddenly got a line on her in Bay City. This friend wants to see his sister before he dies."

"Simple as that?" he asked pushing the clipping back at me. I took it and returned it to my pocket.

"Simple as that," I said.

He looked around to see if anyone was watching and then whispered, "New chief here. Cleaning up. New image. I'd retire now if I had the years in. Collar's killing me. Can't afford to retire without the pension."

"Can I contribute to the pension fund?" I asked.

"Don't see why not," he said. "Private donation. Say, fifteen dollars."

"Say ten," I said, pulling out a ten and letting him see me palm it in my right hand.

"Ten," he said. "Name's not Cash like it says under that picture. Calls himself Dyson. He was on the force here. Quit some time back. You're lucky you ran into me. Most of the young vets around here wouldn't know him."

"How do I find him?" I asked.

He looked around again, held up a finger to show I should wait, and then slouched around the corner. I watched the neatly dressed cops at their desks talking quietly on their phones for about three minutes till the old cop came back. He leaned toward me.

"Four-four-six Oleander Drive. Go back to Central and then right almost to the docks. You'll see Oleander on the right about the same time you see the Pacific. That's his last address. Your guess is as good as mine if he's still there."

I reached over, shook his hand, and felt him take in the ten dollar bill with the skill of an expert. There was nothing more to say. I went back outside and headed down Central.

Oleander wasn't hard to find. It was one of those run-down side streets on which some developer had thrown up one-story white-frame houses back in the 1920's for the first wave of newcomers working in the Bay City shipyard. Ten years after they were built the flimsy one-stories were ready for the wrecker. Twenty years later they were occupied by Negro families where the breadwinners were women who cleaned house for the grifters in the estates higher up in the hills. Thirty years later the houses of Oleander Street were sagging and dying. A few of them had been shorn up and coaxed like punch-drunk pugs into standing up for one more round. Four-four-six Oleander didn't look as if it could take another punch. The porch sagged and the paint flecked. The screen door had been patched so many times that it looked like modern art, and the dirt lawn with only a barren lemon tree on it had long ago given up the hope of grass.

I parked on the curb of the cracked concrete street and looked over at the two Negro kids about six who had been tossing a tin can back and forth till I got out of the car. The boy crinkled his nose at me and the girl squinted. As I hit the steps of four-four-six, I heard the girl say, "He gonna see the witch."

I knocked at the peeling frame of the screen door. The door shook and threatened to come loose. Nothing. I knocked again.

"Keep knockin', mister," called the girl across the street. "They home. They always home."

I kept knocking and eventually I heard a shuffle inside. It stopped. I knocked again and the shuffle moved toward the door and then the door opened, but just a crack.

"What?" came the man's voice.

I couldn't see the face in the shadows through the thick mesh.

"Mr. Dyson?" I asked.

"So?" he asked.

"My name's Marlowe. I'd like to talk to you for a minute. I just came from police headquarters in Bay City."

He hesitated, started to close the door.

"It's about your wife," I threw in.

The door stopped closing.

"My wife isn't well," he said.

"I've got a message for her," I said.

"No," the man said, slamming the door.

"Mr. Dyson," I called through the closed door. "I think you're going to have to deal with me, either now or tomorrow or the next day. I can keep coming back and draw a lot of attention to you, or you can let me in and get it over with."

If he hadn't opened the door, I would have left and gone back to Warren with my report. But he didn't call my bluff.

"That's tellin' him, mister," the girl across the street called.

The door opened and I went through the screen door into a darkened hall. I could see the thin outline of a man in front of me. He backed away and I followed. When we stepped into a small living room, there was enough light coming through the drawn shades to see that the man was dressed in a badly faded blue shirt and equally faded blue pants. His mouth was partly open and his teeth were bad but they were all there and there was a gap. In his right hand he held a Smith and Wesson .38 with a six-inch barrel, a favorite with cops.

The most striking thing about Alton Cash was that I knew he couldn't be more than fifty, but he looked at least twenty years older. His hair was white, his shoulders bent, and his eyes a vacant, faded blue.

"Who are you?" he asked.

"Name is Marlowe, just the way I told you."

There were chairs to sit in, even a sofa, but they were old with a washed out, ghostly pattern and I was sure that dust would rise from them if I sat. He didn't ask me to sit and I didn't want to.

"He sent you, didn't he?" Cash asked, pistol leveled at my stomach. "He sent you to find us."

"He?"

"Her brother," he said.

"I want to talk to your wife," I said.

"No," he said.

Something stirred in the doorway and I turned to the sound of sagging wooden floors. My eyes met the deepest, darkest and most melancholy brown eyes I had ever seen. The eyes were set in a soft balloon of a face resting on a huge, neckless, round body. Louise Hlushka Cash walked with a cane to support her mass. Her breathing was pained and labored.

"He's from Warren," Alton said.

Her eyes opened wide in fear.

"He wants to talk to you," I said.

"We know what he wants with her," Alton said.

"Alton," Louise croaked.

"We've spent our lives hiding from him, Louise," Alton said with almost a sob in his voice. "I'm beginning to think our lives aren't worth that damned much anymore."

With that he gave me his full attention.

"How much he paying you to kill us?" he asked.

"Kill you?" I asked. "He doesn't want to kill you. He wants to see his sister."

"His sister is dead," Louise Cash said, sagging into a nearby chair that groaned under her weight.

"Dead?"

"Her name was Sharon Rose Taylor," Louise said. "My parents adopted Warren. The Taylors adopted Sharon Rose when their mother abandoned them."

"Whole family was a little mad," said Alton. "Sharon Rose thought I was in love with her. She said I'd promised to marry her. Louise and I went to see her where she worked in the Equity Building in Baker. We told her we were getting married, that she had to stop bothering me. And then . . ."

"She acted crazy, threatened," said Louise, her eyes looking beyond me into the past. "I lost my temper . . . I said things . . . and she . . ."

"Went out the window," I finished. "That's . . ."

"Crazy?" Alton said. "Damned right. She'd written to Warren telling him lies about me, about Louise, and when Sharon Rose died he blamed us for it."

"And he was right," said Louise softly.

"He wasn't," wailed Alton. "We didn't know she was that crazy."

"We should have been more gentle with her," said Louise to no one.

"We've been over it and over it," cried Alton. "You want to die now? You want this man to shoot you?"

"I don't care anymore, Alton," she said. "We ran from him when he came for us in nineteen twenty-nine or thirty, and we ran from the other man he sent when the war started, and . . ."

"I'm not here to shoot anybody," I said, but the Cashes weren't listening to me. They were off in a conversation they must have had a thousand times on a thousand nights and afternoons.

"No more, Alton," she said. "No more."

Alton's hand dropped slowly as he spoke and the gun pointed toward the floor. I wanted to tell them to forget the whole thing, that I would just go back to Los Angeles, return what I had of Warren's money, and tell him it was over. And that's what I would have done if Alton had given me a chance to explain. What he did instead was lift his .38 and take aim at me. I recognized the look in his eyes. I'd seen it before. It was a look that said, "I've got nothing to do with what's going to happen next. I'm somewhere else. When it's over, I'll come back and I won't even know what I've done."

The look gave me a fraction of a second to throw myself to the floor before he fired. I rolled further into the room when the second shot came and I heard a wheezing groan, a groan that sounded like a punctured tire. I was on the dusty floor against the wall waiting for Alton to take a third shot at me when I heard his pistol clatter to the floor.

I looked up to see Alton shuffling over to Louise, who was slumped forward, a rivulet of blood snaking down her once-white dress. I got to one knee and lunged for the gun but Alton didn't notice. He was trying to stop the massive body of his wife from sliding onto the floor. He didn't have a chance. I picked up the gun by the barrel.

"She's dying," he wailed.

"She's dead," I corrected, walking over to him as Louise Cash rolled onto the floor.

"I killed her?" he asked, looking up at me.

"You killed her, Alton," I confirmed.

"She'd be alive if you hadn't come."

"That's one way of looking at it. Where's the phone?"

"No phone," he said.

He sat cross-legged on the floor cradling his dead wife's head in his lap. The dust in the house and the taste of death got to me. I went for the door and into the sun still holding the .38 by the barrel. The bright hot day hadn't gone away. Nothing had changed in the few minutes I'd been in the tomb the Cashes had lived in. The two kids across the street were looking at me, probably wondering about the gunshots but not too surprised to hear them in this neighborhood.

"You got a phone?" I asked.

"Nope," said the girl, "but there's one in Robinson's store up the road. Anybody dead?"

"Most of the people who ever lived," I said.

The Bay City police came about twenty minutes after I called them. An address on Oleander gave them plenty of reason to move slowly. I turned the pistol over to the cops, who showed little interest in a routine domestic incident, and said I was just passing through the neighborhood when I heard the shot and went in. I told them I didn't know the Cashes, that I was just a good citizen, a former employee of the Los Angeles district attorney. I gave them Alton Cash's .38 and left a false name and address in L.A. in case they wanted to get in touch with me. Alton was too far out of it to contradict me or pay any attention. He had been waiting and planning to go mad for more than half a lifetime. His moment had come.

I drove back to Los Angeles slowly and made my way to the Cascadia Lounge where Coils Conroy was behind the bar. It was late afternoon and the place was alive with a crew of construction workers who were tearing down an office building nearby. I ordered a Scotch straight and nursed it. Warren Hlushka came through the door about an hour after I did.

"Figured I'd find you here," said Warren behind me over the sound of two of the construction workers arguing about whether a major league baseball team belonged in Los Angeles.

"You figured right," I said without turning around.

"Any luck, Mister Marlowe?" he asked, squirming onto the red leather bar stool next me.

"Not for Louise Cash," I said. "She's dead."

Behind us a construction worker had dropped a couple of dimes in the jukebox. A band blared out and I wanted to leave.

"What?"

"You're too late, Warren," I said. "You can't kill her. She's dead."

"Kill her?" he asked, those eyes wide with confusion. "I didn't want to kill her. I wanted to tell her I forgave her. I was bad to Louise, Mr. Marlowe. I said bad things to her when someone died. I tried once to have someone find her, tell her I was sorry, but she ran away. I tried to find her myself but it was no go. I wanted to forgive her."

"For what she did to Sharon Rose?" I asked over the noise of the jukebox and the arguing construction workers.

"Yeah," he said. "I said bad things and I been real sorry for a long time. I wanted to tell Louise I was sorry."

I looked at Warren and I could see from his battered face that he was telling the truth. Alton and Louise Cash had spent most of a lifetime running from nothing but their own guilt.

"I guess I got no sister now," Warren said. "Had two sisters most of my life. Now I got none."

"You've got change coming, Warren," I said, pulling out my wallet.

He put his hand on top of mine to stop me.

"No favoring," he reminded me.

I shrugged and put the wallet back.

"Let me buy you a drink," I said.

"Just a beer will do," said Warren, looking around the bar in amazement. "You got any brothers or sisters, Mister Marlowe?"

"No," I said, trying to get Coils Conroy's attention.

"Too bad," said Warren softly. "Too bad."

I hardly heard him. The air was full of music.

━━━━━━━━━━━━━━━━━━━

Raymond Chandler is not one of my favorite writers. He is my favorite writer and has been since the day I happened to pick up a paperback copy of The Lady in the Lake *shortly after my fourteenth birthday. I had read detective stories before that day, had listened to Sam Spade on the radio, had seen Mike Shayne movies, but Marlowe on the printed page came alive instantly. I knew what he was feeling, suffered his pain, understood his pleasures, though I could never remember the plots. I still get them confused, but I find the characters unforgettable, especially Marlowe, who carries the burden of living with a cynicism which manages to avoid bitterness. I imagine*

Marlowe with a wry, knowing smile, joking to ease the boredom and to protect his emotions, willing to let his romanticism show enough to help an innocent in distress, knowing that each adventure is destined to result in a tragic loss, a love gone sour, a friend who betrays. When I was fourteen, I sensed the pained author behind the characters and wondered why tales so melancholy could fascinate me. Now that I am an adult I no longer wonder. Chandler captured our world, an immoral world in which everyone has an excuse, a reason, even the worst of villains, for the transgressions they engage in. I am haunted by Chandler's characters in this dark world, his fantasy pleading for understanding from Marlowe, who can understand their pain but do nothing about it. My only regret about Chandler is that he wrote so little. He did, however, spawn others who have tried to carry on and recapture, as much for themselves as for any audience, the world which Chandler created. And for that I am grateful.

Stuart Kaminsky

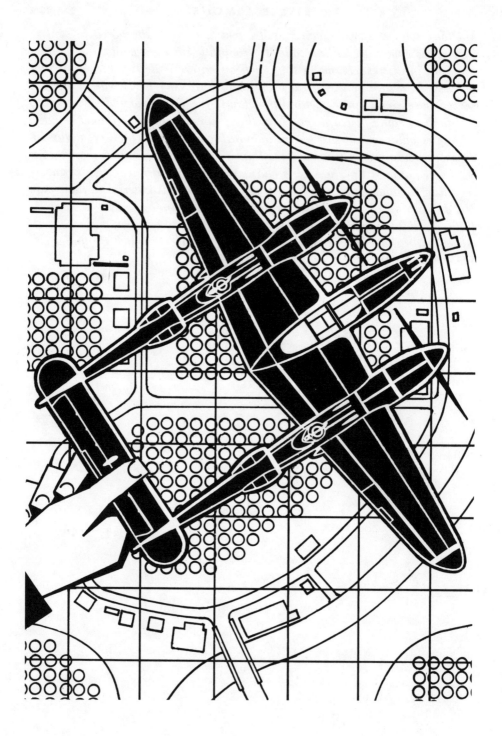

THE MAN WHO KNEW DICK BONG

ROBERT CRAIS

1953

THE WOMAN CAME in first, taking hard fast steps that made her spike heels dig into the linoleum out in the little reception office. She had bright red lips and penciled eyebrows and orange hair that was pinned back on one side and waved forward on the other. She was in a cheap camel suit with big shoulders that looked like it had seen a lot of wear. So did she.

When she saw me she stopped with her hand still on the door knob and said, "Are you Philip Marlowe?"

I would've taken my feet down from where they were napping on the desk, but she had been too fast for me. I let them snooze. "If the price is right."

She gave me a hard grin. "A smart guy. I like that." Knock'm dead, Marlowe.

She said something into the hall and a little boy came in. He had a chubby face and a chubby body and pencil-thin arms and legs. She had him dressed in a plaid short-sleeved shirt and short pants that were too big for his skinny legs and black wingtips that looked like they had never been polished. He was slurping at a grape-flavored Tootsie-Roll Pop and he was hanging onto a little cast tin model of a P-38 Lightning twin-engined fighter plane. You could smell the grape all the way across the office.

She pointed him at the couch beneath the window and said, "Sit over there till I'm finished." He sat. She took the hard chair across from my desk and made a big deal out of looking at my feet. "Are you interested in a little job or is your dance card full?"

I shook my head. "I don't do divorce work."

"What makes you think that's what I want?"

"You've got the look."

She gave a single sharp laugh that I didn't like very much. The boy was sitting quietly on the couch, playing with the little airplane and sneaking peeks at me. She said, "The divorce I got twenty months ago. What I need is someone to collect the alimony and child support that the sonofabitch I was married to owes me."

I glanced at the boy. "Are we talking about the boy's father?"

"You don't think I'd make this mistake more than once, do you?"

When she said it, the boy turned around and stared down at Hollywood Boulevard. His right shoe was on the couch, but I didn't say anything. Worse than that had been there.

Her name was Louise Barris and her boy's name was Robby. She'd met and married an aeronautical engineer named Frank Barris who'd worked in Burbank near the end of the war, but the marriage hadn't amounted to much. Frank boozed, Frank whined about everything, Frank couldn't make the grade as a man, and finally they'd split. Robby was their only child. Louise said, "The sonofabitch hasn't been able to hold a job since the start of Korea, but now he's managed to scrape up some kind of measly little irrigation engineer thing out in Tarzana or Woodland Hills or one of those places. I figure I can't wait. I figure I better get mine before the no-good lush finds another way to get shitcanned."

I looked at the boy again. He was holding the airplane out the window, lost flying in the hot summer sky three stories above Hollywood. I said, "If your ex isn't paying alimony and child support, you don't need me. Go back to court."

She made a face, like I should've been sharper than that. "Going to court costs money."

"So do I. Thirty bucks a day."

She shook her head. "Jesus, things have gone up since the war."

I nodded. Thirty was a backbreaker, all right. "If he's been out of work, maybe he doesn't have it."

"He has it, all right. Don't you worry about that." She dug around in her purse until she came out with a photograph and a yellow piece of paper and put them on my desk. I had to move my feet to get them. "That's a picture of Frank. I wrote down how to get to where he lives and where he's working. There's a little map."

I didn't bother with the map. Frank had a blocky head and a high brow and a pencil mustache under a zucchini nose. The picture looked like a college yearbook picture. Cal State, maybe. Or City College. The boy looked just like him.

She said, "It's not even lunchtime, now. I figure you could get over there just after lunch, lean on him a little, then get back to my place by early afternoon with the money."

"I'm not a hired thug."

"So we're not even talking a full day here, are we? Shouldn't cost more than, what, fifteen dollars?"

I looked at the boy again. "How much does your ex owe you?"

"Nine months at a hundred-fifty a month. Thirteen-fifty. But don't start thinking you can screw me out of a percentage. I need that money." She frowned at the boy. "I got expenses."

I nodded. Fifteen bucks.

She said, "He knows I want it, and he knows he's got to get it to me. We talked about it and he said he would, only now he's double-crossing me. Don't let the no-good piece of shit kid you on that."

The boy turned away from the window, both hands holding the little airplane as if it were flying in a long gentle turn. His lips moved as if he were talking to himself. Pilot to pilot. If I had a son, I wondered, would he look like me the way this boy looked like Frank Barris? I stood up. "I'll see what I can do."

She opened her purse, took out two fives and five singles and put them on my desk. I didn't touch them. "My address is on the little map, too. We'll be expecting you."

I watched her seal up her purse. I said, "Tell me something, you always shit all over your ex-husband in front of the boy?"

She nodded. "Every chance I get."

Louise Barris stood, put out her hand for the boy, and they left.

Frank Barris worked at a county irrigation station in the San Fernando Valley, in Tarzana. I drove up through the Cahuenga pass, then went west along Ventura Boulevard for about a million miles. The further I went, the drier the air became, until my skin felt tight and raw and gritty. It was cooler than I had expected, though. Only about a hundred and fifteen.

After a while, the number of buildings along the boulevard grew spotty and the orange groves began. They stretched up into the valley across desiccated ground, row after row of short, dark-trunked trees, each heavy with bright orange balls. Tarzana. Edgar Rice Burroughs had lived in Tarzana, but Tarzan never had. Everything was flat and dry and empty except for the endless rows of orange trees. No rivers. No alligators. No elephants or lions or friendly chimpanzees. Orange trees would be hell to swing through.

I followed the directions that Louise Barris had drawn on the yellow sheet of paper until I came to the irrigation station. It was a single-story industrial building made out of cement blocks and corrugated tin, with three county trucks and a couple of sedans out front. I went through a big sliding door into a warehouse where the county stored pipes and fittings and valves and pumps and the other equipment they used to fight the desert. A couple of Mexicans were carrying a pump that was too heavy for them, and a bald man was sitting at a dark wood table, smoking and reading the news. The bald man didn't look up. I walked past him and went through the door into a little hall that joined a couple of glass-walled offices. One of the offices was empty, but Frank Barris was in the other.

Barris was lighting a cigarette with a big Zippo lighter and laughing at something that a goof named Lou Mardo was saying when I went in. There were large flat tables in each office with official-looking county irrigation plans spread over them and the sort of T-squares and angles engineers use for drawing, only Barris's looked like they hadn't been used in a while.

Barris saw me first and then Lou Mardo saw me. Lou was holding a short glass with something brown in it. There was another short glass on the desk in front of Barris and a pint bottle of Old Crow. Mardo stared at me until he put a name to the face, then tipped his glass. "Philip Marlowe. My, my."

Lou and I went back. His older brother had been a pretty good peeler, splitting twenty-dollar bills for a living until a couple of psychos tortured him to death with an electric iron. Lou had wanted to take up his older brother's trade, only he didn't have the steady hand. His criminal career had topped out with two-bit burglary and making out he was better with safes and locks than he really was and telling lies. Some guys are born small time. "Hiya doing, Louie. Haven't seen you in a while."

Lou took more of the Crow. Just a couple of guys meeting in a bar. "Korea."

Frank Barris looked nervous. "Who is this guy?"

Lou smiled. "He's a shamus. Forget him."

"I didn't think engineers were your style, Lou." I grinned at Frank Barris. "Usually it's pimps and horse dopers and candy queens."

Barris said, "What's he doing here?" He didn't look any less nervous.

I said, "Lou doesn't have anything to do with this, Frank. This is between me and you."

Frank stared at me and so did Louie Mardo and I wondered what all the staring was about. I also wondered what a guy like Lou Mardo was doing in a county engineer's office. Frank said, "I don't have business with you."

"Your ex-wife."

"Louise?"

I nodded. "She needs the alimony and the child support and she sent me around to see about it." I showed him the private buzzer. "How about it?"

Lou Mardo laughed suddenly and put down the glass. "These dames." He went to the door. "I'll see you later, Frankie. You, too, Marlowe." He went out. There was a slight limp that I hadn't seen before. Korea, maybe.

Frank Barris waited until Mardo was gone, then opened the desk drawer and flipped a maroon checkbook onto his desk. There was a framed diploma on the wall behind him. University of Southern California, College of Engineering. Not bad. Better than I had thought. He said, "You're just here for the check?"

"Sure. Why else would I be here?"

Barris crossed his arms and leaned back in the chair away from the checkbook. You could see the boy in him, all right. Same round face, same wide nose, same high forehead. "Don't worry about it," he said. "How much she paying you to arm-twist?"

"Fifteen dollars."

"Man, you must be big-time." Barris put on a smirk. "She'll haul you in the sack if you like'm that way."

I didn't answer. There was a small photograph of a P-38 Lightning fighter thumbtacked to the wall over one of Barris's drafting tables, the same plane that the boy had played with in my office. The photograph was seven or eight years old, and looked as if it had been handled a lot. I stared at it. When Barris saw what I was looking at, the smirk went away. He uncrossed his arms, dug out a pen, and wrote the check. "I owe her nine months. That's one thousand three hundred fifty. Tell her she would've gotten the damn money without spending any of it on you."

"The kid will appreciate it." It came out harder than I liked.

Barris tore the check out of the book, blew on it, then slid it across the desk. "I've been out of work."

"Sure." I picked it up.

He looked as if there were more to say and he was deciding whether or not to say it. There was something soft in his eyes then, and it made me wonder if he ever called his boy or took him to the park to play ball. It made me think he wanted to. Barris looked at the Old Crow bottle, then lifted his glass and sipped some of it. "Don't ever marry a whore, Marlowe," he said. "You end up doing the damnedest things."

"Sure." I folded the check once, put it in my coat pocket, and went back out into the heat.

Louise Barris lived in a beige stucco bungalow on Whipple Street in North Hollywood, just off Lankershim Boulevard. There was a '38 Ford coupe in the drive and a red Columbia bike lying on the ground by the little front porch. The lawn was brown and ratty because no one watered it and no one mowed it, and the house and the car and the bike and the lawn looked dusty.

I parked behind the Ford and went up to the front door and knocked. Marlowe earning his fifteen dollars.

The boy opened the door. The plaid dress-up-to-visit-the-detective shirt was gone. He was wearing a dirt-stained white tee-shirt with a vee-neck collar, cutoff dungarees, and scruffy black sneakers. He was eating a Mars bar. I said, "Is your Mom home?"

He nodded.

"You think I could see her?"

He said, "My daddy knew Major Richard Bong, America's Ace of Aces." He blurted it out, the way he'd heard it on the newsreels. Richard Bong was America's top fighter ace in World War Two. The last couple of years of the war, a week didn't go by when Dick Bong wasn't in the headlines.

I said, "Yeah?"

"My daddy built fighter planes. He went all over making sure that the planes worked right, and Dick Bong gave him a ride from Brisbane, Australia, all the way to Port Moresby, New Guinea. My daddy had to scrunch down in the back because there's only one seat in a P-38." P-38. The little twin-engined airplane the kid had carried into my office.

"Man," I said. "That must've been something."

The kid finished his Mars bar. "She's in the kitchen. I'll get her."

I went in as he ran back through the tiny living room into the house. The living room wasn't much cleaner than the front yard. There was a tattered davenport opposite a round-screen RCA television with a pecan coffee table keeping them apart. Empty Coca-Cola bottles and plates and dirty napkins were on the coffee table and on the T.V. An ashtray with about fifteen thousand butts in it sat on the couch's arm, and old cigarette burns on the arm looked like furry black caterpillars. There was a copy of *Life* magazine on the floor with Marlon Brando on the cover. I walked over to the coffee table and looked at what was left in the plates. Lunch had been jelly sandwiches.

Louise Barris came out wearing a slip. "Buddy, you work fast. Did Frankie come across?"

I gave her the check. "He said you'll get what's yours. Every nickel."

She looked at the check as if she thought he'd written it in disappearing ink. "If he knows what's good for him, I will. You wait right here. I wanna call the bank and check on this sonofabitch."

She went back into the kitchen. I heard ice in a glass before I heard her dial. Maybe I would ask for overtime.

The boy came in and stood with one foot atop the other and watched me the way you watch something that's on television. I gave him a smile and he smiled back. I said, "You're a pretty big kid. You like to play football?"

He crossed his arms and looked embarrassed. I wondered how long it had been since he'd talked with a man who wasn't over here just to jump his mother.

He said, "Did you see my daddy?"

"Uh-huh. He said to tell you hello."

He looked pleased. "Were you in the war like my daddy?"

"Nothing as classy as building fighter planes. I was in the infantry. In the Philippines."

"Did you know Dick Bong?"

"No."

"How about Tommy McGuire or Pappy Boyington?" Other fighter aces.

I shook my head. "Guys like me watched guys like Bong and McGuire fly by overhead and wished we were up there."

He rubbed at the side of his face with the back of his forearm, smearing what was left of the Mars bar. "You wanta see what I got in my room?"

"Sure."

We went back past a small turquoise bathroom into the boy's bedroom. There was a single bed with a painted iron frame and a chest of drawers and a very old wicker trunk and an oval throw rug on the floor. A small stack of Human Torch comics was on the floor near the head of the bed and a G-Man Big Little Book was on the windowsill and four immaculately painted balsa wood P-38 Lightning model airplanes were on top of the chest. There were pictures of more P-38's pinned to walls and three or four clippings from the *Los Angeles Times* showing Dick Bong, America's Ace of Aces. The papers were old and yellowed but the edges had been neatly trimmed and the clippings had been pinned in place with great care. The models were free from dust and the floor free from litter. There were no dirty clothes scattered about and no clutter. The bedroom was spotless. It was as if this room were not part of the house, as if stepping in here were stepping into someplace special and preserved and private.

The boy said, "My daddy built these models for me. That's Dick Bong's plane. That's Dick Bong right there." He pointed at one of the browned clippings on the wall. A smiling young guy with blond hair and a baby face was standing beside the wicked round nose of a P-38. A girl's portrait had been painted there. Beneath the painting was her name. Margie.

I said, "Dick Bong was something, all right."

"He got forty Japs and the Medal of Honor, see?" Robby ran to another spot on another wall and showed me another clipping. Douglas MacArthur was placing a ribbon around Bong's neck. The headline said *Bravest of the Brave*. "I'm gonna be a fighter pilot just like Dick Bong," he said. "I'm gonna be just like Dick Bong and Tommy McGuire and Pappy Boyington and those other guys my daddy knew. Lookit this."

He ran to the chest and pulled out the bottom drawer and took a flat package from under some clothes. There were two pieces of cardboard, tied together with yellow cord. The cardboard was old and smudged, but strong and stiff. He untied the cord and lifted back the top piece of cardboard like he was lifting the lid on a treasure chest. "My daddy gave me this last year. Dick Bong signed it himself."

It was a simple black-and-white photograph of three men sitting together in a tent, very likely somewhere in the South Pacific. The man in the middle was Frank Barris, ten years younger. The man on his right was Tommy McGuire. The man on his left was Richard Bong. The three of them were smiling, and Tommy McGuire was kidding around by pulling out Frank Barris's ears so he looked like Dumbo. An inscription across the right corner of the picture said *Keep'm flying, Frankie! Your pal, Dick Bong*.

Robby Barris tapped the picture and looked up at me with wide, bright eyes. He said, "You see. I'm gonna be just like Dick Bong. Just like him. You wait and see." He kept tapping. He wanted to be like Dick Bong, all right. Pals with his dad.

Out in the kitchen, Louise Barris yelled, "That son of a bitch!"

She came crashing through the house, first into the living room where she screamed where in hell had I gone, then slapping barefoot back along the hall toward the kid's room. Robby sandwiched the cardboard around the picture and then put it back under the clothes and shut the drawer. When I turned away from him I was in the door and she couldn't get into the room. She expected me to move so that she could come in, but I didn't. Her face was red and her eyes bulged and there was a dribble of spit down her chin. She held up the check and shook it. "The goddamned check's no good! The son of a bitch is trying to screw me."

I spoke quietly. "Not in front of the boy."

"What in hell do you mean, not in front of the boy? He's my boy." She tried to look past me at the boy, and shouted louder. "He's cheating us, Robby! You see how that no-good bastard father of yours cheats us? You see?"

The muscles in my neck and jaws went tight and I moved so that I filled the doorway as much as possible. She took a step back, and you could tell she was thinking that I was a no-good bastard, too, just like every other man she had ever known. I said, "Not in front of the boy."

She leaned close to me and hissed, "You tell Frank his ass is mine. Tell him I'm going to get him for this."

I looked back at their son. Robby had climbed up onto his bed and was sitting cross-legged, face stuck in one of his comic books, eating a Tootsie-Roll that had appeared from God knows where. One cheek was puffed out with candy and his jaw worked furiously and he looked the way he'd look if the guy who drew the comic book had drawn him. Only tears were dripping down from his cheeks onto the pages.

I turned back to Louise and took the check. "I'll go straighten it out."

I left without saying anything.

I drove around for a while and stopped at the Studio City park and watched some kids playing softball. There was a guy selling ice cream out of a little white cart, so I stood in line and bought a bar. I was twice as tall as anyone else in the line. You wonder why people have kids. You think maybe people oughta have to get special licenses or take classes. How to be a good parent. How to love. How to beat up each other without damaging your child. You think maybe there ought to be a special goon squad that goes around checking up on parents and beating the shit out of those who don't measure up. Ah, Marlowe. You crab.

I watched the kids playing softball and ate my ice cream and after a while I drove to a little market on Moorpark at Coldwater and called the Tarzana irrigation station and asked for Frank Barris. The guy who answered the phone told me Barris had taken off for the day. I asked if Barris usually called it quits after lunch. The guy said a couple of Barris's buddies had stopped by in a maroon Caddie and if Barris wanted to go with them that was Barris's business, Barris being the station's chief engineer, though maybe not for long, heh-heh. I asked if the guy knew who the buddies might be. The guy said no, but they looked like a couple of high rollers, maybe I should try Santa Anita.

I hung up and shook my head. Frank Barris, check bouncer and all-American father.

I went into the little market, bought a strawberry soda, then drove over to Frank Barris's apartment. Philip Marlowe, Captain of the Goon Squad.

Barris lived in a ground-floor apartment on Valley Spring Lane in Toluca Lake, a couple of blocks up from Universal Studios. It was a small building, just six units, home for secretaries who worked at film studios and apprentice film editors and people who like things quiet. On a Sunday there would be radios playing and a couple of the secretaries sunning themselves and the smell of suntan oil. Midweek it was empty.

I parked by the hydrant out front, walked back to Barris's apartment, and knocked. After enough knocking I went around to the side of the place and let myself in through his bathroom window.

Frank had two rooms and a bath and not much else. There was a bed and a round wooden dining room table and two wooden chairs and a fridge in the kitchen and a lot of empty beer and Gilbey's bottles. His underwear and socks and things were in a suitcase on the floor by the bed. Two wrinkled suits hung in the closet, and there were dozens of rolls of county blueprints leaning against the walls. Someone had dumped an ashtray of cigarette butts into the toilet and forgotten to flush it, and the heat made the whole place stink sour with booze and cigarettes and sweat. Nice. Just the sort of place for a guy who had known Dick Bong.

On a high closet shelf in the bedroom, there was a kit with a half-completed balsa wood model of a P-38 Lightning. The main body fuselage had been finished, and the right wing along with the right engine nacelle and tail boom had been assembled and sanded and cemented into place. The left engine and tail boom were sanded, but hadn't been put together. When it was finished and painted, it would look just like the models in Robby Barris's room. Only there was dust on the kit. No one had touched it in a long while.

I put the little airplane back on the high shelf and went out into the living room. I went over to the dining table and sat and lit a cigarette and looked around and got ready to wait. There must have been a hundred rolls of blueprints around the little apartment. Most looked like stamped county plans for pumping stations or irrigation site maps or topographic studies. Not aeronautical engineering, but not particularly complicated, either. Maybe just right for a guy with a booze problem and trouble keeping a steady job. I was trying to spell my name with smoke rings when I saw that one of the plans was a little different. It had fallen over and uncurled so you could see the job description. It wasn't a pumping station or an aqueduct. It was a private home, and it belonged to a guy named Leo Pinella. Well, well. Leo Pinella ran a party house in the hills above Glendale. You could gamble, you could have girls, you could watch the kinds of movies they don't show at Grauman's Chinese Theater. You could get or do just about anything that money would allow you to get or do.

I unrolled the plans and looked at them. They were county file plans showing the plot map, the floor plan of Leo's house, his electrical and plumbing layouts, the front and side elevations, and the grading and footing specifications. I rolled them up and put them against the wall where I had found them and wondered why a guy like Frank Barris would have Leo Pinella's house plans lying around. A guy like Barris was just the kind of guy who'd find his way up to Pinella's as a customer and dump what little money he had into Pinella's pockets, but he and Pinella wouldn't be friends. Pinella wouldn't lower himself.

I thought about it some more, then I got up and unfurled the plans again and stared at them. Plans show you how to get in and how to get out. Take a guy like Barris who was hurting for money and mix in a heist artist like Lou Mardo who talked a good game as long as you were buying, and one things leads to another and maybe they start thinking they can take down Leo Pinella. Sprinkle in Barris telling his ex-wife he was going to pay her off and a couple of guys in a maroon Caddie taking him for a ride in the middle of the day and it didn't look good. Of course, maybe it didn't look bad, either. Maybe everything was fine and Barris was out at the track with a couple of his old buddies from the Dick Bong days.

Sure.

I turned to the first page of the plans, tore off Leo Pinella's address, then let myself out through Frank Barris's bathroom window.

Just before the war, Leo Pinella had bought six hundred acres of orange groves north of Los Angeles at the far edge of Glendale where the Verdugo Mountains push up from the valley floor. With mountains and desert behind him and a plain of orange groves in front of him, it was as far as he could get from cops and preachers and parent-teacher associations and anyone else who might object if he built a big place and ran people up there and let them do whatever they had a taste for doing. Leo Pinella had made a fortune.

I drove through Toluca Lake into Burbank where the Santa Monica foothills petered out by Griffith Park, then went north on Olive Boulevard toward Glendale. Up against the Santa Monicas there were little tract houses and movie studios, but further north along Olive the houses and studios gave way to factories and industrial facilities and finally the groves.

I turned off Olive and followed state roads into the trees and drove for a very long time. There was an Eagle filling station and a Simms Feed & Hardware and still more orange trees. The trees swallowed everything and pretty soon there was nothing else, just orange trees and crows and a hot, dry wind rippling the leaves. Out here, you could scream as deep and as loud and as long as you wanted and the trees and the wind would swallow it and give nothing back.

Pinella's house was easy to see from the valley floor. It was a sprawling white hacienda, bright against a mountainside that had not been irrigated. Everything was stone and dust and rock lizards just as the valley had been before the knuckleballers like Mulholland brought the water. I was at the edge of the groves and wondering how best to approach the house when the maroon Caddie nosed its way down the hill.

I reversed off the road and backed into the groves and hoped that the shade and the trunks and the heavy green boughs would hide me. There was a guy with a pushed-in face driving and Leo Pinella sitting in back, but no Frank Barris. Hmmm. Maybe Leo had run out of mixers and Frank was waiting up at the house while Leo and his most trusted bartender sped into town to repair their embarrassingly bare larder. That Leo. He had a fleshy face and long sideburns and what hair he had left was oiled and slicked straight back. He kept a cigar as long and black as a cop's baton in his mouth but he never lit it. I guessed he just sucked on them until they fell apart.

When the Caddie passed I eased back out to the road and continued on to the house. The road climbed quickly and pretty soon I was above the grove and could see forever. You could see the county roads that cut through the orange groves. You could see the Eagle station and Simms hardware. You could see across the valley to Burbank, crawling up the Santa Monica mountains. You could see through the Glendale pass into Pasadena and the Los Angeles basin beyond. You could even see that the maroon Cadillac wasn't going into town. I stopped and got out on the side of the road and watched.

The Caddie had turned off the county road a couple of miles back and was kicking up a rooster tail of dust along an unpaved service road. It turned onto another service road and then another and pretty soon it stopped at a small adobe-brick shed that was the only building around for miles. Not a place to go for mixers or to repair embarrassing social situations. Not a place a guy like Leo Pinella would ever go except for something very important or very secret. When the dust settled, all was still.

I got back into my car and turned around and pushed down the mountain as hard as I could, counting service roads and turnoffs and praying I had the right one when I slewed into the groves. I tried to remember how far the maroon Caddie had gone from the county road and which irrigation road it had turned onto and how it had gotten to the little shed. I drove as hard as I could and I didn't give a damn if anyone saw my dust trail. When the little hut and the maroon Caddie were a hundred yards in front of me, I jerked my car into the trees, yanked off my coat and tie, got the .38 out of the glove box, and ran toward the old building.

It was hot in the grove, and earth that had been watered that morning was already seared crusty and brittle. Tiny flying things swarmed in the trees, clouding around fruit that had fallen or gone bad, and the smell of the bad fruit was thick and bitter. I worked my way to the Cadillac and then across to the shed. It was a small single-story box of adobe brick with a door in the front and a couple of windows on the north side. It might have been built a hundred years ago by some Spanish don who owned all of Verdugo as his rancho. Once a roof for vaqueros, it was now a place to store replacement pipe and harvesting tools, and where itinerant day laborers recovered from the heat before being pushed back to the trees. When I got closer I could smell the chemical fertilizers and bug sprays and the oil they used in the smudge pots. Within the shed there was a radio, Julius La Rosa singing *Eh, Cumpari.*

I looked in the nearest window and there was Frank Barris. He was sitting in a wooden chair with his hands tied behind his back to the chair's rear legs. Leo Pinella and the pug with the pushed-in face were standing in front of him, Pinella gesturing with the mile-long cigar. There was a black guy standing beside Frank. The black guy was short and shirtless and slicked with sweat from the work he had been doing.

Leo lifted Frank's head and jiggled his chin and said, "Where's my fuckin' money?"

Barris mumbled something. His eyes were puffy and rolling around in different directions and his lips were split.

Leo looked disgusted and let Barris's head drop. He said something to the pug that I couldn't hear and the pug took out a Nazi Luger and put the muzzle in Frank Barris's mouth. Leo grabbed a handful of hair on the top of Frank's head and shook him. "That ain't no lollipop in your mouth, bubbe. I wanna know where my goddamn money is."

Frank mumbled something around the Luger.

"What?"

More mumbles.

The black guy said, "Lou Mardo."

Leo smiled like that was a real kick. "What a dumb shit you are, a guy like Lou Mardo." He put the cigar back in his mouth and made a little gesture to the pug. "Blow this bastard's head off."

I leaned through the window and showed them the .38. "Forget it."

The pug with the Luger jumped, but the black guy didn't and neither did Leo Pinella. He rolled lizard eyes toward me and took the cigar out of his mouth. Frank Barris saw me and strained against the ropes. Pinella said, "Who in hell are you?"

"Arthur Godfrey's talent scout. We're looking for people to enter the greasy hair contest." I pointed the gun at the black guy. "Cut him loose."

Pinella said, "Like hell. This fuckin' weasel stole twenty-two thousand bucks from me."

"He got in a tight place, Leo. He got desperate and he did something dumb. You'll get it back." I cocked the gun. "Untie him and we'll get out of here and he'll get the money back to you."

Leo Pinella said, "My ass," took the Luger from the pug, and shot Frank Barris once in the chest.

I shot Leo Pinella in the body as I went in through the window. He dropped the gun and tumbled back into the pug, and the black guy came for me, throwing a handful of something gritty in my face and swinging a piece of pipe. I fired blind, pumping out shots until the black man fell, then dragging Frank Barris and his chair behind some crates. The pug pulled Leo Pinella out the front door, Leo screaming, "You fuck! You fuck!" while his pants grew dark with blood. Then the Cadillac ground to life and sprayed gravel and Frank Barris and I were alone, the only two left alive in the grove.

I untied his hands and packed a burlap shipping bag tight into his chest and told him he was an asshole. I said, "You've got a kid, you dumb shit. You've got a kid, and you go and get mixed up in something like this."

Frank Barris looked at his chest and tried to see the hole and opened and closed his mouth like a fish. I got him up and went out of the little house and down the long straight dusty road to my car. I ran with him in my arms. I ran as fast as a man can run like that, but by the time we got to the car he was gone.

I drove back to the little adobe house and put Frank Barris in the spot where Leo Pinella had shot him. While I was doing that I found some papers in Barris's outside coat pocket. Deposit slips to his checking account in the amount of thirteen hundred and fifty dollars. I kept them. I brought the Luger that Leo Pinella had used to kill Frank Barris outside and hung it safely within the tight branches of a Valencia orange tree. If Pinella's people came, they wouldn't be able to find it. The cops would, though, because I was going to tell them. They would find Frank and the black man and the Luger and it would be hard as hell for Leo Pinella to beat the charge.

When I finished with all of that I put on my jacket to cover the blood on my shirt and I drove to the Eagle station. I washed my face and hands with water from the little hose the attendant uses to fill your radiator and

brushed off as much of the dust as I could. Then I made a couple of calls
and got a line on Lou Mardo and that's where I went.

Mardo was sitting in the bar at Musso's Grill in Hollywood, sipping
neat scotch and craning his head around to watch Donna Reed across the
room, smiling at a couple of studio executives. He was wearing a brand-
new dark blue herringbone suit and a pair of black loafers shinier than a
set of chrome hubcaps and an immaculate snow white brushed felt fedora
with a brim like a broken back. Ah, sudden wealth.

When I climbed onto the stool beside him, Mardo said, "Well, well.
Look what the cat dragged in." Always the sharp line.

I said, "You know something, Lou? The Peeler was a small-time
chiseler, but I liked him okay. He had some heart. But you, you're just
act two, and act two ain't never as good as act one." The bartender came
over but I waved him away.

Mardo gave me what he thought was a hard sneer. "We can go out
in the parking lot and see just how good I am, you want."

"You're scaring me to death, Lou. Here's a guy, knocked over Leo
Pinella, and he's sitting in the middle of Musso's wearing the evidence."

Lou Mardo's right eye began to twitch and he looked at me like he
thought I was kidding him. "What the hell are you talking about?"

I unbuttoned my jacket and opened it enough so that he could see
what was on my shirt. "I just left your partner Barris in an orange grove
up by Pinella's party house, Lou. Pinella and a couple of his thugs were
working on him and he told them you were involved."

Lou Mardo went as white as his hat. He said, "He's lyin'. It wasn't
me."

I shook my head. "Lou, I can see you nine years old saying that.
You've been saying that every day of your life. You gotta think of something
new."

He picked up the scotch, then put it back down. Donna Reed got up
with the two executives and the three of them left. Mardo didn't look at
her now.

I said, "Pinella put a bullet in Frank Barris and killed him. I shot
Pinella, but it looked pretty low in the gut. He might not die. He'll be
with a doctor now and if he makes it, he'll send a couple of his boys to
pay you a visit, Lou."

Lou Mardo began to sweat. There was a film of droplets above his
lip and beneath his eyes and over his forehead. He picked up the scotch
glass again and this time he drained it. He took his hat off and then he
put it back on. He shook his head to himself like he couldn't believe this

was happening. Guys like Lou Mardo never could. "We had that job aced. We got in and out of there on a charm. There must've been a couple of hundred other people up there. How'd he put the finger on us?"

I put my hand on his arm and squeezed, settling him down. "You got twenty-two thousand."

He nodded.

"I want Barris's split."

He looked at me sharply and frowned, still thinking to chisel. "What are you talking about?"

I shifted my stool closer to his and put one foot on the floor and leaned into him. The .38 was in my belt and he could see it now. "I've been through Frank's apartment and it isn't there. Barris didn't even put part of his cut in the bank yet. I'm thinking you were trying to work a way to weasel all of it, and you have the whole nut."

Mardo's mouth got small and his eyes got wide and he blinked a lot, maybe telling himself he had enough to worry about without me, but not yet able to convince himself. "I spent it already."

"You spent your side, Lou. Frank's side is still there."

"I had expenses." A whine.

I reached under my coat and put my hand on the .38 and I spoke very slowly. "Leo's on his way, Lou. Frank had some things to take care of, and now I'm going to take care of them for him, so I need his split."

He looked down at the gun and he lifted his glass again but the glass was empty. He gave a little shrug and put down the glass and said, "Sure."

He paid his bar tab and we went out to his car and he opened the trunk and there it was. What was left of the twenty-two thousand dollars in hundreds and twenties and tens and fives and ones, sitting in an army knapsack in the trunk of a gleaming new 1953 Lincoln Continental Cabriolet. He counted out eleven thousand, all the while shaking his head as if he still couldn't believe that this was happening. He lost count twice.

The small bills filled my pants and my jacket and made each pocket bulge. When I had Barris's split, Mardo looked at what he had left after the clothes and the car and the looking good. It wasn't much to have a guy like Leo Pinella after you. I said, "You still got a little time. There's New York. There's Mexico."

He shook his head. The sky was falling. "We had that job aced. We knew when to go in and when to come out and where Pinella kept the money. We got away clean, Marlowe."

"Sure. For guys like you it's always clean."

Mardo shook his head again. "This wasn't my baby. It was Frankie's. Frankie was a regular at Pinella's since the war. We were talking about all the money Pinella pulled in and what he did with it and where he must keep it and Frankie said he could find out and he did. Then he got the plans from the county and it was a piece of cake. In and out, man. In and out."

"Sure." I had it, then. I could see the whole thing.

Mardo kept shaking his head. "It was supposed to be a snap. Now I'm fucked. I'm fucked."

"Uh-huh."

I left Lou Mardo in Musso's parking lot and drove back to my apartment. I counted the money again and arranged it by denominations and then put it in a shoe box behind the refrigerator. I pulled off my clothes, took a long shower, and dressed. I drank half a tumbler of Tennessee bourbon, and then I drove to Louise Barris's house.

The little boy answered the door. He was wearing the same shorts and the same dirt-smudged tee-shirt as yesterday. He was eating another Mars bar. He smiled when he saw me. It was a good smile, and made me smile back. I wanted to tell him that with all the damn candy he ate he'd better be sure to brush his teeth.

He went into the kitchen and came back with his mother. Her radio was going back there, Tony Bennett singing *Rags to Riches*. When Tony Bennett was on the radio, you couldn't worry about what your boy ate. She said, "Did the sonofabitch cough up what he owes me?"

I made my right hand into a gun and shot the boy with a wink. "Tell you what, Robby. Head outside and give me and your mom a minute to talk."

He left without saying a word or looking at his mother. Come to think of it, I had never heard him say a word in her presence. Maybe he never spoke to her and she never spoke to him. Maybe she ignored him. *I'll never make that mistake again.* I waited until I heard the front door slam, and then I looked at Louise. She didn't look happy. "I don't need any lectures on how to raise my boy from some two-bit peeper."

I said, "Frank's dead. Leo Pinella killed him because he stole twenty-two thousand dollars of Pinella's money."

She stared at me for a solid ten-count, then raised her hands to her head and nodded. She went into the kitchen. I heard water run, then the pipe-hammer you get when you turn the water off too quickly, and then she came back. She said, "I guess I'll have to take care of his affairs. I guess I'll finally get what's coming to me from the sonofabitch." She looked around the seedy little room when she said it, as if everything were suddenly going to change. "What about the twenty-two thousand?"

"I have Frank's split."

She wet her lips. "Well, I guess that should belong to me now."

I shook my head.

Her mouth stretched and the skin around her eyes tightened. "Goddamn it, he was my husband. The bastard had obligations." She shouted it.

I said, "You put the finger on him to Leo Pinella."

She turned the color of steamed clams.

"Frank told me he married a whore and he meant it. He met you when you were working up at Pinella's party house. He took you out of there and married you, but he could never get what you had been out of his head."

She looked at the door as if she expected the boy to come back.

"So Frank hit the bottle and fell apart. Maybe he wasn't all that together to begin with. He was broke and he owed plenty and maybe the scumbags he had for friends helped him get the idea of taking down Pinella's. Only he needed to find out how Pinella ran his operation, and only someone who had worked there would know. That's you. You knew where Pinella had his money room and you went along because if Frank had some money he could pay you what he owed you, and maybe a little extra. Only Frank was still a lush and lushes have a hard time doing what they're supposed to do. When it looked like he was stiffing you with the bad check, you called Pinella. You tipped him that Frank had been the guy who'd taken him down."

"He owed me." Her voice was shrill.

I took out the bank papers that I had taken off Frank Barris's body and threw them at her. "Deposit papers," I said. "Frank was going to cover the check, he just didn't get around to it."

Her mouth worked, and when her voice came out it was hoarse. "I should still get the money. It's mine. I need it."

"You get nothing. I'm going to put the eleven grand into an account for the boy."

She came at me with her hands balled into fists, flailing at me and spitting and telling me I couldn't do that, that the money was hers, that I was a no good sonofabitch just like Frank. I grabbed her wrists and shook her and slapped her hard one time. Her hair was wild and she was breathing deep and if she could've gotten to a butcher knife she would have used it.

I said, "I'm going to put the money into an account for the boy. When he needs it for school or for clothes or for things like that, I'll draw some out and use it. When he's twenty-one, if there's any left, I'll give half to you and half to him. His father's dead and he's going to need you more than ever, now. You're going to be here for him. If you aren't, or if you try to create a problem for me, I will go to Leo Pinella and tell him that you were the person who fingered his money room. Do you understand that?"

She nodded. She looked scared, but she would get used to it.

I said, "I'm going to go now and call the cops. They'll find Frank's body and they'll be by to tell you that he's dead. Play stupid. You're going to have to sit down with the boy and tell him. That's going to be hard, but that's part of being his mother."

She said, "I know what being a mother is."

"All right." I wanted to say something more. I didn't want to just leave. "Maybe you got a raw deal in all of this, too. If Frank was willing to marry you, maybe he should've been willing to accept what you were, and maybe you had a right to expect that he would. If he had, maybe you would've gotten what you wanted and he would've gotten what he wanted and everything would've been just great. He didn't. I can't help you with that."

She crossed her arms and she looked small and pinched and alone. She was not looking at me. "No one ever could," she said. "Go to hell."

I nodded and left then, and drove to Frank Barris's apartment. I went in through the bathroom window again and took a beer out of Frank's icebox and sat at the little dining room table and drank some of it. I called the cops and told them that Leo Pinella had killed a guy named Frank Barris and left the body in an orange grove up in Glendale. I gave them directions to the little adobe shed. I told them where I had put the Luger, and that they would find Leo Pinella's prints on it and that the bullet in Barris had come from that gun. Then I hung up. I sat a little while longer and finished the beer. I felt old and I didn't really want to go home. There was nothing there to go back to.

After a while I got up and went into Frank's bedroom and took the unfinished model of the P-38 out of his closet. I put the pieces carefully in the box, making sure I had the instructions and all of the parts. Then I closed the box and left.

If I took my time, I might be able to do a pretty good job on the little airplane. It would give me something to do in the evenings, and at the end of the week it would be fun to show the boy.

When my veterinarian tells me he's got four orphaned kittens on his hands because the momma cat stood her ground to protect them from a crazed Rottweiler, I cry like a baby and adopt the entire family. When the six o'clock news tells the story of the guy in Michigan who fell through the ice and drowned as he tried to save two children he didn't know, I choke up for the rest of the night. I am a sucker for heroes, and, at a point in my life when I very much needed one, Raymond Chandler gave me Philip Marlowe.

I read "Red Wind" in a broken-backed second-hand bookstore copy of Trouble Is My Business *and went through the rest of Chandler's work as fast as I could find it. What Chandler was doing wasn't just telling lurid stories (which he did, better than almost anyone), he was exploring the ways a good man might retain his goodness in a modern world, and his themes were the themes of courage and duty and personal responsibility. I found this work profound. I still find it so. It caused me, for perhaps the first time, to consciously think about how I wanted to live my life and what would constitute acceptable ethical behavior and who I wanted to be. This reflection and the themes that grow from it recur in my work. Appropriately, they form the basis of "The Man Who Knew Dick Bong."*

Philip Marlowe didn't just help to shape my fiction, he helped to shape my life.

Thanks, Ray.

Robert Crais

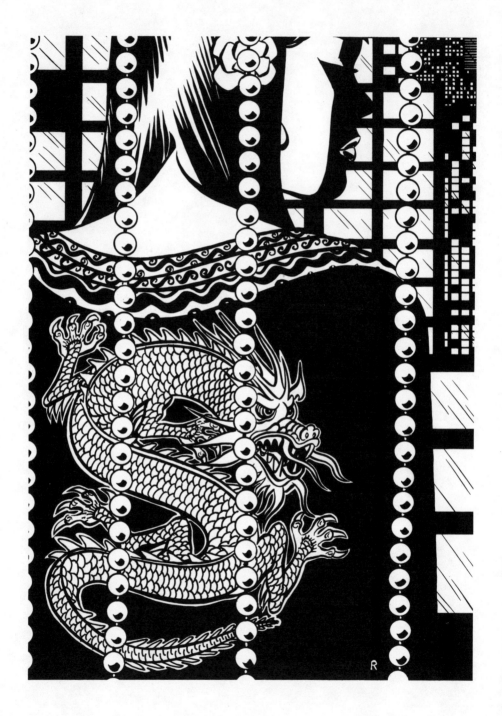

ESSENCE D'ORIENT

EDWARD D. HOCH

1954

WHEN I FIRST saw Jade Kashi she was singing at a nightclub in the Laurel Canyon district, not far from the house I was renting at the time. She was a shapely Oriental girl with straight black hair just long enough to tickle her bare shoulders, and she sang like an angel in a strapless gold gown that was slit up the right leg to her hip.

I was thinking about inviting her over to my table when she finished and maybe she could read my mind. After the last set she gave a deep bow to the audience and headed right for me. "You're Philip Marlowe, aren't you?" she asked in a voice as sweet as her songs.

"Yeah, I'm Marlowe."

"Could I sit down for a moment?"

"Sure. What are you drinking?"

"Nothing, thank you. They told me you sometimes come in here. I want to hire you."

"Who told you? Reggy?" The nightclub was called Reggy's Place, and it was owned by an Englishman named Reggy Maitland. You could find people around town who'd tell you Reggy had mob money behind him, but that was none of my affair.

"Yes, I believe he mentioned it." Her English was flawless. "I have a younger brother named Lien. He travels with a bad crowd and I am worried for his safety. If you could help him—us—I would pay you."

"Just about every woman in this town with a younger brother thinks he travels with a bad crowd," I told her. "Most of them turn out all right."

"His best friend was murdered two nights ago."

"Well, that makes a difference. Was he Chinese like your brother?"

"We are Korean," she corrected me.

"Korean? We just fought a war there."

"I know. I should say our parents are Korean. Lien and I were both

255

born in Hawaii. Our parents still live there. We moved to Los Angeles a few years ago after he finished high school, but my career has advanced faster than his."

"What does he want to do?"

"Act in the movies, but there just aren't that many parts for Orientals."

I gave her a weary smile. I'd been hearing variations on her story all my life. "There's not much I can do. Who was this friend that got himself killed?"

"His name was Mickey O'Brian. He was beaten to death in an alley about a mile from here, Sunday night while I was working."

I thought it odd that a Korean youth and an Irishman had been such good friends. "How'd they know each other?"

"They worked together at a shop that manufactures costume jewelry. The police have some crazy idea they might be linked to recent thefts of real jewelry, and now they're questioning Lien about the killing."

"Who's the detective on the case?" My relations with the L.A.P.D. were far from friendly of late, but I figured it didn't hurt to ask.

"Sergeant Green. Do you know him?"

I nodded. "He's halfway human. He watched another cop beat me once, but at least he didn't join in."

"Will you talk to him, before something happens to my brother?"

"What do you think might happen?"

"Somebody might kill him like they did his friend. Or the police might decide to pin the killing on him."

"Where is he now?"

"At work. He's been going in nights this week. It's the Galaxy Jewelry Company." She gave me the address, in a seedy area of downtown Los Angeles.

Jade Kashi's slit skirt had fallen away from her leg, and I studied the inviting curve of her thigh for a long moment. "I'll look into it," I said finally. "I can't promise anything."

As I was leaving the club a few minutes later, Reggy Maitland himself stopped me at the door. "It's always good to see you, Marlowe. You bring a touch of class to my place."

I waited for him to get to the point. "You need a lot more than I can offer, Reggy."

He smoothed the hair back from his forehead in a familiar gesture. Usually it meant he was nervous about something. "I saw you talking to Jade. You want her to drink with you?"

"I can arrange my own dates, thanks."

"Jade's nice to look at, but I wouldn't want to get too involved with her. She's North Korean, you know."

"The war's over, Reggy."

I went out the door leaving him standing there.

The Galaxy Jewelry Company was on the fringes of Chinatown, not far from City Hall. It was an area of light industry and import-export firms, and there wasn't much doing there after dark. All the buildings on the block were closed for the night, and Galaxy Jewelry was no exception. I walked around the two-story structure, checking the doors, and then got back in my car. Whatever Lien Kashi did at night, he wasn't working at Galaxy.

I turned onto Alameda Street and decided I was only a few blocks from police headquarters. It was as good a time as any to check the reports on the death of Mickey O'Brian. When I got there I asked for Sergeant Green and received a sour look from the other detectives in the squad room. "Green," one of them called out. "You got a visitor."

He came around the partition that separated his office and stared at me. It took him just an instant to remember who I was. "Well, Marlowe! Good to see you again. Come on in."

"There's nobody with a sap waiting to work me over?"

He laughed at that. "The chief is retiring. I think there'll be some changes in the routine soon. What can I do for you?" He had gray-blond hair and patient eyes, waiting to see what I wanted this late in the evening.

"A young guy named Mickey O'Brian was killed two nights ago. I hear it's your case."

"O'Brian, yeah. What about it?"

"He worked with a Korean kid named Lien Kashi. The Korean's sister sings at Reggy's Place and she's worried about him. She asked me to look into it."

"She's got reason to be worried. Right now her brother's a prime suspect in the killing."

"Has he been arrested?"

"Not yet, but we've questioned him. It seems the two of them went to a bar the other night after work. They left the place around ten o'clock and Kashi says they separated at the corner. About an hour later we got a report of an assault in the area. A patrol car found Mickey O'Brian badly beaten and near death in an alleyway. He died a few hours later in the hospital without regaining consciousness."

"Sounds like a mugging to me."

"Yeah, except that his wallet wasn't touched. He had forty-four dollars in it. We're looking into reports that O'Brian and Kashi had been arguing earlier that evening."

"What about?"

Green's eyes hardened a bit. "I've told you enough already. Fill me in on this sister."

"Her name is Jade. She's got a good voice."

"Good-looking?"

"Yes."

"I'll have to go question her myself."

I took out my pipe and began filling the bowl from my tobacco pouch. "Any idea what sort of weapon was used on this O'Brian kid?"

"A length of lead pipe. We found it in the alley."

"Did the people who called in the report give any description of the killer?"

"Someone heard O'Brian's groans a little before eleven and found him in the alley. They didn't see the assault."

"Jade Kashi says you think her brother is involved in some jewel robberies."

"We questioned both Kashi and O'Brian recently. I wasn't involved personally because it wasn't a homicide, but there's a suspicion that Galaxy Jewelry or its employees might be involved in a string of robberies from the homes of movie stars. A Galaxy matchbook was found near one scene. The latest robbery was Sunday night. A big guy with a gun held up Mrs. Roger West, the actor's wife, at her Malibu home and got away with a pearl necklace and some other things."

I puffed on my pipe and thought about it. Finally I said, "Thanks, Green. I'll return the favor someday."

"You can do that by keeping out of my sight, Marlowe."

In the morning I stopped by the office and checked the mail. There was nothing but bills. I took a swig from the bottle in the bottom drawer of my desk and remembered I hadn't even asked Jade for a retainer. I was getting forgetful in my old age.

I drove over to Galaxy Jewelry and parked next to the shiny white Caddy in the lot. It occupied a space next to the front door which was marked Reserved for Mr. Brian Lightner. I went in and asked for him. The blonde receptionist studied me like she was trying to guess the price of my suit. "You got an appointment?"

"No, but I think he'll see me. The name's Philip Marlowe." I passed her one of my cards.

She returned after a few minutes and ushered me down a corridor with bumpy brown linoleum on the floor. Lightner's office was done up in a sort of pseudo-art deco, something left over from a bargain basement in the 1930's. He glanced at me from beneath heavy eyelids and didn't bother to rise. "You're Marlowe?"

"That's right. Thanks for taking the time to see me."

"What is this, an insurance investigation?"

"No, I'm looking into the killing of one of your employees the other night—Mickey O'Brian."

"What's the matter, the police shorthanded?"

"I'm trying to help a client. What can you tell me about the victim?"

Lightner shrugged and bit on his cigar. "I got nearly thirty people working for me. I don't know them all. He did his job."

"What about Lien Kashi?"

"Yeah, the Chink."

"Korean," I corrected, feeling I owed that to my client.

"Same thing. I guess the two of them were friends, from what I hear."

"Is Lien working today?"

"He should be."

"Can I talk to him?"

"I guess so. Come on."

He stood up finally, a squat middle-aged man with food stains on his trousers. "What do you make here?" I asked. "Costume jewelry?"

"Imitation pearls."

"Are those like cultured pearls?" I'd encountered fake pearls on other cases, but I'd decided to play dumb.

He shot me a look that seemed to say he'd love to take my money on the spot. "No, no—cultured pearls are ones induced to form inside an oyster by adding a grain of sand or some other irritant. Imitation or artificial pearls are just painted glass beads."

We passed down a line of male and female workers, mostly young and foreign—Mexicans, Orientals. I wondered how many of them were in the country illegally. I also wondered what someone with a name like O'Brian was doing working among them. Finally we stopped before a slender young Korean. "Lien, here's someone to see you."

I introduced myself and asked him what he was doing with the trays of clear glass beads before him. Lightner took over the explanations. "He's preparing to color the beads by dipping them in a solution called 'essence d'orient.' It's a preparation derived from the scales of fish. There—you see! They emerge from their bath looking like pearls. Now we simply string them together and the result is a fine pearl necklace. It wouldn't fool a jeweler, of course, or anyone familiar with real pearls, but for the costume jewelry market they're just fine."

"This is your job?" I asked Lien Kashi. "You do this?"

"Yes," he answered with a touch of pride. "You want to see me?" His English was good but not quite as pure as his sister's.

Lightner moved on down the line, chatting with the other workers. "I'm working for your sister," I told Lien. "She's worried about you."

His face hardened. "She has no need to worry. She leads her own life."

"She told me about your friend who was murdered. Any idea why it was done?" He hesitated about answering and I gestured toward a coffee machine standing against the nearby wall. "Come on, I'll buy you some coffee and we can chat."

The paper cup of coffee relaxed Lien a bit and soon I had him talking about his sister and his early days in Hawaii. The conversation flowed naturally into his friendship with Mickey O'Brian. "He started working here just a few months ago, but we were good friends from the start."

"Did you ever fight with him?"

"No."

"The police think you argued with O'Brian early on the night he was killed."

"They tell lies! They try to say Mickey and I steal pearl necklace from movie star! They say we fight over loot and maybe I kill him, but none of that is true!"

"All right." I was beginning to get the picture, but the focus wasn't quite sharp enough yet. "Who do you think killed him?"

"There is a bad man named Cusoltz. He threatened us once."

"Cusoltz." The name meant nothing to me. "When was this?"

"One night a few weeks ago. I saw him hanging around the parking lot outside." He was calmer now, more in control. "I asked what he wanted and he shoved me, told me to mind my own business. When Mickey came running up he punched him, knocked him to the ground. He called him bad names."

"Like what?"

"He called him a fairy," Lien answered quietly.

"How did you find out Cusoltz's name?"

"Mickey knew it. He met him in a bar called the Golden Parrot."

I knew the place. It was a homosexual hangout. "They knew each other?"

"Not well," Lien insisted. "Mickey would never be friends with a man like that."

"What does Cusoltz look like?"

"A gorilla!" the Korean spat out. "A big hairy one."

"One more question—where were you last night when you told your sister you were working?"

He looked away. "I went to a bar."

"The same bar where Mickey met Cusoltz?"

Lien glanced around nervously. "I must get back to work. Mr. Lightner is watching us."

I let him go and stopped to speak with Lightner at the door. "He was very helpful."

"Yeah?"

"He mentioned a man named Cusoltz who threatened Mickey and him. Does the name mean anything to you?"

"Not a thing," Lightner replied.

That evening I went back to Reggy's Place to report to Jade Kashi and speak to her about a retainer. I'd been spending more time on her problem than I'd planned, and I couldn't afford free jobs anymore. The sign outside, which I hadn't noticed before, announced, Jade Kashi, the Korean Kutie—Every Night at 8 and 11. Closed Mondays.

I sat through her first show, listening to the familiar renderings of popular show tunes. Tonight she wore a silver gown just as striking as the gold one, and the colored spotlight bathed it in changing hues to complement the style of the song. She was too good for Reggy's Place and I wondered what kept her there.

When she came over to my table after the set I gave her a quick version of what little I'd learned. She sat leaning forward, her hands tightly clasped, as she listened to every word. "I know this man Cusoltz," she said finally. "He used to come around here occasionally. I haven't seen him lately."

"Did your brother ever mention him?"

"Not to me."

I glanced at my watch. "You're off till eleven now?"

"Yes."

"Want to get something to eat?"

She searched my face for some hidden meaning to the invitation, and I wondered if she got this from guys all the time. Finally she shook her head. "I'd better not. Reggy might not like it."

"What's he to you?"

She shrugged. "He pays the bills."

"All the bills?"

"Pretty much."

It explained why she stayed at Reggy's Place. "Does your brother approve of the arrangement?"

"I look after him, but he never says much about my life."

"Too bad you don't have an older brother."

"You applying for the job, Mr. Marlowe?"

I laughed and got up from the table. I could see Reggy Maitland eyeing me from across the room. "I'll see you around, Jade."

"Be careful," she warned.

Maitland intercepted me on my way to the door. "She isn't your type, Marlowe."

"I never said she was."

"Find yourself another client."

"That's always good advice. Thanks, Reggy."

I went outside and crossed the dimly lit parking lot to my car. There was some movement reflected in the car window that warned me in time, and I half turned just as a shiny leather-covered sap swung down at my head. I took the blow on the shoulder, feeling a stab of pain shoot down my arm. I thought it was a cop at first and I hesitated a split second. Then I saw the gorillalike shape of the guy and knew that I'd come face to face with Cusoltz.

I locked onto his arm as he raised it again, and I brought it down hard on the hood of my car. He yowled and dropped the sap, but he wasn't done fighting yet. I backed off but he came at me like a tank, barreling into my gut and knocking the wind out of me. I staggered back, clutching the car for support, and he rammed his hamlike fists into my face. I went down hard on the cinders and lay there waiting for him to come in close.

He fooled me and went for his gun. I tried to turn over and reach my own .38 special, but there wasn't time. I saw the barrel leveled at me like a rat's eye and heard Cusoltz bark, "Say your prayers, Marlowe!"

Then suddenly Jade was behind him, swinging the sap as if it were a baseball bat. It hit the back of his head and he fell on his face. "Are you all right?" she asked, tossing the sap to the ground next to him.

"I am, thanks to you. That was some rescue."

"I saw Reggy talking to you and I followed you to find out what he said. I was just in time to see Cusoltz trying to kill you."

"And we haven't even been introduced." I tried to stand up but I hurt in too many places. "Take my key and get the pint of Canadian Club out of the glove compartment, will you? I could use a swig."

She did as I asked and I took a long one before offering the bottle to her. "No," she declined. "I have to work again. Let me help you up."

I took another swig first and then put the top back on the bottle. She helped me to my feet and I felt better. I bent over Cusoltz to make sure he was still breathing, then went quickly through his pockets. In the inner pocket of his jacket I found a slim jewelry case. I opened it and took out a small strand of pearls. After my visit to Lightner's shop I was adding to my rudimentary skill on the subject, and although these pearls had the right coloring they lacked the nacreous, incandescent quality of the real thing. They were grade-A essence d'orient, and I wondered what Cusoltz was doing with them in his pocket. I decided to keep them and ask Lightner about it.

"What are those?" Jade asked as I slipped the box into my pocket.

"Imitation pearls, from the place where your brother works. It's a connection between Cusoltz and Galaxy Jewelry."

The big man began to stir on the gravel and I decided I'd better get out of there if I didn't want to kill him. "I'll see you later," I told Jade. "Thanks again."

"It was my pleasure, Mr. Marlowe."

By morning I'd decided what to do. After a phone call to Sergeant Green I drove over to Galaxy Jewelry once more. The neighborhood hadn't improved any since my previous visit. A group of teenage kids loitered down the block, setting me to worrying about my hubcaps.

As I was led down the corridor to Brian Lightner's office I glanced into the shop area, but Jade's brother wasn't in sight. Lightner himself seemed to be in a good mood. He rose when I came in and offered me a cigar. I took out one of my cigarettes instead and lit it with a wooden match. "What can I do for you today, Mr. Marlowe?" he asked.

"I have a couple more questions for you. Your man Cusoltz came to see me last night. He made quite an impression on me, outside of Reggy's Place."

"Cusoltz? I don't know the man."

"He seems to specialize in parking lot encounters. Lien Kashi says the man threatened him in your parking lot outside."

"That's impossible."

"Lien would have no reason to lie about it." I slipped the jewel case out of my pocket and tossed it on the desk between us. "I found this in Cusoltz's pocket."

Lightner's eyebrows went up, but he didn't touch the case. "What is it?" he asked quietly.

"A string of pearls." I reached over and opened the lid for him.

"They're some of ours," he said at once. "But what are they doing in the fancy case?"

"That's what I wondered too. You're the first to admit your imitation pearls couldn't fool anyone. They're costume jewelry, lacking the luster of the real thing. So why would Cusoltz carry them around in a fancy box?"

Lightner carefully placed his cigar in the ash tray. "You tell me, Marlowe."

"I think they're real pearls, stolen from Roger West's wife on Sunday night. You gave them a bath in your solution, coating the real pearls with essence d'orient so they'd look like imitations. That way they'd be safe to carry around and sell to a fence. Once the heat was off, they'd get a chemical bath to remove the coating and they'd be good as new."

Lightner studied my face for a moment. "What do you want, Marlowe?"

"The pearls are between you and the police. I'm after Mickey O'Brian's killer. Answer me one question—why does Cusoltz hang out at a bar called the Golden Parrot?"

Lightner shrugged. "It's a homosexual joint."

"I know that. Is Cusoltz one?"

"Look, he likes to beat them up. He gets his kicks that way. Satisfied?"

"That's what I wanted to know."

"You gonna tell the cops about the pearls?"

"I already told them. They're waiting outside with a search warrant."

"You bastard!" His hand went into the desk drawer, but my fist was faster. I caught him on the tip of the jaw.

I sat in Sergeant Green's little cubicle while Brian Lightner was being questioned by the robbery squad. "We found more of the doctored pearls in his office safe," the detective told me. "I guess we owe you our thanks, Marlowe."

"I never thought the L.A.P.D. would be thanking me for anything. What about Cusoltz?"

"Mrs. West just identified his mug shot. He's the one who robbed her at gunpoint in her home Sunday night. We have an arrest order out on him."

"Now I'll help the homicide squad. Cusoltz killed Mickey O'Brian too. O'Brian was a homosexual and Cusoltz likes to beat up on them. Lightner told me so. Cusoltz punched O'Brian in the Galaxy parking lot, and the other night he went a little too far with that lead pipe."

But Green shook his head. "A good theory but it won't wash, Marlowe. Cusoltz couldn't have killed O'Brian."

"Why not?"

"The murder took place shortly after ten on Sunday night, certainly before eleven, when the body was found. Cusoltz was twenty-five miles away in Malibu, robbing Mrs. West, at exactly ten-thirty. There's no way he could have been in both places at once."

I felt like I'd been hit with Cusoltz's sap. "You're sure?"

"I told you she just I.D.'d his mug shot."

I left the police building and drove around for a while. Finally I looked up Jade's address in the phone book and drove over there. She had an apartment on Kenmore Avenue, not far from Hollywood Boulevard. I'd once found a body near there, but Jade Kashi was very much alive as she let me in.

"Thank heavens it's you! Early this morning I saw a car parked outside and I think Cusoltz was in it." She was wearing a red lounging gown with an embroidered dragon on the back.

"He's finished if he shows his face," I told her. "The cops want him for a jewel robbery."

"That doesn't sound like his sort of crime."

"Lien's boss, Brian Lightner, put him up to it." I told her what I knew.

"Does this clear Lien, then?"

"Of the robbery but not of the murder. Cusoltz couldn't have done that."

"Then who did?"

I felt like a drink just then. I felt like I wanted to be somewhere a hundred miles away from there. "I think you did, Jade."

"I—"

"O'Brian was homosexual, and you didn't like what he was doing to your brother. Those nights when Lien was supposed to be working he was at the Golden Parrot or some other place, wasn't he? You followed them Sunday evening and when they parted you lured Mickey into that alley and hit him with a lead pipe, just as you hit Cusoltz with that sap. You kept hitting him, and left him for dead."

"I told you I was working at the time of the killing."

"Yes, you made an unnecessary point of mentioning that, but the sign outside Reggy's Place says you sing at eight and eleven. O'Brian was slugged between ten and eleven. You had plenty of time to do it and get back to the club. You could even have walked the mile's distance."

I hadn't known just how she'd react. Surprisingly, she merely nodded and asked, "Ever had a kid brother?"

"No."

"He's my responsibility, with our parents back in Hawaii. I saw him slipping away from me, from the kind of life we'd always planned for him. He was slipping into something bad. I spoke to Mickey, warned him away, but it did no good. Mickey didn't want to go away. He wanted Lien. Finally I did the only thing I could. Then the police started questioning Lien about the killing, and I went into a panic. I asked for your help, hoping you'd uncover another possible suspect."

I sat there watching the afternoon shadows on the carpet. Finally I asked, "Can I take you downtown to see Sergeant Green?"

She nodded. "Let me get a coat."

We went downstairs and crossed the sidewalk toward my car. That was when I saw Cusoltz come suddenly around the corner of the building. The gun in his hand was pointed at me. "I figured you'd turn up here, Marlowe!" he growled. "This is for last night!"

I tried to grab Jade as I pulled my own gun free, but she seemed to step deliberately between Cusoltz and me. His first shot caught her in the chest. I went down on my knees trying to grab her and then fired twice, knocking him backward with the force of the bullets.

When I was sure he wouldn't be moving I crawled over to her. The blood was running across the sidewalk to the curb and I could see she was dead.

Essence d'orient, I thought.

I knelt there beside her until I heard the sirens coming.

I cannot honestly claim that Raymond Chandler has been a greater influence on my work than, say, Ellery Queen or Graham Greene or John Dickson Carr. But I have long admired his writing and have read every word he ever published, including novels, shorter works, letters, screenplays, notebooks, and even his early poems. I've read most of the novels and stories two or three times by now, and I return to my favorites regularly.

Virtually all of them have their memorable scenes, and especially their memorable closing lines, but I think my favorite remains The Lady in the Lake. *I believe it to be the best plotted of all the books, showing Chandler's craftsmanship at its peak. It's a complex story that's still easy to follow, and even now it reads as if it had been written just last year.*

There's an urgency about much of Chandler's writing that's lacking in most of today's private eye novels. I don't pretend to have captured that mood in my own story about Philip Marlowe, but I'm pleased to have been a part of this project to honor a writer who will probably never be equaled.

Edward D. Hoch

IN THE LINE OF DUTY

JEREMIAH HEALY

1955

THE HORIZONTAL PLAQUE centered at the front of his desk read, Arthur Mims, Manager. Mims stood to greet me. He was maybe five-five, gravity taking whatever shoulders he once had down to his waist, suspenders the color of his tie holding up his pants. He parted his hair in the center and apparently felt enough in charge of things at Golden State Insurance not to wear his suit jacket.

Mims held up a copy of the L.A. *Times* with Monday, March 28, 1955, at the top. "So, who do you like for Wednesday, Garland or Kelly?"

"I'm sorry?"

"The Oscars for last year's films. This is Hollywood, Mr. Marlowe. Movieland. The Academy's giving them out on Wednesday. Who do you think's going to win Best Actress?"

I didn't like people who called Hollywood "Movieland." I did, however, like to work to earn money to buy food and shelter. "Who do you like, Mr. Mims?"

"I say Garland's got it wrapped up for *A Star Is Born*. Kelly was good in *The Country Girl*, but with Judy having the baby on the way and all, you've got to lean toward her."

I hadn't seen either film. "The only thing I remember Grace Kelly being in was *High Noon*."

"Boy, there was a picture, huh? But that really wasn't hers. It was Gary Cooper, standing alone against four bad guys. What more can you want?"

I wanted Mims to get to the point. Finally he folded the paper over, substituting for it a file he pulled from a side drawer.

"You know about the armored car job last week, on Vine?"

It had been tough to miss. "Just a few blocks from my office."

"Yeah, yeah, I know. Well, we carried the insurance for the company, Stanley Security."

"I didn't think the robbers got away with anything."

"They didn't. One of the guards gunned both of them, the bad guys, I mean. Brothers, they were, the robbers were brothers named Hauer. Jailbirds, out of stir maybe a month. Abel was the older, Randy the younger."

"The guard died, too, right?"

"Right. Ex-cop named Behagen, Dan Behagen. That's why you're here. We carried life policies on the guards. Old man Stanley was always a nut on insuring his people. 'It's a dangerous job for damn low pay. Insurance doesn't cost much and they deserve it.' So, they go down in the line of duty, the family gets twenty-five thousand dollars."

"And?"

"And if the guard was in on the heist instead, we're off the hook on the policy." Mims had good eyes, the kind that can see a scam through a foot-thick wall. "We think there might be something fishy about this one."

"Anything specific?"

"This guard, Behagen, he worked at a shipyard since he was fourteen, then joined the Marines, even though the defense job would have kept him out altogether. Served in the South Pacific, killed about a hundred Japs, then went onto the force. He gets married, has a kid, model cop for like ten years. Then he quits, joins Stanley. Two months later he's involved in a robbery."

"And you think the timing stinks."

"Yes and no. You see, this car gets hit kind of early in the morning on a Tuesday, when the other two guards are chowing down in some coffee shop half a block away and there's only fifteen, sixteen thou in the bags. The brothers wait till two o'clock, they're looking at a hundred grand, easy."

"And three guards instead of one."

"Yeah, but if Behagen goes in for a penny, why not a pound? On the other hand, we always put an ad in when we get notice of a claim. You know, 'Anyone having any information about an accident at the corner of Fifth and Main, etc., please contact us at the following post office box.' Doesn't usually lead to anything, but this time a soda jerk was working early on the Sunday morning before the attempt, and he says he thought he saw this Behagen walking around where the truck got hit."

"Walking?"

Mims slid a photostat of a handwritten letter over to me. "We want you to look into it."

I skimmed the letter, noticed it had name and address on it. Creasing the photostat so the text didn't get too cracked, I tamped it into my jacket pocket.

"That's it?"

"No. This Hauer, the older one, Abel. He had a girlfriend. Cops said she didn't know anything, but here's her name and address, too."

I tucked the paper next to the photostat.

"The other two guards you can see at Stanley's headquarters."

I waited.

Mims said, "We pay market rates here, Marlowe." He said it like he thought that was what I was waiting to hear.

"Why me?" I said.

"Why you?"

"Yeah. I'm not one of your own, not even one of your referral free-lancers. Why me?"

"Somebody said you were good."

"Lots of people are good."

"Good with cops, I mean."

"No, Mr. Mims. What you mean is you don't want any of your regulars poking into a cop, even an ex-cop. Might tick off the other cops your regulars need favors from."

"I don't think my motives are the question here."

"You don't?"

"No. I think the question here is whether you need our money bad enough to risk getting the cops ticked at you."

Mims reached back into the drawer for his newspaper. I decided he was good enough not to worry about wearing his suit jacket.

Stanley Security operated from a postwar building on Broadway near Sixth, just past spitting distance from the district attorney's offices on West Temple. The other two guards assigned to the truck that morning were Wylie and Green. Wylie's nose had the exploded vein look you get from drinking Four Roses for breakfast. Green was more the boy next door that your daughter won't date because he plays the accordion and the other girls would laugh.

I decided to start with Green. Some junior executive whose name I didn't catch shunted us into a small office that was enough like an inter-rogation room to be to my liking.

"My name's Philip Marlowe. Your company's insurer hired me to look into the robbery the other day."

"Attempted robbery."

"Attempted robbery. Why don't you tell me what happened."

"Sure. Dan, Wylie, and me were assigned to car seven. It's kind of a milk run till the early afternoon, so we generally take turns eating breakfast. One man stays on the truck. We parked the truck by this coffee shop on Vine shy of Franklin, down by the bus station, and Wylie and me go in to eat. We're just about finished when I hear the shots."

"How many?"

"Two or three at first. That's when we jumped up. From the door of the restaurant I could see at least one back door of the truck was open, and a guy's flat on his back on the pavement."

"Behagen?"

"No, no. This guy wasn't in uniform." Green flicked a hand at his gray blouse and trousers. "He was just stretched out. I barely saw him when this car screeches up, fifty-three or fifty-four Ford, hard to tell because I couldn't see the taillights, and this other guy jumps out, firing into the truck, like through the open door, get me?"

"I can picture it."

"I draw my gun as I'm coming out of the restaurant, but it was too late. Dan returned fire at the second guy from inside the truck, and the guy gets lifted up off his feet and back against his car. He started sliding down it like he was a kid, playing at getting shot. I never saw anybody actually take a bullet before, but it wasn't like the movies, you know? I mean, this guy really bled. Buckets of blood."

"Then what?"

"Then I go to the truck. Dan's all folded over, holding his stomach like he was cradling eggs or something. He looked . . ."

"Go on."

Green pursed his lips. "He looked like he knew, like he knew the guy had killed him, but he just wasn't dead yet."

"Behagen say anything to you?"

"No."

"Didn't say, 'Get an ambulance,' or anything?"

"No. I'm not sure he could. Talk, I mean."

"You said he was shot in the stomach."

"Right."

"Not the throat or face."

"No. Dan just looked, I don't know, like a man who knew it wouldn't do any good."

"Was Behagen a particular friend of yours?"

"No. Why?"

"You called Behagen 'Dan,' but you call Wylie by his last name."

"Dan told me to do that, call him by his first name. He was a real cop, Mr. Marlowe, but he was down to earth, you know? Not like some other guys around here, getting by more on age than experience."

I took that to mean Wylie. "So how come it was you and Wylie instead of you and Behagen in the coffee shop?"

"Dan wasn't feeling too well, didn't want to eat anything."

"Sudden sickness?"

"Huh?"

"Behagen been sick for a while or did it just hit him that morning?"

"Oh, no. He had some kind of allergy, some days worse than others with coughing and stuff."

"What was your procedure for gettting back into the truck?"

"After we ate, you mean?"

"Yes."

"Well, the one of us would get in the cab to drive, and the other would ride shotgun."

"In the cab, too?"

"Yeah. Like on a stagecoach, you know?"

I paused for a moment. "Look, I know you liked Behagen, but I've got a job to do here. Was there any reason he'd have for opening the rear doors?"

Green moved his tongue around inside his mouth, like he'd been thinking about that himself and hadn't come up with a good answer. "Not without recognizing one of us knocking."

Wylie had breath you could walk on. I tilted back in my chair but couldn't get far enough away, so I stood up and questioned him from my feet.

"I understand from Green that you and he were eating when the Hauer brothers made their move."

"I was eatin'. I didn't see nothin'."

"When you heard the shots you got up, right?"

"Yeah."

"And went to the door?"

"No. Just Green."

"What did you do?"

"Went to the back, phoned the cops."

"Leaving your buddy out on the street?"

"If Behagen'd stayed buttoned up, he wouldn't had no problem, see? How was I supposed to know he was gonna open the doors?"

"What about Green?"

"What about him?"

"Wouldn't he have been exposed, coming out of the restaurant like that?"

"Kid wants to play John Wayne, fine with me. I'm not gonna cover him. I wanna retire in two years, mister. Kid like that don't know what it means to die."

"He does now."

Garth Peevey was sixteen years old and worked in a drugstore on Vine, diagonally across the street from the coffee shop. At six feet and maybe a hundred and thirty counting the pimples, the Peevey fit him better than the Garth.

Elbows on his counter, he said, "Yeah, mister, right over there was where they say it happened."

"You weren't here the day of the robbery?"

"Nah. I had school. But I was here the Sunday before, and that's when I saw the guy."

"You know Behagen from somewhere?"

"Nah, but his picture was in the paper, remember? He looked a lot younger in the photo, but it was him. He came right up to this window."

"What were you doing?"

"Taking inventory. My uncle owns the place, so he trusts me to count things right. He had me do it on Sunday, paid me extra and all, so I figured, hey, get it over with, no sense killing the whole day, right?"

"Right. What time was this?"

"Early. Early early, maybe six-thirty, seven. I was just getting started, coming out from the storeroom, when I see this guy, his back to the window there. Scared me a little, tell you the truth."

"Why?"

"Well, that time of morning down here on a Sunday, it's like a ghost town. I mean nobody on the streets, not even cars going by. So I freeze, and I don't think he sees me because he's concentrating so much."

"Concentrating?"

"Yeah. Like he's looking hard at one spot. Then he shifts around a little, and looks hard at another. Then he walked across the street toward the coffee shop, but real funny."

"You said that in your letter."

"Yeah, that's why I took so much time to look at him and could recognize him from the newspaper. I thought he was a crazy, you know?"

"He was walking crazy?"

"No, no. I mean, not like wild or a raving lunatic or anything." Peevey came out from behind the counter. "I mean he went up and down the sidewalk, going like this, and then he'd look at his watch."

Peevey took exaggeratedly long strides and glanced melodramatically at his wrist, causing a man on an end stool to stare at him and two older women at the magazine rack to look up and then away quickly.

To me, Peevey said, "See?"

"He was stretching out his steps?"

"Yeah. But more like he was counting them or timing it."

"Counting his steps and timing them?"

"Yeah, yeah. Like in a treasure hunt. 'Take twelve steps north from the stone gate,' you know?"

The next day, I left my house on Yucca Avenue at nine. By the time I got to the office on Cahuenga, the air was so heavy it seemed the heat was sitting on me. Bad sign for only late March.

I spent the morning cleaning up paperwork. After lunch downstairs, I drove to the Hollywood Division on Wilcox, where Dan Behagen had worked as a detective before signing on with Stanley Security. A uniform I knew at the desk told me Behagen's former partner was named Cuellar.

It was a large squad room, but Cuellar wasn't hard to spot. He was the only olive-skinned man there that wasn't handcuffed. He shared a back-to-back desk arrangement with another cop who hung up the phone and was leaving as I approached.

"Detective Cuellar?"

"Yeah?" He had a square face and a pompadour that Brylcreem could use in a television commercial. He also looked ragged, like trying to be better than the rest of the squad in order just to tread water was getting him down.

"My name's Marlowe. I'm investigating a claim for Golden State, and I'd like to ask you a few questions."

His expression remained neutral, but the eyes glowed a little brighter. "I never met you before, right?"

"Far as I know."

"You got anybody here who'll vouch for you?"

I gave him some names, enough so he didn't feel he needed to call them on me.

"Sit down. What can I do for you?"

"Your partner, Dan Behagen."

Cuellar's lips flared, but all he said was "Go ahead."

"I'd like to know more about him."

"Like for instance?"

"How long were you partnered with him?"

It wasn't the question he'd been expecting. "Four years."

"Did you know him before that?"

"Yeah. We went through the academy together just after we got . . . just after the war."

"You were in the Marines with him, too?"

"Right. That's how we met."

"I'm really sorry. About his death, I mean."

"Thanks."

"Why'd he quit?"

Cuellar was expecting that one. Sooner or later. "I don't know."

"He didn't talk with you about it?"

"No."

"Not even in general?"

"No."

"My guess is he was giving up fifteen hundred, maybe two thousand a year to go from the force to Stanley Security. He never talked about why?"

"No."

"You've got to know what I'm thinking."

"Marlowe, I know guys with no teeth don't talk so good anymore."

Just then the officer from the other desk came back and said, "Jeez, Vic, good to hear you talking like a cop again. Finally beat the hangover?"

"Yeah."

"Can't blame you none. I lost a partner once. Nothing I could do either, guy drowned out fishing somewheres, but I got plastered for three days anyway. Lieutenant asks, I'm out on the Steinberg case."

"Okay."

After the other cop left, I said, "He's right, you know. There wasn't anything you could do."

"Look, Marlowe, I was friends with the guy, all right? Doesn't mean we were like brothers. I knew him from the war and all. Things worked out we were partnered. But he had his own life, like I got mine. I'll tell you this, though—he was a good cop. As good as they come."

"And he proved it by going down in the line of duty?"

"What do you mean?"

"I mean I'd like to know if Behagen was involved in the robbery before the Hauer brothers hit the truck."

"Dan never took a dime in his life. That's . . ."

I waited while Cuellar thought of a different sentence than the one he was going to say.

"That's the truth."

I said, "You don't want to talk to me, fine. I can talk with other people."

"You going to see Karen?"

"If that's his wife's name, you know I am."

"Be nice to her, Marlowe. I find out you haven't been, you're gonna think God's shitting bricks on you."

Behagen's home was a stunted ranch on a block of houses so identical even the numbers didn't help much in telling them apart. Everything looked washed and swept, but up close the driveway was cracking and the paint was peeling, a process that had started well before last week.

I knocked on the screen door. The inner one opened, and for a minute, through the mesh, I thought Mims's talk about Grace Kelly had gotten to me. She was that beautiful in the blonde, classy way.

"Yes?"

I took twice as long as usual to introduce myself and show her my identification. She opened the screen door to examine it, shifting a book awkwardly in her hand, an index finger crooking to mark her place. Without the screen between us, she looked older, the kind of aging that worry and heartache bring on early.

She told me to come in, and I saw why things had been wearing down. For a long time.

There was an iron lung in the living room, leaving very little space for much of anything else. The head of a boy of six or seven stuck out from a diaphragm that closed around his neck like a collar. The back of his head lay on a yellow vinyl pad. His face stared at me upside down from an angled mirror at the top of the machine.

She said, "Kenny, this is Mr. Marlowe."

Kenny said, "Hi, Mr. Marlowe."

I said, "Hi."

"Kenny, Mr. Marlowe and I are going to talk in the kitchen for a while. Yell if you need anything."

"Right, Mom."

As we moved past him, I could see the bellows contraption at the foot end that breathed for him. It moved back and forth, making a noise like the swish of doors in a supermarket.

In the kitchen, Mrs. Behagen set down her book and I sat in a chair. "Coffee?"

"No, thank you."

Her back toward me, she poured herself a cup and tried to sound casual. "Something wrong with the insurance, Mr. Marlowe?"

"Just some routine questions. I'm sorry to have to ask them of you now."

She sat down with the coffee, stirring it past the point of blending in the milk and sugar. "Dan always said that was what he'd tell the people who were in the most trouble."

"Before he quit the force."

She stopped stirring. "That's right."

"Why did he quit, Mrs. Behagen?"

"Just tired of it, I guess."

"And became an armed guard because he got tired of being a cop?"

"I guess."

"And a pay cut with all the expenses . . ."

I stopped. She said, "All the expenses of a son like Kenny to take care of?"

"I'm sorry."

"No need to be sorry. Polio isn't something you did. It's just something that happened."

"Did your husband act differently in any way lately?"

"Yes."

"How?"

"He went from being a cop, dealing with the dregs of the city, to being a relatively normal, typical working guy."

"Who worked around a lot of money."

She laughed. "Yes, a lot of money. Too bad he never brought any home, huh?"

I watched her drink her coffee. She was good, almost as good as Mims.

Abel Hauer's girlfriend was named Monica. "After the pier," she said. Short, with choppy brown hair, she had that cheap but alluring look that sours with the thirtieth birthday. She'd been souring for about five years.

Monica reluctantly clicked off Red Skelton on the RCA when I suggested we could do without the competition. "So what do you want to know?"

"How long had you known Abel Hauer?"

"Hah, me and Abel, we go back a long ways together." Catching herself, she added, "Of course, I was real young for him then. Too young, if you catch my drift. How about a drink?"

"Sure."

"Scotch okay?"

"Fine."

For three glasses we covered her miserable childhood and aborted acting career. Then I said, "So you knew Abel before he went to prison?"

"Oh, yeah. Way long before." She took a healthy slug. "He was a good guy then, always looking after Randy 'cause they didn't have no ma and pa, you know. Fact, even after they went to prison, he looked after Randy. Some kinda funny guys in prison, if you catch my drift."

I got the feeling Monica's drifts were never too hard to catch. "What were they in for?"

Monica looked at her drink, her head bobbing a bit. "Bank. They tried to do a bank. Jerks."

"What happened?"

"Held it up, of course. Got away, too. But they killed . . . The cops said they killed this hick sheriff out in the valley someplace, getting away. They got caught finally, but they didn't have a gun on them that killed the sheriff, so they only went up for the bank robbery. Still, seven years ain't exactly a walk on the beach, you know?"

"Both Abel and Randy are dead now. You can tell me the truth, can't you?"

Monica lifted her chin and hooded her eyes, giving me a saucy smile. "Some guys, I tell everything to."

"Abel killed the sheriff, right?"

"I wasn't there myself, of course. But that's how I heard it."

"Supposedly Abel and Randy weren't out too long before they went after the armored car."

"Brother, you said it. That Abel, he had me on my . . . He stayed with me for about three days, tops. Then he started working on a new caper. Always a new caper with Abel."

"You have any idea how he decided on an armored car?"

She lifted her chin again, but not coyly. "What did you say you were again?"

"An investigator. A private investigator."

"So you're not a cop, right?"

"Right."

"And what we're talking about here, this doesn't get back to the cops, right?"

"My word on it."

"Well, that's good enough for me. You see, Abel—pour me a little more of that, will ya, honey?"

"Sure."

"Thanks. That's just right." She finished half of it. "What was I— oh yeah, that Abel, he had the brass of a . . . a . . . I don't know what. But in the brains, he wasn't so good. He needed . . . I don't know, a leader, I guess."

"And he found one."

"Yeah. Or one found him. He said it that way, that the guy found him. Don't know how."

"Then what?"

"Guy sets this up, this whole thing up for Abel and Randy, but it stinks, turns out it . . ." She started crying, swiping her forearm over her eyes, smearing the mascara. "It stinks and they get killed. Why'd they have to get killed like that, tell me?"

I was losing her. "Who did Abel say set it up?"

"I didn't tell the cops."

"I know you didn't."

"I didn't tell them."

"Sure. What'd they ever do for you, right?"

"No, no, you jerk. I didn't tell them because Abel told me."

"Told you what?"

"Told me it was a cop. A cop set it up. What did you think?"

The Public Library is one of the best buildings we've got in L.A. I know because a friend of mine from Massachusetts once walked by it and complimented me that he could drop it into the middle of Boston and it wouldn't even look out of place. I was there the next morning as they opened the doors, bothering the poor guy in charge of periodicals.

I used Monica's hazy memory as a gauge and started with 1948, figuring it might be front page stuff. I found the second story about the dead sheriff in the September 18th issue, then backtracked to September 17th for a page 10 story on the bank robbery. I recognized no one mentioned except the Hauers themselves.

The last paragraph of the September 18th story gave a trial date in November. Flipping forward, I found the accounts of the five-day hearing. Monica was right: they were found guilty on the robbery, innocent of the killing. The reporter noted the particularly incensed face of one officer who had responded to the robbery scene and who had testified "in unbroken English." A young patrolman named Victor Cuellar.

◆ ◆ ◆

Staking out a police station is tricky. Staking out a house is a lot easier. I figured he'd show up sooner or later. It turned out to be later. I looked away from his headlights to preserve my night vision. As he walked up the path to the little ranch, I could see his pompadour gleaming in the moonlight.

I gave them a while to settle in, then went up and knocked on the door.

Maybe I hadn't given them long enough. As Karen Behagen led me silently through the living room and past a sleeping Kenny, she was fully, correctly clothed. Entering the kitchen, I looked down at Cuellar. He was rotating a grape jelly glass of jug red wine in his hand, but except for his jacket over the back of the chair and a pulled-down tie, he was perfectly presentable. And not a little angry.

Cuellar started to say, "Marlowe, this better—"

"Vic," she said softly, cautioningly. "Kenny?"

Cuellar took in a long breath, letting it out slowly and with some effort. But when he spoke again, it was a whisper. "Why did you follow me?"

"I didn't. I was waiting here for you."

He said, "Karen is my partner's wife. She needs somebody at night sometimes, with Kenny."

"Let me tell you a bedtime story then. Only wait till I finish before you draw down on me or punch me out, okay?"

Cuellar and Mrs. Behagen just looked at me.

"You fall in love with your partner's wife. Nobody means for it to happen, it just does. He finds out about it, or suspects it, and can't abide it. He can't trust you or he can't stand you, but he can't make you quit the force either, so he does. He goes into security work because it's close to being a cop, as close as he can get on short notice maybe. But if you're no longer partners, there's no excuse for you seeing Karen anymore, and that eats at you. Then you think of the Hauer brothers, and you get a bright idea."

Karen Behagen said, "Please stop."

Cuellar said evenly, "No. Keep talking."

"You get the idea of setting up your ex-partner, to get him out of the way and have a little nest egg from the insurance all at the same time. The Hauers like to rob things, and you know they killed a cop once and got away with it, so they're not shy of the idea. You set it up with them to look like a robbery, but they're really in it just to kill Behagen, for some cut of the policy from you and maybe to grab whatever they can off the truck. But you've got to be sure it doesn't look like Behagen is in on it, because that would void the insurance. So you have them hit the truck when it's not carrying that much, when an insider like Behagen wouldn't have planned it, and when he's not feeling too well so he'll be in the truck alone while his buddies are grabbing some breakfast. How am I doing so far?"

Karen Behagen covered her face with her hands. "Please, please just stop this."

Cuellar said, "Finish it, Marlowe."

"Abel Hauer even arranges it so his younger brother can make his first kill. He was always looking after him that way. But Behagen is too good, and gets both brothers, saving you the trouble of knocking them off or facing blackmail for the rest of your life. I'm betting there's a file clerk somewhere who'll have a receipt or a memory of you asking for the Hauers' jackets well before the robbery, around when they got out of prison. What do you think?"

Mrs. Behagen dropped her hands and said, "Vic, we've got to tell him."

Cuellar said, "No."

She laid one of her hands on his and squeezed. He turned to look at her. Something passed between them. Affection certainly, maybe love, and even guilt. But not passion. And suddenly I knew I was dead wrong.

Cuellar turned back to me, worked his jaw a few times, and said, "You're right about the jackets on the Hauers, Marlowe. You'd be able to trace that I looked them over. I don't think that'd be enough, but if Karen can't stand this anymore, neither can I."

He rubbed her knuckles with his thumb. "Dan was dying. He told everybody it was some allergy or other, but it was down in his lungs and he was coughing, on and off. The doctor told him some disease, got more syllables in it than Tippecanoe and Tyler, Too. Doc thought it was from the shipyard work Dan did, because the Doc sees a lot of guys from the old days in the shipyard with it."

"From what, fifteen, twenty years ago?"

"That's what Dan said."

Mrs. Behagen said, "That was all he could think about."

I said, "So your husband leaves the force, and Cuellar here scans the files for a likely robbery team. Then what?"

Cuellar said, "I knew the Hauers iced that deputy seven years ago, and they walked on it. Dan had killed a lot . . . in the war. He had a lot of nerve that way. So when the Hauers got out, Dan contacted them with a cock-and-bull story about leaving the force and being bitter, and they set up the heist, Dan doing all the planning."

Part of which Garth Peevey saw from the drugstore on the Sunday morning. "And that's why the back door of the armored car was open."

"Right. The Hauers thought Randy was supposed to go in first, slug Dan to make it look good, then take off with what Dan told them would be a hundred, a hundred twenty grand. Instead Dan . . ." Cuellar stopped, looked sideways at Mrs. Behagen. "Instead Dan shot Randy, knowing it would make the older brother Abel go nuts and come after him instead of taking off."

"Which Behagen couldn't tolerate because then there's somebody who could tell the cops what happened."

"Right. And . . ." Cuellar glanced toward Mrs. Behagen again.

She said, "And Dan needed Abel to come after him, too, Mr. Marlowe."

I finally saw it. "So Abel could shoot your husband. So he could qualify for the insurance."

Her head drooped toward her chest. "The insurance would cover the mortgage and help me enough with Kenny to let us get by."

I thought about Dan Behagen, shooting Randy and then waiting for Abel, not just to drive up but to draw and fire, waiting for Abel's bullets to hit him somewhere he knew would be fatal, then having enough left to drill Abel, kill him for sure.

Cuellar said, "That's it, Marlowe. Now what?"

I shut my eyes, but all I could see was a doubly dying man in a gray uniform, clutching his stomach and counting himself out in silence. "You got anything stronger than wine?"

Thursday morning Mims said, "Sit down, Marlowe. You look like hell."

"Hangover."

"On our time?"

"Not exactly."

"You find out anything?"

"I did."

He folded his paper and put it away. "Well?"

"Behagen's clean as a whistle. No connection. It'll all be in my report."

"Then how come you came here in person?"

"I knew it was important to you. Wanted to ease your mind."

Mims tried to tell if I was kidding him. "Why, I appreciate that. Especially after last night."

I couldn't read him. "Last night?"

"The Oscars, man. Where were you, Mars? Judy Garland lost out to that Kelly girl."

I stood up, told Mr. Mims how much I'd enjoyed working for him, and left.

I know I saw movies based on Raymond Chandler's works before reading any of his books. Struck by the version of The Big Sleep *starring Humphrey Bogart and intrigued by the version of* The Long Goodbye *starring Elliott Gould, I began reading the novels themselves. Chandler's straightforward, declarative tone in both narrative and dialogue appealed to the trial lawyer I was then. Many attorneys are criticized, correctly, for a prolix style in drafting contracts, wills, and other documents. Chandler came across as closer to the litigator than the obfuscator, as an author who had to make his points clearly for the wide audience of nonspecialists he attracted.*

Chandler, John D. MacDonald, and Robert B. Parker were the authors I was reading when I started writing my first private investigator novel. A person who lived in the South when he or she began to speak tends to have a southern accent. I think Chandler and the other masters necessarily influenced me in a similar fashion. I just hope my efforts prove half so successful.

Jeremiah Healy

THE ALIBI

ED GORMAN

1956

HE FIRST TIME I ever saw Robert
Hutchings, he was lying on a fancy leather couch in a fancy hotel just off
Hollywood Boulevard. Across from him on the seventeen-inch screen of a
blond Admiral television console, Douglas Edwards was telling us all about
a Negro named Autherine Lucy who was trying to enter the University of
Alabama. She was not having any notable success. It was a feeling I was
familiar with. My business—Philip Marlowe, Investigations—was not exactly going through a golden age, either.

Closer by Hutchings, on a love seat that seemed made especially for
the properly rounded bottom of a princess, perched a tall, recklessly beautiful, dark-haired woman in a gray gabardine suit meant to make her beauty
seem not quite so reckless. But her slight overbite and the moontide gravity
of her dark eyes made that impossible. She was thirty-five perhaps, and
she would have exuded sexuality inside a steel coffin that had been dropped
straight down into the Pacific. Or would under normal circumstances, anyway. At present her condition appeared to be one of clinical shock and so
her sexual appeal was operating at one remove, like a museum statue that
could only suggest the real thing.

There was one other person in the room, a shabby man in need of a
shave, a clean suit, and a brand new life. His name was Donald Hanratty
and there had been a time, back in his days on the force, when he'd been
shiny as a new dime. But that had been before a wife had died of cancer
and a son had wrapped a '46 Ford convertible around the unremitting
finality of a light pole. Hanratty, good cop, good man, good husband, good
father, had died a death of sorts right along with them—the death of bottled
spirits, that peculiar half-life that is lived out in tears and rage and the
bleeding stomach of the alcoholic. He'd stayed on the force until "nerves"
had forced him to retire, and since then he'd sold shoes, parked cars, and

worked—laughably and sadly—as a bouncer at a juke joint where a male starlet had broken his jaw one night. For the past few years, Hanratty had been calling himself a private investigator.

Hanratty, lighting his third Chesterfield in less than ten minutes, said, "She killed him."

Somebody had killed him, anyway. An especially nasty looking butcher knife had been plunged hilt deep into Robert Hutchings' chest. The blood was completely ruining the fancy brown leather couch. There were some hotels in L.A. where they would just hose down the room and go back about their business. This wasn't one of them. Here, when the management found out, there would be a lot of shrieking, a lot of cursing, enough cops to go around for a policeman's ball, and plenty of press. Plenty. Robert Hutchings had been, after all, Captain Starman on the television.

I moved over closer to the woman. Her eyes told me she was still someplace else, someplace where small-time T.V. stars didn't get butcher knives shoved into their chests. She reminded me just then, with that vacant but somehow melancholy look filling her eyes, of Jean Simmons in Olivier's *Hamlet*. I don't spend all my time reading *Confidential* magazine.

"She has blood on her hands and her suit," I said.

"I know," Hanratty said.

"And you haven't called the cops in yet? Why not?"

"I needed time to think. Because of this—" He nodded to the blood-soaked chest of Captain Starman. "This doesn't make me look real good, Philip."

It wasn't quite the proper thing to say with a dead television star no more than six feet from us and a woman in clinical shock sitting even closer by.

Still, his remark made me more than casually curious. "What kind of jobs have you been doing, Hanratty?"

I spoke softly. Ten years ago, my investigator's license under serious and perhaps terminal review by some very unfriendly types up in Sacramento, Hanratty had written me a letter of endorsement that would have melted the heart of a hanging judge. I owed him and I'd never repaid him.

He sighed. He sounded as if Pat O'Brien all got up in a Roman collar was about to walk him down an echoing corridor to the electric chair. "I kind of watch over stars."

" 'Watch over'?"

"Take care of any problems they have."

"Which stars?"

He had some more Chesterfield. When he took it from his mouth you could see the wet spot on the white paper where he'd lipped it. A fleck of paper remained behind on his lip. "Not big stars, Philip. Nobody in the movies, I mean. But T.V. people, you know. Like that." He looked dog sad and dog whipped.

"And you were 'watching over' Hutchings?"

"Yeah. Or I was supposed to. He was supposed to be meeting her in this suite and he was afraid to be alone with her."

Hutchings had been a strapping blond, just the sort of machine-tooled Muscle Beach product who'd wind up playing Captain Starman. No doubt he'd had as many faults as a defrocked minister, but physical cowardice wasn't likely to have been one of them.

"He was afraid of her?" I asked.

"She tried to shoot him two days ago."

"Why?"

"He was playing around on her and she didn't like it."

"Who was he playing around with?"

He shrugged. "His wife."

Wandering over to the window, I looked down on the April afternoon. They didn't let you into this section of the city if you drove anything less than a Packard and then it had better have been waxed and buffed and polished within the past twenty-four hours. I glanced over the suite once more. In the vast marble lobby below, an area that suggested a set from *Quo Vadis* gone slightly to seed, there were photographs of the stars who'd stayed over the years—the young Douglas Fairbanks, Jr., Clark Gable, and Garbo herself. I tried to imagine them sitting in this staid, icy room laughing their silver Hollywood laughs, but somehow the stiff worked against my sense of nostalgia.

I turned back to him, putting my pipe in my mouth. "Hanratty, what the hell's going on?"

"You know what I said I wouldn't do?"

"Yeah."

"I did it."

I said a word that sounded particularly vulgar on the refined air of this room. Five times in three years I'd taken Hanratty to and from those discreet little motel-like hospitals where they strap drunks to beds and let them scream long past midnight. Five times he was supposed to have been "cured." Five times. I suppose it was my way of trying to pay him back for helping me with my license.

He had tears in his eyes now. I nearly did, too. "It's easy enough, Philip. She—Susan Ames here—was to be the next Mrs. Hutchings. But then the first Mrs. Hutchings—Darla—started looking good to him again.

A couple days ago he tried to break it off with Susan and that's when she tried to shoot him."

"No police again?"

"No police. He's a hero to the kids. He can't afford this kind of publicity." He shook his head. He didn't have to say it. It was sadly plain. "Well, I sat in the other room there while Hutchings and Susan were talking and—" He pawed at his face again.

"You had a bottle?"

"Yeah."

"How much of a bottle?"

"Pint."

I said the dirty word again. "So you started drinking and—"

"It was only supposed to be a couple belts, Philip. Honest."

"You passed out."

He paused. "Yeah."

"And while you were passed out—"

He finished it for me. "She killed him."

Now I could see why he didn't want any publicity about this job. You didn't get a lot of bodyguard work when you were known for drinking yourself to sleep. Or when the person you're supposed to be watching gets killed.

He had a croak in his throat and as soon as he started to talk, he started crying. He looked old, the kind of old that can scare you to see, the kind of old you hope you don't live long enough to ever become. "How do I get out of this mess?"

"Walk me through it."

"Huh?" He was starting to shake.

"Walk me through it. Show me where you were and where they were and just how you found them."

"Oh," he said, "right." He pushed his shoulders back and wiped at his runny red nose with the back of his hand and then put another Chesterfield between his lips. "It was pretty simple."

It took us ten minutes to go through the whole thing. When he'd awakened in the next room, he'd heard sobbing, and when he'd come out, he'd found Susan Ames sitting next to Hutchings. Hutchings was long dead. Susan was deep into some kind of traumatic withdrawal.

When he finished walking me through it all, I ended up where he'd ended up, right next to the Ames woman.

I sat down and took her cold hand in mine. I touched one of her cheeks gently with my fingertips, then moved her face toward mine. "I need to talk to you, Susan. I need to talk to you."

But there was nothing in the eyes. Hers was the beauty of the department store mannequin, the ironic vacancy in the perfect erotic shell.

"Susan," I said again. "Susan."

But I knew better. Much better.

As I stood up, Hanratty said, "Can you keep my name out of the papers?"

Now I found myself shaking my head. "God, Hanratty, I'll try, but you aren't exactly talking to the mayor, you know."

"But people know you, Philip. Important people."

"Yeah," I said, "like my landlord on rent day."

He said it one more time. "I just need a little help, Philip. Just a little."

In the hallway, I heard the squeaking of shiny shoes on thinning carpet. The sound gave me an idea. "Wait here."

"Huh?"

"Wait here," I said.

There was light at the far end of the hallway where dust motes tumbled in rich yellow afternoon sunlight. A Negro maid pushed a cart with the weariness of plantation days, and a dapper young couple, just finished with one of those disposable adulteries almost mandatory here, went whistling toward the elevators.

Bent over an ice machine, his gray trousers shiny, his red jacket shabby, was a bellhop whose tiny monkey cap looked silly perched on his greasy hair. I believe the kids call the hairstyle a duck's ass. The guy was at least thirty.

"You been working on this floor most of the afternoon?" I said.

"Who wants to know?"

"I want to know."

"So you want to know. So big deal, pal." He raised a hand to turn up the volume on a small white plastic radio. "Elvis," he said. "I dig him."

A kid with the unlikely name of Elvis Presley was singing a pretty standard Tin Pan Alley song named "Heartbreak Hotel" and the world was treating it as if Christ had just sent the whole planet a letter.

I put my hand on the bellhop's wrist and said, "I'm a Glenn Miller man, myself." Then I put a crisp five dollar bill in the handkerchief pocket of his silly red coat.

"My hearing just got better."

"It isn't your hearing I'm worried about," I said. "There's a woman in six-oh-two."

Obviously he'd seen. Obviously he'd liked her. "There sure is." He grinned. "A babe."

"You see or hear anything of her this afternoon?"

"Nope."

"You see or hear anything in the room?"

"Nope."

"You sure?"

"Why would I lie?"

I nodded to the radio. "I'm not sure I trust anybody who likes music like that."

"Hey, pal," he said. "It's one way people like us can stay young."

"If that's young, give me my rocking chair."

He bent over the ice machine again and scooped up cubes into a plastic bucket. After three scoops he started shaking his hands. "Fingers get cold. I should start wearing gloves." Then he said, "Hey, gloves."

" 'Gloves' what?"

"Reminds me of what she said."

"Who said?"

"The babe in six-oh-two."

"I thought she didn't say anything."

"I guess I just kind of forgot. About her dropping her purse and all."

"She dropped her purse?"

"Yeah, as the three of them were going into the room."

"Who were the three?"

"Well, the dame, this guy about my age who looked like he'd probably been a cop at one time or another, and this pretty boy who plays Captain Starman or some candyass thing like that."

"So she dropped her purse?"

"Yeah, and her gloves fell out and then this little bottle of pills. And that's when Captain Starman goes apeshit."

"Why would he do a thing like that?"

He shrugged. The tassels on his epaulets swayed back and forth like a skirt on a hula girl lamp. "Said she wasn't supposed to be taking them with booze."

"That's all?"

"They closed the door. That's all I heard."

"You didn't hear them arguing or anything?"

"Not really arguing. He just got kind've p.o.'d was all. Then, like I said, they closed the door." He nodded to his container of ice. "We about done, pal?"

"Yeah, pal, we're about done."

Back in the room Hanratty said, "He's starting to smell."

"So I noticed."

"We're gonna have to call the cops, aren't we, Philip?" He was shaking again.

I took him over and planted him in a chair. He looked very bad. "You got any left?"

He knew exactly what I was talking about. He measured out about an inch and said, "In there." He nodded to the bedroom.

I went in and got it out. It was cheap stuff, about what you'd expect. I put it in his hands. He drank it quickly and without shame. The way his throat worked when he was gulping it down was almost obscene. I had to look away to Susan Ames. If she'd moved at all, you would have had to use a tape measure to prove it.

"I've got to call the cops," I said.

He grabbed my hand. Lepers grab at the pope this way. "Can you keep my name out of it, Philip? Can you, Philip, huh?"

I sighed. "I'll try. That's all I can say."

He shot up from the chair before I could push him back in it.

"Why the hell don't you sit down and let me call the cops and get this thing rolling?"

"I gotta pee, Philip. I'm sorry. Ever since my rookie days, when I get nervous, I have to pee. I can't help it."

I sighed. "Okay, but hurry up, all right?"

"All right."

Harcourt was far happier than he should have been about standing next to a corpse. He was a detective and he was young and he looked, from a certain angle, not unlike the actor John Derek, over whom any number of teenage girls were ready to ruin their lives.

Harcourt had good reason to be happy. He was the man in charge of investigating the death of Captain Starman. Of just such fortuitous opportunities are entire careers made.

All the people you expected to see were there, from the medical examiner's team looking like a pair of dour pharmacists in their white jackets to eager newspaper photographers who kept peering inside the suite's front door until one of the uniformed boys threatened to slam the door in an act of legal decapitation.

You could tell that Harcourt was a college man because he said "ain't" only three times in his first four sentences, which is far below average for an L.A. cop.

"So you're in this room," he said.

"So I'm in this room," I said.

"And you see her with blood all over her clothes and hands."

"And I see her with blood all over her clothes and hands."

"And Hanratty's over there?"

I nodded.

"And then you call the police?"

I nodded once again.

He had a grin as big as a crooked politician's. "So that, I guess, is that." He pointed to the Ames woman, who looked, if anything, comatose by this point, and had two uniformed men lead her away.

There were flashbulbs exploding and endtables being dusted for prints and a fat uniformed cop yawning. Even murder can get tedious.

"And you'll testify to all this?" Harcourt asked me.

"Yes."

Harcourt, who wore a crewcut and the sort of black horn-rimmed glasses prep schools hand out on registration day, glanced at Hanratty and said, "Some goddamn bodyguard he is."

Hanratty, insulted, started up out of his chair as if he were going to punch Harcourt. Obviously thinking better of it, he sat back down and glared at me with an I-told-you-so look deep in his eyes.

I made a show of patting my pockets. "Nuts."

"What?" Harcourt said.

"No cigarettes."

He reached in his suitcoat pocket and came back with a red and white package of Cavaliers. "Have one of mine."

"Afraid I'm a sissy these days. Filters only. Think I'll go downstairs and buy myself a pack."

"I'm not through with you."

"Five minutes is all I'm asking. I'll even get a note from my Mom."

Harcourt said, "Five minutes."

Before the police had come, and after Hanratty had gone into the bathroom again, I'd checked through Susan Ames's purse, finding her driver's license and all sorts of interesting data. I figured it wouldn't hurt to know a little something about her.

More helpful than her license had been the bill from a Doctor Farnham. It was stamped OVERDUE in bold, ominous letters. The letterhead gave no indication of what sort of doctor this Farnham was. My naturally suspicious mind got very suspicious indeed.

Which is why, when I reached the lobby on my supposed mission to get a pack of filter-tips, the first thing I did was angle myself into a phone booth and call Doctor Farnham.

The secretary, who had apparently studied under Hermann Goering, was about as cooperative at first as a nun at an orgy. But then when I told her a little white lie about being with the L.A.P.D., she put some sunshine in her voice.

Doctor Farnham came on twenty-three seconds later.

We had a brief but most instructive chat about Susan Ames. In not much time at all, I was thanking the doctor and hanging up.

Then, because stars, even television stars, don't have listed numbers, I phoned the Screen Actors Guild and asked for the name of Robert Hutchings' agent. From that man, again floating my little white lie, I got Hutchings' home number and called.

Knowing that what I was doing was as risky as asking Liberace about his sex life, I dialed the number and said in as Hanratty-like a rasp as I could summon, "It's all done and the cops are here." I spoke very quickly, hoping the speed would help.

From the woman on the other end of the phone, I heard, "Thank God."

"I'll be wanting the rest of the money."

She got a little snappish. "You know our deal, Hanratty, you—"

I hung up and went back upstairs in an elevator as fancy as the inside of a rich man's coffin.

Harcourt had now allowed the press in. He was smiling as much as those pretty boys in toothpaste commercials.

One of the reporters was talking about how crushed his six year old was going to be when he heard that Captain Starman was dead. He was right. I could still remember the day when my mother told me that Fatty Arbuckle might go to prison. Young minds shouldn't have to deal with things like that.

"Yes," Harcourt was pontificating, "it's open and shut. She was jealous because he was going back to his wife and so she killed him."

I went over to Hanratty where he sat in a chair staring out the window. I said, "I know what happened, Hanratty. Why the hell did you do it?" I was trying to whisper but the way people snapped toward us, I could tell I was doing a lousy job.

I stepped into the ring of reporters and said, "Hanratty killed him."

For the second time in less than twenty minutes, Hanratty came up out of the chair as if he were going to thrash somebody.

I said, "He was working with Mrs. Hutchings. They knew that Susan Ames had a history of mental problems and was occasionally given to violence, and so she was the perfect patsy for a setup like this. She was under the care of a Doctor Farnham, a psychiatrist, if you want to check this out.

"Mrs. Hutchings no doubt stood to collect a lot of insurance money on her husband. So she got hold of Hanratty, whom her husband had hired as a bodyguard, and made a deal with him. If Hanratty killed her husband and made it look as if Susan Ames did it, then Hanratty got a big chunk of the insurance money. Isn't that how it went, Hanratty?"

Before he could respond, I said, "And he brought me in as a witness. I would come up here and see that everything looked as if Susan Ames had in fact killed Robert Hutchings. Then Hanratty would have a kind of second-hand witness to back up his story. I would testify that everything looked to me as if she was the killer. I'd make a reasonably credible witness on the witness stand and Hanratty knew it. In a sense, I'd be his alibi."

Harcourt, not a man to be upstaged, said, "And that's exactly why I kept Hanratty right in this room." Like any good political hack, he sensed that a bandwagon was starting to roll, and he wanted to jump on.

"But you said that Susan Ames was the killer," a kid who had one of those squeaky Jimmy Olsen voices said to Harcourt.

"Only because I wanted to lull Hanratty here into a false sense of security." He glanced at me anxiously. "Right, Marlowe?"

"Right," I said. "Harcourt here knew about it all along."

"Man," the kid with the squeaky voice said. "This is some story." He gave the impression he'd just graduated from journalism school last week.

I rode down the service elevator with Hanratty and his handcuffs and two beefy, silent cops.

Hanratty was pretty bad off. I tried not to look at the way he was shaking.

"I wish I knew what to say, Philip."

"Yeah."

"You mad?"

"We shouldn't talk about it, Hanratty. We shouldn't talk about it at all."

"I never was crooked. Not on the force, I mean."

"I know."

He was starting to cry. "You know what my wife said to me when she was dyin', Marlowe?"

"No," I said. "No, I don't." My voice didn't sound much better than Hanratty's and I knew in that moment why I'd always liked him. He was an older version of myself. In younger days, when he'd been dapper and successful, he'd been somebody I'd wanted to be. Now, he was somebody I feared I would be.

"She said, 'You never been the man you coulda been.' You know, Marlowe, she was right."

He started crying so hard he was choking. He fell into me and I held him. The two cops looked at each other and shook their heads.

When he got hold of himself again, there in the tiny oil-smelling elevator, he said, "I don't know what to say. I really don't."

"That's the hell of it," I said, just as the elevator bumped to a stop and the ornate doors began to open. "There isn't anything to say, Hanratty. There really isn't."

We walked outside into the afternoon that was dying grandly—with purple and amber streaking the sky and the cricket-clack of palm fronds chattering in the breeze—and they put him in the car and he didn't look back at me. He didn't look back at me at all.

He did us both a hell of a favor.

More than any writer except Hemingway, Raymond Chandler taught me that language matters at least as much as story and perhaps as much as character. Proof of this is simple enough—think of the hundreds of private-eye tales told and now utterly forgotten. Why do we, all these long years later, remember Chandler? For his stories? In most cases, he was not an especially gifted tale spinner. For his characters? Yes and no. A few were brilliantly rendered, but most were little more than stereotypes, and movie stereotypes at that. I always wondered—were there really so many gangsters in the world? No, we remember Chandler for the way his sentences made the familiar special and the trite brand-new. His socks with the clocks. His tarantula on the angel food cake. The overheated hothouse and the crippled tyrant with the blanket on his lap. In addition, he gave us at least one great novel, arguably the best private-eye novel ever written, The Long Goodbye. *It is mystery fiction's* Gatsby, *and one can't say much more than that.*

Ed Gorman

THE DEVIL'S PLAYGROUND

JAMES GRADY

1957

SUPLEE WAS A weathered trio of adobe buildings on a sunbaked plain of sand and scrub brush 224 miles northeast of L.A. where a state road crossed US91. Two box houses sat on one side of the state road. Across that black snake was a truck stop cafe and gas station. My car was up on the rack in the garage and I was nursing a cup of coffee in the cafe, pretending to study the menu while I considered my next move, when she walked in.

We all turned to look: the beatnik couple at the next table, the trucker perched on a counter stool reading a newspaper, the waitress filling the trucker's mug at the coffee urn, and the beefy man behind the cash register. She had wind-twisted long brown curls, wore an Air Corps leather jacket over a snap-buttoned cowboy shirt, khaki slacks, and battered black flats. Her purse was black and bulky and probably went to the prom. When she brushed the hair off her face she was maverick beautiful, with wide lips, a fine nose, and bright green eyes. The air around her was electric. She got her bearings, went to the counter, and drank the glass of water beside the trucker.

"Broke down," she said, putting the empty glass on the counter, "about a mile back. You got a wrecker?"

"Thirsty?" cracked the waitress without a smile.

"Get Billy," the man behind the cash register told the waitress. An open door connected the cafe to the garage bay. The wheels of my car were visible six feet off the cement. The waitress walked to that door and yelled at the kid in overalls.

"Mister," Billy said to me as he walked in from the garage, "I pulled off two tires, but ain't found . . ."

Billy saw the girl, lost his voice. The calendar said they were about the same age, but the calendar lied.

"She needs a wrecker," said the cash register man. " 'Bout a mile back north. That right?"

"Yes," said the girl. "My brothers are with the car."

The trucker's toothpick changed corners in his mouth.

"You mean you got two men in the car, 'n' they let you walk it out?" he said.

"Sure." She smiled at Billy. He blushed.

"What the hell kind of men are they?" said the trucker. "Letting a woman walk. This out here ain't safe like the city."

"Hank," said Billy to the man behind the register, nodding toward me, "I ain't figured what's making noise in this guy's car. He's still up on the hoist."

"Go ahead and pull them in," I said, grateful for the luck. "I'm in no hurry."

"Be right with you!" he told the girl.

"Go without me," she said, and Billy's face fell. "It's the only broke-down car between here and there. The guys will take care of you."

Billy left in the wrecker. The girl sat one stool away from the trucker, her back to the counter, watching the rest of us. The trucker ordered a hot roast beef sandwich. The beat couple whined about no club sandwiches on the menu, ordered hamburgers.

"What about you?" asked the waitress when she got to me.

"Steak sandwich," I told her.

"What's wrong with your car?" Her name tag read Anna.

"Ask Billy," I said. "Many people live in this town?"

"Not enough to be a *town*," Anna said and we laughed. "Me and Billy drive over from Baker."

The girl took her purse and went into the bathroom.

"Who does live here?"

"Looking to move?" I smiled, and she said: "Just Hank, the owner, Sal, the cook, and a sheepherder and Hell, he's a drunk."

"Lot of people 'round here use the bus?" I asked, nodding to the Greyhound sign on the wall.

"Ain't a lot of people around here. You gotta drive to get here, so if you got a car, why take the bus? How come you want to know?"

"No special reason."

It was one of those high desert days when the thermometer says you should be in shirt-sleeves but the wind carries a dry chill and a thousand needles of sand. I'd drained my coffee and was considering taking off my suit coat when the girl came out of the bathroom. Billy would have blushed again. She'd combed her hair until it fell evenly to her shoulders, washed her face, and painted her lips dark red. She stared out the windows.

"That's an awful lot of nothing out there," she said.

"The map calls it the Devil's Playground," said Hank.

"He don't need no special place," she told the world.

"Know all about that, do you?" cracked Hank.

"Enough," she answered. She nodded to the cooler behind the register. "You got any beer?"

"You got any I.D.?" Hank leered at her.

She pouted, gave him her back, and sat on a stool.

"The boys will want beer," she told everyone and no one.

Out the front window I saw the wrecker turn off the highway, a red Dodge in tow. Billy backed the Dodge toward the empty bay. Two men jumped out the wrecker and headed to the cafe.

They walked in like they owned the place. The leader wore a Levi jacket over a white tee-shirt, rolled cuffed blue jeans, and black engineer boots with heels designed to make him feel six feet tall. He was a pretty boy, with dirty blond hair greased up and combed back, pale skin, a wild grin, and dancing blue eyes. His companion wore an old-fashioned canvas duster that covered him past his knees. His face implied an I.Q. well into double digits. He walked with a gimpy left leg.

"How we doin', Nora?" asked pretty boy. He stayed by the door. His eyes sized up the room. The gimp walked to the register, asked Hank for a beer. Hank opened the cooler.

"So you're the two heroes who sent a girl for help," said the trucker, spinning round on his stool to face pretty boy.

"We figured nobody would tell her no." Pretty boy smiled.

"Maybe she should ride with more man behind the wheel."

The girl named Nora cautioned: "Jesse."

"She's fine with what she's got," said pretty boy Jesse.

At the register, the gimp laughed.

The trucker shook his head with disgust, turned back to his meal and newspaper.

"How we all doing today?" Jesse asked us. The beatniks ignored him. I shrugged.

The door to the garage bays opened and Billy came in.

"Mister," he said to Jesse, "I checked your engine and—"

"I told you not to mess with it." Jesse's voice was cold.

"Hey, fixin' cars is what I do. Did you know you got a couple holes punched in your radiator?"

"No," said Jesse.

"How in the hell couldn't you know?" continued Billy. The gimp leaned against the window, watched Hank and Anna behind the counter. "Almost looks like somebody shot your car."

The trucker stood, dropped a couple of bills on the counter beside his newspaper. He kept his eyes off Nora two stools away and walked toward the front door where Jesse stood.

"Where you going?" said Jesse.

"Back on the road." The trucker's voice was strained. "Gotta make Texas by midnight."

"You got plenty of time," said Jesse. "Sit a spell. I'll buy you a cup of coffee."

The trucker swung hard from his hip. His fist smashed into Jesse's jaw and the small man crashed to the floor. The trucker leapt over Jesse's legs and grabbed the door handle, all while I was getting to my feet. Jesse rolled, came up with a revolver. The gun cracked three times. Two red circles popped up on the trucker's back and a crimson line creased the side of his head. He fell half in, half out the door.

The gimp pulled a police riot gun from under his duster—now I knew why he'd limped. The shotgun swung from Hank to us and back again.

Nora sat on her stool, clutching her purse.

"You!" Jesse screamed at Billy, who stared at the fallen trucker, mouth open, face pale. "Drag him back in here!"

When Billy didn't move, Jesse slapped him. Billy pulled the trucker inside the cafe.

The beatnik woman screamed.

"Shut up!" yelled Jesse. To Hank: "Who's out back?"

"Just . . . just the Mex cook!"

"Scooter!"

The gimp motioned Hank and Anna from behind the counter, then ran into the kitchen.

The beatnik woman screamed again.

"Shut her up!" yelled Jesse. Her man pressed his hands over her mouth.

"All of you! Over there!"

They joined me by the wall.

"Take him with you."

Billy and I pulled the trucker into our group. His head wound wasn't deep, but he was unconscious.

"Is he dead?" asked Jesse.

"No," I said. "So far it's just assault."

Jesse laughed. Scooter herded a curly black-haired man out of the kitchen and over to us: Sal, the cook. His skin was olive. Sal wore a long-sleeved white shirt.

"Who else is in this town?" Jesse asked Hank.

The cafe owner stammered, pointed to one of the two houses across the highway.

"J-just a rummy. Louis. He's probably in there."

"Invite him over, Scooter."

Scooter ran out.

"Well, now," said Jesse, the revolver dangling from his hand, "I bet this isn't what any of you expected."

"What do you want?" cried the woman. "Our money—"

"Good idea. Nora, get their wallets."

Billy stood at my side; when Nora got to us, she whispered: "Be careful!"

Jesse swung a chair around cowboy-style, sat down. Nora brought him the wallets. He kept one eye on us and used his free hand to pull out the green. My luck held, and he didn't flip my billfold open and find the special deputy's badge.

Scooter pushed a disheveled man through the front door and into our group: Louis, the sheepherder, reeking of whiskey.

"This isn't exactly what we planned," said Jesse.

"What *plan*?" snapped Nora.

"You ain't got no complaints so far," said Jesse. She frowned, stared at her shoes.

Scooter whined: "When we gonna get out of here?"

Jesse smiled. "We just got here."

"There'll be troopers."

"Maybe there will, maybe there won't."

"They'll see that one in the ditch, find his car."

"These are lonesome roads," said Jesse. "You never know who you're going to find. Or when."

The wind rattled the screen door.

"You hungry?" asked Jesse. Scooter nodded. Jesse wagged his pistol at the owner. "Fix us some burgers, man."

"I ain't the cook," said Hank. He nodded to the curly-haired man. "Sal is."

"You hire him 'cause he cooks good?" asked Jesse.

"I hired him 'cause he came along. He does the cookin' and I do the bossin'."

"Bet you're a fair man, too, ain't ya?" Jesse smiled.

"Damn right!" insisted Hank. For a moment, he forgot about the guns. "I ain't like some. I work 'em all fair, colored or Mex, long as they know their place."

"You're a good man," said Jesse. "Ain't he, Sal?"

"I've known worse," answered the cook. He had a thick accent, more guttural than most Mexicans.

"Maybe we should get him to give you a raise," Jesse said.

"I just want to be left alone," Sal replied.

"Can't oblige you, *amigo*," said Jesse. "Scooter, take Sal back to the kitchen, have him fry us some burgers. On your way, get the green in the till. And check around there real good."

"We gotta get going," whined Scooter, but he waved the shotgun at Sal.

"You be good now," Jesse told the cook. "Follow orders."

"I know how to do that." Sal walked toward the kitchen. Scooter called him up short while he cleaned out the till. Scooter smiled, reached beneath the counter, and came up with a Winchester .30-.30 lever-action saddle rifle.

"Expecting Indians?" said Jesse. Scooter laughed. Shotgun in one hand, Winchester in the other, he marched Sal back into the kitchen. "Any more iron around?"

The owner shook his head.

"Mister," said Anna, the waitress, "I'm going to get the first-aid kit under the counter and tend to this man."

"Knock yourself out, sister."

The trucker lay on his back, pale, his chest slowly moving. I rolled him over, tore away his shirt. There should have been more blood coming out of the two holes in his back.

Jesse waved his .22 revolver. "He's lucky I wasn't packing more gun."

"Oh, he's real lucky," I said as Anna came over with the tin first-aid box.

"I'll help," said Nora. Jesse frowned as she left his side to stand next to me. "I've never seen a man shot before."

"Sure you have," I whispered. If Jesse heard me, he made no sign. Nora blushed. "How many have you guys gunned so far?"

"Hush," she whispered back. "He'll hear us."

Anna and I stuck compress bandages over the holes in the trucker's back, put some tape over the crease on his skull. Nora watched us for a few moments, then drifted to the kitchen.

"Give me a hand," I said to the beatnik man. He wore a green corduroy jacket, khaki pants, a black turtleneck to match the one worn by his pale blonde woman friend. He had a beard, shaggy hair, and thin wrists. The trucker gurgled when we lifted him, and the beatnik woman began to cry. From the kitchen came the spatter and crackle of frying meat.

"Holy cow!" whispered Billy, color returning to his face.

We laid the trucker across tables Billy pushed together.

"Who are you people?" said the beatnik woman. "What do you want?"

"Lady," said Jesse, "we are whoever we want to be."

"Why are you doing this?" she whispered. "We're just on our way to San Francisco—"

"*Why?*" Jesse spread his arms wide. "Because we can."

"Mister," said Billy, "you're in real trouble with the police."

Jesse laughed, held his forehead to keep from crying.

"That's probably what it says in the newspapers," I said, nodding to the folded journal the trucker had left beside his plate.

Those blue eyes raised up from Jesse's hand; he walked backward to the counter and picked up the paper.

"So that's what put a burr under his saddle!" Jesse read the paper to us: " 'Police in five Western states are searching for three young murder suspects believed headed for California.'

"Ain't everybody headed to California?" He grinned, continued: " 'Police in Riverton, Wyoming, say Jesse Edwards shot and killed Harley Benson, the stepfather of his girlfriend, Nora Benson, two days ago. Authorities say the girl may be a victim' . . . Hah! . . . 'a victim Edwards kidnapped. Before fleeing in a stolen car, Edwards stopped at the city jail, where his reform school roommate, Eugene Pandono, also known as Scooter, was in custody for burglary. Edwards shot and killed the jailer, and fled with Pandono. The stolen car was abandoned in Idaho, where police found the body of a salesman but not his car.'

"Hear that, folks? We're famous! Hey, babe!" he called out to the kitchen. "We're really going places now!"

"Where?" I asked.

"America, you know?" Jesse smiled. "It's a big place."

Sal and Nora walked out of the kitchen, carrying plates of hamburgers, french fries. Scooter came behind them carrying artillery. He left the Winchester on the counter, grabbed three beers from the cooler, and walked to the food table. They sent Sal to join us. Scooter and Jesse sat with their eyes our way.

"Hey, man," whined Scooter. "Let's go, huh?"

"It's lunchtime!" Jesse nodded to Hank. "You got a jukebox in here?"

"There's a radio by the coffee urn," said waitress Anna.

"Well, sister," Jesse told her, "let's have some tunes."

Anna slowly walked past the seated trio, behind the counter. She turned on the radio, got the news: Joe McCarthy was dead, the Teamsters were being thrown out of the AFL-CIO for being run by crooks, there was trouble in the Middle East.

"Did you hear England's got the bomb?" Jesse asked us over the commercial for life insurance. He grinned. "It's 1957: now everybody can die."

Anna glanced at the rifle lying on the counter.

Without looking at her, Jesse said: "Forget it, sister."

Anna turned the radio louder and came back to my side.

"You people spread out in a line so I can see all of you," said Jesse, and we complied. "You can sit down."

I pulled a chair next to Anna's. If we whispered, I didn't think they could hear us over the radio.

"You did the smart thing," I told her.

"Somebody ought to shoot that bastard," she said.

"Somebody will. Are there any more guns in here?"

She shook her head.

"How long you known these guys? Not them," I added, ruling out the trio. "Hank. The sheepherder Louis. The Mexican cook."

"Sal maybe ain't Mex. Anybody who ain't white, black, or Indian is Mex to Hank. What the hell do you care?"

"Just curious," I lied.

"I just came to these parts five years ago," she said. "I should've stayed in Butte."

Billy sat next to me, his hand thrust in his overalls. "Hank's been here since I was born. He should have kept a pistol under there. Maybe they'd've missed it. Maybe I . . ."

"You stay smart, too," I said. The trio were intent on their lunch. Through the side door to the garage I saw my car up on the hoist. "Where's the switch to drop the hoist?"

"Mister, you got no tires on . . ." My glare cut him short. "The operating switch is by the bay door. There's a master hydraulic switch right around the corner there. You could flip it standing in here and it'd drop like a giant snowflake, but . . ."

"I know where it is," said Anna.

"It won't make any sound coming down," I said. "If either of you can, when they aren't watching, drop my car."

"Who are you, mister?" said Billy.

"Come on, Jesse!" Scooter, whining again. "Let's grab one of their cars and go!"

The radio played "Seventy-Six Trombones."

"Scooter," said Jesse, leaning back in his chair, "you gotta think more. That's why you always end up in trouble."

I stood, and Scooter's shotgun swung my way.

"Mind if we walk around a little back here?" I nodded to the trucker stretched out on the tables. "Check him out?"

"Move slow," said Jesse, "or you'll end up beside him."

"Let me help," said Nora. She brought her purse and met me beside the trucker. Her green eyes walked up and down my frame.

The trucker was cool and dry. His ribs were still and I felt no heartbeat. Nora watched me.

"He's okay," I told Jesse. "Out, but he'll make it."

And Nora knew I'd lied.

"You're real smart," she whispered to me. "I need a real smart man to get me out of this."

"You got Jesse," I told her.

"It isn't like it looks," she said. Bit her lip.

Sal the cook and the grizzled sheepherder were sitting at a table apart from the others. I sat down between them.

"Ain't never seen nothin' like this," said Louis the sheepherder. His hands shook as he tried to roll a cigarette. Tobacco rained on the floor. Nora stared at me, then sat in a chair between her friends and the rest of us. "Ain't never."

"You sure?" I asked.

"So how we going to get out of here?" whined Scooter.

"Saw a boy cut up in a bar in 'Bama," Louis told me. He succeeded in filling the papers with tobacco. Used both hands to hold the papers to his lips, licked them shut. "Saw a bear rip up a herder on the mesa in forty-two, but I ain't never seen no one shot."

I settled in my chair.

"Scooter," said Jesse, "you're right. There'll be cops, sooner or later. Probably roadblocks." Jesse's eyes roamed over us, over the cafe walls. He saw the Greyhound sign. Smiled.

"They'll be stoppin' every car," Jesse nodded to the trucker, "every truck. We take one of their heaps, we're no better off'n now. This piss ant place is a bus stop, ain't it?"

Hank nodded.

"When's the next bus?" said Jesse.

"The four-oh-two," answered Hank. "Goes to Los Angeles."

"Hey, baby!" Jesse called to Nora. She looked at him impassively. "Hollywood! You always wanted to be a star!"

Sal, the cook, sat to my left. His white shirt-sleeves were buttoned on his wrists, and his hands were crossed in his lap. I've smelled a lot of fear on a lot of men, in my own sweat, but nothing like that came off of Sal. He sat there like a curly-haired doll. Waiting without much wonder for whatever would happen.

"Sal's a funny name for a Mexican," I whispered.

"It's good enough for Hank." His accent was soft, and like no Mexican I ever heard. "Somebody must stop them."

"Somebody will," I told him. "It's not always easy to know what to do."

"That's a lie," he said. "A lie we tell ourselves so we don't have to face the truth. We know what to do, but we pretend we don't so we don't have to do anything."

"We'll just get on that bus," Jesse told his companions, "and ride it through the roadblocks and into the bigtime."

"We ain't got no tickets," said Scooter seriously.

Jesse laughed. He lifted Scooter's shotgun barrel.

"Sure we do," he said.

"It's only one-thirty," said Scooter. "What are we going to do till then?"

"Till then?" Jesse smiled at us, like a cobra at a rabbit. "Till then, we'll just have to keep ourselves amused."

"What if you do the wrong thing?" I whispered to Sal.

"Then you carry it through life," he said. "If you're lucky, you die so people can forget you, get on with their lives."

"What's going to happen to us?" the beatnik man asked Jesse.

"Nothing," I quickly and loudly said. Jesse's eyes locked on me. "Nothing at all. Because they're smart. Whatever's behind them is behind them. They're running, and they don't want to make the law dogs any madder, any hungrier for 'em than they already are. Hell, here they just shot up a guy a little. No big deal. Nothing to change their hand."

Beside me, I heard Sal sigh in disgust.

"You're pretty smart," said Jesse. "You don't look like no salesman or tourist. What's your name?"

"Marlowe. Philip Marlowe."

"Honey," he told Nora, "dig through those wallets and find me Mr. Philip Marlowe."

She did. He flipped it open. Found the badge. When he held it out for all to see, Scooter swung his shotgun at me.

"Keep looking," I said. "That tin is only for suckers."

"Well, well, well," said Jesse, pulling my photostat from the wallet. "You're a private detective.

"Hey, honey!" he yelled to Nora, who'd moved back between us, her green eyes staring at me. Her red lips were open. "He's a private eye! Like, we're in the movies!

"And he might be packing a gun. Check him out, sugar."

Nora walked over to me as I stood, pulled my jacket wide. She came close. Her hands slid over my chest, down along my sides. When they reached my belt, she slid them around to my back. Her breasts brushed my shirt. Her hair was thick and musty below my chin. She wore dime-store lilac perfume and nothing before or since has ever smelled so sweet. Jesse's eyes burned.

She stepped back, whispered, "Help me."

To Jesse, she said, "He doesn't have a gun."

She walked away from me slow and easy, her pants tight across her round hips. She looked back over her shoulder. The red lips smiled.

"So, Marlowe," said Jesse, "what's a big-time L.A. dick like you doing in a nowhere town like this?"

"I'm looking for a man," I said.

"You lookin' for *me*?" Jesse tapped his chest.

"You're not my business," I told him.

"So you're lucky. Who you looking for?"

"I don't know," I answered.

Jesse flipped open the cylinder on his .22 revolver. He flicked out the three spent shells from the trucker, fished three fresh bullets from his jacket pocket, reloaded the cylinder, snapped it shut. The gun stared at me.

"You better know," he told me. "And you better come across with it. I don't like dicks doing what I don't know."

"My client is the wife of a movie producer—"

"See, babe?" said Jesse. "I told you you'd be a star."

"She's from Germany," I said. "Jewish. When she was a girl, her father sent her, her mother, brothers and sisters, and cousins to America. Get away from the Nazis. Her father stayed behind. Her uncle, his older brother, ran the family business. The uncle figured it would be just another pogrom, rough but survivable. He convinced the father to stay behind, too, and help mind the family store."

"That wasn't so smart," said Jesse.

"No," I agreed. "They rode the train to Auschwitz."

"Your client hire you to kill Nazis? Here?"

"Two weeks ago, a man came into the big synagogue in L.A. He bought two Yahrzeit candles. One for her father, Abraham Muller. One for her uncle, Saul Muller. My client hired me to find out who's lighting candles for her dead kin."

"Why light candles for the dead?" said Nora softly. "It's the living who need them."

"Why look for that guy here?" asked Jesse.

"All the rabbi got out of him was that he had a four hour and twenty minute bus ride from L.A. to where he was going. This is the third bus stop about four hours and twenty minutes from L.A."

Jesse shook his head. He stood.

"Marlowe, you ain't so big-time after all. Come on," he waved his pistol. "Let's you and me look outside. Maybe we'll find your candle lighter."

He made me lead the way. Outside, by the gas pumps, he told me to turn around. He kept three long steps away.

"Kind of dumb thing to do," he said.

The wind blew bullets of sand in our faces, but none closed his eyes. We squinted at each other.

"What?" I asked him.

"Take your pick," he said. "Playin' with the Nazis. Hunting somebody who lights candles for ghosts."

"Killing a trooper," I said.

Jesse shrugged. "He shouldn't have caught us."

"What about the others?"

"The paper didn't mention I stole a car from some folks who were nice to us. They walked."

"I get the idea."

"Yeah, well, maybe you do and maybe you don't. I seen you looking at Nora."

"I couldn't help it. You sent her to me."

"Man, nobody sends her nowhere. She goes where she wants. You best remember that. You also better remember what all I done for her. Her old man, always hasselin' me. Stepfather, and he didn't want no man around her. Specially me. 'Tween you and me . . . I think he had the taste for her himself."

"She could give it to anybody."

"Yeah," he shook his head. "He come down to my shack. Shouldn't ever bother a man at his place."

"No," I agreed, "you shouldn't."

"What you said back there. About the law dogs. They catch us, you think maybe we can walk? Couple years, sure, but . . ."

"You killed some badges, a salesman, her old man." I shrugged while I racked my mind for an answer he'd believe. "If that stops now, if they catch you alive or you surrender . . . you got a chance to cop a crazy plea."

He laughed into the wind.

"Crazy? Man, all I been is *sane*. The world's crazy! People always messing with me, never letting me have what I want, thinking they's *better*. Nora, she knew me, knew I'd get her old man off her back and her out of that two-bit town, but no, they had to go messin' with me. And Scooter, lockin' him up. Jesse don't forget his friends. Or his enemies. Crazy? Hell, no, I ain't crazy!"

"When they catch you," I said, "it's worth a shot."

"*If* they catch me, Marlowe. And there's only one kind of shot makes any sense."

"Can we go back inside?"

"Sure," he said. "I figured you for a wiseguy, but you don't know nothing I don't know."

As we walked toward the cafe, I said, "Does Nora know how deep in trouble you got her?"

"I warned you about her." Jesse laughed. "Does Nora know? Just 'cause she looks that good don't mean she's stupid. An' she knows she travels with me till I say no."

As my hand touched the cafe screen door, Jesse said: "Hey, Marlowe. You go getting sweet on her, remember: she called her old man and told him where we were."

"Jesse," said Scooter when we walked through the door, "what are we going to do? It's two hours till the bus comes!"

"You got T.V. here?" asked Jesse.

"Not yet," said Hank, shaking his head. I sat next to Sal, the cook.

"Hell, Scooter! We got beer, we got a radio." He grinned at Nora. Her stare back was cold and hard. "We'll have us a party."

The radio played "Young Love."

"Hey, babe!" Jesse shuffled across the cafe floor to where Nora sat. "They're playing our song!"

He tucked his pistol in his belt and pulled Nora to her feet. Whirled her into his arms. The song had a tangled rhythm for dancing, but they didn't seem to mind. He was wild smiles and flashing eyes. She leaned back into his arms, swung her hair.

"What will they do to us?" the beatnik woman whispered to her man.

"They'll let us go. We'll be okay," he replied. "We just have to do what they say."

"Follow orders?" It was Sal, the cook. Whispering to no one in particular as we watched the mad dance. "*Trust* them?"

"We don't have much choice," I said. "Not yet. If we can make a better chance . . ."

"What chance? You wait like sheep and you die or go on living and be better off dead, better dead to the world."

"Bide your time," I hissed to him. "We'll make it."

The song ended. Nora left Jesse in the middle of the dance floor. She shot me a glance all we prisoners saw, a plea.

"What about me?" whined Scooter.

I glanced to my right. Billy and Anna the waitress sat closest to the door to the garage. They saw my look.

"You? Hell, Scooter! Grab yourself a girl!" Jesse looked us over, said, "Ain't nobody here gonna complain."

And I went cold. Knew.

Scooter put his shotgun on the table by Jesse. Licked his lips, ran his hand through his greasy black hair. The radio played a commercial for laundry soap. Scooter walked over to Anna.

"You'll have to shoot me first." She stood up, put her back against the wall. Ten feet from the side door.

"You're too old and skinny anyway," he said.

Scooter swung his beady eyes to the beatnik woman. She had heavy breasts beneath her black sweater. Scooter held out his hand. She started to cry.

"No," she moaned softly. "Please. No."

"Just a dance," yelled Jesse. He lifted Scooter's shotgun off the table. "Hey, Scooter—you need this big long thing?"

The beatnik woman looked at her man. He stared at the floor.

Scooter jerked her out of her chair. The radio played "Love Letters in the Sand."

She was taller than Scooter. He ground his hips into her, dug his chin into her shoulder, her right hand twisted down and trapped in his. Over the music, we could hear her sobbing.

In the reflection of the windows, I saw Anna reach through the side door. Jesse was laughing, watching his buddy paw the beatnik woman. My car slowly, silently slid down the hoist.

The song ended. The woman tried to break away, but Scooter pulled her with him. Headed outside, toward the houses across the highway. She cried, dragged her feet. Pleaded, *"No!"*

"All this stops!" yelled Sal. He stood. "Let her go! Get out of here!"

"Sit down!" yelled Jesse. His hand rested on his pistol. "Mind your own business or—"

Anna moved from the door. I stood, turned my back to Jesse, and tried to push Sal down in his chair. He shrugged me off, moved me aside— moved me closer to the door. I kept my feet, backed toward the wall as if I was distancing myself from the cook.

"Or what?" shouted Sal. "Your bullets can't kill me. Now let her go and get out!"

Sal walked toward Jesse, toward the beatnik woman and Scooter. Nora moved out of the way.

"You ain't very smart for a Mexican," snapped Jesse.

Sal lunged toward Jesse.

The beatnik woman broke free from Scooter.

Jesse was on his feet, backpedaling. He shot at Sal's chest. Fired again. By the time he fired the third round I was at the door. Jesse yelled: "Get Marlowe!" and fired again. Sal draped his body on the gun that Jesse emptied into him. I ran into the garage. The beatnik woman screamed as I jerked open my car door, dove across the seat, opened the glove compartment, found the Luger I hadn't needed to carry on a simple ghost hunt. Behind me in the cafe I heard a crash: Billy jumped Scooter, got knocked down by the shotgun butt. Billy bought the seconds I needed. I'd rolled to my back, was sitting up when Scooter and his shotgun filled the doorway. I shot him and shot him and shot him, and he fell.

Screams echoed inside the cafe as I squirmed out of my car. I sent a round high through the door to keep them inside and scurried out the garage to the front of the building, ducking low behind the beatniks' car and circling toward the cafe windows.

When I stuck my head up and looked through the window I saw Jesse. He had the Winchester aimed at the side door to the garage. I zeroed him, squeezed the trigger.

The window shattered—but the thick glass deflected my bullet. Jesse whirled. The Winchester roared my way. The slug screeched across the hood of the car and crashed into a gas pump.

A sane man would have stayed inside the cafe and picked me off with the rifle. But Jesse was wrong, he must have been crazy. He kicked open the cafe door and sent another bullet my way. It missed the car, but it, too, hit a fuel pump. Gas fumes filled the air. Jesse swore. Huddled behind the car, I knew he was coming toward me, rifle raised, waiting for his shot. The closer he got the more likely it became that even if I shot him, he'd put one in me. Another rifle bullet slammed into the car metal between us. I tried to remember how many rounds a Winchester held.

When he was maybe ten feet away, he fired again, trying to angle the bullet down over the hood. The slug ricocheted on the concrete apron, sparked off the metal handle of the gas hose.

An explosion of heat knocked me against the car and turned the world orange. Where the gas pump had been was now a roaring flame twenty feet high. Acrid black smoke swirled around me. The heat seared my face and hands, my eyes were tearing, and I had no choice. I stuck the Luger over the hood of the car, squeezed off a blind round and ran toward the highway. My feet hit the pavement. The two houses were ahead. I looked back toward the cafe.

Saw Jesse zeroing me with the rifle. I ducked. He fired. The rifle bullet ripped a line across my shoulders and flipped me off the road. I hit the ditch on my back. My wind blew out, the Luger spun from my hand.

Ten, twenty seconds of agony. The air I sucked into my lungs stank of burning gasoline and sand. I rolled to my stomach. Jesse walked toward me, rifle in hand. Behind him hurried a girl clutching a purse. A pillar of flame rose into the sky.

Jesse stopped in the center of the highway, raised the rifle to his shoulder.

"Later, Marlowe," he said.

Nora was six feet behind him. From her black purse that had gone to the prom she pulled out the revolver they'd taken off the trooper they killed. She shot Jesse in the back. He staggered forward a few steps, sagged to his knees, fell dead on the road.

It took a week for me to get to my feet. Nora held the revolver at her side. Billy ran toward us from the cafe, Scooter's shotgun in his hands.

"I saved your life," she told me as I took the gun from her. "Remember that. Tell them that."

"Sure," I said.

"Marlowe!" She reached for me, but I knocked her hand away. "You owe me! I saved you!"

She got twenty-five years. She should have hung.

A line of fire burned across my back. My shirt was sticky. I was wobbly, nauseous. I left her standing there for Billy to guard, shuffled past the giant flame to the cafe. The living had fled into the desert. The dead trucker waited inside. Scooter. And a man called Sal. He lay on his back, his white shirt soaked red. I rolled up his left sleeve, found the tattooed numbers. My client believed me when I told her I found nobody and that she should forget and leave the dead to their own heaven or hell.

Raymond Chandler made journeys to the dark alleys of America legitimate for American literature in general and for me in particular.

Chandler's keen eye, cool prose, and timeless popularity beat the critics into accepting him as a "legitimate" author in the 1950's, when I was a boy in Montana dreaming of being a writer. For me, being a writer meant—and means—telling stories that say something about good and evil, stories that show some small truths of how we live and that take a stand in a world of violent moral and physical chaos. When I was growing up, the stories of Chandler—and of Dashiell Hammett and others—did that for me. They did it without sacrificing entertainment, without preaching. When I set forth to write my first novel, I chose to travel those dark and fruitful alleys they'd shown me, and wrote Six Days of the Condor.

But I worried, felt embarrassed that I had not penned an East of Eden. *My book was good, the best I could then do, but was it enough?*

In the months before Condor *came out, I worked as an aide for U.S. Senator Lee Metcalf. One cold and dreary February afternoon in 1974, I muttered about the lack of "weight" of my first novel to the senator's legislative assistant. She was tough, smart, and broked no nonsense. With a cigarette dangling from her lips, she said: "Kid, if you can ever write something half as good and important as 'Killer in the Rain,' you're all right."*

And I still believe her.

James Grady

ASIA

ERIC VAN LUSTBADER

1958

ANGELA CARTER WAS the most beautiful girl in the world. She had creamy skin the color of peaches, her long hair was the color of cornsilk, and her huge eyes had that warmth that reminded you of summer days when you had nothing better to do than lie beneath an apple tree and stare at an endless sky.

Angela Carter was something, all right. She was also dead.

The mournful wail of a siren along Hollywood Boulevard reminded me of the cruelty of wasted youth. Angela Carter's youth.

I had just wrapped up the case. Angela Carter had come into my office six months ago, her face pale with fear. Someone, she had said, was terrorizing her over the phone.

It had turned out that Angela Carter's half-brother, the professional baseball player she had idolized, had been making the obscene calls. I had found out too late. He had strangled her in a fit of rage, when, half drunk, he had seen a man coming out of her apartment at three a.m. But not before he had raped her, as he had confessed he had dreamt of doing all along.

It was that kind of world, I told myself, as I stood with my head against the glass of the office window. Three in the morning, an empty bottle of Scotch in my fist, and I was so tired I wanted to sleep for a month solid.

Then what was I doing here in the office with no one to talk to but the roaches and the mice? I watched the cop car, red lights revolving, careening around a corner. The siren was no more than a sigh. The smoke from my cigarette clung to the glass, smearing the neon into artist's colors. Maybe, I told myself sourly, it was because I could no longer bear to be in the company of human beings. Maybe it was because after all these years of being knee-deep in murder, blackmail, and drug running I had finally begun to figure it was time to get out of this crummy business.

I could still feel my hands on Angela Carter's half-brother as I reluctantly pulled myself back from the brink of the red abyss that had almost caused me to empty my gun into his belly. Instead, I had obligingly handed him over to gimlet-eyed Lieutenant Oliver, and the case was over. Ashes in my mouth.

All of L.A. was glittering outside my window, and on this clear, star-spangled night it had never been more beautiful. Then why was it that all I could see was the image of her once-perfect body lying on the coroner's slab?

Somewhere swells in tuxes were escorting tall blondes into neon-lit nightclubs, somewhere couples swayed to bossa nova beats, somewhere frails laughed at the jokes their men made. But not Angela Carter, and not me.

I threw the bottle in the garbage and grabbed my coat and hat. Like it or not, it was time to get out of there—if only because I was out of Scotch.

But I didn't go home. I think I'd intended to, but I must have gone left on Cahuenga instead of right, because before I knew it, I'd taken the boulevard all the way to Bay City.

I ended up on the Pacific Coast Highway, five hundred feet above the ocean, at a joint I'd been to once or twice on this case or that. It was the kind of place that didn't open until midnight, and who knew when it closed. It was called The Glass Slipper, which was apt in this city of disconnected souls, products of aborted ambitions and burnt-out dreams.

It smelled. It was as if the club was steeped in orchids and lavender. Maybe they wanted it to smell like a boudoir. Outside, stucco walls faced off what was left of the ocean view, and often, the calling of the seagulls still drowned out the sounds of traffic. Some things never changed.

Which was more than you could say for The Glass Slipper. The rose-colored banquettes were the same, as were the black formica tables, the translucent glass bar at which dusty figures sucked at their drinks as if they were memories. They'd had a wheezy, crepe-paper-faced bartender who knew all there was to know about baseball. But now a tall, slim Japanese woman with pouty, half-parted lips was dispensing drinks with appalling adroitness.

The place was half empty, but you would have zeroed in on her if the joint had been as crowded as Grauman's Chinese. She was a spotlight in a roomful of candles. She had huge, glittery eyes and luxuriant blue-black hair held back from her oval face by a pair of decorative pins.

"What'll it be?" she asked, as I slid onto a black vinyl-covered barstool. She was wearing a tight-busted number in snakeskin Lurex. Too much for most places, but not here.

"What's your name?"

"What would you like it to be?" She gave me the smallest smile I'd ever seen. She was a little bit more than beautiful. She had that kilowatt look Lana Turner and Susan Hayward used so well, the kind of magic starlets who came to Hollywood by the truckload would kill for. So what was she doing tending bar in a cheap after-hours joint on the road to nowhere?

"Scotch," I said, pointing to the good stuff. "And leave the bottle up."

Her lips pursed in a moue, and I was dazzled by an image of that face blown up ten times lifesize on the silver screen. She poured me a double. "Bad day at the races?"

"Bad day, period," I said, downing the Scotch.

" 'If it wasn't for bad luck,' " she sang softly, " 'I'd have no luck at all.' " She had a voice, too.

I watched her as she poured me another double, then went off to fill the order of a couple of narrow-eyed men at the other end of the bar. I wondered if she knew anything about baseball—or baseball players. The all-American sport.

The same tired Mexican orchestra that always worked this place started playing "Begin the Beguine" as if in its sleep. She swayed while she worked, giving life to an off-tempo beat that should have been put to sleep years ago.

"You ought to be in pictures," I told her.

She laughed, pouring me another drink. She said: "I'm Japanese. No one wants me, let alone would put my image up on a screen."

"I would."

She put her elbows on the bar and, leaning over, pressed her palms against my eyes. They were as cool and hard as marble. "Go to sleep," she said. "When you wake up, you'll no longer be crazy."

Three hours later, I was still drinking Scotch, staring into the mirror behind the bar. When I looked around, the staff was putting the chairs atop the tables, and the place had cleared out. I put a twenty on the bar, went out into the parking lot.

The sea breeze was stiff and, in the east, you could just see a sliver of shell pink creeping along the horizon like a woman's arm carelessly thrown across the back of a sofa. The night was no longer black.

I started up the car and drove west along the rising, snaking road.

Not more than a mile on, I spotted a car—a white '58 Corvette—in the overlook fronting the sheer cliff down to the Pacific.

I would have passed it by, but inside, I saw the bartender. She was just sitting there in the front passenger's seat, staring straight ahead.

I drew in behind her, wondering if she had a flat or engine trouble. I walked over and rapped my knuckles on the window. Her head jerked around so hard I swear I could hear the crack of vertebrae.

The fright on her face lasted so short a time I wasn't even sure it had ever been there. Then she rolled down the window and said, "So you finally finished drinking."

"I haven't started yet."

"Yeah. I can see that." She put her head back against the seat. "You look like you just danced fifteen rounds with Patterson."

"You're quite a knockout yourself."

She groaned, but she smiled, too. It seemed like the nicest thing that had happened to me in weeks.

"Will you tell me your name now?"

"Asia."

"Mine's Marlowe. Philip Marlowe."

I was about to follow that up, when a black Fleetwood limousine running very fast came around the hairpin turn from up above and swung into the overlook.

Two men were out before the big car, rocking on its shocks, slid to a stop. Both were armed and had that Cro-Magnon look endemic to the underworld. The only difference was these two were Japanese.

One pointed his gun at me, while the other went quickly to Asia's car and dragged her out. She seemed paralyzed, walking on stiffened legs.

"What is this?" I said, and the ape swung the barrel of the gun into my mouth. I spat onto the ground and took a step toward him.

"I would seriously advise against any aggressive action."

A man had emerged from the Fleetwood limousine. He was a middle-aged Japanese dressed in a black sharkskin suit with a white shirt and a silver tie that matched the color of his close-cropped hair. He was a bantam of a man, powerful looking, with a bullet head dominated by coal-black eyes that seemed to see right through you.

He moved away from the door of the Fleetwood as the second ape shoved Asia inside and disappeared after her. "It would be discouraging for me if I was obliged to kill you now. My loss of face would be great."

"Do I know you?"

"It doesn't matter, Mr. Marlowe." He beckoned me into the Fleetwood. "I know you."

I started to walk away. "I don't think I want to play this game."

The bullet-headed man said something I couldn't quite catch, and the ape who had hit me moved. I had been watching his gun hand, so when his other hand brushed against the side of my neck I didn't think much of it.

A moment later, I didn't think much of anything. I had fallen down a hole so deep I knew I was never going to climb out.

I awoke to the sound of waves lapping against a hull. A soft rocking cradled me. I was on a boat. I opened my eyes and groaned. I wondered whether I'd been K.O.'d in the fifth or the sixth and then remembered that it had been Asia who had said I looked like I'd gone fifteen with Patterson.

She was sitting across the stateroom, her legs crossed, smoking a cigarette.

"I could use a little of that," I croaked.

She came across and, kneeling by the side of the bunk, put the cigarette between my lips. I blew out a cloud of smoke.

"Don't try to get up," she said. "They've handcuffed you to the metal stanchion."

" 'They' also know who I am."

"It doesn't surprise me." She took out another cigarette, lit up. "You're a detective. You're dangerous to them."

I closed my eyes and wondered whether this was the way Alice had felt when she dropped down the rabbit hole. What did everyone else know that I didn't? "Start at the beginning," I said, "and don't stop until you've come to the end."

Asia went back and sat on the cane chair. She was showing a lot of leg, but I was in no position to take advantage of it. My head felt as if Santa and all his reindeer had landed on it. On the other hand, it was the first time in a long while I hadn't been thinking of Angela Carter.

"The man who spoke to you is Tono Kuruma. He owns a conglomerate in Tokyo that makes steel, chemicals, and plastics. He's enormously wealthy." Smoke curled up around her like an adder, obscuring one side of her face. "He's followed me here all the way from Japan."

I asked the obvious question. "Why?"

"I made the fatal mistake of falling in love with his son."

"Is that bad?"

She got up, walked back and forth in the small room, as if she was abruptly nervous. "It is worse than bad. It is forbidden."

I looked at her. "I don't understand."

"Of course you don't." She turned to me, and I got another high-voltage dose of her. "It is a matter of face. As we Japanese know it, a point of honor. Honor is the most important element in our lives, Philip. Without it, we are nothing.

"Yoshi—he is Tono Kuruma's only son—and I planned to marry secretly. Tono Kuruma caught us. Now he wants to kill me."

"For wanting to marry his son?" I said skeptically. "I'd think he'd be delighted. What man wouldn't give his left arm to have you?"

Now Asia seemed to collapse onto the cane chair. She was hunched over, and the smoke, the cascade of her hair, hid her face completely. "The Kurumas are of samurai blood. They are aristocrats. I, however, am something else. My mother is a geisha. I never knew who my father was, but it is clear I am not of noble parentage. Tono Kuruma feels only shame that Yoshi and I are in love. If we married it would be a great loss of face for him and his entire family."

"But is this a reason to want to kill you?"

Her head came up, and I could see she had been crying. "It is, if you are carrying Yoshi's child, the heir to the Kuruma fortune."

For a while, I listened to the lapping of the waves against the side of the boat. I wondered how far we were from land. I tried to judge the depth of the swells by the movement of the boat. All I knew was that we weren't moored at a dock.

"I need two things," I told her. "A key and a gun."

I could see the hope blossoming in her eyes. "Tono Kuruma thinks I have hired you to get me away from him."

"I'm surprised either of you know me from Adam."

"Tono Kuruma has many interests in Los Angeles, Philip. He has been here many times. As for me, I read the papers. You found Angela Carter's murderer."

"I must be the world's most famous private eye." I recognized the irony in my voice, and didn't much care for it. It reeked of self-pity.

Asia crouched close to me. "I have very little money, but you are welcome to whatever I have."

"Keep it," I said. "When the kid is old enough, buy it a car, something in red and chromium."

She smiled, and the room lit up like it was New Year's Eve. "You're very kind, Philip." There it was again, the way she said my name. It would be easy to fall in love with how she spoke.

I watched her as she took one of the long pins from her hair. She inserted the tip of it in the handcuff lock, and did a bit of fiddling. The concentration turned her face into a little girl's, the way kids are, totally unselfconscious, when they are sure no one's looking. In a moment, I heard a tiny click, and the manacles fell away.

I sat up, rubbing the red skin of my wrists. I wondered how come she didn't know how to get out of here. She knew everything else.

I went over to the stateroom door. It was locked. "Give me that pin," I said. Then, as I heard the sound of approaching feet outside, "Wait." The scrape of a key in the lock. "I've got a better idea."

I took off one shoe, moved to a spot just behind the door. When it opened and one of Tono Kuruma's apes walked through, I cold-cocked him behind the right ear with the steel-edged heel of my shoe.

As I took his .38 I saw he was the one who had put me out. It gave me a good feeling to see him lying there. I put on my shoe, dragged him over to the berth. I handcuffed him to the stanchion. Then we got out of there.

"What are you going to do?" Asia whispered as we took the companionway up.

I didn't know. If I had known, I'd be smart, and at that moment I wasn't feeling in the least bit smart. I'd had a few teeth shaken loose, been knocked unconscious, and been chained to a bed, and I wasn't even getting paid for it. This wasn't a case, it was a mission of mercy. Now I was sure it was past time for me to get out.

And yet, for the first time since I had seen Angela Carter on the slab, I knew that I didn't want out. Not now, not ever. Maybe I was already half in love with Asia. I knew I was in love with the danger.

On deck, the moon was up. A whole day had passed. The smell of the ocean was everywhere. To the west, I could see the lights of Catalina Island. The City of Angels was far away, across the Pacific where the cormorants were dipping and wheeling. They were clowns, anyway. They didn't know how serious life could get.

We were on a luxury yacht. Brass fittings gleamed in the moonlight and, ahead, I could see shadows moving past the lights inside the forward cabin. I heard a bumping, and leaning over the side, I saw a small motorboat tied up alongside.

I motioned Asia to stay in the shadows where she was, then moved forward. I didn't speak until I had Tono Kuruma in my sights. "Come on out, Asia."

He turned unhurriedly as she appeared from out of the darkness, and he said in a cool voice, "I see you have found your samurai." If he was concerned by the .38 he didn't show it.

"What has she told you?"

"Enough."

His eyebrows shot up. "Indeed."

I waved the gun as one of his goons came up from belowdecks. "I'm putting her on the launch. Don't do anything stupid."

A frown creased his face. "Mr. Marlowe—"

"Shut up," I said. "Tell the animal to keep his hands out of his pockets." Tono Kuruma said something in Japanese.

"All right, Asia." I felt her close behind me. "Do you know how to start an outboard?"

"Yes."

"Steer for the marina lights. It shouldn't take you more than twenty minutes."

"Thank you, Philip." I could feel her arms around me and, for a moment, I was waist deep in orchids. "I'll never forget you." She kissed me, and I didn't want to let go. So I watched Tono Kuruma and the ape as I heard the sounds of her heels diminish along the deck.

After a moment, an engine coughed to life. I could smell the rich diesel fumes, and then the pitch of the motor changed and I knew she was away.

Tono Kuruma's face fell. He rubbed his forehead as if it had begun to hurt. "I forgive you, Mr. Marlowe," he said, "because you have no idea what you have done. But now I must take this boat after her."

"Make a move and you're dead."

Tono Kuruma sighed. "What did she tell you?"

"All of it." I repeated what Asia had told me about her background and his, about her love for Yoshi, Tono Kuruma's son, and about the baby she was carrying.

Tono Kuruma smiled ruefully. "She knows well how to weave fact with fiction. It is true that my son loved her. It is true they planned to marry. But it was with my blessing." His face had gotten as craggy as Mount Rushmore. "Asia comes from as noble a samurai family as exists in Japan. Her father and I were business rivals waging a war that nearly destroyed both of us. Until my son, Yoshio, came to me with this solution: that he and my rival's daughter should marry, thus uniting our companies in an alliance that could never be broken.

"Asia had a duty to comply. It is a matter of honor—of face."

"She ran away?"

"In a manner of speaking." I could see he was holding himself together by a great force of will. "She killed my son. She put one of her abominable pins through his eye."

I remembered how adroit she was at using the pin to open the hand-cuffs. I was starting to feel sick to my stomach, but I didn't think it was seasickness. "Then it's true," I said softly. "You want to kill her."

"I cannot." I thought I had seen pain in a human being, but what was etched on Tono Kuruma's face went beyond that. "She is carrying my son's child. My heir. I am by honor enjoined from harming her."

I needed to test him. I had to see who was telling the truth, the lady or the tiger. I put down the .38, looked east toward the pink glow of L.A. I thought I saw the pale phosphorescence of the launch's wake.

No one drew a gun. No one moved against me. With a sigh, I holstered the gun in my shoulder harness. "She suckered me."

"You aren't the first," Tono Kuruma said. "I daresay you won't be the last." He swung out of the cabin. "I'll never find her now. It was only by the sheerest good fortune that I discovered her whereabouts this time."

I walked over to the railing, gripped it so hard my knuckles turned white. "What were you going to do with her?"

Tono Kuruma joined me at the rail. "You know, Mr. Marlowe, in the old days samurai, forbidden to act in certain ways by bushido, their code of honor, hired others to carry out those acts. These people were sometimes called 'ninja.' Private eyes, of a sort."

"Forget it," I said, disgusted. "I know what you're thinking."

He shook his head. "No, Mr. Marlowe, I don't believe you do. I wish to hire you to find Asia. I see now that she is like certain animals: incapable of surviving in captivity.

"It is my grandchild who matters to me." Tono's eyes had that moist, incomprehensible look you see in new parents when they trot out the billfold full of baby photos. "I want you to make sure that she does not abort its life. You see, Mr. Marlowe, I believe that is why she came to Los Angeles. To screw up her courage, as you would say, to find a doctor who would—"

I looked at him, and he dug in his jacket pocket. He handed me a card. "I found this in Asia's pocketbook."

I knew the name all too well. One of those sleazy lizards who call themselves doctors, who take money to perform their butchery.

"Of course, she's too smart to go to him now. But she'll find another."

I let it go, and the card disappeared into the night.

"What about justice? She murdered your son."

"You and I, Mr. Marlowe, have differing ideas of justice. But consider this: is there not justice in seeing Yoshi's child grow into adulthood? Penance may be paid in a variety of forms."

He had a point. Or maybe I was just losing my mind.

"I want my grandchild," Tono Kuruma said.

I knew what he was asking of me, and I wasn't at all sure I liked it. "I think you've got the wrong man," I said.

He smiled. "On the contrary, Mr. Marlowe. Though you are *gaijin*, a foreigner, you possess honor, the most important quality a man can have. Such a man finds a way to honor his commitments."

"I wasn't aware that I had any commitment to you or to Yoshio."

Tono Kuruma said: "You're quite right. If you don't feel it, then you haven't any."

I watched him, the moonlight shattered against his sharkskin suit. I wondered what it was like to lose a son, and hoped that I would never find out.

"Do you know what Asia will do when she sees the baby? She may not want to give it up."

Tono Kuruma's face was utterly expressionless. "Mr. Marlowe, neither of us knows what she will do. We can only be aware of what she is capable of."

I thought about that for a moment. I couldn't get Lieutenant Oliver to put Asia in jail; she hadn't broken any laws while she was here. But she had committed murder in Japan, and I wondered how I'd feel for the rest of my life if I told Tono Kuruma, No, and just walked away when we docked. I knew I couldn't do that either. So what was left?

"I'll see that she has the baby," I said, knowing that I had just answered my own question.

"And after that?"

"When the time comes, I'll have to see," I said. "What I have to do now will be tough enough."

Tono Kuruma nodded. "You have made the honorable choice, Mr. Marlowe. I have full confidence in you. L.A. is, I think you say, your turf. Besides, it has not escaped my notice that over a short period of time you and she have developed—what shall we say?—a rapport. In Asia's case, that is highly unusual—and for you useful, *neh*?"

Well, he was right about one thing: L.A. was my turf. I knew every square inch of it. I knew I'd find Asia, all right, but what then? Was the rapport Tono Kuruma spoke of real or another of her illusions? She had already killed once. Talk about the beauty and the beast.

One thing at a time, Marlowe, I told myself. You've just come back from the dead, and you've got the case of a lifetime.

What more could you want?

When I came upon Raymond Chandler's work for the first time, I was electrified. Here was a master stylist who brought to life with astonishing clarity the fevered, almost surreal atmosphere of Los Angeles. The rather sad, rather tawdry underpinnings revealed by Chandler's neon-glow prose painted a realistic portrait of a city traditionally regarded as having no soul. He breathed character and life into an American icon, making of it a legend.

Chandler's work showed me the ultimate importance of atmosphere. His novels and short stories compelled me to realize the power such beauty can have to enlighten and enthrall a reader.

Eric Van Lustbader

MICE

ROBERT CAMPBELL

1959

T HEY MADE ME feel a little funny. I don't mean ha-ha. I mean the feeling you get when someone doesn't seem quite right but you can't put your finger on what it is at first. It's like a kind of lurch in the stomach, a bad oyster going down before you can cough it back up, a slice of guilt when you start figuring out what's not right and then a slab of pity which isn't even as honest as the first two.

I stood there watching them and finally felt a good feeling like the one you get watching children with their innocent eyes always ready to laugh or cry.

They were what some people still call Mongoloid idiots, though they never were idiots, just slow and capable of only so much. And they never were exclusively Asiatics, in spite of their flat faces and narrowed eyes, but simply people suffering from Down's syndrome.

I reckoned them to be somewhere in their late twenties, pretty old for what ailed them, since they don't usually live much beyond their teens. The man seemed older than the woman, but it might just as easily have been the other way around.

They looked like brother and sister. That's another thing about Down's syndrome, it makes everybody look related. Maybe if we all looked like members of the same family we wouldn't be so quick about killing each other off. On the other hand, there's more violence among family members than among unrelated people. Ask any cop.

I noticed them right after I left Poodle Springs and went back to Los Angeles, walking up and down Franklin Avenue looking for a place to set up housekeeping by myself again.

I'd tried marriage. It went sour in six months. Maybe it was because my wife was rich and I was poor. Maybe it was because Linda wasn't happy without a couple of dozen people kissing her hand, even if she knew they were trying to steal her rings, and I wasn't happy unless there were just the two of us. Even then I wasn't really happy unless there was just the one of me. At least that's what Linda accused me of.

So she was there in the sun and I was here in the drizzle. It was a toss-up if I'd get to wanting her so badly that I'd give up holy poverty and go back to the Springs, ready to be the pampered husband of a woman with several million bucks, floating in the swimming pool, highball in hand, watching my toes turn brown, or if she'd get to wanting me so badly that she'd join me in the only town I ever called home and wait for me while I went out and sorted through the wreckage of a society that made garbage better than it made anything else.

I'd homed back to Franklin Avenue like a pigeon to the loft. I'd lived there just before my one great leap of faith into that mystery called marriage, maybe hoping that it would work some magic and put things back into perspective. I didn't really want to give Linda up and I'd left a lifeline trailing in the water in case I wanted to climb back into the boat.

There was nothing available at the Hobart Arms, where I used to live, so I went up one side of the street and down the other, a block at a time.

It's a nice street of shade trees, the occasional palm, and fairly new garbage cans lined up at the curb on pickup day, which looked like it was going to be tomorrow.

I say that because these two I'm talking about were struggling up the three steps from the basement of an apartment house with a garbage can between them, laughing when they tripped and bumped the railings as though hard work was nothing but pure pleasure.

It all made a hell of a racket and I stood there for a minute, well back from the basement well, letting those feelings I just described go flashing through me.

When they spotted me they laughed harder, exaggerating their pleasure, inviting me with their grinning mouths and crinkled eyes to get in on the fun. I couldn't help but laugh myself, now that I knew I hadn't fallen into a trance and found myself among trolls or dwarfs in some enchanted land.

Then, just as in any decent fairy tale, the ogre stepped into the frame. A man with a head like a dum-dum bullet, flat and scarred, a fringe of aging black hair hanging over his ears and down his neck like moss, bull's neck and bull's nose, came into sight like a disembodied horror. He was standing below the level of the steps, but even so, I could tell he wasn't much taller than the man lugging one half of the garbage can by the handle.

He yelled at them with curses half English, half Spanish. The word he beat them with the most was "feebs."

They cringed like a couple of abused dogs. His fury cut off their laughter like he'd ripped out their tongues and wiped the smiles off their gentle kissers like you'd wipe a message of joy off a blackboard with a felt eraser. They looked at me as though they felt even worse because their master was scolding them in front of a stranger.

I was ready to walk on so my presence wouldn't add to their humiliation when the bullet-headed sucker lifted his hand as though meaning to strike the woman. He was holding a sawed-off piece of broomstick. She startled and threw her head aside, dropping the handle of the garbage can and crying out.

The can dropped on the step and tipped over before her companion could wrestle it straight, and several pounds of wet garbage, fish carcasses, chicken bones, orange rinds, coffee grounds, tin cans, and soggy newspapers went spilling into the areaway.

It made an already angry bull madder than ever.

He started slapping the air near the man's head with the broomstick, missing, but coming closer and closer.

I walked over and said, "Don't do that."

He looked at me as though I'd called his mother a filthy name. "Who you?"

"My name's Marlowe."

"I know you?"

"You don't stop bullying that man, you're going to know me pretty good."

"Go mind your own business."

I raised my hand to him like he'd raised his to them. I swung it one way and the other, slapping air, but coming closer and closer, letting him know what it felt like to be treated with such contempt.

He swung the stick right back and cracked me one on the wrist. When I snatched my hand back, I scraped my knuckles on the railings. I slapped him across the mouth then, and he ran into the basement.

I felt bad a second after. He'd had it coming, but I knew I could have handled it better. Nothing's gained answering a threat with a threat, violence with violence.

"What's his name?" I asked the two people, who were looking at me as though I was something heroic.

The man pointed to himself and said, "Benny. Her name's Minnie."

"No. What's that other guy's name?"

Benny stood there with his tongue poking out of his mouth, working it out. Minnie whispered in his ear.

He grinned and said, "Mr. Januaria."

"He your boss?"

"He takes care of us."

"You mean he's your guardian?"

They looked at one another. The word was too much for them. They shrugged their shoulders, grinned, threw their heads back, and looked at me for a minute. Then they lost interest and started picking up the muck. Making a game of that, too.

"You happen to know of any apartments to rent around here?"

They stopped what they were doing. They couldn't move and think at the same time. They held another whispered conference. This time Minnie pointed across the street.

I turned around and saw the sign in a window on the first floor.

In fifteen minutes I was signing a lease and handing over a check to a Mr. Bochos, a Greek with a happy face.

"Leases is okay," he said, "but in my country we share a glass of wine to seal a bargain."

"I honor the customs of all nations," I replied.

While we were having our wine, Bochos looked at me and said, "I saw what you done. That was very kind."

"Does Januaria do that sort of thing very often?"

"Ah," he said, as though making small of that kind of man. "He don't actually hit the mice. At least not that I know about."

"Mice?"

"That's what I call the dummies. I say to the wife, 'They ain't got the brains of a couple of mice.'"

"If you did actually know that he hit those people, would you do anything about it?"

The look of admiration and appreciation for what I had done left his face. "I don't know. Januaria's a violent man, I think. He might not actually hit the mice, but I don't know about people like me or you."

I could tell that Bochos was afraid of the janitor across the street, but I didn't want to press it any farther. It would have done no good and there was no reason for me not to have friendly relations with the building manager.

"Are Benny and Minnie related to him some way?"

Bochos shrugged. "I don't think so."

"Where'd they come from?"

He shrugged again. "I don't know. I notice them hanging around the block, over by the empty lot on the corner, every once in a while. Sometimes I see them picking through the dumpster behind the supermarket down on Hollywood Boulevard. You know the one I mean?"

"I think so."

"So I started wondering about who they was and where they come from. I was just going to call the police and see what about them when I see them working over there for Januaria. So then I think I'll mind my own business."

"That's not a bad idea," I said, knocking back the wine. "I think I'll do the same."

I went upstairs to my new apartment on the third floor. There was an overhead fixture with one working bulb out of three in the living room and another with a dead bulb in the bedroom. The fixtures on either side of the bathroom mirror worked too.

The water ran rusty into the basin for a minute and then cleared up. I washed my face with my hands and dried them on my handkerchief.

I'd rented the place unfurnished. There wasn't a stick in the place except for two unmatched wooden chairs in the kitchen. I carried them into the living room in front of the gas fire. I took a wooden kitchen match from my pocket and lit it. I sat down in one chair and put my feet up on the other. I sat there as evening settled into night outside the window, thinking what a damn fool a man was who valued his pride and independence and solitude more than a lovely woman with bags of money.

You start feeling that way, sitting in a dark, empty room feeling sorry for yourself, and the next thing you know you're looking for a puddle to stick your nose in and drown. So I stood up and looked down into the street hoping to see some action, a delivery boy dropping off a pizza or a dog lifting his leg against a tree.

In the well of the entryway to the basement across the street I could see a glow. It took me a second to get adjusted to it and then I saw that it was somebody sitting there hunched over his knees and shining a flashlight on a magazine or newspaper. While I watched, the basement door opened up. Somebody was standing in the doorway partially blocking the light. There was a minute and then another dark shape passed by the first one and the rectangle went black again.

I wanted to know who was sitting there reading by the light of a flash. I wanted to know who it was went inside the basement. I didn't want to be alone in an empty room right at that minute.

I went downstairs and strolled across the street, stopping in front of the railing and looking down into the well.

Benny was crouched on an old mattress, his legs covered with a tattered blanket against the chill. He was reading so intently he didn't even know I was there until I cleared my throat. Then he looked up like a startled deer and his hand with the flashlight in it started to shake.

"Hey, excuse me, Benny. I didn't mean to scare you," I said.

"You gave me a start, you did," he said.

"What you reading?"

He hesitated, then handed it up to me. "You need my flashlight?"

"There's enough light from the streetlamp over there for me to see," I said, as I looked the magazine over.

It was a comic book, boldly drawn and brightly colored. The title on the cover was *Survival*. Inside there were stories about trekking through the mountains with nothing but a knife, living in the desert with nothing but a plastic tarp, and defending yourself to the death with nothing but a stick or your bare hands. I'd seen similar magazines before in candy stores and drugstores. The kids bought them by the ton, the new comics for children born under the shadow of the bomb.

"This is pretty exciting stuff, Benny."

"Oh, yes. I read it every night."

"You read pretty good?"

"Well, I don't really read it, but you can tell what's going on from the pictures."

"Where'd you get it?"

"I found it in a dumpster. I didn't steal it," he said defensively.

"I didn't think you did. I was just asking."

"Oh, that's all right, then."

"Where's Minnie?" I asked, handing the magazine back to him.

"I take care of Minnie."

"That's good."

"She takes care of me. We take care of each other."

"That's really good. So where is she?"

A strange expression passed across his face, like the face of a kid who'd just learned what it was to feel shame. "Mr. Januaria come out and asked was she cold. She said she wasn't, but he made her go inside anyway."

"Why'd he do that?"

"He wanted her inside with him. That's part of the deal."

"What deal's that, Benny?" I asked, getting a sick feeling in the pit of my stomach.

"He lets us sleep here at night. Sometimes he gives us coffee and bread or what's left over from his supper. He lets us use the sink and toilet in the basement."

"And what do you have to do for all this generosity?"

"We work around the building. We carry out the garbage cans and sweep the hallways. And sometimes, when Mr. Januaria tells her to, Minnie goes inside his apartment with him."

He was staring at me as though waiting for a reaction, as though seeing disgust on my face would finally make it impossible for him to kid himself that nothing bad was going on inside Mr. Januaria's apartment. I tried not to show anything, but I guess he read the anger rising up in my eyes and that was enough to squeeze his heart.

"She shouldn't have to go into his apartment when he wants her to, should she?" he said in the smallest voice you can imagine.

"I could talk to him, if you wanted me to."

"No, no. Oh, don't do that."

"But if he's abusing her in some way. If he's taking advantage, maybe a word from me would put him wise that he better cut it out."

He was terrified again.

"Oh, no, it'd only make him mad and he could beat us again."

"Benny, at least let me call the cops."

"He was crying now, begging me not to do anything like that. "They'll put us away in different places. I'd never see Minnie again."

I calmed him down and went back to my empty flat and my two straight-backed kitchen chairs. I took off my shoes and went to lie down in the corner. Using them for a pillow and my jacket for a blanket I thought about what some human beings will suffer in the name of love. Somehow I could understand better what Benny was doing, sleeping in the areaway, than what I'd been doing, sleeping on satin in Linda's king-sized bed.

It was just breaking dawn when a hammering on the front door woke me up. I was as stiff as a week-old corpse. I was a bundle of broken bones shuffling across the floor to see who was being so insistent so early in the morning.

Nobody had to tell me the two characters standing there were plain-clothes cops. It was written all over their kissers. One smiled and the other didn't. One was polite and the other wasn't.

The one without the smile walked right past me and looked the place over without asking my permission. The smiling one said, "Mr. Marlowe?"

"Mr. Bochos give you the introduction?" I asked, patting my pockets, looking for a cigarette. All I found were the usual two or three wooden kitchen matches.

He took out a pack of Camels and offered them. "My name's Menafee. That's Schindler over there."

I took a cigarette, noting the unfiltered brand. "I see you're not afraid to die."

He took out a lighter and spun the wheel. "I'm a fatalist, I guess. When you're going to do it, you're going to do it."

I waved the lighter away and snapped a kitchen match alight. "A little taste of sulfur starts the first one of the day off right."

"A little assault and battery start the day off pretty good, too?" Schindler asked, talking from behind me.

I turned around to face him.

"I answer questions better when I can see the person asking them."

He reached out and grabbed my wrist, pulling my hand with the scraped knuckles up closer to his face. I jerked it away, glad that he let go as quick as he did, because big as he was, and worn out as I was, I would have lost a bout of arm wrestling.

"You've just moved into the neighborhood, isn't that right Mr. Marlowe?" Menafee said.

"That's right."

"You got a private ticket, ain't that right, Marlowe?" Schindler said.

"You're pretty quick for so early in the morning."

"The name rang a bell right away, Mr. Marlowe," Menafee said, the smile never leaving his face. "You've got a reputation."

"A reputation for being pretty violent, pretty tough. Are you pretty tough?" Schindler said, moving his lips in what I figured was supposed to be a sneer. "You get tough with a little man across the street?"

A little shock wave went through me.

"Something happen to Benny?"

"I don't know if Benny's Mr. Januaria's first name," Menafee said.

"Benny's the dummy we found hiding in the cellar with his dum-dum girlfriend," Schindler said.

"You're a prince, you are," I said.

Even Menafee didn't seem to like the way his partner had called them dummies. "Ah, for God's sake, Schindler."

"It was the spic janitor got it," Schindler went on, determined to play the bigot right to the wire.

"And you're asking me who did the job?"

"Mr. Bochos tells us you had a little fight with Januaria just last evening," Menafee said, working it smooth and easy again.

"We had a little discussion. He was leaning on Benny and Minnie, so I waved my hand in his face."

Schindler started reaching for my wrist again so I pulled it back. "I missed and scraped my knuckles on the railings."

"Just waved your hand in his face?" Menafee said, pleasantly.

"That's all."

"We hear it that Januaria hit you with a stick and you slapped him in the mouth," Menafee said.

"And that was the end to that."

"Except later on you took a little stroll across the street."

"Bochos?"

"Yes, Mr. Bochos saw you."

"Then he saw me stroll right back again."

"Well, no, his wife called him into the kitchen at the back of the apartment. He didn't see you come back."

"We got no doubts you come back," Schindler said. "I mean you're here, ain't you? But we're wondering did you stay across the street long enough to take that stick he hit you with away from Januaria and poke him in the gut and kidneys with it enough times to kill him."

"That how it happened?"

"The examiner's finishing up his prelim even as we speak, but that's the way it looks," Schindler said.

"Would you like to walk over with us and see if he's found out anything new?" Menafee asked, as polite as a Poodle Springs gentleman asking a lady to a dance.

They waited for me while I put on my shoes, washed my face, and shook out my jacket.

Across the street Januaria's body was sprawled on the concrete steps leading down into the basement well. The medical examiner was squatting awkwardly alongside him, one foot higher than the other. He'd opened up the janitor's shirt. The bruises across his chest and belly were the color of watery schoolhouse ink.

The three of us stepped around and over Januaria and gathered at the bottom in the well.

"Anything extra?" Menafee asked.

The examiner struggled to his feet with some difficulty, looking at me as though knowing that we shared some of the same aches and pains of approaching age.

"One of the blows ruptured his spleen. That would've done the jump in short order. But the immediate cause of death was a broken neck. He fell and landed on the steps like you see. It was enough."

"The blows with the stick had to be delivered by a strong man?" Menafee asked.

The examiner wouldn't be led. He smiled and said, "A woman or a healthy child could kill with a stick used the right way. It's a matter of engineering and physics. Pounds per square inch delivered through the tip of a small, blunt surface. Could kill anybody if they got in the first couple of lucky shots or the victim wasn't defending himself."

I looked over at Benny, who was in the corner, standing with Minnie on their makeshift bed, his arms around her and her arms around him, looking wide-eyed, looking scared. But looking triumphant, too, somehow.

The examiner told the ambulance crew to bag the body and put it in the wagon. When they had Januaria safely stowed away, the examiner said, "One other thing."

We waited like a nightclub audience waiting for the comic to deliver the punch line.

"He was killed during or just after an act of sex."

"If I were you," I said, looking at Menafee and then at Schindler, "I'd start looking around for a violent husband or boyfriend."

"You could be right," Menafee said.

Nobody even glanced at Benny and Minnie standing there, holding on to one another. Not many people think about people like Benny and Minnie even knowing anything about sex.

"I got a bad feeling about this one," Schindler said. "This is going to be one of them unsolved homicides."

"Nobody saw anything? Nobody heard anything?" I asked.

"Nobody who can tell us about it," Schindler said, his eyes flicking toward Benny and Minnie. "This is going to be a bad one."

"You could be right," Menafee said again. "You going to be around in case we want to talk to you again, Mr. Marlowe?"

"I'm going right out this morning to buy a bed and a coffeepot."

"That's okay," he said, as he followed Schindler up the flight of steps.

I started to follow them, but first I reached down and picked up a comic book that had been under Januaria's body. I handed it to Benny.

"Here you go, Benny," I said. "Why don't you toss this in the garbage can?"

I did go out to buy a bed, a coffeepot, a cup, a saucer, and some utensils. I even bought a pretty good used couch, an easy chair, and a floor lamp. Some towels and a washcloth.

That night I made myself some hamburger and beans in my new frying pan. Then I went into the living room and sat in the easy chair, under the floor lamp beside the window, and read the late edition.

Once I glanced down across the street and could see Benny's flashlight shining in the dark.

Benny, Minnie, and me were at home.

———————————————

I never did like the idea that Marlowe settled down to marriage, rich wife or otherwise. It just ain't natural. The classic private eye is essentially a loner. How else would he develop the angst to make him go out trying to clean up the garbage dumps and abattoirs when he knows the job is impossible? How else could he afford to work for spit? How else could he present every woman he meets with a challenge and every villain he meets with the threat that they are fighting a man who has absolutely nothing to lose?

If Chandler instructed mystery writers in anything, it was in that. He was one of those pioneering few who took the lonely cowboy, the archetypical American hero, off his horse and put him behind the wheel of a Ford or more commonly still out walking the mean streets.

Robert Campbell

THE PENCIL

RAYMOND CHANDLER

HE WAS A slightly fat man with a dishonest smile that pulled the corners of his mouth out half an inch leaving the thick lips tight and his eyes bleak. For a fattish man he had a slow walk. Most fat men are brisk and light on their feet. He wore a gray herringbone suit and a handpainted tie with part of a diving girl visible on it. His shirt was clean, which comforted me, and his brown loafers, as wrong as the tie for his suit, shone from a recent polishing.

He sidled past me as I held the door between the waiting room and my thinking parlor. Once inside, he took a quick look around. I'd have placed him as a mobster, second grade, if I had been asked. For once I was right. If he carried a gun, it was inside his pants. His coat was too tight to hide the bulge of an underarm holster.

He sat down carefully and I sat opposite and we looked at each other. His face had a sort of foxy eagerness. He was sweating a little. The expression on my face was meant to be interested but not clubby. I reached for a pipe and the leather humidor in which I kept my Pearce's tobacco. I pushed the cigarettes at him.

"I don't smoke." He had a rusty voice. I didn't like it any more than I liked his clothes, or his face. While I filled the pipe he reached inside his coat, prowled in a pocket, came out with a bill, glanced at it, and dropped it across the desk in front of me. It was a nice bill and clean and new. One thousand dollars.

"Ever save a guy's life?"

"Once in a while, maybe."

"Save mine."

"What goes?"

"I heard you leveled with the customers, Marlowe."

"That's why I stay poor."

341

"I still got two friends. You make it three and you'll be out of the red. You got five grand coming if you pry me loose."

"From what?"

"You're talkative as hell this morning. Don't you pipe who I am?"

"Nope."

"Never been east, huh?"

"Sure—but I wasn't in your set."

"What set would that be?"

I was getting tired of it. "Stop being so damn cagey or pick up your grand and be missing."

"I'm Ikky Rossen. I'll be missing but good unless you can figure something out. Guess."

"I've already guessed. You tell me and tell me quick. I don't have all day to watch you feeding me with an eye-dropper."

"I ran out on the Outfit. The high boys don't go for that. To them it means you got info you figure you can peddle, or you got independent ideas, or you lost your moxie. Me, I lost my moxie. I had it up to here." He touched his Adam's apple with the forefinger of a stretched hand. "I done bad things. I scared and hurt guys. I never killed nobody. That's nothing to the Outfit. I'm out of line. So they pick up the pencil and they draw a line. I got the word. The operators are on the way. I made a bad mistake. I tried to hole up in Vegas. I figured they'd never expect me to lie up in their own joint. They outfigured me. What I did's been done before, but I didn't know it. When I took the plane to L.A. there must have been somebody on it. They know where I live."

"Move."

"No good now. I'm covered."

I knew he was right.

"Why haven't they taken care of you already?"

"They don't do it that way. Always specialists. Don't you know how it works?"

"More or less. A guy with a nice hardware store in Buffalo. A guy with a small dairy in K.C. Always a good front. They report back to New York or somewhere. When they mount the plane west or wherever they're going, they have guns in their briefcases. They're quiet and well dressed and they don't sit together. They could be a couple of lawyers or income-tax sharpies—anything at all that's well mannered and inconspicuous. All sorts of people carry briefcases. Including women."

"Correct as hell. And when they land they'll be steered to me, but not from the airfield. They got ways. If I go to the cops, somebody will know about me. They could have a couple Mafia boys right on the city council for all I know. The cops will give me twenty-four hours to leave town. No use. Mexico? Worse than here. Canada? Better but still no good. Connections there too."

"Australia?"

"Can't get a passport. I been here twenty-five years—illegal. They can't deport me unless they can prove a crime on me. The Outfit would see they didn't. Suppose I got tossed into the freezer. I'm out on a writ in twenty-four hours. And my nice friends got a car waiting to take me home— only not home."

I had my pipe lit and going well. I frowned down at the one-grand note. I could use it very nicely. My checking account could kiss the sidewalk without stooping.

"Let's stop horsing," I said. "Suppose—just suppose—I could figure an out for you. What's your next move?"

"I know a place—if I could get there without bein' tailed. I'd leave my car here and take a rent car. I'd turn it in just short of the county line and buy a secondhand job. Halfway to where I'm going I trade it on a new last-year's model, a leftover—this is just the right time of year. Good discount, new models out soon. Not to save money—less show off. Where I'd go is a good-sized place but still pretty clean."

"Uh-huh," I said. "Wichita, last I heard. But it might have changed."

He scowled at me. "Get smart, Marlowe, but not too damn smart."

"I'll get as smart as I want to. Don't try to make rules for me. If I take this on, there aren't any rules. I take it for this grand and the rest if I bring it off. Don't cross me. I might leak information. If I get knocked off, put just one red rose on my grave. I don't like cut flowers. I like to see them growing. But I could take one because you're such a sweet character. When's the plane in?"

"Sometime today. It's nine hours from New York. Probably come in around five-thirty p.m."

"Might come by San Diego and switch or by San Francisco and switch. A lot of planes from both places. I need a helper."

"Damn you, Marlowe—"

"Hold it. I know a girl. Daughter of a chief of police who got broken for honesty. She wouldn't leak under torture."

"You got no right to risk her," Ikky said angrily.

I was so astonished my jaw hung halfway to my waist. I closed it slowly and swallowed.

"Good God, the man's got a heart."

"Women ain't built for the rough stuff," he said grudgingly.

I picked up the thousand-dollar note and snapped it. "Sorry. No receipt," I said. "I can't have my name in your pocket. And there won't be any rough stuff if I'm lucky. They'd have me outclassed. There's only one way to work it. Now give me your address and all the dope you can think of—names, descriptions of any operators you have ever seen in the flesh."

He did. He was a pretty good observer. Trouble was, the Outfit would know what he had seen. The operators would be strangers to him.

He got up silently and put his hand out. I had to shake it, but what he had said about women made it easier. His hand was moist. Mine would have been in his spot. He nodded and went out silently.

It was a quiet street in Bay City, if there are any quiet streets in this beatnik generation when you can't get through a meal without some male or female stomach-singer belching out a kind of love that is as old-fashioned as a bustle or some Hammond organ jazzing it up in the customer's soup.

The little one-story house was as neat as a fresh pinafore. The front lawn was cut lovingly and very green. The smooth composition driveway was free of grease spots from standing cars, and the hedge that bordered it looked as though the barber came every day.

The white door had a knocker with a tiger's head, a go-to-hell window, and a dingus that let someone inside talk to someone outside without even opening the little window.

I'd have given a mortgage on my left leg to live in a house like that. I didn't think I ever would.

The bell chimed inside and after a while she opened the door in a pale-blue sports shirt and white shorts that were short enough to be friendly. She had gray-blue eyes, dark red hair, and fine bones in her face. There was usually a trace of bitterness in the gray-blue eyes. She couldn't forget that her father's life had been destroyed by the crooked power of a gambling-ship mobster, that her mother had died too.

She was able to suppress the bitterness when she wrote nonsense about young love for the shiny magazines, but this wasn't her life. She didn't really have a life. She had an existence without much pain and enough money to make it safe. But in a tight spot she was as cool and resourceful as a good cop. Her name was Anne Riordan.

She stood to one side and I passed her pretty close. But I have rules too. She shut the door and parked herself on a sofa and went through the cigarette routine, and here was one doll who had the strength to light her own cigarette.

I stood looking around. There were a few changes, not many.

"I need your help," I said.

"The only time I ever see you."

"I've got a client who is an ex-hood, used to be a troubleshooter for the Outfit, the Syndicate, the big mob, or whatever name you want to use for it. You know damn well it exists and is as rich as Midas. You can't beat it because not enough people want to, especially the million-a-year lawyers who work for it."

"My God, are you running for office somewhere? I never heard you sound so pure."

She moved her legs around, not provocatively—she wasn't the type—but it made it difficult for me to think straight just the same.

"Stop moving your legs around," I said. "Or put a pair of slacks on."

"Damn you, Marlowe. Can't you think of anything else?"

"I'll try. I like to think that I know at least one pretty and charming female who doesn't have round heels." I swallowed and went on. "The man's name is Ikky Rossen. He's not beautiful and he's not anything that I like—except one thing. He got mad when I said I needed a girl helper. He said women were not made for the rough stuff. That's why I took the job. To a real mobster, a woman means no more than a sack of flour. They use women in the usual way, but if it's advisable to get rid of them they do it without a second thought."

"So far you've told me a whole lot of nothing. Perhaps you need a cup of coffee or a drink."

"You're sweet but I don't in the morning—except sometimes, and this isn't one of them. Coffee later. Ikky has been penciled."

"Now what's that?"

"You have a list. You draw a line through a name with a pencil. The guy is as good as dead. The Outfit has reasons. They don't do it just for kicks anymore. They don't get any kick. It's just bookkeeping to them."

"What on earth can I do? I might even have said, what can *you* do?"

"I can try. What you can do is help me spot their plane and see where they go—the operators assigned to the job."

"Yes, but how can you do anything?"

"I said I could try. If they took a night plane they are already here. If they took a morning plane they can't be here before five or so. Plenty of time to get set. You know what they look like?"

"Oh, sure. I meet killers every day. I have them in for whiskey sours and caviar on hot toast." She grinned. While she was grinning I took four long steps across the tan-figured rug and lifted her and put a kiss on her mouth. She didn't fight me but she didn't go all trembly either. I went back and sat down.

"They'll look like anybody who's in a quiet well-run business or profession. They'll have quiet clothes and they'll be polite—when they want to be. They'll have briefcases with guns in them that have changed hands so often they can't possibly be traced. When and if they do the job, they'll drop the guns. They'll probably use revolvers, but they could use automatics. They won't use silencers because silencers can jam a gun and the weight makes it hard to shoot accurately. They won't sit together on the plane, but once off of it they may pretend to know each other and simply not have noticed during the flight. They may shake hands with appropriate smiles and walk away and get in the same taxi. I think they'll go in the same taxi. I think they'll go to a hotel first. But very soon they will move into something from which they can watch Ikky's movements and get used to his schedule. They won't be in any hurry unless Ikky makes a move. That would tip them off that Ikky has been tipped off. He has a couple of friends left—he says."

"Will they shoot him from this room or apartment across the street—assuming there is one?"

"No. They'll shoot him from three feet away. They'll walk up behind and say 'Hello, Ikky.' He'll either freeze or turn. They'll fill him with lead, drop the guns, and hop into the car they have waiting. Then they'll follow the crash car off the scene."

"Who'll drive the crash car?"

"Some well-fixed and blameless citizen who hasn't been rapped. He'll drive his own car. He'll clear the way, even if he has to accidentally on purpose crash somebody, even a police car. He'll be so damn sorry he'll cry all the way down his mongrammed shirt. And the killers will be long gone."

"Good heavens," Anne said. "How can you stand your life? If you do bring it off, they'll send operators after you."

"I don't think so. They don't kill a legit. The blame will go to the operators. Remember, these top mobsters are businessmen. They want lots and lots of money. They only get really tough when they figure they have to get rid of somebody, and they don't crave that. There's always a chance of a slipup. Not much of a chance. No gang killing has ever been solved here or anywhere else except two or three times. The top mobster is awful big and awful tough. When he gets too big, too tough—pencil."

She shuddered a little. "I think I need a drink myself."

I grinned at her. "You're right in the atmosphere, darling. I'll weaken."

She brought a couple of Scotch highballs. When we were drinking them I said, "If you spot them or think you spot them, follow to where they go—if you can do it safely. Not otherwise. If it's a hotel—and ten to one it will be—check in and keep calling me until you get me."

She knew my office number and I was still on Yucca Avenue. She knew that too.

"You're the damnedest guy," she said. "Women do anything you want them to. How come I'm still a virgin at twenty-eight?"

"We need a few like you. Why don't you get married?"

"To what? Some cynical chaser who has nothing left? I don't know any really nice men—except you. I'm no pushover for white teeth and a gaudy smile."

I went over and pulled her to her feet. I kissed her long and hard. "I'm honest," I almost whispered. "That's something. But I'm too shop-soiled for a girl like you. I've thought of you, I've wanted you, but that sweet clear look in your eyes tells me to lay off."

"Take me," she said softly. "I have dreams too."

"I couldn't. I've had too many women to deserve one like you. We have to save a man's life. I'm going."

She stood up and watched me leave with a grave face.

The women you get and the women you don't get—they live in different worlds. I don't sneer at either world. I live in both myself.

At Los Angeles International Airport you can't get close to the planes unless you're leaving on one. You see them land, if you happen to be in the right place, but you have to wait at a barrier to get a look at the passengers. The airport buildings don't make it any easier. They are strung out from here to breakfast time, and you can get calluses walking from TWA to American.

I copied an arrival schedule off the boards and prowled around like a dog that has forgotten where he put his bone. Planes came in, planes took off, porters carried luggage, passengers sweated and scurried, children whined, the loudspeaker overrode all the other noises.

I passed Anne a number of times. She took no notice of me.

At 5:45 they must have come. Anne disappeared. I gave it half an hour, just in case she had some other reason for fading. No. She was gone for good. I went out to my car and drove some long crowded miles to Hollywood and my office. I had a drink and sat. At 6:45 the phone rang.

"I think so," she said. "Beverly-Western Hotel. Room 410. I couldn't get any names. You know the clerks don't leave registration cards lying around these days. I didn't like to ask any questions. But I rode up in the elevator with them and spotted their room. I walked right on past them when the bellman put a key in their door, and went down to the mezzanine and then downstairs with a bunch of women from the tea room. I didn't bother to take a room."

"What were they like?"

"They came up the ramp together but I didn't hear them speak. Both had briefcases, both wore quiet suits, nothing flashy. White shirts, starched, one blue tie, one black striped with gray. Black shoes. A couple of businessmen from the East Coast. They could be publishers, lawyers, doctors, account executives—no, cut the last; they weren't gaudy enough. You wouldn't look at them twice."

"Faces?"

"Both medium-brown hair, one a bit darker than the other. Smooth faces, rather expressionless. One had gray eyes, the one with the lighter hair had blue eyes. Their eyes were interesting. Very quick to move, very observant, watching everything near them. That might have been wrong. They should have been a bit preoccupied with what they came out for or interested in California. They seemed more occupied with faces. It's a good thing I spotted them and not you. You don't look like a cop, but you don't look like a man who is not a cop. You have marks on you."

"Phooey. I'm a damn good-looking heart wrecker."

"Their features were strictly assembly line. Each picked up a flight suitcase. One suitcase was gray with two red and white stripes up and down, about six or seven inches from the ends, the other a blue and white tartan. I didn't know there was such a tartan."

"There is, but I forget the name of it."

"I thought you knew everything."

"Just almost everything. Run along home now."

"Do I get a dinner and maybe a kiss?"

"Later, and if you're not careful you'll get more than you want."

"You'll take over and follow them?"

"If they're the right men, they'll follow me. I already took an apartment across the street from Ikky—that block on Poynter with six lowlife apartment houses on the block. I'll bet the incidence of chippies is very high."

"It's high everywhere these days."

"So long, Anne. See you."

"When you need help."

She hung up. I hung up. She puzzles me. Too wise to be so nice. I guess all nice women are wise too.

I called Ikky. He was out. I had a drink from the office bottle, smoked for half an hour, and called again. This time I got him.

I told him the score up to then, and said I hoped Anne had picked the right men. I told him about the apartment I had taken.

"Do I get expenses?" I asked.

"Five grand ought to cover the lot."

"If I earn it and get it. I heard you had a quarter of a million," I said at a wild venture.

"Could be, pal, but how do I get at it? The high boys know where it is. It'll have to cool a long time."

I said that was all right. I had cooled a long time myself. Of course, I didn't expect to get the other four thousand, even if I brought the job off. Men like Ikky Rossen would steal their mother's gold teeth. There seemed to be a little gold in him somewhere—but little was the operative word.

I spent the next half hour trying to think of a plan. I couldn't think of one that looked promising. It was almost eight o'clock and I needed food. I didn't think the boys would move that night. Next morning they would drive past Ikky's place and scout the neighborhood.

I was ready to leave the office when the buzzer sounded from the door of my waiting room. I opened the communicating door. A small tight-looking man was standing in the middle of the floor rocking on his heels with his hands behind his back. He smiled at me, but he wasn't good at it. He walked toward me.

"You Philip Marlowe?"

"Who else? What can I do for you?"

He was close now. He brought his right hand around fast with a gun in it. He stuck the gun in my stomach.

"You can lay off Ikky Rossen," he said in a voice that matched his face, "or you can get your belly full of lead."

He was an amateur. If he had stayed four feet away, he might have had something. I reached up and took the cigarette out of my mouth and held it carelessly.

"What makes you think I know any Ikky Rossen?"

He laughed and pushed his gun into my stomach.

"Wouldn't you like to know!" The cheap sneer, the empty triumph of that feeling of power when you hold a fat gun in a small hand.

"It would be fair to tell me."

As his mouth opened for another crack, I dropped the cigarette and swept a hand. I can be fast when I have to. There are boys that are faster, but they don't stick guns in your stomach.

I got my thumb behind the trigger and my hand over his. I kneed him in the groin. He bent over with a whimper. I twisted his arm to the right and I had his gun. I hooked a heel behind his heel and he was on the floor.

He lay there blinking with surprise and pain, his knees drawn up against his stomach. He rolled from side to side groaning. I reached down and grabbed his left hand and yanked him to his feet. I had six inches and forty pounds on him. They ought to have sent a bigger, better-trained messenger.

"Let's go into my thinking parlor," I said. "We could have a chat and you could have a drink to pick you up. Next time don't get near enough to a prospect for him to get your gun hand. I'll just see if you have any more iron on you."

He hadn't. I pushed him through the door and into a chair. His breath wasn't quite so rasping. He grabbed out a handkerchief and mopped at his face.

"Next time," he said between his teeth. "Next time."

"Don't be an optimist. You don't look the part."

I poured him a drink of Scotch in a paper cup, set it down in front of him. I broke his .38 and dumped the cartridges into the desk drawer. I clicked the chamber back and laid the gun down.

"You can have it when you leave—if you leave."

"That's a dirty way to fight," he said, still gasping.

"Sure. Shooting a man is so much cleaner. Now, how did you get here?"

"Nuts."

"Don't be a fool. I have friends. Not many, but some. I can get you for armed assault, and you know what would happen then. You'd be out on a writ or on bail and that's the last anyone would hear of you. The biggies don't go for failures. Now who sent you and how did you know where to come?"

"Ikky was covered," he said sullenly. "He's dumb. I trailed him here without no trouble at all. Why would he go see a private eye? People want to know."

"More."

"Go to hell."

"Come to think of it, I don't have to get you for armed assault. I can smash it out of you right here and now."

I got up from the chair and he put out a flat hand.

"If I get knocked about, a couple of real tough monkeys will drop around. If I don't report back, same thing. You ain't holding no real high cards. They just look high," he said.

"You haven't anything to tell. If this Ikky came to see me, you don't know why, nor whether I took him on. If he's a mobster, he's not my type of client."

"He come to get you to try and save his hide."

"Who from?"

"That'd be talking."

"Go right ahead. Your mouth seems to work fine. And tell the boys any time I front for a hood, that will be the day."

You have to lie a little once in a while in my business. I was lying a little. "What's Ikky done to get himself disliked? Or would that be talking?"

"You think you're a lot of man," he sneered, rubbing the place where I had kneed him. "In my league you wouldn't make pinch runner."

I laughed in his face. Then I grabbed his right wrist and twisted it behind his back. He began to squawk. I reached into his breast pocket with my left hand and hauled out a wallet. I let him go. He reached for his gun on the desk and I bisected his upper arm with a hard cut. He fell into the customer's chair and grunted.

"You can have your gun," I told him. "When I give it to you. Now be good or I'll have to bounce you just to amuse myself."

In the wallet I found a driver's license made out to Charles Hickon. It did me no good at all. Punks of his type always have slangy aliases. They probably called him Tiny, or Slim, or Marbles, or even just "you." I tossed the wallet back to him. It fell to the floor. He couldn't even catch it.

"Hell," I said, "there must be an economy campaign on, if they send you to do more than pick up cigarette butts."

"Nuts."

"All right, mug. Beat it back to the laundry. Here's your gun."

He took it, made a business of shoving it into his waistband, stood up, gave me as dirty a look as he had in stock, and strolled to the door, nonchalant as a hustler with a new mink stole.

He turned at the door and gave me the beady eye. "Stay clean, tinhorn. Tin bends easy."

With this blinding piece of repartee he opened the door and drifted out.

After a little while I locked my other door, cut the buzzer, made the office dark, and left. I saw no one who looked like a lifetaker. I drove to my house, packed a suitcase, drove to a service station where they were almost fond of me, stored my car, and picked up a rental Chevrolet.

I drove this to Poynter Street, dumped my suitcase in the sleazy apartment I had rented early in the afternoon, and went to dinner at Victor's. It was nine o'clock, too late to drive to Bay City and take Anne to dinner.

I ordered a double Gibson with fresh limes and drank it, and I was as hungry as a schoolboy.

On the way back to Poynter Street I did a good deal of weaving in and out and circling blocks and stopping, with a gun on the seat beside me. As far as I could tell, no one was trying to tail me.

I stopped on Sunset at a service station and made two calls from the box. I caught Bernie Ohls just as he was leaving to go home.

"This is Marlowe, Bernie. We haven't had a fight in years. I'm getting lonely."

"Well, get married. I'm chief investigator for the sheriff's office now. I rank acting captain until I pass the exam. I don't hardly speak to private eyes."

"Speak to this one. I need help. I'm on a ticklish job where I could get killed."

"And you expect me to interfere with the course of nature?"

"Come off it, Bernie. I haven't been a bad guy. I'm trying to save an ex-mobster from a couple of executioners."

"The more they mow each other down, the better I like it."

"Yeah. If I call you, come running or send a couple of good boys. You'll have time to teach them."

We exchanged a couple of mild insults and hung up. I dialed Ikky Rossen's number. His rather unpleasant voice said, "Okay, talk."

"Marlowe. Be ready to move out about midnight. We've spotted your boyfriends and they are holed up at the Beverly-Western. They won't move to your street tonight. Remember, they don't know you've been tipped."

"Sounds chancy."

"Good God, it wasn't meant to be a Sunday school picnic. You've been careless, Ikky. You were followed to my office. That cuts the time we have."

He was silent for a moment. I heard him breathing. "Who by?" he asked.

"Some little tweezer who stuck a gun in my belly and gave me the trouble of taking it away from him. I can only figure they sent a punk on the theory they don't want me to know too much, in case I don't know it already."

"You're in for trouble, friend."

"When not? I'll come over to your place about midnight. Be ready. Where's your car?"

"Out front."

"Get it on a side street and make a business of locking it up. Where's the back door of your flop?"

"In back. Where would it be? On the alley."

"Leave your suitcase there. We walk out together and go to your car. We drive by the alley and pick up the suitcase or cases."

"Suppose some guy steals them?"

"Yeah. Suppose you get dead. Which do you like better?"

"Okay," he grunted. "I'm waiting. But we're taking big chances."

"So do race drivers. Does that stop them? There's no way to get out but fast. Douse your lights about ten and rumple the bed well. It would be good if you could leave some baggage behind. Wouldn't look so planned."

He grunted okay and I hung up. The telephone box was well lighted outside. They usually are in service stations. I took a good long gander around while I pawed over the collection of giveaway maps inside the station. I saw nothing to worry me. I took a map of San Diego just for the hell of it and got into my rented car.

On Poynter I parked around the corner and went up to my second-floor sleazy apartment and sat in the dark watching from my window. I saw nothing to worry about. A couple of medium-class chippies came out of Ikky's apartment house and were picked up in a late-model car. A man about Ikky's height and build went into the apartment house. Various other people came and went. The street was fairly quiet. Since they put in the Hollywood Freeway nobody much uses the off-the-boulevard streets unless they live in the neighborhood.

It was a nice fall night—or as nice as they get in Los Angeles' climate—clearish but not even crisp. I don't know what's happened to the weather in our overcrowded city, but it's not the weather I knew when I came to it.

It seemed like a long time to midnight. I couldn't spot anybody watching anything, and no couple of quiet-suited men paged any of the six apartment houses available. I was pretty sure they'd try mine first when they came, but I wasn't sure if Anne had picked the right men, or if the tweezer's message back to his bosses had done me any good or otherwise.

In spite of the hundred ways Anne could be wrong, I had a hunch she was right. The killers had no reason to be cagey if they didn't know Ikky had been warned. No reason but one. He had come to my office and been tailed there. But the Outfit, with all its arrogance of power, might laugh at the idea he had been tipped off or come to me for help. I was so small they would hardly be able to see me.

At midnight I left the apartment, walked two blocks watching for a tail, crossed the street, and went into Ikky's drive. There was no locked door, and no elevator. I climbed steps to the third floor and looked for his apartment. I knocked lightly. He opened the door with a gun in his hand. He probably looked scared.

There were two suitcases by the door and another against the far wall.

I went over and lifted it. It was heavy enough. I opened it—it was unlocked.

"You don't have to worry," he said. "It's got everything a guy could need for three-four nights, and nothing except some clothes that I couldn't glom off in any ready-to-wear place."

I picked up one of the other suitcases. "Let's stash this by the back door."

"We can leave by the alley too."

"We leave by the front door. Just in case we're covered—though I don't think so—we're just two guys going out together. Just one thing. Keep both hands in your coat pockets and the gun in your right. If anybody calls out your name behind you, turn fast and shoot. Nobody but a lifetaker will do it. I'll do the same."

"I'm scared," he said in his rusty voice.

"Me too, if it helps any. But we have to do it. If you're braced, they'll have guns in their hands. Don't bother asking them questions. They wouldn't answer in words. If it's just my small friend, we'll cool him and dump him inside the door. Got it?"

He nodded, licking his lips. We carried the suitcases down and put them outside the back door. I looked along the alley. Nobody, and only a short distance to the side street. We went back in and along the hall to the front. We walked out on Poynter Street with all the casualness of a wife buying her husband a birthday tie.

Nobody made a move. The street was empty.

We walked around the corner to Ikky's rented car. He unlocked it. I went back with him for the suitcases. Not a stir. We put the suitcases in the car and started up and drove to the next street.

A traffic light not working, a boulevard stop or two, the entrance to the freeway. There was plenty of traffic on it even at midnight. California is loaded with people going places and making speed to get there. If you don't drive eighty miles an hour, everybody passes you. If you do, you have to watch the rearview mirror for highway patrol cars. It's the rat race of rat races.

Ikky did a quiet seventy. We reached the junction to Route 66 and he took it. So far nothing. I stayed with him to Pomona.

"This is far enough for me," I said. "I'll grab a bus back if there is one, or park myself in a motel. Drive to a service station and we'll ask for the bus stop. It should be close to the freeway."

He did that and stopped midway on a block. He reached for his pocketbook and held out four thousand-dollar bills.

"I don't really feel I've earned all that. It was too easy."

He laughed with a kind of wry amusement on his pudgy face. "Don't be a sap. I have it made. You didn't know what you was walking into. What's more, your troubles are just beginning. The Outfit has eyes and ears everywhere. Perhaps I'm safe if I'm damn careful. Perhaps I ain't as safe as I think I am. Either way, you did what I asked. Take the dough. I got plenty."

I took it and put it away. He drove to an all-night service station and we were told where to find the bus stop. "There's a cross-country Greyhound at two twenty-five a.m.," the attendant said, looking at a schedule. "They'll take you, if they got room."

Ikky drove to the bus stop. We shook hands and he went gunning down the road toward the freeway. I looked at my watch and found a liquor store still open and bought a pint of Scotch. Then I found a bar and ordered a double with water.

My troubles were just beginning, Ikky had said. He was so right.

I got off at the Hollywood bus station, grabbed a taxi, and drove to my office. I asked the driver to wait a few moments. At that time of night he was glad to. The night man let me into the building.

"You work late, Mr. Marlowe. But you always did, didn't you?"

"It's that sort of business," I said. "Thanks, Jimmy."

Up in my office I pawed the floor for mail and found nothing but a longish narrowish box, Special Delivery, with a Glendale postmark.

It contained nothing at all but a freshly sharpened pencil—the mobster's mark of death.

I didn't take it too hard. When they mean it, they don't send it to you. I took it as a sharp warning to lay off. There might be a beating arranged. From their point of view, that would be good discipline. "When we pencil a guy, any guy that tries to help him is in for smashing." That could be the message.

I thought of going to my house on Yucca Avenue. Too lonely. I thought of going to Anne's place in Bay City. Worse. If they got wise to her, real hoods would think nothing of beating her up too.

It was the Poynter Street flop for me—easily the safest place now. I went down to the waiting taxi and had him drive me to within three blocks of the so-called apartment house. I went upstairs, undressed, and slept raw. Nothing bothered me but a broken spring—that bothered my back.

I lay until 3:30 pondering the situation with my massive brain. I went to sleep with a gun under the pillow, which is a bad place to keep a gun when you have one pillow as thick and soft as a typewriter pad. It bothered me, so I transferred it to my right hand. Practice had taught me to keep it there even in sleep.

I woke up with the sun shining. I felt like a piece of spoiled meat.

I struggled into the bathroom and doused myself with cold water and wiped off with a towel you couldn't have seen if you held it sideways. This was a really gorgeous apartment. All it needed was a set of Chippendale furniture to be graduated into the slum class.

There was nothing to eat and if I went out, Miss-Nothing Marlowe might miss something. I had a pint of whiskey. I looked at it and smelled it, but I couldn't take it for breakfast on an empty stomach, even if I could reach my stomach, which was floating around near the ceiling.

I looked into the closets in case a previous tenant might have left a crust of bread in a hasty departure. Nope. I wouldn't have liked it anyhow, not even with whiskey on it. So I sat at the window. An hour of that and I was ready to bite a piece off a bellhop's arm.

I dressed and went around the corner to the rented car and drove to an eatery. The waitress was sore too. She swept a cloth over the counter in front of me and let me have the last customer's crumbs in my lap.

"Look, sweetness," I said, "don't be so generous. Save the crumbs for a rainy day. All I want is two eggs three minutes—no more—a slice of your famous concrete toast, a tall glass of tomato juice and a dash of Lea and Perrins, a big happy smile, and don't give anybody else any coffee. I might need it all."

"I got a cold," she said. "Don't push me around. I might crack you one on the kisser."

"Let's be pals. I had a rough night too."

She gave me a half smile and went through the swing door sideways. It showed more of her curves, which were ample, even excessive. But I got the eggs the way I liked them. The toast had been painted with melted butter past its bloom.

"No Lea and Perrins," she said, putting down the tomato juice. "How about a little Tabasco? We're fresh out of arsenic too."

I used two drops of Tabasco, swallowed the eggs, drank two cups of coffee, and was about to leave the toast for a tip, but I went soft and left a quarter instead. That really brightened her. It was a joint where you left a dime or nothing. Mostly nothing.

Back on Poynter Street nothing had changed. I got to my window again and sat. At about 8:30 the man I had seen go into the apartment house across the way—the one about the same height and build as Ikky—came out with a small briefcase and turned east. Two men got out of a dark-blue sedan. They were of the same height and very quietly dressed and had soft hats pulled low over their foreheads. Each jerked out a revolver.

"Hey, Ikky!" one of them called out.

The man turned. "So long, Ikky," the other man said.

Gunfire racketed between the houses. The man crumpled and lay motionless. The two men rushed for their car and were off, going west. Halfway down the block I saw a limousine pull out and start ahead of them.

In no time at all they were completely gone.

It was a nice swift clean job. The only thing wrong with it was that they hadn't given it enough time for preparation.

They had shot the wrong man.

I got out of there fast, almost as fast as the two killers. There was a smallish crowd grouped around the dead man. I didn't have to look at him to know he was dead—the boys were pros. Where he lay on the sidewalk on the other side of the street I couldn't see him—people were in the way. But I knew just how he would look and I already heard sirens in the distance. It could have been just the routine shrieking from Sunset, but it wasn't. So somebody had telephoned. It was too early for the cops to be going to lunch.

I strolled around the corner with my suitcase and jammed into the rented car and beat it away from there. The neighborhood was not my piece of shortcake any more. I could imagine the questions.

"Just what took you over there, Marlowe? You got a flop of your own, ain't you?"

"I was hired by an ex-mobster in trouble with the Outfit. They'd sent killers after him!"

"Don't tell us he was trying to go straight."

"I don't know. But I liked his money."

"Didn't do much to earn it, did you?"

"I got him away last night. I don't know where he is now, and I don't want to know."

"You got him away?"

"That's what I said."

"Yeah—only he's in the morgue with multiple bullet wounds. Try something better. Or somebody's in the morgue."

And on and on. Policeman's dialogue. It comes out of an old shoebox. What they say doesn't mean anything, what they ask doesn't mean anything. They just keep boring in until you are so exhausted you slip on some detail. Then they smile happily and rub their hands, and say, "Kind of careless there, weren't you? Let's start all over again."

The less I had of that, the better. I parked in my usual parking slot and went up to the office. It was full of nothing but stale air. Every time I went into the dump I felt more and more tired. Why the hell hadn't I got myself a government job ten years ago? Make it fifteen years. I had brains enough to get a mail-order law degree. The country's full of lawyers who couldn't write a complaint without the book.

So I sat in my office chair and disadmired myself. After a while I remembered the pencil. I made certain arrangements with a .45 gun, more gun that I ever carry—too much weight. I dialed the sheriff's office and asked for Bernie Ohls. I got him. His voice was sour.

"Marlowe. I'm in trouble—real trouble," I said.

"Why tell me?" he growled. "You must be used to it by now."

"This kind of trouble you don't get used to. I'd like to come over and tell you."

"You in the same office?"

"The same."

"Have to go over that way. I'll drop in."

He hung up. I opened two windows. The gentle breeze wafted a smell of coffee and stale fat to me from Joe's Eats next door. I hated it, I hated myself, I hated everything.

Ohls didn't bother with my elegant waiting room. He rapped on my own door and I let him in. He scowled his way to the customer's chair.

"Okay. Give."

"Ever hear of a character named Ikky Rossen?"

"Why would I? Record?

"An ex-mobster who got disliked by the mob. They put a pencil through his name and sent the usual two tough boys on a plane. He got tipped and hired me to help him get away."

"Nice clean work."

"Cut it out, Bernie." I lit a cigarette and blew smoke in his face. In retaliation he began to chew a cigarette. He never lit one, but he certainly mangled them.

"Look," I went on. "Suppose the man wants to go straight and suppose he doesn't. He's entitled to his life as long as he hasn't killed anyone. He told me he hadn't."

"And you believed the hood, huh? When do you start teaching Sunday school?"

"I neither believed him nor disbelieved him. I took him on. There was no reason not to. A girl I know and I watched the planes yesterday. She spotted the boys and tailed them to a hotel. She was sure of what they were. They looked it right down to their black shoes. This girl—"

"Would she have a name?"

"Only for you."

"I'll buy, if she hasn't cracked any laws."

"Her name is Anne Riordan. She lives in Bay City. Her father was once chief of police there. And don't say that makes him a crook, because he wasn't."

"Uh-huh. Let's have the rest. Make a little time too."

"I took an apartment opposite Ikky. The killers were still at the hotel. At midnight I got Ikky out and drove with him as far as Pomona. He went on in his rented car and I came back by Greyhound. I moved into the apartment on Poynter Street, right across from his dump."

"Why—if he was already gone?"

I opened the middle desk drawer and took out the nice sharp pencil. I wrote my name on a piece of paper and ran the pencil through it.

"Because someone sent me this. I didn't think they'd kill me, but I thought they planned to give me enough of a beating to warn me off any more pranks."

"They knew you were in on it?"

"Ikky was tailed here by a little squirt who later came around and stuck a gun in my stomach. I knocked him around a bit, but I had to let him go. I thought Poynter Street was safer after that. I live lonely."

"I get around," Bernie Ohls said. "I hear reports. So they gunned the wrong guy."

"Same height, same build, same general appearance. I saw them gun him. I couldn't tell if it was the two guys from the Beverly-Western. I'd never seen them. It was just two guys in dark suits with hats pulled down. They jumped into a blue Pontiac sedan, about two years old, and lammed off, with a big Caddy running crash for them."

Bernie stood up and stared at me for a long moment. "I don't think they'll bother with you now," he said. "They've hit the wrong guy. The mob will be very quiet for a while. You know something? This town is getting to be almost as lousy as New York, Brooklyn, and Chicago. We could end up real corrupt."

"We've made a hell of a good start."

"You haven't told me anything that makes me take action, Phil. I'll talk to the city homicide boys. I don't guess you're in any trouble. But you saw the shooting. They'll want that."

"I couldn't identify anybody, Bernie. I didn't know the man who was shot. How did *you* know it was the wrong man?"

"You told me, stupid."

"I thought perhaps the city boys had a make on him."

"They wouldn't tell me, if they had. Besides, they ain't hardly had time to go out for breakfast. He's just a stiff in the morgue to them until the I.D. comes up with something. But they'll want to talk to you, Phil. They just love their tape recorders."

He went out and the door whooshed shut behind him. I sat there wondering if I had been a dope to talk to him. Or to take on Ikky's troubles. Five thousand green men said no. But they can be wrong too.

Somebody banged on my door. It was a uniform holding a telegram. I receipted for it and tore it loose.

It said: ON MY WAY TO FLAGSTAFF, MIRADOR MOTOR COURT. THINK I'VE BEEN SPOTTED. COME FAST.

I tore the wire into small pieces and burned them in my big ashtray.

I called Anne Riordan.

"Funny thing happened," I told her, and told her about the funny thing.

"I don't like the pencil," she said. "And I don't like the wrong man being killed—probably some poor bookkeeper in a cheap business or he wouldn't be living in that neighborhood. You should never have touched it, Phil."

"Ikky had a life. Where he's going he might make himself decent. He can change his name. He must be loaded or he wouldn't have paid me so much."

"I said I didn't like the pencil. You'd better come down here for a while. You can have your mail readdressed—if you get any mail. You don't have to work right away anyhow. And L.A. is oozing with private eyes."

"You don't get the point. I'm not through with the job. The city dicks have to know where I am, and if they do, all the crime reporters will know too. The cops might even decide to make me a suspect. Nobody who saw the shooting is going to put out a description that means anything. The American people know better than to be witnesses to gang killings."

"All right, but my offer stands."

The buzzer sounded in the outside room. I told Anne I had to hang up. I opened the communicating door and a well-dressed—I might say elegantly dressed—middle-aged man stood six feet inside the outer door. He had a pleasantly dishonest smile on his face. He wore a white Stetson and one of those narrow ties that go through an ornamental buckle. His cream-colored flannel suit was beautifully tailored.

He lit a cigarette with a gold lighter and looked at me over the first puff of smoke.

"Mr. Philip Marlowe?"

I nodded.

"I'm Foster Grimes from Las Vegas. I run the Rancho Esperanza on South Fifth. I hear you got a little involved with a man named Ikky Rossen."

"Won't you come in?"

He strolled past me into my office. His appearance told me nothing—
a prosperous man who liked or felt it good business to look a bit western.
You see them by the dozen in the Palm Springs winter season. His accent
told me he was an easterner, but not New England. New York or Baltimore,
likely. Long Island, the Berkshires—no, too far from the city.

I showed him the customer's chair with a flick of the wrist and sat
down in my antique swivelsqueaker. I waited.

"Where is Ikky now, if you know?"

"I don't know, Mr. Grimes."

"How come you messed with him?"

"Money."

"A damned good reason," he smiled. "How far did it go?"

"I helped him leave town. I'm telling you this, although I don't know
who the hell you are, because I've already told an old friend-enemy of
mine, a top man in the sheriff's office."

"What's a friend-enemy?"

"Lawmen don't go around kissing me, but I've known him for years,
and we are as much friends as a private star can be with a lawman."

"I told you who I was. We have a unique setup in Vegas. We own
the place except for one lousy newspaper editor who keeps climbing our
backs and the backs of our friends. We let him live because letting him
live makes us look better than knocking him off. Killings are not good
business any more."

"Like Ikky Rossen."

"That's not a killing. It's an execution. Ikky got out of line."

"So your gun boys had to rub the wrong guy. They could have hung
around a little to make sure."

"They would have, if you'd kept your nose where it belonged. They
hurried. We don't appreciate that. We want cool efficiency."

"Who's this great big fat 'we' you keep talking about?"

"Don't go juvenile on me, Marlowe."

"Okay. Let's say I know."

"Here's what we want. He reached into his pocket and drew out a
loose bill. He put it on the desk on his side. "Find Ikky and tell him to
get back in line and everything is okay. With an innocent bystander gunned,
we don't want any trouble or any extra publicity. It's that simple. You get
this now," he nodded at the bill. It was a grand. Probably the smallest
bill they had. "And another when you find Ikky and give him the message.
If he holds out—curtains."

"Suppose I say take your grand and blow your nose with it?"

"That would be unwise." He flipped out a Colt Woodsman with a short silencer on it. A Colt Woodsman will take one without jamming. He was fast too, fast and smooth. The genial expression on his face didn't change.

"I never left Vegas," he said calmly. "I can prove it. You're dead in your office chair and nobody knows anything. Just another private eye that tried the wrong pitch. Put your hands on the desk and think a little. Incidentally, I'm a crack shot even with this damned silencer."

I flipped the nicely sharpened pencil across to him. He grabbed for it after a swift change of the gun to his left hand—very swift. He held the pencil up so that he could look at it without taking his eyes off me.

I said, "It came to me by Special Delivery mail. No message, no return address. Just the pencil. Think I've never heard about the pencil, Mr. Grimes?"

He frowned and tossed the pencil down. Before he could shift his long lithe gun back to his right hand I dropped mine under the desk and grabbed the butt of the .45 and put my finger hard on the trigger.

"Look under the desk, Mr. Grimes. You'll see a .45 in an opened holster. It's fixed there and it's pointing at your belly. Even if you could shoot me through the heart, the .45 would still go off from a convulsive movement of my hand. And your belly would be hanging by a shred and you would be knocked out of that chair. A .45 slug can throw you back six feet. Even the movies learned that at last."

"Looks like a Mexican standoff," he said quietly. He holstered his gun. He grinned. "Nice work, Marlowe. We could use a man like you. I suggest that you find Ikky and don't be a drip. He'll listen to reason. He doesn't really want to be on the run for the rest of his life."

"Tell me something, Mr. Grimes. Why pick on me? Apart from Ikky, what did I ever do to make you dislike me?"

Not moving, he thought a moment, or pretended to. "The Larsen case. You helped send one of our boys to the gas chamber. That we don't forget. We had you in mind as a fall guy for Ikky. You'll aways be a fall guy, unless you play it our way. Something will hit you when you least expect it."

"A man in my business is always a fall guy, Mr. Grimes. Pick up your grand and drift out quietly. I might decide to do it your way, but I have to think about it. As for the Larsen case, the cops did all the work. I just happened to know where he was. I don't guess you miss him terribly."

"We don't like interference." He stood up. He put the grand note casually back in his pocket. While he was doing it I let go of the .45 and jerked out my Smith and Wesson five-inch .38.

He looked at it contemptuously. "I'll be in Vegas, Marlowe—in fact, I never left Vegas. You can catch me at the Esperanza. No, we don't give a damn about Larsen personally. Just another gun handler. They come in gross lots. We *do* give a damn that some punk private eye fingered him."

He nodded and went out by my office door.

I did some pondering. I knew Ikky wouldn't go back to the Outfit. He wouldn't trust them enough even if he got the chance. But there was another reason now. I called Anne Riordan again.

"I'm going to look for Ikky. I have to. If I don't call you in three days, get hold of Bernie Ohls. I'm going to Flagstaff, Arizona. Ikky says he will be there."

"You're a fool," she wailed. "It's some sort of trap."

"A Mr. Grimes of Vegas visited me with a silenced gun. I beat him to the punch, but I won't always be that lucky. If I find Ikky and report to Grimes, the mob will let me alone."

"You'd condemn a man to death?" Her voice was sharp and incredulous.

"No. He won't be there when I report. He'll have to hop a plane to Montreal, buy forged papers, and plane to Europe. He may be fairly safe there. But the Outfit has long arms and Ikky won't have a dull life staying alive. He hasn't any choice. For him it's either hide or get the pencil."

"So clever of you, darling. What about your own pencil?"

"If they meant it, they wouldn't have sent it. Just a bit of scare technique."

"And you don't scare, you wonderful handsome brute."

"I scare. But it doesn't paralyze me. So long. Don't take any lovers until I get back."

"Damn you, Marlowe!"

She hung up on me. I hung up on myself.

Saying the wrong thing is one of my specialties.

I beat it out of town before the homicide boys could hear about me. It would take them quite a while to get a lead. And Bernie Ohls wouldn't give a city dick a used paper bag. The sheriff's men and the city police cooperate about as much as two tomcats on a fence.

I made Phoenix by evening and parked myself in a motor court on the outskirts. Phoenix was damned hot. The motor court had a dining room, so I had dinner. I collected some quarters and dimes from the cashier and shut myself in a phone booth and started to call the Mirador in Flagstaff.

How silly could I get? Ikky might be registered under any name from

Cohen to Cordileone, from Watson to Woichehovski. I called anyway and got nothing but as much of a smile as you can get on the phone.

So I asked for a room the following night. Not a chance unless someone checked out, but they would put me down for a cancellation or something. Flagstaff is too near the Grand Canyon. Ikky must have arranged in advance. That was something to ponder too.

I bought a paperback and read it. I set my alarm watch for 6:30. The paperback scared me so badly that I put two guns under my pillow. It was about a guy who bucked the hoodlum boss of Milwaukee and got beaten up every fifteen minutes. I figured that his head and face would be nothing but a piece of bone with a strip of skin hanging from it. But in the next chapter he was as gay as a meadowlark.

Then I asked myself why I was reading this drivel when I could have been memorizing *The Brothers Karamazov*. Not knowing any good answers, I turned the light out and went to sleep.

At 6:30 I shaved, showered, had breakfast, and took off for Flagstaff. I got there by lunchtime, and there was Ikky in the restaurant eating mountain trout. I sat down across from him. He looked surprised to see me.

I ordered mountain trout and ate it from the outside in, which is the proper way. Boning spoils it a little.

"What gives?" he asked me with his mouth full. A delicate eater.

"You read the papers?"

"Just the sports section."

"Let's go to your room and talk about it."

We paid for our lunches and went along to a nice double. The motor courts are getting so good that they make a lot of hotels look cheap. We sat down and lit cigarettes.

"The two hoods got up too early and went over to Poynter Street. They parked outside your apartment house. They hadn't been briefed carefully enough. They shot a guy who looked a little like you."

"That's a hot one," he grinned. "But the cops will find out, and the Outfit will find out. So the tag for me stays on."

"You must think I'm dumb," I said. "I am."

"I thought you did a first-class job, Marlowe. What's dumb about that?"

"What job did I do?"

"You got me out of there pretty slick."

"Anything about it you couldn't have done yourself?"

"With luck—no. But it's nice to have a helper."

"You mean sucker."

His face tightened. And his rusty voice growled. "I don't catch. And give me back some of that five grand, will you? I'm shorter than I thought."

"I'll give it back to you when you find a hummingbird in a salt shaker."

"Don't be like that." He almost sighed, and flicked a gun into his hand. I didn't have to flick. I was holding one in my side pocket.

"I oughtn't to have boobed off," I said. "Put the heater away. It doesn't pay any more than a Vegas slot machine."

"Wrong. Them machines pay the jackpot every so often. Otherwise— no customers."

"Every so seldom, you mean. Listen, and listen good."

He grinned. His dentist was tired waiting for him.

"The setup intrigued me," I went on, debonair as Philo Vance in an S. S. Van Dine story and a lot brighter in the head. "First off, could it be done? Second, if it could be done, where would I be? But gradually I saw the little touches that flawed the picture. Why would you come to me at all? The Outfit isn't naive. Why would they send a little punk like this Charles Hickon or whatever name he uses on Thursdays? Why would an old hand like you let anybody trail you to a dangerous connection?"

"You slay me, Marlowe. You're so bright I could find you in the dark. You're so dumb you couldn't see a red, white, and blue giraffe. I bet you were back there in your unbrain emporium playing with that five grand like a cat with a bag of catnip. I bet you were kissing the notes."

"Not after you handled them. Then why the pencil that was sent to me? Big dangerous threat. It reinforced the rest. But like I told your choir-boy from Vegas, they don't send them when they mean them. By the way, he had a gun too. A Woodsman .22 with a silencer. I had to make him put it away. He was nice about that. He started waving grands at me to find out where you were and tell him. A well-dressed, nice-looking front man for a pack of dirty rats. The Woman's Christian Temperance Association and some bootlicking politicians gave them the money to be big, and they learned how to use it and make it grow. Now they're pretty well unstoppable. But they're still a pack of dirty rats. And they're always where they can't make a mistake. That's inhuman. Any man has a right to a few mistakes. Not the rats. They have to be perfect all the time. Or else they get stuck with *you*."

"I don't know what the hell you're talking about. I just know it's too long."

"Well, allow me to put it in English. Some poor jerk from the East Side gets involved with the lower echelons of a mob. You know what an echelon is, Ikky?"

"I been in the Army," he sneered.

"He grows up in the mob, but he's not all rotten. He's not rotten enough. So he tries to break loose. He comes out here and gets himself a cheap job of some sort and changes his name or names and lives quietly in a cheap apartment house. But the mob by now has agents in many places. Somebody spots him and recognizes him. It might be a pusher, a front man for a bookie joint, a night girl. So the mob, or call them the Outfit, say through their cigar smoke: 'Ikky can't do this to us. It's a small operation because he's small. But it annoys us. Bad for discipline. Call a couple of boys and have them pencil him.' But what boys do they call? A couple they're tired of. Been around too long. Might make a mistake or get chilly toes. Perhaps they like killing. That's bad too. That makes for recklessness. The best boys are the ones that don't care either way. So although they don't know it, the boys they call are on their way out. But it would be kind of cute to frame a guy they already don't like, for fingering a hood named Larsen. One of these puny little jokes the Outfit takes big. 'Look, guys, we even got time to play footsie with a private eye.' So they send a ringer."

"The Torrence brothers ain't ringers. They're real hard boys. They proved it—even if they did make a mistake."

"Mistake nothing. They got Ikky Rossen. You're just a singing commercial in this deal. And as of now you're under arrest for murder. You're worse off than that. The Outfit will habeas corpus you out of the clink and blow you down. You've served your purpose and you failed to finger me into a patsy."

His finger tightened on the trigger. I shot the gun out of his hand. The gun in my coat pocket was small, but at that distance accurate. And it was one of my days to be accurate.

He made a faint moaning sound and sucked at his hand. I went over and kicked him hard in the chest. Being nice to killers is not part of my repertoire. He went over backward and stumbled four or five steps. I picked up his gun and held it on him while I tapped all the places—not just pockets or holsters—where a man could stash a second gun. He was clean— that way anyhow.

"What are you trying to do to me?" he whined. "I paid you. You're clear. I paid you damn well."

"We both have problems there. Your's is to stay alive." I took a pair of cuffs out of my pocket and wrestled his hands behind him and snapped them on. His hand was bleeding. I tied his show handkerchief around it and then went to the telephone and called the police.

I had to stick around for a few days, but I didn't mind that as long as I could have trout caught eight or nine thousand feet up. I called Anne and Bernie Ohls. I called my answering service. The Arizona D.A. was a young keen-eyed man and the chief of police was one of the biggest men I ever saw.

I got back to L.A. in time and took Anne to Romanoff's for dinner and champagne.

"What I can't see," she said over a third glass of bubbly, "is why they dragged you into it, why they set up the fake Ikky Rossen. Why didn't they just let the two lifetakers do their job?"

"I couldn't really say. Unless the big boys feel so safe they're developing a sense of humor. And unless this Larsen guy who went to the gas chamber was bigger than he seemed to be. Only three or four important mobsters have made the electric chair or the rope or the gas chamber. None that I know of in the life-imprisonment states like Michigan. If Larsen was bigger than anyone thought, they might have had my name on a waiting list."

"But why wait?" she asked me. "They'd go after you quickly."

"They can afford to wait. Who's going to bother them? Except when they make a mistake."

"Income tax rap?"

"Yeah, like Capone. Capone may have had several hundred men killed, and killed a few of them himself, personally. But it took the Internal Revenue boys to get him. But the Outfit won't make that mistake often."

"What I like about you, apart from your enormous personal charm, is that when you don't know an answer you make one up."

"The money worries me," I said. "Five grand of their dirty money. What do I do with it?"

"Don't be a jerk all your life. You earned the money and you risked your life for it. You can buy Series E Bonds—they'll make the money clean. And to me that would be part of the joke."

"*You* tell *me* one good sound reason why they pulled the switch."

"You have more of a reputation than you realize. And suppose it was the false Ikky who pulled the switch? He sounds like one of these over-clever types that can't do anything simple."

"The Outfit will get him for making his own plans—if you're right."

"If the D.A. doesn't. And I couldn't care less about what happens to him. More champagne, please."

They extradited "Ikky" and he broke under pressure and named the two gunmen—after I had already named them, the Torrence brothers. But nobody could find them. They never went home. And you can't prove conspiracy on one man. The law couldn't even get him for accessory after the fact. They couldn't prove he knew the real Ikky had been gunned.

They could have got him for some trifle, but they had a better idea. They left him to his friends. They just turned him loose.

Where is he now? My hunch says nowhere.

Anne Riordan was glad it was all over and I was safe. Safe—that isn't a word you use in my trade.

ABOUT THE AUTHORS AND ARTISTS

RAYMOND CHANDLER was born in Chicago in 1888 and educated at Dulwich College, England. He worked at various times as poet, teacher, book reviewer, accountant, oil executive, and pulp writer, before writing his first Philip Marlowe novel, *The Big Sleep*, in 1939. It was followed by *Farewell, My Lovely*, *The High Window*, *The Lady in the Lake*, *The Little Sister*, *The Long Goodbye*, and *Playback*. Raymond Chandler lived most of the last decades of his life in Southern California. He died in 1959.

SIMON BRETT is the author of twelve crime novels featuring actor-detective Charles Paris and three other crime novels, including *A Shock to the System*, which was nominated for the Best Novel Award by the Mystery Writers of America.

ROBERT CAMPBELL has three different detectives with three different voices working in three different series. Whistler and Jimmy Flannery and Jake Hatch. There is only one of Campbell. Like the classic private eye, he lives alone. Like most of the classic private eyes, he rarely uses a gun.

MAX ALLAN COLLINS is the author of the Nathan Heller historical detective novels, the first of which, *True Detective* (1983), won a Shamus. He is also the author of three other popular suspense series, Nolan, Quarry, and Mallory, as well as a new series of novels about real-life "untouchable" Eliot Ness.

ROBERT CRAIS writes the popular *Elvis Cole* novels. His first book, *The Monkey's Raincoat*, was nominated for both the Shamus and Edgar awards. Additionally, Crais has written numerous scripts for such influential and critically acclaimed television series as *Hill Street Blues*. His TV work has received several awards, including an Emmy nomination.

LOREN D. ESTLEMAN's first novel was published in 1976. At present he has published twenty-eight books, including the Amos Walker detective novels and numerous westerns. He is a past winner of the Western Writers of America Golden Spur Award (twice) and the Private Eye Writers of America Shamus Award (twice), as well as a nominee for the American Book Award and the Pulitzer Prize.

ED GORMAN has written books in several fields. His most recent novel, *The Autumn Dead*, features actor and private investigator Jack Dwyer. He has been nominated for the Shamus, and his historical novel *Guild* was called by the Western Writers of America "disturbing and memorable."

JAMES GRADY worked as an investigative reporter in Washington, D.C., covering politics, espionage, organized crime, and drug trafficking. Grady began his novelist career with *Six Days of the Condor*. His ninth and latest novel is *Steeltown*.

JOYCE HARRINGTON's first story, "The Purple Shroud," won an Edgar from the Mystery Writers of America in 1973. Since then, she has written somewhere between forty and fifty stories and three novels. She's been nominated for short story Edgars three more times, and her latest novel, *Dreemz of the Night*, was published in June 1987.

JEREMIAH HEALY's first novel, *Blunt Darts*, was selected by *The New York Times* as one of the seven best mysteries of 1984. Healy's second book, *The Staked Goat*, received the Shamus Award from the Private Eye Writers of America as the best novel of 1986.

EDWARD D. HOCH is a past president of the Mystery Writers of America and the author of more than seven hundred and fifty short stories, mainly in the mystery field. His thirty-one published books include *The Shattered Raven* and three other novels. In 1968 he won an Edgar for his short story "The Oblong Room."

STUART M. KAMINSKY is the author of more than twenty published mystery novels and numerous short stories. His novels include the Toby Peters series, the Inspector Porfiry Petrovich Rostnikov series, and the Xavier Flores series. He was nominated in 1984 for an Edgar Award by the Mystery Writers of America for his novel *Black Knight in Red Square*.

In addition to his Nero Wolfe Award winning *Sleeping Dog*, and the current *Laughing Dog*, DICK LOCHTE has written for numerous publications and for motion pictures and television. For ten years he was a book columnist for the *Los Angeles Times* and is presently drama critic for *Los Angeles* magazine.

JOHN LUTZ was awarded a Shamus Award in 1982, and an Edgar in 1986. He is the author of two private detective series. One features Nudger, a somewhat reluctant P.I. with a nervous stomach, who operates in St. Louis. The other series is about Fred Carver, a lame former Orlando cop who solves his cases in Florida.

FRANK MacSHANE is the author of *The Life of Raymond Chandler* and editor of *Selected Letters of Raymond Chandler*. He is also the author of a number of other books including biographies of Ford Madox Ford, John O'-Hara and James Jones. He is Director of the Translation Center at Columbia University and also a professor in the School of the Arts at Columbia.

JOHN MARTINEZ has been working as an illustrator in New York City for the last ten years. His work has appeared on book covers and in various advertising campaigns. He has also published a number of limited-edition posters.

FRANCIS M. NEVINS, JR., is the author of about forty short stories of crime and suspense and of four mystery novels, the most recent of which are *The 120-Hour Clock* and *The Ninety Million Dollar Mouse*. He has also written a number of nonfiction works on the genre, including the Edgar-winning *Royal Bloodline: Ellery Queen, Author and Detective*.

SARA PARETSKY began writing plays when she was five; she continued writing for her private entertainment throughout adolescence and adulthood. Her first novel, *Indemnity Only*, published in 1982, featured Chicago private eye V. I. Warshawski. Her fifth Warshawski novel, *Blood Shot*, was published by in 1988.

W. R. PHILBRICK is the author of the mysteries *Slow Dancer, Shadow Kills,* and *Ice for the Eskimo*, and three crime novels featuring Florida Keys fishing guide T. D. Stash: *The Neon Flamingo, The Crystal Blue Persuasion,* and *Tough Enough*. He recently completed *Deadwalkers*, a thriller.

ROBERT J. RANDISI has published seven P.I. novels, more than twenty mystery novels, and over twenty-five short stories. He is the author of *The Disappearance of Penny, Eye in the Ring,* and *Full Contact*, all featuring Manhattan P.I. Miles Jacoby. In 1982, he created The Private Eye Writers of America (PWA) and the Shamus Award.

PAUL RIVOCHE has been doing free-lance illustration in Toronto for ten years. His work can be found in advertising, animation, and numerous books including the bestselling series *Isaac Asimov's Robot City*. He was involved in creating the well-known graphic novel *Mr. X*.

Born in Madrid, Spain, JAVIER ROMERO now works in New York City as a graphic illustrator and instructor at the School of Visual Arts. His editorial clients include *The New York Times, Fortune* and *Business Week;* and he also works for various advertising agencies, record companies, and corporate clients such as Estée Lauder.

BENJAMIN M. SCHUTZ is the author of three novels featuring private eye Leo Haggerty. His fourth one, *The Things We Do for Love*, will be published soon. He is a clinical and forensic psychologist and lives in the suburbs of Washington, D.C.

ROGER L. SIMON's first Moses Wine detective novel, *The Big Fix*, won awards from the Mystery Writers of America and the Crime Writers of Great Britain as the best crime novel of the year. His novel *The Straight Man* was nominated for an Edgar Award. Simon is also a screenwriter and the president of the newly formed International Association of Crime Writers.

JULIE SMITH is the biographer of two sleuths—Rebecca Schwartz, a San Francisco lawyer, and Paul McDonald, an ex-reporter who writes mysteries. Schwartz appears in *Death Turns a Trick, The Sourdough Wars,* and *Tourist Trap;* McDonald in *True-Life Adventure* and *Huckleberry Fiend*.

PACO IGNACIO TAIBO II is the author of twenty-eight books, of which seven belong to the genre of crime literature: *Dias de combate, Cosa facil, Algunas nubes, No habra final feliz, De paso, Sombra de la sombra, La vida misma*. He is recognized in Mexico as the founder and a key figure in the new Mexican crime literature.

JONATHAN VALIN has written seven novels featuring a private eye named Harry Stoner, a character he modeled on Philip Marlowe. Currently, he is finishing his eighth Stoner book, *Extenuating Circumstances*.

ERIC VAN LUSTBADER has written seven major internationally best-selling novels, including *The Ninja, Shan,* and *Zero*. He graduated from Columbia College with a B.A. in sociology. He has worked in the music and entertainment industries.

California-based DENNIS ZIEMIENSKI has been doing illustrations professionally since 1973. His work has appeared in a number of national advertising campaigns, as well as some of this country's leading magazines.

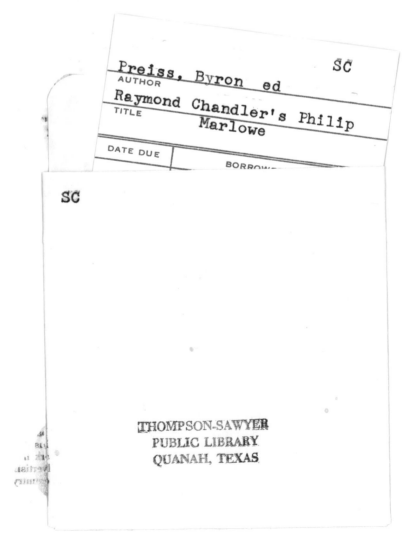

PHILIP MARLOWE'S
LOS ANGELES

LAUREL CANYON

VENTURA BOULEVARD

5

CAHUENGA BOULEVARD

MULHOLLAND DRIVE

BOULEVARD

13

1

3

YUC

2

HOLLYWOOD

11

SANTA MONICA BOULEVARD

14

LA CIENEGA BOULEVARD

CRESCENT HEIGHTS

HIGHLAND AVENUE

WILSHIRE BOULEVARD

OLYMPIC BOULEVARD

BOULEVARD

PICO BOULE

WASHINGTON BO

SAN VICENTE BOULEVARD

8

26TH STREET

WILSHIRE BOULEVARD

SANTA MONICA BOULEVARD

OLYMPIC BOULEVARD

LA CIENEGA BOULEVARD

BAY CITY

18

PACIFIC COAST HIGHWAY

23

PICO BOULEVARD

SEPULVEDA BOULEVARD

7

OCEAN PARK BOULEVARD

LINCOLN BOULEVARD

17